SLACK/TAUT

A Day in the Life of Ford Aston

SLACK/TAUT

A Day in the Life of Ford Aston

J. A. Huss

OTHER BOOKS BY J.A. HUSS

Science Fiction Series

Clutch
Fledge
Flight
Range
The Magpie Bridge
Return

Rook and Ronin Books

TRAGIC
MANIC
PANIC
SLACK
TAUT
BOMB
GUNS

Ford Aston is not too picky about what he wants out of Christmas. He's not into this holiday—like at all. He doesn't do presents, or family dinners, or parties, or church.

He does pets. And he's got one lined up for Christmas Eve. In fact, it's the highlight of his day. And if he can get through drop-in visits, nosy twelve year olds, an inappropriate conversation with his best friend's girlfriend, dinner with a family that's not his, and a party at his mother's house—well, he might just get home in time to enjoy himself with a stranger and make it all OK.

SLACK: A Day in the Life of Ford Aston, is a prequel to TAUT: The Ford Book, and can be read as a standalone novella.

Dear Readers,

What is this, you might be thinking. Or maybe not—but I think this bundle deserves a little note from the author, so here it is. SLACK is a novella about Ford. It takes place before Fords book TAUT happens, and after all the events that occurred in the Rook & Ronin 1-3 series. I mention that stuff at times, but neither SLACK nor TAUT require you to know anything about those books. It's all background you can absorb, or not. It's not important to understand TAUT. If you read my other books, then SLACK plays a huge role. But for now, it's just a character study of one day in Ford's life. What he does, who he talks to, how he acts. It's a good "before" snapshot of the man he *is* as he sets out on his journey in TAUT to find the man he *becomes*.

Also, SLACK is a sort of prequel to COME BACK, book two in my Dirty, Dark, and Deadly series that features Merc, Sasha, Harper, and James. So, if you're into that series, SLACK is fun as it drops so many clues. But again, not necessary to the plot of COME BACK, I tell you what you need to know in that series, as you need to know it.

Ford is quite a guy and I hope you appreciate his weirdness as much as I do. :)

Read on…

SLACK

A Day in the Life of Ford Aston

J. A. Huss

ONE

I cross Park Avenue at a full run and head down Stout where it intersects with Broadway. My breathing is not even heavy. It's difficult to get a decent run in this flat city without the Coors Field steps to challenge me.

My building looms in front of me, contributing to the Denver skyline. This pre-dawn run is the only peace I'll get today, so I might as well try and enjoy what's left of it. I pick up my pace and run harder, desperately trying for the endorphin rush, but there's just not enough distance. Not enough incline. Not enough time.

I slow as I cross the street and then walk up to the doorman. He welcomes me back with small talk and gratitude for the Christmas tip I authorized via my personal accountant. I ignore his *thank yous* and get in the elevator, then key in the code to the penthouse so the doors will close.

I count the floors as they ding. Too many. But it allows me to feel removed from society so I don't hold it against the condo. The doors open right into my space, but it's not the actual condo. It's a hallway that has a pet mat—which at this moment has a kneeling and naked pet on top of it—a closet, and a poinsettia plant that someone who is not me, put there.

Most likely it was my mother, and most likely it was her subtle way of reminding me that midnight mass is tonight. I have no idea why she bothers. I never go. I haven't gone to church since I graduated high school. As a Jesuit student I was required to attend mass and take theology, but that was the very first change I made in my adult life. No more church. I'm not a believer. It's been almost eight years, so the fact that my mother continues to ask me to attend midnight mass with her every Christmas Eve I'm in town, is just annoying.

I shake it off because she does her best, I guess. I'm weird. Her only child is probably a huge disappointment. She probably figures she'll never get a wedding out of me. She'll never have grandkids.

It's gotta sting.

"Stay here, pet. I'll be back later."

The girl on the pet mat says nothing, which is mandatory. I do not want to hear them speak. At all. Not one word. Some moaning, some squealing, small whimpering and tears during punishments—all that is fine. But if they talk, they are asked to leave.

I enter the condo and take it in. It never did feel like home because nothing in this condo is mine. The only thing I feel a connection to is the view outside. The furniture is white with black accents, the walls are a light gray that looks a little too pink for my taste, and there's floor to ceiling windows visible from the front door as you walk in. The penthouse terrace faces west so I have an unobstructed view of the mountains.

I close the door and walk quickly to the shower, wash off, and then pull on a pair of jeans and make my way back to the kitchen. I press the button on the machine and it spits the one-cup instabrew out into a mug. I take it, and a bowl of cut strawberries, over to the dining table and swipe my finger across the tablet so I can read the *Wall Street Journal* after I finish with the pet.

I walk back over to the door, open it, and then bend down and whisper in the pet's ear. "Count to ten, come in, shut the door behind you, and then crawl to the table." I walk back over to the table and take my seat. Her ten seconds are up and she stands, walks through the door, closes it softly behind her, then drops to her knees and crawls across the hard stone tiles.

She never once looks at me.

Another rule.

Her hair is long and blonde. It hangs down and brushes against the floor as she crawls. When she reaches me, I open my legs and pat my thigh. She rests her cheek on my leg and assumes the position.

The position is kneeling, legs open, head straight, hands on her thighs. My pat is a command she knows, so that's why she rests her head on my leg. She's been here about two dozen times. I have no idea what her name is, how old she is—other than legal age—where she lives, what she does, what this means to her, or why she does it.

And I could care less about any of that personal stuff. My assistant in LA sets the pets up for me, and much of the time I have no knowledge about the particulars, beyond fucking them, of course. Occasionally I take one out to eat or to a function that requires a date, but not often. I prefer to do almost everything alone.

"Are you hungry?"

She nods.

I pick up a small piece of cut strawberry from the bowl in the center of the table. "Open."

She lifts her head slightly and opens her mouth. I place the wet fruit on her tongue and she closes her mouth and chews slowly, then licks her lips to get a drop of juice.

I like that. I'm hard already. This girl is a fair submissive. She made a few minor mistakes when she first came, but over the past couple months she's learned fast. She takes the punishments, she likes it in the ass, and she comes for me on command.

She's good.

Good enough, anyway.

She's about as far away from my type there is. Because my type is Rook. Dark hair, dark eyes—I make allowances for Rook's blue eyes because they are striking. Much too beautiful to dismiss as a fault.

But the pets are never dark. The pets are always light. Blonde or red. It's a requirement.

"More?" I ask.

She nods again and I detect a small smile forming on her lips as I pluck another strawberry piece from the bowl, and place it on her tongue. She moans this time and I wonder how real that is. Does she enjoy this?

"Stand up," I command. She obeys immediately and I slip my fingers between her legs. She's very wet. "Good girl," I tell her in a low voice. Her skin prickles, like I just gave her the chills. I open my palm and flatten it against her sex, then push two fingers inside her. This makes her moan again.

"Kneel, please."

She does, and my fingertips slip out of her pussy and drag her wetness up her stomach and across her breasts as she moves. She's got her head down so I tip her chin up with my finger, still slick with her juices, and then press it against her lips. She opens and licks, then wraps her lips around my finger and gently sucks—her tongue caressing it seductively. I slouch back in the hard dining room chair and unbutton my jeans. "Proceed."

She leans in and grabs the zipper with her teeth, chancing a quick look up to see if I'm pleased.

I give her nothing, so she looks back down at her task. Once the zipper is down she leans back and waits. The first time she did this, she made the mistake of touching me. Her palms flattened against my thighs and she got a swift smack on the ass with the riding crop, hard enough to make her yelp.

"You're a good pet," I praise her for not repeating that

mistake.

She sighs with satisfaction as I grab my dick and free it from the jeans. "Begin," I whisper.

She's eager and a moment later her hot breath is teasing me as her face moves slowly towards her goal. Her lips part and then her tongue darts out and licks my tip. Her whole mouth opens up and she descends on me, the combination of her warmth, wetness, and desire makes my balls tighten and my shaft stretch. My left hand clamps down on her head while my right hand slides across her throat. She hesitates slightly. I've never touched her throat before and I've got her wondering, no doubt.

Breath play is not something I do and if she read her contract carefully, she'd know that. But she remains stiff until I remove that hand. I force her down on my cock, a punishment for disappointing me, and then try that throat again. She stiffens and then gags because she's lost her concentration. I ease up on her head and let her pull back, but she dives back in before I have a chance to dismiss her.

This one catches on quick.

I've dismissed her before. The first two times she came over. Once for gagging and once for talking. Since then she's held the gag reflex in check, and she never again uttered a word.

Like I said, quick learner.

"I don't like the gagging, pet." She opens her mouth further and devourers my cock, burying it into her throat. I reach down and palm her neck again, feeling for the muscle strain as I force her to take more. She breathes through her nose, my hard thickness blocking her airway, and then I explode into her, the semen bursting out as I press my hand against her throat. She swallows… *once, twice.*

I let go of her head and she withdraws. Licking her lips and eyes cast down. "Look up," I command.

She lifts her head, but her eyes do not meet my gaze. She's not allowed to do that either. I stare at her for a few moments. Her make-up is smeared down her cheeks from the tears.

SLACK

"Sit in my lap."

She stands, sniffling a little, and perches herself on my thighs. I reach around and play with her clit and this makes her forget her tears and begin to moan. "I'm going to leave you frustrated today. Would you like that?"

She nods out a yes.

"Good. If you want to come back later tonight, I'll be here at ten."

This is not customary. I rarely make dates. Pam, my assistant does almost all the scheduling. The pet turns her head to the side, almost like she's about to ask me something. But then she faces forward again and keeps her mouth shut.

"You were a good pet today. If you come back tonight I'll show you how much I appreciate your obedience." I push her up and smack her behind. "Go."

Her ass sways slightly as she walks. Not in a flaunting way— she knows better than to tease me. I spanked her for that the last time she was here. No, this is just her natural sexy gate. She is sexy, I conclude. Even though her cheeks are not red with my hand prints, I like the view from behind.

"Ten," I remind her. "Unless you have plans for tonight?"

She stops at the door, probably stunned that I asked her a question. She shakes her head no, and then she takes a deep breath. Uncertain. Wondering if I took that as a *no, I'm not coming.* Or *no, I have no plans.*

"You have plans?" I ask to clarify.

She shakes her head no.

"I'm surprised, really. You're pretty."

Why does she do this? Why does she participate in this… this… this *totally* fucked up arrangement? And it's not the submissive thing that makes me wonder. Lots of women enjoy being submissive. That's not weird. What's weird is that she allows me to treat her like she's worthless. I've never understood this.

I love it, don't get me wrong. I love that there are women who will put aside their own needs and submit to my whims. Not speak to me, not touch me with their hands—and still pleasure me sexually. But what could she possibly get out of it? More often than not I pay no attention to them. I've left this pet sitting on the mat outside the door for hours. Twice. And once I never even showed up. I have no idea how long she stayed waiting because I couldn't even be bothered to check the security footage to find out.

I am the first to admit that my rules are unreasonable. My behavior is atrocious. My indifference is derogatory. But if the pets don't care, why should I?

She contemplates my statement, probably wondering if she's supposed to actually address it. But she decides correctly that I really do not give a fuck, and she exits quietly.

I tuck my dick back into my pants and reach for my coffee and take a sip.

What a productive morning.

I grin widely.

The coffee's still hot, I ran, I got a blowjob, and I'm ready for whatever the fuck this stupid Christmas Eve decides to throw at me.

Life could be worse.

TWO

My phone rings and I glance over at the screen. "Fuck." I pick it up and swipe my fingers. "What's up?"

"I need a small, you available?"

He sounds paranoid and this means I can mess with his head, so I take a loud slurping sip of coffee and swallow. "I have a date tonight. Will we be finished by ten?"

"Shut the fuck up and come get me, you freak. I'm at DIA, west terminal, parking garage level two, behind a blue station wagon, near the south elevators. Do the call and I'll come out when you get here."

"Merc, I swear, if you complicate my life today, I'll be—" I get the three quick beeps on my phone that tells me the line went dead. I hope he hung up on me and didn't get caught in whatever scheme he's involved in this time.

Goddammit.

I walk to the bedroom and pull on a white t-shirt. I wanted to wear a suit today but Merc will be looking like a vagrant, and a suit would make us stand out. So this is it. I open the patio door and check the temperature, it's still mild. Not as warm as it was when I was running this morning, the cold front is getting closer. But still forties, easy.

I grab my leather jacket and stuff my keys and phone into the pockets. There's a small bag sitting on the pet mat and I bend down and pick it up. What the hell? She's leaving me things? I open it up and I'm accosted with the scent of homemade cookies. I take one out and bite, chewing as I wait for the elevator. They're pretty good. When the ding comes and the doors open, I toss the bag back down on the pet mat and leave it for later.

Someone gets on a few floors below. Woman with a dog. She nods and I'm just about to turn my head and ignore her when Rook comes to mind. I smile and dog lady starts chatting about the weather.

"Yes," I say, agreeing with her about the coming snow.

See, this is why I ignore people. They talk to you if you acknowledge them. But Rook is friendly, so maybe she likes friendly guys? Ronin is friendly. And Spencer even more so. So I figure if I want Rook to like me, then I should try to emulate the other people in her life whom she likes. Ronin is her number one and Spencer is not far behind. She's always smiling with Spencer. He makes her laugh. Ronin makes her blush.

And me? I make her uncomfortable.

The elevator doors open and I nod at the chatty dog woman as she gets off. "Nice talking to you," I say amicably. She sets her dog down and hurries off, calling out a *good day* to me as she goes.

Well, that wasn't so bad.

The doors close and I descend to the parking garage and then make my way over to the Bronco, Rook still on my mind. I sigh as I picture her with Ronin. Why? Why him? Of all people? I like Ronin these days, he's not a bad guy. But why does he always get the fucking girl?

I met Ronin on his first day of high school. Spencer and I grew up together—he lived across the street from us, in fact. We both went to St. Margaret's for elementary and middle school, so Spencer graduating up to the Catholic high school was something I looked forward to. Since I had my truck, I picked him up on his first day of ninth grade. Ronin came along as part of the package. I'm two years older than them, so I was already in high school when Spence and Ronin were putting the Team together back at St. Margaret's.

Spencer got in the front seat, looking like a fucking linebacker for the Broncos—that's how big he was at fifteen, and Ronin got in the back, looking like a fucking Calvin Klein underwear model.

He was too young for that kind of modeling back then, but I know for a fact he did jeans and sportswear. His life was bizarre. And not in a bad way, but bizarre in a way that makes people jealous. He never spent the entire school year in *actual* school. And our high school was pretty strict about attendance, but did Ronin Flynn have to abide by the rules?

No.

Antoine fucking Chaput stepped in and glossed it all over so Ronin could leave every month or so for a few days to go shoot in New York or LA for his own work, or just travel with Antoine and Elise for Chaput Photography. The girls went wild over him. Our school was co-ed, but the boys and girls were separated for classes, and the only time we got to mix was during lunch or at afterhours events.

Sitting with Ronin at lunch was enough to give any guy an inferiority complex, but add my social limitations to that mess, and it was torture for me.

I get in the Bronco and start her up. It's not too cold so I don't bother letting the engine warm up, just put her in gear and head out towards Denver International. The drive is long. They made this airport a while back and it was in the middle of the Denver expansion. That was their excuse for why the fucking place had to be an hour outside of the damn city. It takes forever to get there. Literally in the middle of nowhere. Which means I have all this time to sit and stew on why Ronin gets the girls and I get the pets.

Fucking pets.

Not that I don't enjoy them, I do. I like the sex, they're good at it. And the girl this morning is not bad. She's pretty in her blonde way. She's trying hard to please me. She keeps her mouth shut. She's acceptable.

But I want Rook.

Rook is all those things the pet is, times a million. She's obedient, she's submissive, and she's beautiful—far, *far* more beautiful than the girl this morning. And Rook is smart. She might not think so, she's always down on herself about school. But she's smart in all the ways that count. Plus, she likes to run. I love that. *Love that.* I miss her running with me so fucking bad. It kills me to run alone after having her as a partner for half the year. I hate it. It takes all the joy out of it.

I miss her.

I really, *really* miss her.

The traffic on I-70 is horrific—must be an accident up ahead. Colorado has the worst drivers. They say California drivers are bad, but that's not true. California drivers know what they're doing. They might speed the hell down the freeway, but they can cut over six lanes of traffic, find a song on the iPod, check their teeth in the mirror, and flip off the slow driver they're passing, without even blinking.

Here—every day is a major fuck-up on the freeway. And there is really only one way to get to DIA from Denver unless I want to drive up north and cut back around on the toll road. And I don't. So I sit in traffic.

Back to Ronin. God that guy just pissed me off from the minute I met him. Getting into my truck, chatting and laughing with Spencer like they're best friends since birth or something.

I was Spencer's friend all growing up. Spence comes from money, like me. My parents inherited our house and Spencer came from the same situation. Our families have lived across the street from each other for close to fifty years. But there was Ronin, inserting himself between us like he belonged, even though he wasn't even *from* Park Hill. He was from fucking Five Points. The slum of Denver. And he was practically the son of a porn photographer.

I mean, looking at it objectively, that's exactly what the situation was.

I inch past the accident and finally the freeway opens up just past the 225. I get over in the right lane so I can get on Pena. One long-ass road that only leads to one lonely-ass place. The airport.

But every girl at school loved Ronin the minute he got out of the truck that day. It was like something out of a movie where the action is all slow-mo, the dude drags his hand through his perfectly messed up, yet still coiffed, hair, and all the girls drop their Trapper-Keepers and gawk at him with their mouths open.

I hated him.

I still might hate him a little. Maybe even more than a little.

He's just lucky that loyalty is my number one moral value. Maybe my only moral value. I do, after all, steal, cheat, lie, and lust. I have most of the vices covered. But for some reason, my whole worldview begins and ends with this absolute dedication to Spencer and Ronin. I'm not even sure how it started since I hated him immediately.

But it's there. I can't *not* be loyal to Ronin. I simply can't change it. We're bound together in this life whether we want to be or not. I'm sure he hates me as well. Maybe even more, since he knows Rook loves me in her own way, and there's nothing he can do about it.

DIA eventually shows up off in the distance. They say the white peaked roof is supposed to remind people of the snow-capped Rocky Mountains, but it looks like some futuristic circus tent of you ask me. I always get a strange craving for cotton candy when I come here.

I get in the lane for the west terminal garage and then follow the road around to the ticket station. Fucking Merc. Making me get a ticket and pay for parking. Why can't he just show up like normal people instead of being all paranoid and stealthy? Now security will have my plates when I leave because I have to stop at the exit and pay as they take pictures of my car. If he would just stand out at *Arrivals* like everyone else, then I could swoop in, pick his ass up, and swoop back out. No plates. No pictures. No payment.

I pull up in front of the stop gate and roll my window down so I can take a parking ticket. The gate lifts and I drive through, trying to get my bearings on which way is north so I can find the south elevators on level two.

In California, west equals the ocean. In Denver, west equals the mountains. I find the mountains so I know where south is, and then take the ramp up to level two. This place is packed since it's Christmas Eve, and there are holiday travelers everywhere. Kids are crying, moms and dads are stressed, and grandparents are happy to be with them, even though it's an all-out nightmare trying to get in and out of this garage.

I drive past the south elevators, looking for a station wagon and come up short. So I try the old-fashioned method. I roll the window down and yell, "Merc!"

Every set of stressed-out eyeballs turns at my call and stares at me.

I stare back and have to tuck down the urge to say something nasty.

Then the passenger door opens and a man slides in, half ducking down thinking no one can see him, and tugging on his hat to cover his eyes. Merc is a huge guy, at least six foot four and two hundred pounds. So him thinking he can duck in the seat and hide himself is almost funny. His hazel eyes are darting all over the place, checking the parking lot. His hand rubs the stubble on his chin, and his cropped brown hair is covered by a trucker hat that proclaims he's a bacon lover.

"Good going, Rutherford. Just call out my fucking name in one of the busiest airports on the planet, on one of the busiest days of the year."

"You said call you."

"No, I said, do *The Call*, Ford. Not just scream out my name."

"I do not scream. And the last call we had together was a duck. Quacking out a duck call in an airport parking garage is gonna be less conspicuous than your name?"

"Whatever," he says as he turns to check behind us like the paranoid freak he is, "just drive."

"Well now we have to stop at security to get our fucking pictures taken, so this is all moot anyway. You should've stayed in *Arrivals*."

"Fuck that, I saw a few suspicious people back there. One on the plane and one in baggage. I went to baggage because it's what people do and I was blending in, plus I wanted to see if this guy would follow me. And he did."

"Let me guess, he picked up bags from baggage as well? Suspicious."

He sneers his lip at me in typical Merc fashion. "Don't patronize me, just take me to your rig. I got a smallish-big, I said."

"You said you have a small, Merc. Not some smallish-big."

"Yeah, well, think of it as a biggish-small then. Roll with it, dude."

I'm gonna regret this, I can already tell. "Nice to see you again, Merc."

He grunts. People think I'm anti-social? This guy, he's the anti-social one. He's OK one on one, but get this asshole in a group and I won't take responsibility.

I make my way down to the first level and follow the signs to the exit. Since it's a busy day, I wait in line for ten minutes as every car is photographed and matched to the picture they took at the parking garage stop gate. They do that under the guise of collecting the fee money to use the garage, but really, they are just cataloging your vehicle in case you're a terrorist.

"My rig's up in Fort Collins still. I have a place there."

"Perfect," Merc says as he lights a cigarette. He blows the

smoke out of his nose and mouth at the same time. "I got a gun deal up in Cheyenne later, so that's perfect. You can take me up to Wyoming, right? I mean, you have no plans today. It's Christmas Eve for Christ's sake."

I shoot him a look for the blasphemous humor. "I said I have a date at ten."

"Yeah, but that was a joke, right?" I look over at him and he's got one of those *you-fuck-with-me-I'll-fuck-with-you-back* grins on his face.

I glare at him.

"You owe me, Ford. So just get over it. You're in."

"Fine, but this is beyond my debt, so you owe me a *big* once this is over. What's the job, anyway?"

"Some senator's sixteen-year-old daughter was kidnapped last night. Some kind of pathetic wanna-be militia in the hills between Laramie and Cheyenne is responsible. I'm going in."

He says all this like he just said, *I'll have eggs for breakfast.* "Why not the Feds?"

"Hush, hush, you know. The girl's caught up in something bad. Drugs, sex, something. Who the fuck knows, who the fuck cares. They didn't really kidnap her from the way I see it. I figure she went on her own volition, but the senator is having none of that. All I know is that if I can get her out alive with no media involvement, I get five hundred tax-free grand." He takes a long draw on his cigarette and lets it out through his grinning teeth. "Fuckin-a, I'm in."

"What if the media gets involved?"

"Penalty," he says though a puff of smoke. "They knock off twenty percent for media fuck-ups. I'll shoot you ten grand for the lift, though."

"Fuckin-a then, I'm in too."

Why the hell not? Wyoming is not that far, it's Christmas Eve, I'm a total *Scrooge*, and my pet date is twelve hours from now. I got plenty of time to make ten grand and get back home in time to plan some dirty sex.

THREE

It's a lot easier to get the hell out of DIA if you're going north than it is if you're going south. There's an expensive toll road almost no one uses that shuttles you past all the worst I-25 traffic, and spits you out just before you hit Longmont. From there, it's a fifteen minute ride to my apartment on the southern outskirts of Fort Collins. I pull into the complex driveway and Merc starts laughing. "You live *here*? In this suburban singles complex?"

"Guess what I do here, Merc?"

He lights up another smoke. Fucker's been chain smoking since we left. If this was a high level job, he'd never smoke. Leaves a scent on his clothes that can give his ass away when he's sniping. So he must feel this one is no big deal.

"Eat, sleep, shit, and fuck?"

"No, I said guess what *I* do here. Not what most people do here."

He tilts his head, interested. "Fuckin tell me then."

I say nothing. Just park the Bronco in the spot numbered E33, then get out and head towards the stairs that will take me up to my third floor apartment. Merc follows behind, his cigarette still smoldering. I open the door and wave him in, then reach out and snatch the smoke from his lips and toss it over the balcony. "No smoking in my gear room."

He hands me a sly smile and I follow him in and close the door. From the entry it's just your basic shit apartment, albeit, in a luxury suburban setting. Nondescript brown couch, two dark wood end tables with matching lamps on either side. Dark wood coffee table, an over-sized chair and matching ottoman, and a dining table.

"No TV, Ford?"

"Fuck TV."

It's got three bedrooms, but only one has a bed. I open the last door on the right and let Merc walk in ahead of me. "The rig room, eh?" he says as he looks over his shoulder at me.

"You bet. The rig room."

The rig room is one long stainless steel table with one laptop and a metal stool.

"Sparse, dude."

"It's all I need."

"Right, then." He sighs his frustration with me. We've been friends since senior year of high school. He knows me well. All my strengths and all my weaknesses. "Get to it. I need info on…" he rattles off names as I pop off an electrical wall cover plate, fish around inside the wall for the end of the cable, then pull it through the hole and plug it into my laptop. I sit down in the chair and open the rig and start typing. The external drive inside the wall contains all my scripts, but its password protected and has an automatic trip. If you get the password wrong, just once, it nukes the drive.

We spend almost an hour in the rig room getting the deets on who may or may not be inside the 'compound' in the desolate hills between Cheyenne and Laramie, where this girl has apparently run away to. Just as we're walking out, Merc asks the question I'm sure has been on his mind since he got here. "So what's behind door number three?"

He gives me a knowing grin.

"Books," I deadpan. *And guns.* I say to myself. Spencer has a stash here. For some reason, that paranoid fucker insists on having weapons in every place I inhabit.

"Yeah?" Merc says with interest. "Like I actually believe you have books in that fucking room, Aston. Please."

"Believe what you want." We descend back down the stairs and head to the Bronco. I know what he thinks is in there. Same thing that Rook thought was in there when she first questioned me about the apartment last fall. They both think I bring pets here, but that's not why I got the apartment. I got it to bring dates. Regular dates. Like—*normal girls.*

I never even came close to bringing a normal girl home. Not even close.

We get in the truck and I head back towards the I-25 and get on going north. Merc is studying the notes he took back in the rig room, so I'm left with thoughts of my sorry attempt at a normal love life last October.

I gave it a shot. Thirty days. One solid month of trying. I went on eight dates. Hell, I had a shitload of inquiries on my Match. com account. I was even featured on the home page a few times. Under an assumed name, of course. Ford Aston is infamous in these parts. A one second Google search brings up thousands of hits and four years' worth of questionable shit.

No. These girls went in blind. Which speaks to the stupidity of online dating. You just never know who you're getting. Of course, I have credit cards under assumed names and most people don't. But every one of those women wanted to have sex with me after our date. Two of them made very convincing arguments with their provocative dresses and dirty mouths as we got drunk at a local bar.

A threesome sorta defeats the purpose of the whole experiment, right? I can get two pets for a threesome and never have to exert an effort at conversation. So those two were a dead

SLACK

end the minute they walked into the bar together.

But the truth of the matter is, all those women were established. They were my age, they had degrees, they had jobs, they were looking for sex, sure. But they were also looking for all that other shit. Houses, and rings, and kids. And maybe they were just hiding their freak because it was a first date, but somehow I doubt it. Every one of them was respectable.

Every one of them was *boring*.

I ended four dates early, the two-for-one lasted until the bar closed, but that was all drinking and bull riding. Yes, FoCo is quite the rodeo town. There are no urban cowboys here, they're all one hundred percent real. And these two cowgirls took me to the only bar I know of that has bulls out back for the cowboys to ride. It was one of the most entertaining nights of my life.

But none of those girls were for me.

I gave up after thirty days and admitted defeat. I'm a freak looking for a freak. A freak that can relate to me. And the pets are the closest thing I've come to so far.

Besides Rook, of course. She's not a freak. Her sick ex tried to make her into one, but she's not a freak. She wants the fairytale—I'd go for that if I could have Rook. I would. I'd give her the fairytale if she wanted it. I'm not *against* the fairytale. I'm not against marriage and all that shit. I'm just picky. I want what I want and I refuse to settle. I'd rather be alone than settle.

But, I sigh, there is only one Rook and her heart belongs to Ronin.

"So…" Merc tries for conversation as we head north. Cheyenne is only forty-five minutes away and there's no traffic on Christmas Eve. Hell, there's no traffic on any eve. Or any *day* for that matter. It might be the capitol of Wyoming, but I'm not sure Cheyenne even qualifies as an urban center. In fact, I think Fort Collins has double the population of Cheyenne in every season except summer, when the college students go home. "How's life, Ford? You keeping busy?"

"I'm busy today, and today is the only day that matters."

"Your date tonight is your mom, right? Midnight mass and all that shit."

I laugh a little. "Please, do not even mention it. I've been avoiding her calls all fucking week."

"But she's your date, right?" he prods.

"How pathetic do you think I am?" I roll my eyes at him. "A pet I've used for a while. She agreed to come, so why not? Keeps me out of church and takes my mind off the holiday at the same time."

"Yeah, hear ya, dude. That's why I took this job, ya know? I fucking hate Christmas. Fucking hate it."

"I'm just the ride? Or you counting on backup? Do I need to call Pam and cancel the pet?"

"When we get up there, hang out for a few while I discuss the details, if that's alright. I'll let you know if I can use you. If you want in, of course."

"What if she didn't run away?"

He takes a long drag on the cigarette and blows it out the crack in the window. "That's what the weapons are for. But I think this girl ran away. One of the members is a guy she dated on and off for a while. Only makes sense."

"But, on Christmas? I mean, *we* hate Christmas, but sixteen year old rich girls generally don't. They like big boxes wrapped in bows."

"Yeah, well, we'll see. Head east on 16th when we get into Cheyenne. The pick-up is in one of those antique malls."

I shoot him a look.

"What? It's perfect."

"Did the senator sanction the weapons too?" He doesn't answer right away and this is my first real clue that he's not as comfortable with this job as he's making it out. "What?" I ask. "What's the deal, Merc?"

He shakes his head a little, like he's thinking about lying or holding it in. But we've been friends too long, so the words come out anyway. "It's just strange. All of a sudden I start getting a string of high priority jobs from people with position, ya know? This senator. The last job was collecting a debt owed to a millionaire from Miami. Had to go to Columbia for that one. And the one before that was stealing some data from a small European government."

"Virtually, I hope?" I have insane hacking skills, like Merc here, but unlike him, I'm no soldier. I can shoot and I can fight. And if I do either of those two things you can be sure someone will end up dead by the time it's over. But I am not a soldier.

"Nah, real time dude. Boots on the ground."

"Hmmm…. maybe it was that mercenary ad you ran in *Soldier of Fortune*?"

He puffs out some smoke with his chuckle. "Hey, I was twelve."

"As if that makes it any less ridiculous." We both laugh. Fucking Merc. "Well, your name's on a list somewhere. And you seem pretty popular and the shit's sanctioned, so enjoy it I guess."

"Yeah, I guess."

Cheyenne comes into view after that and Merc takes out his notes and studies them again. I don't blame him for being paranoid. I do this shit as a side thing. This is his life. This *is* his day job. He has nothing else *but* this. So knowing that people with power have a list with your name on it is not comforting in the least. Because one of these days, the target and the gun might switch places.

I get off the freeway and had east on 16th like he said. This town looks like it got stuck in 1940 and nothing has changed. There's a rail yard on one side of the street and a shitload of old fashioned shops on the other. I park in front of one of the brick buildings and look up at the sign. *Roundhouse Antique Mall.*

"Why is this place even open, it's fucking Christmas Eve. Isn't everyone home with their families doing family shit and eating crap by the handfuls, wishing that everyone's kids would just shut the fuck up and fall into a post-sugar coma?"

"Jesus Christ, you really are a *Scrooge*. Last minute shopping,

Ford. You'd know that if you ever bought a Christmas present in your life. Let's go."

I sigh as his door slams. But I give in and get out. I've got nine hours until my pet date, so what the fuck. I'll stick around for an illegal arms deal. Why not?

FOUR

I've never been in an antique mall. I know they exist, there's one on the west side of Denver on the side of the freeway, and the sign is huge and gaudy. But I can say with one hundred percent certainty, that entering that building has never crossed my mind. I'm not a snob about old things. I don't mind old things when they're mine. But as I walk down the many, many, *many* aisles in this huge-ass fucking building filled with *crap*—the first thing I think of is how many hands have touched these items.

The second thing I think is, why? Why would you come here to shop for Christmas presents?

I can only shake my head.

I follow Merc though an endless maze of booths filled with the oddest things—books, fabric, postcards, furniture, art, photographs, frames. The list goes on and on. But Merc stops in the way-way-back of the place and we end up at what appears to be a mini Cabala's store. If said store was contained within a fifteen by fifteen foot booth, and it only had scratch-n-dent items.

SLACK

I sigh and try my best to appear professional.

"Wait here," Merc says as he enters the booth. "I'll be back in a minute."

"Right." With Merc, be back in a minute can mean anything from five minutes to half an hour. I pick up a knife in a basket on the counter and check it out. It's just a folding knife, but I have nothing better to do, so I flip it open and inspect the blade.

"That knife sucks," a girl's voice says from behind me.

I turn towards the voice. The child is sitting in a chair in the corner of the booth across the aisle, reading *Little House in the Big Woods*. She's about twelve, she's smiling so I can see a full mouth of braces, and her hair is up in long, blonde pigtails. She's wearing a camo hoodie and some black tactical pants. "I wouldn't buy that one," she says.

I check the knife for a brand. None. Then check the blade. Dull. "Yeah, this is crap." I put it back in the basket.

"Wanna see the good ones?"

I turn again, but she's right up next to me now. "Good ones?"

"Yeah, the Emersons. We have a few left. They're a very popular Christmas present." She slides past me and opens a case, then removes a box and sets it on the counter.

"Are you allowed to open that?" I ask.

She never looks up at me, just picks up the thin black box. "This is my dad's booth." She nods over to the booth she came from. "That one over there is mine." And then she looks up at me with her pre-teen eyes and pouts. "I always get left out of the back-room deals too. So I know how you feel."

I laugh. "What makes you think there's some kind of back room deal going on?"

"You came in with a hunter," she says, nodding to the back room where Merc disappeared. "Hunters make deals. And since you're out here and not back there, you're not making the deal, that other guy is."

"What makes you think we're hunters?" I have no camo on and neither does Merc. "Do you see an orange vest on me?" I flap my jacket open and turn for her.

She smirks at my joking and points her finger to my face. "Not *that* kind of hunter," she giggles. "You know," she whispers, "the *hunters*."

I raise my eyebrows at her.

She raises hers back. "Your friend is buying guns from my *dad*, doofus. Do I look stupid? I know what you guys do." And then she takes her attention back to the box and removes an absolutely gorgeous Snubby CQC and presents it to me on her flattened palm.

I take it from her outstretched hand and admire it, try the weight, then flip it open and inspect the blade. "Yeah, this is nice. How much?"

"*Wellllll*," she says drawing out the word with a smile. "Since it's Christmas Eve, I can give you that for two-seventy-five."

I raise an eyebrow at her. "Two-twenty-five is more like it."

She smiles. "Two-fifty."

"Two-forty."

"Deal." She sticks her hand out and for a moment I just stare at it. "Shake, doofus. That's how you seal the deal."

I look at her again, then her hand. "This knife is only worth two-twenty-five, the rest is a tip for entertaining me."

Her hand remains outstretched. "Shake."

I shake and she flashes her braces at me. I open my wallet and grab the cash and hand it to her.

She shoves the bills in her pocket and takes the knife and places it back in the box. "Gift wrap?"

"Nah, I might use it today."

She nods conspiratorially. "Oh, big job on Christmas Eve. Must be someone important."

What the fuck? Who lets their twelve-year-old daughter in on their secret arms dealing business?

"What did you get your girlfriend for Christmas? Maybe you need something else while you're here?"

"I don't have a girlfriend."

SLACK

"Yeah," she says with a sigh. "You guys never have girlfriends. I used to think your work looked exciting, but then I figured out you had no lives. No offense," she says with a shrug.

"I have a life. I'm not a hunter, I'm just a helper. I have a girl who's a friend. She counts."

She squints her eyes in disbelief. "What'd you get her for Christmas?"

"Nothing. I don't do Christmas."

"Oh, boy." Her breath comes out in a half laugh. "You really need help. Did you at least get your mom and dad something?"

"My dad's dead and no, I just told you I don't do Christmas."

"Oh, sorry about your dad. I have a dad but no mom. Wouldn't it be nice to have both?"

She says this like one parent families are normal. That makes me a little sad. "I did have both, but my dad died two years ago."

Her head bobs in understanding. "My mom died when I was born. So…" she waves her arm around at the hunting supplies. Outdoor gear fills every bit of space in her dad's booth. As if to say, *This is what my childhood was like. All hunting, all the time.* "We're the same almost, you and I. Only opposites." She pauses to look up at me. "And I do Christmas, so that's different too. I got my dad a new longbow. We're gonna bow hunt next year if I do well at State."

"Do well at what?"

"Archery. I'm the Wyoming State champion in both trap and .22 rifle but I'm not a good enough archer yet." She looks wistfully at a bow on the wall. "There's always next year."

I just stare at her. She's like a twelve-year-old *La Femme Nikita*.

Fucking Wyoming. What do I expect? Shooting is practically the state sport.

She shakes herself out of her funk and looks back to me. "Wanna buy your mom something while you're here? Make her happy this Christmas?"

"I'm pretty sure my mother would not appreciate the finer

40

points of an Emerson folding knife."

She laughs so all her braces show. "No, doofus. I have that booth over there. I have jewelry your mom might like. Wanna see it?" She doesn't wait for an answer, just grabs my new knife, pushes past me, and walks across the aisle where she sets the knife down and busies herself pulling out some jewelry. She lies it all down across the glass counter top and then looks up and smiles.

It's infectious, so I smile back as I walk over. What a cool kid. If all kids were like this girl, I might like them more.

"I'll help you pick. Is your mom earthy or fancy?"

"Definitely fancy."

"OK, then these ones are out." She removes a beaded necklace and some feather earrings. "How about this one?"

It's a string of pearls. "My mom would love it, but she'd never wear it. They're not real."

"Oh, then she's classy, not fancy."

"Yeah, that's about right."

"Hold on," she says as she raises her pointing finger. "I have classy stuff too." She reaches into her pocket and produces a key for a tall metal cabinet, then unlocks it and brings out another box. "This is the good stuff. And I know just what you need." She shuffles through it and places an antique bracelet on the glass. "Those pin pricks of silver? Those are marcasite. It's not expensive, but it's pretty don't you think?"

"It is, very pretty," I answer back as I watch her. She's smiling down at the jewelry. "Are those emeralds?" I point to the little green gems.

"Yes," she whispers. And then she looks up at me. "They're small, but they're real. I bought this for my mom for Mother's Day once. It was symbolic, you know. I was missing her and wanted to give her a present. So I worked really hard to sell a lot of stuff that month and I got this bracelet from a lady who used to run a booth on the other side of the mall."

God, how sad.

SLACK

"But I've been thinking about it lately and I'd like for it to go to a mother, even if it can't go to *my* mother. Do you think your mother would like this?" She lifts it up towards my face and then smiles one of those sweet, innocent little girl smiles at me.

Holy shit that almost cracks my black Grinch heart. "Absolutely," I say. "My mom would die to have this bracelet. How much?"

"I have it marked at seventy-five, but since—"

"Done." I grab some more cash from my wallet and lay it out on the counter. "Seventy-five is a steal."

"Want me to gift wrap it?" She looks up at me smiling. "I'll put it in a pretty jewelry bag. With ribbons and everything. And make a card too. I'll be fast." And before I can even answer yes, she's got the ribbon and scissors out. "You should look for something for your friend who is a girl." And then she stops mid-cut and looks up at me. "If she's just a friend, you don't give fancy things. Something small that *seems* insignificant, but really isn't. OK?"

Relationship advice from a twelve-year-old. My life couldn't be any more pathetic. But I do browse for something to give Rook. I walk inside the girl's booth a little farther and start to take things in. "What's your name?" I ask her, as she busily ties ribbons to the jewelry bag.

"Sasha Alena Cherlin."

"Not Nikita then?" She laughs, like she got the joke, and that makes me like her even more. "I don't have a middle name, so Ford will have to do. Ford Aston. Sign my name on the card, OK? I have terrible handwriting. And sign yours too, so my mom knows it came from you as well."

"Awww… that's so sweet, Ford. I'm gonna put little pink hearts on the tag too."

"Do it up right, Nikita."

"Sasha!" she squeals.

"Right—" I stop mid-sentence because I see the perfect gift for Rook. "I want that for the girl who is a friend."

She puts her stuff down and walks over to me. "Eric Cartman? For a girl? I'm not sure…"

"No, I'm sure. It's perfect." The little Eric Cartman figure has mirrored shades, a cop uniform, and he's holding a nightstick. I laugh out loud as I picture Rook saying, '*Respect ma authora-tay*' when she sees it. Can't cost more than five bucks, but this is the perfect gift for Rook. Something small that seems insignificant, but really isn't.

"Gift wrap?" Sasha asks.

"Yeah, but better leave your name off this one, OK?"

"For sure, Ford," she winks at me. "I'm a woman, I totally get it."

Just as Sasha is finishing up the gift wrap, Merc peeks his head out from behind the curtain that leads to the back. "Ford!" he yells over to me. "You can take off man, this job just got complicated."

I give him a little salute, but he's already disappeared.

"You really aren't a hunter, then?"

I look down at Sasha and smile at her. "I told you I wasn't."

"So now you have time for me to gift-wrap your knife." She grabs the box and takes it over to the little table that's doubling as a makeshift wrapping station.

"It's for me, Sasha. It doesn't need to be gift-wrapped."

"It's like a present to yourself, Ford. Just go with it."

Just go with it. I laugh. "You're kinda funny. Why are you working on Christmas Eve? Because my friend had a deal with your dad?"

"No," she says softly as she continues to wrap my knife case very carefully. "We always work until noon on Christmas Eve, just in case people wander in and need help. Like you." She looks over her shoulder and smiles before going back to her cutting and twisting. "Then we drive to my grandparents ranch near Sheridan."

"That's a long drive."

"Yeah, I love the drive. I just look out the window and think about my grandparents and how fantastic it will be to see them. We'll have early calves this year for my 4H project and I get to stay up there and help." She stays silent for a few seconds. "I love the babies. Why are you working on Christmas Eve?" she asks, as she turns with my packages.

"I don't do Christmas Eve. I usually just try to avoid the whole holiday."

"Well," she huffs, "you failed. You have a present to unwrap and two people you love will get a gift from you this year." She flashes me her braces and I smile back as she pushes my packages across the glass.

I stuff them in my coat pockets and shoot my finger at her, Spencer style. "Merry Christmas, Sasha Alena Cherlin. Hope you do well at State next year so you can tag that deer. And may your calf be the biggest one at weaning."

She covers her mouth to laugh and I turn around and walk away grinning.

"See ya around Ford Aston," Sasha calls out after me. "Tell your mom I said Merry Christmas too!"

Yeah, yeah... I walk out and stuff my packages into the glove box, then laugh at what just happened. I feel like I should be saying, *bah humbug*. But I don't. Because I still got a pet date in about eight hours.

FIVE

think about Sasha and what her life might be like all the
way back down into Colorado. Daughter of a gun dealer.
Sharpshooter at age twelve. 4H calf-raiser. Reader of *Little
House* books.

That's quite a combination.

I'm the son of a psychiatrist, socially unacceptable genius,
con-man hacker, film producer.

That's quite a combination too.

Why can't I find a twenty-five-year-old Sasha? Now she...
is a *freak*. But in the best kind of way. Why can't I find a well-
adjusted freak?

Signs for Fort Collins appear on the side of the road and
I get off on Mulberry and head towards downtown. I might as
well go empty out the few things I have up at Spencer's house in
Bellvue before I go home. Nothing better to do. I still have seven
hours until my pet date tonight. I turn right at College and head
north, glancing over at Anna Ameci's when the smell of Italian
food makes my stomach go ape-shit. And who do I see? Veronica

SLACK

Vaughn walking out of the restaurant, hanging on the arm of a well-dressed man.

Hmmm.

I know Spencer and Ronnie have had their difficulties, but I haven't seen either of them since the Shrike Bikes show ended a few weeks ago, so I had no idea they broke up. I pull into one of the many empty parking spaces and get out to go butt into her business. Veronica is dressed like a runner, but I know better. Ronnie does not run. The man leans down and kisses her on the cheek and then walks off, leaving her standing in front of the restaurant. He gets into a new Buick Lacrosse, and drives away.

Being the good best friend that I am, I memorize the plate for future evaluation.

Veronica is daydreaming when I walk up and tap her on the shoulder.

She whirls around. "Holy fuck, Ford! What the hell? You scared the shit out of me!"

"It was intentional."

She rolls her eyes. "Well, what do you want?"

"That did not look like Spencer."

"Wow, you really are a genius," she snaps back at me. "That guy is the farthest thing from Spencer there is. He's polite, attentive, and interested. Need I say more?"

"So you and Spencer broke up? Because I'm pretty sure he has no idea you're seeing other men."

"I don't have time for this," she says pushing past me. "Spencer can go fuck himself. I'm done waiting on him to grow up. He's almost twenty-four years old and he still acts fourteen." She walks down the sidewalk towards Laurel, then stops at the light and pushes the walk-button repeatedly.

I follow her.

"What are you doing? Go home, Ford."

"I was on my way to Spencer's actually. To clear out my shop apartment. Wanna come?"

"Spencer's in Denver with his family and since I'm not part

of his family, I'm gonna walk home and spend Christmas Eve with my *brothers*."

"I have the codes, I can get in everywhere."

She stops anxiously shuffling her feet and looks up at me. Spencer's Veronica is tall and tough, has big blonde hair, perpetual red lips, suicidal high heels, and a never ending E-cig.

But this other man's Veronica looks small and fragile, has no make-up on, her hair is straight and up in a ponytail, and she's not puffing.

Something is definitely wrong.

"Come with me. I'll let you snoop through all his stuff."

The light turns and her walk signal flashes, but Ronnie stands still. "Yeah, right. You'll probably record me and post it on YouTube so Spencer will break up with me."

I point my finger at her. "So, you admit you're still in a relationship with him!"

She shakes her head and then starts to walk across the street. I reach out and grab her arm before a car comes barreling around the corner. "Shit, Ronnie. Watch where you're walking. You die on my watch and I get the blame."

"Your watch?" she sneers.

I shrug. "I'm with you, I'm responsible for you. Which is why I'd like to know what's going on with that man you just kissed."

"I didn't kiss him, he kissed me. On the cheek."

"Same thing."

She plants her fists on her hips and taps her foot. "Ford, what the hell do you want?"

"Come with me to Spencer's. I'll drop you off at home when we're done."

"Why? So you can pump me for information?"

I chuckle. But it's my diabolical chuckle. The one that says *Don't fuck with me or your life might take unexpected and unwelcome wrong turns.* "No, Ronnie. So you can talk me out of going to my FoCo apartment, looking up your man's license plate using my DMV crawler, then calling Spencer and giving him that man's address, so he can show up on his doorstep tonight and start asking questions. Because that's pretty much where I'm at right now. I do not cover for anyone outside the Team."

"Right," she snaps back. "And since Spencer can't commit, I'm not on the team. I'm nobody, I'm—"

I cup my hand over her mouth because her last few words came out rather shrill, and people are starting to stare. "Come with me or I do the crawl and make the call." She huffs air into my palm and then mumbles something incoherent. "What was that? Was that a yes?" She nods her head and I remove my hand. "Great, I'm parked down here."

I walk off and she follows, slowly, but she follows.

We get in the Bronco and slam our doors at the same time. She folds her arms against her chest and pouts.

"Buckle up. It's the law."

"Fuck you, Ford." But she does buckle up and I back out and continue up College until I get to the turn off for Bellvue. Ronnie stares out the window the entire thirty-minute drive to the shop. I park in my old spot under the carport attached to the house, and glance over at Rook's custom Shrike Bike. Spencer made it for her last summer when she was doing his body art modeling campaign.

"He never gave *me* a bike, you know."

"No?" I get out and Ronnie follows. The weather is still fairly mild, but the clouds are really rolling in, the threat of a storm is over and it's just about here. I look at the bike again as we walk past and then I code the lock on the back door and hold it open for Ronnie. "You know why, though, right?"

"Why what?"

"Why he never gave you a bike."

She stands in the kitchen, her arms still folded in defiance. "Because I'm not important. Because he never gives me anything. Because I'm just another fuck-buddy to him. Because he has no feelings for me. Take your pick, Ford."

"No, that's not why," I say back. "Because he doesn't want you to ride it, Veronica. Because he'd go crazy with worry if he had to think about you riding around on a motorcycle. Because you're his number one, he's just caught up in some shit right now and he doesn't want you involved. And believe me, I saw his face last summer when you almost got killed. He didn't even know how to process it."

"Right," she snorts. "He processed it just fine. He was on the road to Sturgis the very next day with you guys."

"Yeah, but that was business. You're not business, Ronnie. You're personal. He's totally in love with you."

She just stares at me for a few seconds and then blinks. "What?"

"Come on, I'll show you." I walk into the living room and then head into the hallway towards Spencer's office. "I don't have the real code for this door, but I hacked it last summer when I was bored." Veronica grunts behind me as I key in the codes. The door beeps and I push it open and wave her in.

She hesitates. "I've never been in here before, Ford."

"I know, that's why I'm taking you in here now." I flip on the lights and she gasps, then walks across the forbidden threshold.

And gasps again. "What the hell is all this?" she asks, panning her arms wide.

I look up and try and imagine myself as her, seeing it for the first time. But I'm no good at that empathy shit, so it's no use. "Well, Ronin and I call it pussy-whipped, but you can call it the *Veronica Vaughn Shrine*." I laugh privately at my joke as she takes in the walls. Every one is adorned with images of her as Spencer's body art model. He stopped using her last year, then gave that last job to Rook, so none of these are recent. But she was his model for several years—they even went to some international contests, and Spencer has all those awards prominently displayed in a glass case behind his desk.

"I don't get it," she says, perplexed.

"What's not to get?"

"Why? Why the fuck does he treat me like *shit*!" She yells that

49

last part and I wince. "Ford!" she says turning to me, her little hands clasping onto the front of my leather jacket. "Why. The. Hell? He lets me come around once a month, if that! He forgets to call me back, he snuffs me on our dates, he hasn't fucked me in three goddamned months, Ford!" She's shaking me now and I'm desperately trying to pry her hands off my coat before I start freaking out from her touching. "*Three months*! Do you have any idea how fucking horny I am! I'm gonna fuck that banker, Ford. The minute he asks, because my goddamned vibrator is broken and the fucking mall sold out of the fucking Hitachi model I like, and won't be getting any more in until after fucking New Year's! I can't even find them online! Not even on eBay!"

She finally lets go and turns back to the wall art.

Holy shit. Veronica is *intense*.

But she's forgotten about me now and her attention is one hundred percent on the walls. There's six life sized photographs of her. All in body art paint, which means she's totally naked in every one of them. If it bothers her that I'm looking at her naked body, she doesn't let on. But honestly, it bothers me.

I do not want to start picturing them together.

It gives me the shivers.

"This one," she says pointing up at a photo, still a little bit hysterical, but calmer than she was about the lack of Hitachi vibrators at the FoCo Mall, "was in Austria. We won two prizes for it."

She's pointing to the one with her painted up as the cyborg chick that Rook loved so much last summer. That was Ronin's favorite picture of Rook once the STURGIS contract was all said and done. Spencer is trying to talk Ronin into letting Rook be his model for Comic-Con this year. But even though Ronnie doesn't see it yet, Spencer tells her no for the same reason Ronin will put his foot down this time as well.

No one wants their woman being displayed naked in front of thousands of men.

That's just the facts. And even though this is such a fucking no-brainer to us men with even the slightest bit of protoplasmic possessive gene, for some stupid reason, the girls never seem to get it.

Allow me to spell it out.

"Ronnie, Spencer is a man. He doesn't do feelings, he does caveman. When he says 'No, Ronnie, you may not have one of my custom Shrike Bikes.' What he really means is, 'Are you fucking insane? I refuse to spend every Goddamn night wondering if you're dead in a fucking ditch somewhere. You may *not* have a bike and you will *never* get a bike with my name on it as long as I'm alive, so fucking help me, *God*.'"

"But he gave Rook a bike!"

"Yeah, because it made Rook happy and she's got Ronin to reign her in when she talks about riding it. And after she took off to Illinois alone on that fucking Shrike Bike, you see where it is now? Sitting under the fucking carport out here in the middle of nowhere, being ridden by no one. Rook will never *sit* on that bike again, let alone ride it. Ronin put his foot down and it's over. Now, do you need me to spell out why he refuses to let you model for him anymore? Because I will. I think you're smart enough to figure that shit out on your own, but I'll hold your hand tonight and not make fun of your idiocy because it's Christmas."

"Nice bedside manner, Ford. You really have a way with words." She stays silent for a few seconds, mulling this over as she looks up at her glory days as a body art model for Shrike fucking Bikes. "I'm not ready for that to be over yet. I'm just not. I'm young, I'm pretty, I'm funny and I might have a little bit of freak in me with the blood phobia, but I'm not that far away from normal. I still want to have fun and I want to have fun with *him*. I'm not ready to just give that up yet."

"No? I thought you wanted him to be serious. You can't have it both ways, Ronnie. You can't be the slutty model at the shows who attracts the buyers and lookers. You can't be the reckless biker chick with no responsibilities. You can't be the wild tattoo artist with red lips and black stilettos who will hygienically tattoo a penis if a customer walks through the door asking for it."

"I've tattooed hundreds of people and only one of them wanted his penis adorned."

I sigh. She's so thick. "My point *is*… you can't be these things and be the kind of girl Spencer wants to settle with. Because eventually, he will settle down and when he does, he wants a wife." I shrug. I know how it sounds, but fuck it. She needs to hear the truth. "He wants dinner and kids and all that shit."

"He never said any of that to me Ford," she replies shaking her head. "He's never talked about a family at all."

"Yeah, but we were raised up together, Ronnie. I know him. We all want the same thing, we just want it in different ways. Ronin wanted to settle down right away because his life has been one exciting event after another. Spencer wants to check life out a bit, explore his options, and then settle down."

"Fuck that," she says as she stomps out of the office. I follow, flicking off the lights and pulling the door closed behind me. "If he can explore his options, then I can explore mine, too. Go ahead and tell him whatever you want, Ford. I don't care. He's hurting me with these other girls he dates. Hell, *dates*? He's fucking them and don't try and tell me he's not! So I'm done with him. I'm gonna call him tonight and tell him it's over and then tomorrow I'm meeting that guy and having a late dinner with him. And you know what, Ford? He'll probably bring me a present. Flowers or something. Spencer never buys me anything. Nothing! He might as well be you, Ford! Hell, if I was your pet at least I'd be getting *fucked*!"

I raise my eyebrows at her.

She winces and backs away. "Sorry. Too far?"

I nod. "Let's go get my things from my apartment and I'll drop you off at home." I usher her out of the house and we get back in the Bronco and drive down to the shop. It's not far, but I have a few boxes of stuff to load up, so I take the truck.

Ronnie sheepishly follows me upstairs to my apartment over the shop. It's pretty bare bones. Just some mismatched furniture and my leftover boxes of casual clothes and personal items. Ronnie grabs a box and I grab two, then we go back down to the Bronco and load it up.

She is silent the whole time. And I know why she's angry. Spencer is distant, but it's got nothing to do with her. He loves Veronica Vaughn. I know this, I've watched him with her on many occasions. And last summer when she accidentally got involved in that con we ran on Rook's ex, she almost got shot and Spencer was freaking out. That's how I know he loves her.

But I also know he'll never tell her as long as we have all this legal shit hanging over our heads. There's too many risks right now. We're all in this together—Rook, Ronin, Spencer, and me— until we know we won't be killed or put in jail.

And if certain people knew how much Spencer Shrike cares about Veronica Vaughn, then her life might be in danger too. And it's not fair to involve her. She's got nothing to do with any of these illegal jobs we've been doing.

We ride back to Fort Collins in silence and I'm still trying to figure out if I should call Spencer and tell him about this, when I hang a right on Mountain Avenue. Ronnie is the only female member of the Vaughn family—which consists of her, her four brothers, her dad, and her grandfather. All of whom are tattoo artists and have owned a shop in Fort Collins, called *Sick Boyz Inc.*, since the early Sixties. They live in a gigantic old house in the historic district right off downtown. If I had left her at the restaurant she could've walked home in five minutes.

I almost feel bad for Ronnie. Spencer is serious about not involving her in the business and that means he does generally ignore her. And he's been especially aloof this past fall. But Ronnie has a point too. Why should she wait around for him if he's not providing for her?

I slow down to gather my thoughts because what I'm about to suggest might be a betrayal to one of my best friends, and it takes a little getting used to. But then Veronica's house comes into view and her brothers are all out in the front looking at one of their many cars, so I make a snap decision. "OK, look Ronnie. I won't tell Spencer because I get it. You're tired of waiting. I'll even hint around that you need some attention. And you're both going to Antoine's New Year's party, so you know for sure you'll see him then."

"I'm not even going as his *date*, Ford. Rook invited me, not Spencer! What if he brings a girl?"

"He's not gonna bring a girl to a party you'll be at, Ronnie. Don't be ridiculous." But in reality, Spencer is not all that astute when it comes to relationships. I might need to pull him aside and make sure he doesn't piss Veronica off. "Just give it until the trials are over in the spring, can you do that? Just wait a few months until all this legal shit is behind us?"

"I don't know, Ford. It just seems pointless."

"Well, at the very least, don't call him up and tell him. If you keep it secret, I'll cover for you. But shit, Veronica, if you push his buttons you know you'll piss him off, and the first place he'll go is that guy's house. So I hope that banker has a gun."

She squints at me and then we're at her house. Her brothers descend on the Bronco like a pack of wolves and open her door.

"Ronnie where the hell have you been?" Vinn Vaughn, her middle brother, asks first.

"Ford," Vic, the oldest Vaughn brother says, "what the fuck are you doing with my baby sister?" All Ronnie's brothers are tatted up like, well, tattoo artists. Veronica has no tatts and that always surprised me. She's got a very strange blood phobia, so her continuing the trade never made sense. But she did get on board. She's one of them. And it was her talented hands that created Spencer's own body art. Every bit of it is Veronica's work.

"I saw her out jogging, picked her up and gave her a lift. She had a cramp in her side. She needs to work on her endurance." I look over at Ronnie when I say this. "Stamina, Veronica Vaughn. Slow and steady."

She smiles sweetly and looks me right back in the eye. "Thank you so much Ford, how about you stay for dinner?"

The Vaughn family is serious about their dinners and once you get invited, it's a done deal. You have no way out. Her brothers are on me like carrion. "Yeah, Ford. Come inside. The whole family's here. We got a little party going."

"Noooo—" But Grandpa Vaughn is already walking up to the Bronco waving at me.

Shit. How the hell do I start my day one hundred percent in control of this holiday and end up spending time with an old friend, buying presents from a cute kid, consoling my partner-in-crime's almost girlfriend, and invited over for dinner with the Vaughn clan?

I put the truck in park and give in.

Screw it. I still got five hours until my pet date and a man's gotta eat.

SIX

Christmas Eve dinner with the Vaughn family is not some sit-down with turkey and stuffing. No. It's a mass conglomeration of men and girlfriends milling about the house, drinking too much, smoking too much, and talking way too loud. Ronnie and I are the only ones with no dates. Even her grandpa has a lady friend over.

I think that's cute.

Ronnie's father, Vern, has the barbecue fired up and is cooking enough meat to feed a small village. I doubt there'll be leftovers.

I get jostled around between the various first floor rooms, talking to her brothers and then her grandpa—who fills my head with the most gruesome war stories I've ever heard—and then eat and make a swift exit. Swift is relative since, I spend a few hours hanging out here.

Ronnie shoots me the stink eye as I wave goodbye to them.

Yeah, Spencer needs to take care of this shit. Because she is not happy. At all. And I don't blame her, he's being a selfish dick.

SLACK

He could at the very least explain himself.

I take College down to Harmony and hang a left towards the freeway. My apartment complex is down this way and I want to bring my computer home to fuck around with tonight after the pet leaves. I'm gonna look up that guy Veronica was with. Just in case. If I never need to tell Spencer, fine. But it's better to have the info ready than be scrounging around for it after the fact.

There's almost no traffic today and I hit every green light all the way down to my apartment. I turn into the driveway and park in my spot. The jog up the steps feels good after so much driving today and I hope the snow isn't too bad tonight so I can run in the morning. Keep the routine. I like a routine.

The apartment is cold and empty. I never liked the place and if it wasn't for Spencer's guns hidden away in the third bedroom, I'd clear it out and be done with it. Chalk it up to a failed experiment with normalcy. But Spencer thinks it's necessary, so I paid up the rent for a year.

My phone buzzes in my jacket and I sift through the gifts and my new knife to find it. "Yes, Pam." She's my assistant in LA. Runs my whole life—from buying me clothes to setting up the pets.

"The studio called Mr. Aston. You're expected to show up on January fourth and pilot filming commences in New Zealand on the fourteenth for six weeks. Do you want me to book a flight for you on the third?"

"Well, that's good news, eh? We're finally getting somewhere with this shitty career." I sigh and take a seat on the couch as I picture leaving Denver for two months. I'm not ready to leave, to be honest. I'm not ready to let Rook go. I've enjoyed her too much and I've missed her even more this past month. I've barely seen her at all. Not since the last taping of Shrike Bikes. "Did we hear back from The Biker Channel on a Season Two?"

"Yes, sir. They said second week in March."

"During the trials?"

"Yes, sir. I think they specifically scheduled it that way for ratings."

"Of course they did. OK, well I'll call you back and let you know about the flight."

"Merry Christmas, Mr. Aston. If you need anything, I'm on call as usual."

"Yes, thank you, Pam." I press end and drop the phone on the cushion. Well, this is it. Life is changing. The only question is, what will I do with it?

I'm not sure yet. All I know is that I'm the only one of my inner circle that is spending this day alone.

Well, that's not quite true, I've seen a ton of people today. But all of them are home or on their way home. I'm the only one who has nowhere to go.

Well, that's not true either. My mother has a party every Christmas Eve and I'm always on the guest list.

But I'm not in the mood for a party and I'm not in the mood to go home. I'm avoiding home. But my reprieve is up. I have nowhere else to go. And maybe if I didn't have that pet coming over I might be tempted to sit Christmas out up here. There's no distractions. No one would look for me here. I'd definitely be left alone.

But after all these years of successfully spending Christmas by myself, I suddenly have some apprehension about it. And this apartment is not a good place to sit and get drunk. At least my Denver condo is in the middle of the city. I could go join other pathetic loners at whatever place is open. And there is always one place open nearby, no matter where I am in the world. There's always some bar owner who relates to us loners and agrees to house the rejected for a night of drowning away one's loneliness.

But the pet *is* coming over and if I'm being perfectly honest, I'm looking forward to her. She's not bad as far as pets go. She's got a nice body and she's trained well enough. So I grab my phone and my computer, and go back outside into the newly chilled air, climb into my Bronco, and head south.

The snow starts as soon as I hit I-70 and the drive into Denver is slick with ice as the wet roads freeze over. I get off the freeway and make my way down Broadway to my building. It's nine PM and I'm just getting into the turn lane when my phone buzzes.

"Now what the fuck?" I get stuck at the light so I grab my phone and find my mother's face staring back at me. I reluctantly press answer. "Hi Mom."

"Ford?"

"You called me, Mom. You know it's Ford. I'm the only son you have."

"It's just an expression, Ford. Can you go to the store and pick up some shallots? I thought I bought them yesterday, but they're not here."

"Shallots? Where the hell am I gonna find shallots at nine o'clock on Christmas Eve?"

"Eli's Market is open. I called him and he's waiting for you now, shallots in hand. He's that nice Jewish man—"

"I know who Eli is. He's lived next door to us for twenty years." I huff out a breath and then my turn-light goes green. "Fine, I'll swing by Eli's and bring you some shallots."

I hang up, annoyed. It's a ploy, I know it. To get me to go to church. But it's not gonna work. I flip a bitch and make my way over to Park Hill where my mom's house is. Eli's Market is a couple blocks down from us, off Colfax. Twenty minutes later I pull up to it and true to her word, Eli is standing there in the blowing snow, bag of shallots in hand. I pull up to him and roll my window down like this is a drive-up vegetable stand. "Thanks Mr. Maus," I say as I grab the bag, simultaneously hand him a twenty, and tell him to keep the change as I roll the window back up. I have forty minutes to get back home for my pet date.

Our street is lined with old trees that tower above the houses. Not all the houses are huge like ours. Spencer's, for example, is just a modest four bedroom bungalow.

Modest is not the word I'd use to describe our house. Pretentious, that's more like it. A huge American foursquare— which is almost a contradictory statement, since foursquares are supposed to be humble. It has symmetrical windows on the first, second, and third floors, and I suspect this is why my mother wanted it. We both like orderly designs. The porch is deep and massive, spanning the entire front of the house. It has a wide, welcoming opening, and thick columns on either side of the steps that lead to the front door. It's got seven bedrooms, six bathrooms, a carriage house where I lived for my senior year in high school, and an elaborate basement set up for dinner parties so the first floor can be used for chatting.

It's walled in with brick on all sides with a massive wrought iron gate that is open at the moment. There are parking attendants waving me off-property for parking, but I pull in anyway. I roll the window down and he immediately goes into his spiel about no parking in the driveway. "I live here. I'm pulling up, get out of my way."

Maybe my tone is a little much for a Christmas Eve party, or maybe he sees the flash of anger in my eyes—but his eyebrows go up in surprise and he moves off to the side. I pull up the driveway and park next to the kitchen door, then get out with my bag of shallots, and head inside.

It's like the North Pole threw up in here, that's how fucking festive it is. People are laughing, someone is playing Christmas songs on the piano in the front room, the whole house smells like food, and the commercial kitchen is packed with cooks and servers.

"Who needed shallots?" I call out to them.

They stare at me, and then ignore me.

"Right." I set the shallots down on the counter and go find my mother. Traditionally, foursquare homes are divided into four rooms per floor, which includes the kitchen, the formal dining room, living room, and family room. Our living and family rooms have been remodeled, so it's just one great-room. My mother is standing in front of the windows, next to a man playing the piano. In fact, she's standing a little too close to this man playing the piano. She's laughing down at him with a

SLACK

twinkle in her eye and she's got a champagne flute in her hand.

Could my day get any more fucked up? Since when does my mother have a boyfriend?

Maybe if you came around more than twice a year you'd know.

People are talking to me as I make my way across the long front room, but they know better than to touch me or get too personal, so I glide right past them and tap my mother on the shoulder.

My mom is kinda on the small side. Petite, I guess. She's got her auburn hair piled up on her head and she's wearing a conservative red dress that ends mid-calf. She turns and throws her hands up in excitement. "You made it!"

"No," I growl. "I came with your shallots but no one in the kitchen knows what I'm talking about."

"Oh," she turns to the man playing the songs. "Gary, go tell the cooks what to do with the shallots, would you please?"

He gets up and leaves, and then my mother turns back to me with a smile. "I wanted you to meet him. Can you say hello at least?"

I just blink at her. "*Meet him?*"

"Yes, Ford," she says in her soothing mom voice. "I've been dating him for three months."

I turn away and walk out. I'm done with this fucking day.

I don't even know how I get back to my apartment garage, but I'm already here, sitting in my Bronco, trying to come to terms with what just happened. My mother has moved on.

Shit that fucking stings like bad.

I check my watch and it's ten minutes past ten. Fuck. I grab my computer and get out. I jog over to the elevator, pressing the button repeatedly, hoping that will make it appear quicker. The doors finally open and I key in my penthouse code, then tap my foot the entire way up.

The doors open and the naked pet is walking to the closet on the far end of the hall where I have them leave their clothes. She stops mid-stride and stares at me, her brows a bit furrowed.

She might be pissed. I've left her waiting lots of times, but it *is* Christmas Eve.

"Sorry," I say as I quickly walk to my apartment door to unlock and open it. "If you're staying, follow me in, close the door behind you, and stand at attention."

I go inside and drop my keys on the foyer table and then walk straight to the office to lock up my computer.

The front door closes quietly behind me and her bare feet make a small padding sound as she walks into the living room.

I smile.

Finally. *Finally*, after all the bullshit I had to do today, I'm gonna get some satisfaction.

SEVEN

When I return to the living room my pet is standing ready in front of the window, not facing me. This is where I like them at night because the window is like a mirror and if they want, they can watch me walk up behind them. The rules state they will not look at me. But this pet cheats. Every single time. I can see her eyes trained on me like a target as soon as I appear in the living room. She knows I can see her and yet, she never averts her eyes—bowing her head is also against the rules and I'd definitely spank her for it tonight. I like an even chin with downcast eyes.

This is how I know she's playing a game. And not a sexual one, but a power one. Because if all she wanted was a spanking, she could bow her head and get it over with. But that's not all she wants. She wants me to punish her on her terms, but she's not in charge here. I am. So I've restrained myself for months.

I take my white t-shirt off as I walk up behind her. I can see the color of her eyes—green—that's how visible it is that she's watching me. Her lips part, form a seductive *o* shape, and the smallest of moans comes out as she licks her lips.

I squint my eyes down into slits as I consider what I'd like to do with her tonight. "Do you want to play, pet?" Her eyes in the window lift up a little so she can stare into my own through the glass. "You know I can see you, so why do you do it?"

She looks away at this, but not because she was caught, but because she's thinking. Considering if she should risk talking.

If she talks, she's out. She knows this.

"Because you're trying to tell me something?" I guess.

She nods and holds my gaze.

"Because you're trying to tell me you're not a pet?"

She shakes out a no for this one, and I let out a breath as I lean into her neck and nip the tender skin near her nape. "Right answer, pet. But is it true?"

She lets out a squeal and lifts her head. My hand automatically slides around the front of her throat. I palm it gently, then reach up under her jaw and press my thumb into the hollow under her ear, forcing her to turn her head towards me. She meets my gaze directly this time. In full defiance. And then she falters and takes a deep breath, letting it out slowly, to calm herself. "Do I make you anxious, pet?"

She swallows and nods.

"But you can leave any time you want. And yet, you never do. Why?"

She squints her eyes at me.

"Why do you come here? Why do you let me treat you like this? Why do you put up with me?" I wait to see if she'll talk so I can throw her out and be done with it, but she holds her silence and redirects her gaze so it's not trained on me. I rest my hands on the top of her shoulders and she shivers as I push my chest into her back. My hands drop down to her nipples and I twist them, not hard, just enough to make her moan. One hand remains on her breast but the other caresses its way down her stomach and rests on her hip. "Come with me," I whisper in her ear.

I lead her over to the buffet table in the dining room and remove a pair of handcuffs from a drawer. She presents her hands behind her back before I even ask, and my dick begins to grow as I fasten them carefully around her wrists. "You know what to do," I tell her softly.

She backs up a little, then bends over so her face is turned to the side, resting on the buffet, her arms are restrained in the small of her back, and her legs are slightly apart.

"Open your legs more, pet. I need to know you want it, or I'll send you home craving."

She widens her stance and then widens it again. Her eyes are open, looking up at me in defiance.

"Do you realize it's against the rules of play to look me in the eye?" I ask her.

She considers me, almost thoughtfully. Like I just asked her what she wanted for dessert. And then she nods yes.

"I should throw you out right now. Do you want me to be done with you?"

She shakes no.

"Then look away, *bitch.*"

That word is like a slap and she closes her eyes, opens them, and redirects her gaze to the muted gray-colored walls. I smack her hard on the left cheek as soon as she relaxes and she yelps.

She's allowed to cry out in pain or pleasure, so I ignore this and pull her hair with my other hand, forcing her head back. "Now you may look at me, *whore.*" She does. She knows my patience has run its course. "You want to press me? You want the nice spankings? You want to come in here and try and control me?" My hand comes down hard on her ass and the redness appears at the same moment she cries out and pulls away. But I've still got a tight hold on her hair, so that snaps her back to attention.

I lean into her neck again and whisper, "You forgot to count, pet." And then I smack her twice and her fingers silently call out the numbers. *One. Two.* I pull her hair again and she whimpers this time. I've been rough with this pet before, but never angry. I rarely get angry, but I feel it tonight. I *want* to be angry.

I step back and take a breath because I don't want to send her away yet. I want to fuck this bitch. *Bad.* She's been testing me for months and she's still mine at the moment, so I will take her. But I need to get a hold of this anger, at least long enough to get off and send her on her way. I grab the key to her cuffs and turn towards the bedroom. "Follow," I call out as I walk away.

Her feet slap against the polished tiles as she runs to catch up with me. Once inside the bedroom I point to the bed. "Sit." She takes a resolving breath and sets herself atop the white down comforter.

Once again I ask myself why? Why the fuck do these bitches put up with me? I sit down next to her, close enough to make her whole body move with my weight on the mattress. "Lie across my lap." She puts her knees up on the bed and then bends over, sticking her ass way out, because her hands are still bound behind her back, so she's forced to lower her face to my thigh and slide herself up into position. Which also forces her face to drag along my hardened dick, only the fabric of my jeans between her hot breath and my cock.

This takes the anger away a little, because that right there, *that* was clever. And it tells me a lot of things. *One*—she's OK with my insults. *Two*—she's still not giving in to me, regardless of how well she's following the rules. And *three*—she wants to be fucked just as bad as I want to fuck her.

I'm not into being mean for the hell of it. I like them to submit, that's all. I like to be in control. I like to call the shots. I like to be obeyed unconditionally. And almost all of the girls who make it beyond the first appointment do that, and do it well. But this girl has been skating on the edge of compliance the entire time she's been my pet.

She needs to go.

Tonight is her last night, so I'm going to enjoy her to the fullest before I send her packing.

I unlock her handcuffs and slide them off, tossing them on to the floor with a hard clunk. "Ready, pet?"

She nods yes.

"I'm going to turn your cheeks bright red for your disobedience. But I'll make it worth it if you're a very good girl." She starts nodding her head when my hand comes down full force on her ass again, making both her legs kick up as she signs off a *one*. I slap them back down. "That's not a good example of perfect behavior, pet." I smack her again, harder, and this time she buffers the pain by sinking into my lap. I caress her ass for being good, rubbing her roundness, then stroking the back of her thighs, stopping in the dent behind her knee where I trace small, light circles.

She relaxes and I push her legs open, making one fall to the floor, and then smack her open pussy hard. My hand slips right between her legs and presses against her sex until she moans. I smack her again and now her entire ass is flaming red. Her hands do the sign for *two*. She lets off a sob and that means she deserves a gently probing finger around her asshole. She squeezes her hole closed, trying to take some control back, and the next smack elicits a loud cry. "Don't. Your ass belongs to me and if I want to play with it, I will." I slip my finger inside and her whole body goes stiff, but she does not resist.

Victory for Ford.

I ease it out and grab her hair with the hand that has been holding her down. I force her head up by pulling and yes, sure enough, she's got tears. "You're defiant. I'm getting rid of you." She stares at me, then more tears come out and she looks like she might start wailing. I flip her over quickly and then move down the bed until her ass is flush with the edge of my thigh and her legs are draped over my lap. "You can get up and leave now if you want. You're never coming back. You refuse to submit and I'm tired of training you. It's a waste of time."

She's silent for a few seconds. "Or?" she asks quietly. Her voice is small and sweet. It's too bad, really. That she came here as a pet. I like her. But whatever her reason for being here, that in and of itself is enough to make me never want her in a serious way.

That and she's blonde.

They're always blonde or red because the last thing I want is any future woman I love to remind me of the shitload of pets I used up and threw away.

"Or I take away all the rules and we just fuck. All the dirty shit we've been doing is on the table. All of it. But when we're done, you leave and don't come back."

Her eyes narrow with her glare. "Why are you such an asshole?"

I laugh. "You can talk if you stay, but I'm not going to pretend I like you for your witty conversation. I like you for your pussy and I'd like to fuck you tonight. I'm tired of playing. Stay and have fun or get the hell out."

She stares up at me, then she bends her legs, points her toes, and lifts them up and back, wrapping her arms around her calves so her pussy is open to me.

I look down at her puffy lips, all swollen with desire and red with the rush of adrenaline, and then I grab her ankles and push them towards her head so I can smack her clit. She cries out, her back arching up off the bed, and I smack her again, making her struggle to get free this time. I stand up and grab her arm before her legs can fall and then I turn her body around until her ass is hanging off the mattress, her feet on the floor.

I kick open her legs. She bites her lip and stifles a moan as I slide a finger into her sopping wet pussy and pump her hard before inserting another finger. "Oh God," she says, her voice heavy with desire.

"Did you get yourself off when you went home this morning?" She writhes as my fingers sweep back and forth against her sweet spot, then slide up and down her slit, rubbing her clit, creating the hard friction that has her panting out, "*Yes, yes, yes.*"

"Yes, you did?"

"*No,*" she gasps as I thrust into her. "No, I didn't, but I want to come," she says in desperation, looking me in the eye. "Right now."

"No one's stopping you, pet." I lean down and tickle her nub with my tongue and suck until she screams and tries to clamp her knees closed. I push against her inner thighs and spread her wide open, sucking on her folds, her lips, her clit, and then tongue fuck her pussy until she gushes into my mouth and twists so hard she breaks free. Her knees slide to the floor as her chest rests on the bed.

I take advantage of her presentation and stand her up so her ass is in the air and her lips are peeking through her closed thighs.

It's my turn to say, "Yes." Because this is how I like my women. I grab a condom from the nightstand, tear the wrapper open, and slide it down my cock. Then I stand up, lift her up by the knees and set them back down on the bed so her ass is at my waist. "Keep your head down and your ass up," I command. She's trying to answer me when I thrust into her, rocking her forward, her face sliding against the sheets. I smack her red ass and she yelps, squirming to get away. But I grab the front of her thighs and pull her towards me, burying myself inside her, all the way up to my balls. I fuck her like that, her crying out with each spanking, wriggling, only to have my arms clamp down on her—holding her still as she moans—begging me to make her come again.

My balls begin to tighten and just before I explode I reach around and stroke her clit, sending her into a screaming fit of "*Oh, oh ohhhhh.*" I push her forward on the bed and then collapse next to her as I try to catch my breath.

My day suddenly sucks a little less.

I close my eyes and before I know it, I'm blinking awake as this fucking pet tries to rest her head on my chest.

I push her off me and sit up. "Time to go, girl. Out."

I don't wait for an answer, hell I don't even know if she's

awake. I just get up and go to the bathroom, slipping the condom off and throwing it into the toilet before I start the shower. I glance down at the clock on my vanity. Fuck, it's only eleven. I waited all fucking day for forty-five minutes of sex.

It's hardly worth it.

"Mind if I join you," the ex-pet asks from the doorway. She's leaning against the door jamb, twirling her hair like she's trying to be sexy.

I narrow my eyes at her nerve. "I told you to go. There's no shower, there's no goodbye, there's no *Thanks for the fuck*. Just get out."

Her whole face changes with these words. It goes from soft and satisfied to chiseled hardness instantly. "I'm not sure who the hell you think you are or why you feel you're so special you can treat people like shit. But you know what? You're one disturbed, messed-up *freak*." She whirls around to leave but I catch her by the upper arm. My reaction surprises me but it positively scares the shit out of her. "Let me go," she growls. But I know her bravery is fake, I can feel her pulse quicken in her brachial artery.

My voice is calm when the words drip out. "*I'm* the freak? You're the one who shows up here, removes your clothes in my hallway, presents your pussy to me by lying on a mat in front of my door, and then allows yourself to be treated like shit just so you can what? Why the fuck would you ever agree to my conditions? Why? Other than you're a much more disturbed individual than I am. At least I'm the one who maintains some fucking dignity during our encounters. *You*—you just open your legs to a complete stranger. The same stranger you think is one disturbed messed-up freak. What you see in me is what you see in you. You're looking in the mirror, honey." I give her a shove towards the door and let go of her arm. "Now get out."

She lifts her chin up and smiles. I figure this is her pathetic attempt to save face, but there's a small gleam in her eye that says she really does feel superior. "Well, all that might be true. But if you really want to know why I do this, I'll tell you." She walks to the bedroom door to put some distance between us and then turns, still smiling as she drums her fingertips along the side of the door. "I do it because I need the money." And then she walks out.

What?

I pull my jeans back on and follow. She's already in the hallway half-dressed when I catch up with her. She buttons her jeans and slips her feet into her snow boots as she tugs the shirt over her head.

I stare at her. Hard. "I do not *pay* for sex."

"Right," she says pulling her hair out of her shirt and shrugging on her coat. "That may be true, but I certainly have been getting paid to show up here on command for the past two months." She huffs out a laugh. "What? You think you're so fucking special you can get nice girls like me to come be your sex slave just for the orgasms?"

I glare at her.

"I mean, sure, I had a few good ones. But come on? Get real, *Aston*. Pam pays me to come here, you dumbass. She pays all of us to service you and your fucked-up fetishes."

She punches the button on the elevator and shoves her hands in her pockets. Then her gaze goes back to the pet mat. I follow that gaze because her expression becomes livid. "And you know what? I baked those fucking cookies for my kid. And you took one bite and threw that bag down on the ground like they were trash. Well, fuck you. I only do this job to pay for my babysitter while I go to school during the day, you self-absorbed, emotionless, pathetic excuse of a man. And my naive kid was the one who said I should bring my boss cookies on Christmas Eve to make him happy."

The elevator opens and she tugs her purse over her shoulder and enters. She doesn't look at me again, just hides in the corner where the buttons are, and allows the doors to close without another word.

EIGHT

I *seethe.*

Positively seethe.

I want to call Pam up and fire her ass. I want to chase that little pet bitch down and fuck with her head, fill it with insults and half-truths so filled with venom, she'll need therapy for years to get over it.

I want to throw things through the fucking living room window.

I take a deep breath instead.

Because nobody. *Nobody*—especially not that skanky little cunt who sold her body for money—*nobody* can make me lose my temper.

It's just not possible. If there's one thing I control in my life, it's my reactions. I have complete control over my reactions and this bitch will not take that away. I take a deep breath and remember my shower is still running. I go back to the bathroom and strip, then douse myself in hot water to wash away the smell of slut.

SLACK

When I'm done I wrap the towel around me and call Pam. She answers on the first ring. "I already heard. I'm so sorry, Ford."

That little tramp will not ruin my only real relationship I have in this world since my father died. Pam keeps my whole life from unraveling—she picks up all the slack. This woman holds me together professionally, and even if I'm not quite all there personally, no one ever knows because Pam is my cover. She's family to me and I would never throw away our five year working relationship over a *whore*. "Forget it, Pam. Forget it, OK? No more pets. Cancel all of them. I'm done." I end the connection and the home screen flashes a missed call at me.

"Great." My fucking mother. I huff out a laugh. That's just what I need. To think about my mother and her new piano playing boyfriend. The asshole's probably after her money. *Prick.* I press the voice mail icon and it begins to play. "*Ford, I'm sorry. I don't want you to be upset. I've told Gary it won't work. I'm sorry.*" She pauses here to sigh.

It's a *very* sad sigh.

"*I have to get ready for church. Maybe you will find time to come by tomorrow? Have dinner?*"

I press end. *Fuck.* This day has gone to shit. I pick up the remote and flip on the TV to break the suffocating silence. This TV came with the apartment. Biker Channel pays for this place, and this condo is one of the few luxury perks written into my contract. The local news comes on and I sit back to think.

Goddamn it. I run my fingers through my hair and glance at the clock. Not even midnight yet. The fucking day's not even over. I'm sure something else will go wrong if I just hang out a little longer. I might as well just go to bed. I point the remote at the TV to turn it off when I see the headlines. *Nine killed in military-style attack on home-grown terror cell west of Cheyenne.*

Holy shit, I totally deserve to see that. That's what I get for turning the TV on. I point at it again to turn it off and then stop.

The whole world fucking stops.

Sasha Alena Cherlin's face flashes across the screen. *Wounded in the firefight,* is all it says.

What fucking firefight?

I just stare at the TV for a few seconds, trying to process this new reality. She's in the hospital after being attacked in a family hunting cabin twenty-five miles north of Cheyenne. There's no mention of Merc or the gun deal, no names of the dead are released, but poor Sasha. The reporter says her grandparents are picking her up and taking her home tonight—and that can only mean one thing. Her father is one of the unnamed dead.

I almost can't think straight as I try to come to terms with what this means for that smiling little girl this morning.

She sold me a present she bought for her mother, just so I could give it to my mother. And my mother will probably never see it because I'm an anti-social freak who can't bring himself to celebrate a holiday with his own family.

Family. That's something I take for granted, even after all that shit with my dad. I bet Sasha would kill to have a mother calling her up on Christmas Eve.

What kind of piece of shit am I?

I look back over at the clock. Eleven forty-two. I know where my mom will be in twenty minutes. Hell, she's probably there now. I walk back to my room and flip the light on in my closet. I put on a gray suit, comb my hair back, slip on my navy cashmere topcoat, and grab my keys and phone.

I'm going to church.

NINE

St. Margaret's is a traditional brick Catholic church with massive cathedral ceilings, dark wooden pews, the gigantic organ up in the corner, the lavish altar, and the stained glass windows. I haven't been in here in years, but as soon as I walk in the smell of incense overtakes my senses and I feel like I never left.

We have a spot where we sit. In fact, almost everyone has a *spot*. Midnight mass is tricky in this regard, because our spot on Saturday evening mass might be someone else's spot on Sunday morning. But when I look over at our spot, there's my mother.

Sitting alone.

I am such a bad son.

The interior is set up in a circular configuration. The altar is the top of the circle, then there are three sets of pews that span out from there. It's not a half-circle of pews, even though that's the best way to describe it. It's slightly more than half a circle, and to my mind this never made sense. It bothered me when I was six and it bothers me now. I can't stand asymmetrical or uneven designs.

SLACK

I do realize this is not normal. To hate this place because the architect wanted the pews to take up more than one-half of a circle so more people can fit in for the service. But I do. I *hate* this room.

It makes me uneasy just to be in here.

But I suck it up and walk to our pew and say, "Excuse me," in my most polite voice as I inch my way past the people already sitting in their *spots*, and plop down next to my mom. She likes to sit in the middle. Not just the middle of this section, or this pew, but the middle of the entire church.

I guess I take after her in that regard, because sitting here almost cancels out the uneven layout of the pews.

"Ford," she says in her soft church-whisper voice. She leads by example and I was always a little too loud as a child, so that voice was practiced to no end.

"Sorry I walked out earlier. I didn't mean it the way it looked." I pause. "If it looked like I disapprove, then I didn't mean it that way. You have a right to be happy."

She looks up at me surprised.

"I hope he didn't stay away because of me. I'd feel terrible." Of course the reason she's alone is because of me, but it's done. Nothing I can do about that, so I don't dwell. She appreciates the sentiment and if the guy's worth a shit, he'll still be available tomorrow when she calls to smooth things over.

Then the choir starts up and the ceremony begins so our conversation is cut short. I look over at the section of pews at my left and through a small break in the crowd, I see Ronin smiling at me. Laughing at me, I think. Elise is on one side, and Antoine on the other side of her. And on Ronin's other side is Rook. She's belting out *Hark the Herald Angels Sing* like she owns it.

God, I love that girl.

She is my herald, a living proclamation that my life can get better.

Rook is so beautiful I constantly want to stare at her. Tonight she's wearing a cream colored suit and she has a red scarf around her neck. Her hair is down and flows over her shoulders in big bouncy curls. She looks up for a moment, to watch the priest and his attendants ascend the steps to the altar, and her bright blue eyes flash in the low light.

She takes my breath away. I reluctantly redirect my gaze over to the other side of the church where Spencer's family sits. Mass begins as I gawk at all the familiar faces. Spencer's parents are still together and they sit on either side of him. He's an only child as well, which was why we gravitated to each other as children. His eyes wander my way and when he spots me sitting in the pews, he fakes an exaggerated look of surprise. Or maybe not so exaggerated, since I haven't been here in years. Then he shoots me with his finger and someone behind me flicks my ear.

Spencer laughs when I wince but I don't even turn around. I know who it is. Sister Anne Catherine.

My childhood nemesis.

She does not accept my silent surrender and leans in to whisper, "Rutherford, behave yourself."

My mother looks over at me with disapproval, Spencer shoots his finger again and covers his fake laughing mouth like he's ten, and when I look over at Ronin, he's smirking.

Rook is reading the bulletin intently, like she's studying for a test.

God, I love her.

My heart begins to beat wildly and I suddenly have the need to flee, but my mother grabs my coat sleeve when I make to rise, and I settle back down.

"You're here now, Ford," she whispers. "Just relax and enjoy it."

And that is how I spend the wee hours of Christmas Day. Desperately wishing I was anywhere but church as I kneel, sit, stand, wish Sister Nemesis peace, and then force myself not to freak out when she grabs my hand to shake it.

She does that on purpose.

There's no way I'm taking communion, so as soon as our

row gets up for it, I pat my mother on the shoulder as my only warning, and make my escape out the back. I stuff my hands into my coat pockets, sorta proud of myself that I lasted a whole hour in there, and then spy Ronin's black truck across the street from my Bronco.

I could put Rook's present in the truck. I walk over to the Bronco and open up the glove box.

Oh, God. Looking at Sasha's gift wrapping handiwork almost makes me feel sick. What must she be thinking right now? I grab both presents and my knife and stuff them all in my pockets. I jog back over to Ronin's truck. The doors are locked but the back glass window slides open when I try it. I hop in the bed, reach my hand in, and drop the little Eric Cartman package on her seat.

I hope she doesn't sit on it, but if she does, she'll definitely know it's there. I close the window and hop out, then spy my mom's Mercedes down the street. Sasha would definitely be disappointed in me if I never gave that bracelet to her. And since I'm not sure if I'll go home tomorrow for dinner—that's asking a lot, even if it *is* Christmas—I better drop it off now, too.

I have a remote on my key chain that unlocks her car, so I slip in the driver's seat and prop the little gift bag in the ledge of her GPS console, and then get out and lock it up.

I feel a little bit like Santa Claus and some of the dread and unease melts away as I walk back to my Bronco. I pocket my gift-wrapped knife and drive home. It stopped snowing and the sky is clear and black, with more stars showing than you usually see in the city.

When the elevator opens to my penthouse hallway, I'm half expecting that psycho-pet to be here waiting, but she's not. I'm alone again. I'm not sure how getting rid of the pets will affect me. I'm not even sure if I'm serious about it. I'll probably call Pam up tomorrow begging for one. Surely she can't have scheduled one for Christmas Day. There's still time if I want to change my mind.

I'm just not sure.

I hang up my coat and change out of my suit and into some

sweats and a t-shirt.

What a fucking day.

I pour some whiskey into a rocks tumbler and take a long slow sip. This is what I've needed since this morning. Teach me to drive all over two fucking states. My phone buzzes an incoming call and I look at the time. Almost one thirty. And it's my mom.

"Mom?" I ask, like she does every time I call, as if she didn't have caller ID and know for a fact that it's me.

"Ford," she says with a lightness in her voice. "You have caller ID, why do you always ask if it's me?"

I laugh.

"I just wanted to thank you for the gift, Ford. It's lovely. And who may I ask is Sasha?"

My laugh dies. I forgot she signed the card. "She's a kid who sold me the bracelet." I tell my mom the story of where it came from because Sasha would've wanted me to, and I can tell she's choked up about it. I even tell her what happened with her dad and the news broadcast. My mom is smart. She's not delusional, she knows what I do. She knows that somehow I'm connected to this girl's father. She knows Spencer, Ronin, and I are guilty as fuck of just about everything they say about us on TV. She knows. But she accepts me. My parents have always accepted me. The weirdness was never a factor. We chat for almost eight minutes. I don't think I've ever talked to my mother on the phone for so long in my life.

"I'm so sorry that happened, Ford," she says as the conversation winds down.

"Yeah, me too. I might drive up there tomorrow and see if she needs anything so you should probably just get Gary to come keep you company all day."

She sighs. "I miss your father every day, Ford. I do. He was my whole life. But he's been gone for two years now and I'm lonely."

I nod, like she can see me. "I understand. It's OK." I'm not really sure that it is OK, but she needs to hear that, so I say it anyway. I'm not capable of much empathy, but I can fake it. And they never know the difference, so what the fuck. It doesn't cost me anything to pretend to understand and be nice.

We say our goodbyes and hang up.

TEN

Everything seems to be changing all of a sudden. This morning I had a routine. I'm not sure if it was a good routine or a healthy one, but it was there. Running, pets, solitude.

And now, I'm not sure where I am, let alone where I'm going.

I turn the TV off and leave my whiskey on the coffee table. My bedroom feels sterile to me. The only hint that someone actually sleeps here is the rumpled duvet from my earlier fuck with psycho-pet. I'm just about to turn off the light and give up on this day when my phone buzzes.

What could my mother want now?

I pick it up and look at the face.

Rook.

Life improves instantly.

"Miss Corvus," I rumble out smoothly. Even I can hear the want in my voice. "I realize you don't need beauty rest, but some of us do."

She snorts at me. "Ford, you are so, so stupid! I just called to tell you I found this little Eric Cartman toy on my seat. In fact,

I sat on it and it made me jump." I picture this in my head and I wish I was there to see it. "And imagine my surprise when I opened it and found that card."

Busted. I didn't write the card, Sasha did. "I have no idea what you're talking about. Tell me what the card says."

"It says," she stops to clear her throat. "*To Ford's friend who is a girl. He likes you a lot, but I'm gonna try and steal his heart when I get my braces off, so you better move fast. Merry Christmas, Sasha and Ford Forever. XXOO, heart, heart, flower.*"

I laugh. I laugh so hard it echoes off the walls in this stupid ultra-modern condo. "Well," I tell her, "that pretty much made my whole day. If I could have you and Sasha together, my life might be complete."

"I got you something too, Ford. But I was afraid to call it a gift. Ronin says you don't like holidays."

"Some people make some holidays more tolerable than others. What did you get me?"

She takes a deep breath. "I talked Ronin into letting me do another season of Shrike Bikes. But I'm not gonna do it unless you're the producer. So if you're out, I'm out too. Because I never realized how much we do together until we were separated this month. When I don't run with you every day, I feel a little lost. You kinda ground me, Ford. I need it. I need that show and I'm really looking forward to all of us being together again."

I breathe deeply to calm my racing heart. "I just heard today that Season Two is on. My assistant called from LA and said they want to film during the trials. I know it'll be hard, but we'll manage it, OK? Ronin, Spence, and I will make sure we come out of this looking squeaky clean."

"I've never doubted you guys, Ford. Never. I look at my life today and I think to myself—Rook, how the hell? Ya know? Just how the hell did you get here? Remember when you asked me that last summer?"

"Yeah," I say as I think back to that day. I was falling in love with her and I didn't even know it. "Last Christmas I was in Japan, all alone, producing a game show. Two Christmases ago I was still enjoying the fact that I had two parents, even if I did take them for granted. Three Christmases ago I was fighting with Ronin and Spencer so bad, we stopped talking completely. Four Christmases ago Mardee was dead from an overdose. Five Christmases ago I was running cons with Ronin and Spencer like we were invincible. I feel like I'm going in circles, ya know? Ending up right back where I started. But you, Rook. You've changed my life."

I stop there because I'm very close to telling her how I really feel and I'm not gonna confuse her like that on Christmas. She loves Ronin, not me. If I was a good guy I'd leave her the fuck alone, just move on to my next job and get over it.

"Well," she says to slice through my silence. "Five Christmases ago I thought Wade Minix was my forever guy. Four Christmases ago I thought Jon Walsh was my forever guy. Three Christmases ago I was getting the shit beat out of me by my soon-to-be husband. Two Christmases ago I thought I was going to be a mom." She stops here to pull herself together and it almost breaks my heart listening to her talk about the baby she lost. "And last Christmas we had this big party at our house in Illinois. It was a nice party actually, but I can only really remember two things. My body was very sore from Jon beating me the night before and I was very cold because I was standing outside in the middle of the night, looking up at the stars. Like I am right now."

"You're outside?"

"Mmmhmm. I saw this star that night. It was so, so bright. And it had a bluish color to it. And maybe I've never really looked before, but I've never seen a blue star. It struck me as special, ya know?"

I grab my coat from the front closet and slip outside on my balcony so I can look at the stars as she talks. "I'm outside now too. It's fucking cold out here, Rook!"

"I know. But I wanted to look for that star when I called you, can you help me find it?"

SLACK

"Was it in the south?"

"Ummm, yes, I think. I was standing next to Jon's car, looking up over the trees behind the house. That's South, right?"

I don't want to think about that house but I force myself to picture it on the satellite image Spencer and I used to find Rook when she took off last fall. "Yeah, the woods were south, so you would've been looking southwest. Where are you now? On Ronin's balcony or the garden terrace?"

"Garden terrace."

"Walk over and look at Coors Field."

"OK"

"Then look left a little bit, then up at the sky. It's twinkling tonight."

"I see it! Oh my God, Ford, how do you know this shit?"

How I love to make this girl happy. I've never wanted someone to be happy so much in my life. "It's called Sirius. It's the brightest star in the sky and it's prominent in the winter. An educated guess, that's all."

She's silent for a few seconds. "I wished on that star, Ford. I asked Santa Claus or God or someone, it didn't matter to me who it was. I just wished on that star and I asked it to make my life change. Because I couldn't live like that anymore, Ford. I was thinking bad things last Christmas. It was a very dark time for me. But I wished on that star that my life would change. It didn't even have to be a *good* change, but it just couldn't stay the same. And it did. I took a lot of chances. I accepted a lot of risk to get here, but here I am. I feel like I'm home now."

I nod, but inside I'm devastated. "I understand, Rook, I do."

Ronin's voice calls out to her from a distance. He must be in the doorway to the studio.

"Well, that ball and chain is barking at me to come inside and go to bed. Will I see you tomorrow, Ford?

There is nothing I want more than to see you tomorrow. I want you every day. These words try to come out, but I hold them back with great difficulty. "No, I think I have plans tomorrow. With a girl up in Wyoming."

"Would that be Sasha?" she chuckles.

"Yeah—" I want to tell Rook everything. Every single thing that happened to me today from Merc to Sasha, to Veronica and Spencer, and my mom and her new boyfriend. So much happened today and I have no one to share it with. No one. I just want someone to listen to me for once.

"You'll be at the New Year's Party for sure, though, right? Exit interviews for Shrike Bikes Season One? You know how I hate those…"

"Yeah," I say softly. "I know. And for sure I'll be there."

"OK, Ford. Merry Christmas. I'll see you soon. Bye."

The phone beeps that the call has ended and I'm alone again. I look up at Rook's Christmas star and make my own wish. I need something new. I need *someone* new. I need change, good or bad, like Rook said. I just need *this life* to stop being mine.

I take a deep breath and go back inside to my totally empty, ultra-modern, sterile, cold and lonely condo.

The knife I bought from Sasha is still wrapped up in pretty Christmas bows and paper, so I pick it up and sit on the couch to open it. I untie the gold ribbon and then carefully peel back the red paper. It's stupid to be excited, I know what the gift is, I bought it for myself. But even so, Sasha made it special.

Inside the case is the Snubby CQC . But that's not all that's in there. I smile as I pick up the silver flash drive all decorated up with mini stickers. Snowflakes, Santa faces, reindeer, and a few guns.

Fucking Nikita.

I grab my computer from the office and set it on the coffee table so I can plug the drive in and see what's on it. It can't be anything personal, she didn't have time. But the curiosity is killing me.

It's got an autorun program that pulls up a welcome screen. It's bobbleheads with transposed pictures of Sasha and her father's faces on them, bobbing their heads to Jingle Bells.

SLACK

The menu almost breaks my heart. This must be a photo CD of trips Sasha and her dad took. I click a link and it cycles through a series of images set to Christmas music.

I bet that little girl is kicking herself for giving me this drive. I get up and go to my closet safe and get out the external drive I keep here with my scripts on it and run a Wyoming DMV crawl for the name Cherlin. There's a few of them, one in Cheyenne, obviously Sasha's father. A few in Laramie, obviously not cattle ranchers since they are within city limits on the satellite map. And one family up in Big Horn, just south of Sheridan. I memorize the address and blow out a long breath of air.

Sasha will never have another happy Christmas. She will never live through this day without thinking of how her father was killed, how she was left in a cabin to wait out some fucked up black-ops job, how she ended up in the hospital—*orphaned*.

I can't do this anymore. I can't do this. I can't be this guy, I can't live this life, I can't stay here tonight. I walk into my bedroom and stuff a backpack full of clothes. I grab my toothbrush and some toiletries, shoving them inside as well. And then I pull on a pair of jeans and a hoodie, shrug myself into my boots and leather jacket, and walk out the door.

I can't change the fact that Sasha got her dad taken away from her on Christmas Eve, but I can be the guy who shows up on Christmas Day, trying his best to make this fucked up shit just a little bit easier.

END OF BOOK SHIT

Can we all agree that we love Ford? :) I'll let you in on a secret—Ford was supposed to be the bad guy. I tried very hard, but as soon as he stood there in the darkness of Antoine's studio and Ronin passed by him in the beginning of Manic, I knew. There's no way Ford was a bad guy. Maybe he's got issues, but there's something about him that's tragic in all the right ways.

Ford is waiting near the studio windows when I walk in, his back to me, his stick-up-his-ass posture as erect as ever. It's been years and still the sight of him makes me want to punch his face in.

"Where'd you find her?" he asks without turning around.

"She found me."

"What's wrong with her?"

"She's a nice girl, Ford. So stay back. She'll do her job, don't worry."

But my favorite Ford scene in Manic was this one, where Rook finds her inner bad-ass and puts him in his place. And after I wrote that chapter I was like—*holy shit, where did that even come from*? I might be in love with Ford.

"Makes you feel what, Rook? Used?"

I stop again. "Yeah, OK? You make me feel like he's using me. And he's not, you are! You're using me to mess things up between us and…"

"And what?"

I hold that in and keep walking.

"And keep you for myself? Is that what you think, Rook?"

"No, Ford. That's not what I think."

"Then your instincts are off, because that's exactly what I'm

doing."

I stop again. "Holy shit! You are such an asshole!"

And then he smiles. And it's not a smile I've ever seen on him before. It's like all his other smiles were fake and I'm just now seeing real happiness on his face for the first time.

It disarms me. Completely. And he knows it because he moves closer to me, not touching me, but very close. It makes me uncomfortable and I look around, feeling guilty. There's no one else in the parking lot. There are a lot of cars on the street, but we're still a good hundred yards from the street.

"I won't touch you, Rook, don't worry," he whispers. "I'm not a runner and I'm not a cheater, either. Life is long, you are young, and I'm very, very patient."

My expression hardens, all traces of insecurities disappear in an instant and I look him in the eyes. "I'm not worried, Ford. Because if you touch me, I'll knee you in the balls so hard it'll be weeks before you can run stadiums again."

In fact, I think every Ford scene is my favorite. In Panic it was the epilogue that you just read in this book that made people fall in love with him. He stole the show in that scene. But before the epilogue, Ford spent most of the book desperately trying to get Rook to see the real him…

"May I cut in?" I laugh as Ford's voice comes from behind me. "I promise to give her back."

Ronin smiles down at me. "I dunno, Ford. She's looking pretty content right now."

I peek back at Ford and smile. "Oh, absolutely, Ford. Because I want to know all about that date you brought. Like every single detail."

We all look over at her at the same time. She's… older. Mid-thirties, older.

I turn to Ronin. "I need that story. Come save me from His Weirdness in five minutes."

He hands me off and Ford slides in next to me without even breaking the little shuffling dance Ronin and I were doing. "Is she the... girlfriend?"

A smirk from Ford. "I told you, I'd never call them girlfriends."

I look at her again as Ford turns us on the patio. She's tall, blonde, thin, and wearing an elegant white dress that goes just past her knees but hugs all her curves. Her hair is piled into a sophisticated up-do that even Josie would envy. "What's her name?"

"She has no name."

I laugh. "Ford."

"I'm serious. I never get their names."

"Is she a call-girl?"

He scowls. "No, I don't pay for sex, Rook."

"Hmmmm. I'm not sure what to think."

"I told you, I do not give a fuck about people. I wasn't kidding. I use them, they use me. Everyone is happy."

"But you're not using me."

"Of course I am. You're filling the friend role for now."

TAUT is Ford's story. It's his past, his present, and his future. All the weirdness is on display and all the reasons behind it come out. He truly is an asshole. But he's got his reasons and it's not something he's proud of, it's just... *his nature.* And he's got a lot of self-loathing, but no one need know that but him. He also has his pride.

TAUT

The Ford Book
(Rook and Ronin Spin-off)

J. A. Huss

Find me at
New Adult Addiction
www.jahuss.com

Interior Design by E.M. Tippetts Book Designs
Edited by RJ Locksley
Cover design by J. A. Huss

ISBN-978-1-936413-64-5

Ford Aston is known for many things. Being an emotionless, messed up bastard, a freakishly smart social outcast, and a cold, domineering master who keeps "pets" instead of girlfriends.

And after Rook broke his heart, he plans to keep it that way.

Ashleigh is known for nothing, and that's exactly what she's got going for her. She's broke, stranded in the mountains with a three month old baby, and Ford Aston is screwing with her head.

Big. Time.

And she plans to mess with his right back.

It's a coy game at first, filled with flirting, and innuendo--but Ford soon realizes something is not quite right with Ashleigh. In fact, something is seriously, seriously wrong and the closer they get to their final destination, the closer Ford gets to the truth.

One night of devastation, self-loathing, and emptiness turns into the best thing that ever happened to Ford Aston. But one day of in-your-face reality threatens Ashleigh's whole existence.

PROLOGUE

New Year's Eve

The Chaput New Year's Eve party is famous in Denver. I'm not a party person and for me New Year's Eve is a time to be alone, so I've only ever been once besides this year. I wouldn't even be here tonight if we weren't filming for the season finale of Shrike Bikes, but Rook disappeared almost the entire month of December with Ronin. First the GIDGET runway show in LA, then a week in Cancun, then Christmas.

So, here I am, trying to pin her ass down and get this over with.

I'd rather be anywhere but here. I'd rather talk to anyone but her.

The entire studio has been cleared of equipment and replaced with tables and a dance floor. The band is playing, the lighting is moody and atmospheric, and there are almost three hundred people here all dressed in black. I've finished the exit interviews for everyone except Rook, but she's conveniently made herself scarce.

A waitress walks by with a tray and I tap her on the shoulder as she passes. "Have you seen Miss Corvus?" I ask politely. I creep her out, I can tell, because she immediately pulls away from me and then points wordlessly over the crowd to Antoine's office.

She's gone before I can thank her.

It's quite difficult to be polite and when I'm handed rudeness in return, it makes me want to morph back into the old me.

I drop that thought as I make my way through the throngs of people and spy Rook standing just inside the door with Veronica. They are thick as thieves these days. If I were Spencer I'd watch out. They will be into trouble soon, if they're not already.

Ronnie is wearing a short black dress with very high heels. Her look says she takes her fun seriously.

Rook, on the other hand, is dressed like a dark princess. Her dress is not a dress. It's a gown. A long midnight-blue gown that breaks the black only rule, but no one cares because she is stunning. The dress has a tight strapless bodice and elaborate skirts that touch the ground. Her hair is flowing down her back in long waves and atop her head is a shiny blue cardboard tiara.

Just as she turns and spies me, the light catches the blue of her eyes and her crown at the same time. It's like a flashbulb and my mind takes a picture.

"Rook," I say loudly and with a smile. She winces and it's official. She's been avoiding me. "It's your turn, let's go." Veronica pats her on the shoulder like she needs her sympathy and that makes me angry. But I strike through that emotion and beckon my friend with a finger.

"Ford," she starts. "I'm not in the mood. I'm tired of talking. I'm sorta drunk. I'm not ready for this. I'm—"

She goes on and on like that but she follows like a good girl and I just tune it out. We exit the studio and walk down the hallway to the room where I've set up the camera. When I wave her through the doorway she's still talking about waiting guests and Ronin missing her if she stays too long.

I nod. *Yes, yes, yes, I get it*, that nod says. I motion for her to sit. She sits. She always does as she's told when I'm the one asking.

It should make me feel good, that I have this control over her. But it doesn't.

I sit across from her and sigh.

And it's only then that she notices. I'm surprised it took her so long, her skills at reading body language are astute.

"What?" she asks. "What's going on? Did something happen?"

"I'm not going to tape an exit interview of you, Rook. We have so much footage of you from the news, there's no need."

She smiles and the knife slips in. She gathers her dress in her fingertips and rises out of the chair. "Good, then I'm not needed here and I'll just be going," she says, twisting the knife just a little.

"I'm leaving," I say quickly.

"What?" she asks, halting her fleeing feet mid-stride. "But it's not midnight yet."

"I just want you to know I did it all for you," I say, ignoring her statement. "And I'd do it again if that's what makes you happy. I only ever wanted what's best for you."

Her whole body softens at my words. "Ford…"

"And I understand why you wanted to stay in community college and finish your general ed classes and not transfer into Boulder just yet. Online classes are better. The weirdoes and haters are thinning, but they're still out there, so that keeps you safe. I'm proud of you, I want you to know that. Whatever makes you happy makes me happy."

She sits back down, rests her elbows on her knees and props her chin up in her hands. Surely she knew this would have to end eventually.

"If it were anyone else, anyone but you who wanted me to give them so much for so little in return, I would've walked away and never looked back a long time ago. But you make it so, *so* difficult to turn away. And I couldn't let the sadness and pain touch you. It drives me mad when you're unhappy. I lie awake at night wishing I could bring Jon back to life and torture him myself. I wanted to kill that Abelli asshole for even entertaining the thought of selling you. I want to pull you into my chest right now and keep you for myself. Because, Rook, I just want you." I stop to study the shock on her face for a moment before continuing.

"I. Fucking. Want. You," I say, my voice a deep rumble in my throat. "If I'd found you first instead of Ronin, you'd be mine right now. And I'd never let you go. I know what you think of me, of the girls I have, of my"—I look away for a fraction of a second, then drag my heated stare back to her slumped shoulders and sad face—"idiosyncrasies. But I am nothing like Jon. I have never been anything like those men on that list."

"I know that, Ford," she says softly as she reaches out to touch my arm.

"Don't." I pull away before she makes contact with my suit coat. "You can*not* touch me. If you touch me…" I shake my head, unable to continue.

"If I touch you what?" she asks with an air of challenge.

My own mother hasn't even touched me as many times as Rook has, so this probably does deserve an explanation. "If you touch me I'll touch you back. I'll cup your face and kiss your mouth. I'll hold you close and make you choose me." I stop and swallow hard and then lean into her space and whisper, "I'll ruin everything if you touch me. I'll ruin us. I'll ruin this. I'll ruin you, just like you said. I'll ruin you and I'll ruin your life. And I love you too much to ruin you. So I'm leaving."

Her shoulders slump a little more. "I don't want you to leave, Ford. I'm not sure life without you is possible."

"And I'm not sure life with you is possible. I can't watch you with him, Rook. I'm seething with jealousy. It infuriates me that time and time again he gets what he wants. Ronin pulls love towards him like he's gravity." I stop to laugh. "He only has to ask and love appears in his life. And me? I beg for it. I want love more than anything, yet everyone thinks I'm insufferable."

I kneel down in front of her and shake my head. "Everyone but you, Rook. You are the only person on this entire Earth I care about. And you belong to someone else. And if it were anyone but him I'd just take you and say fuck the consequences. But you chose one of two people who will stand by me no matter what I do. And even though these days I count Ronin as a friend, and I would never betray him, I'm so fucking jealous. His life since Antoine has been one long string of lucky breaks. And every day I ask myself, why? Why does he get you? Why does he deserve this luck and I'm always left with nothing?"

I shrug and stand up and her eyes follow me, making her head tilt.

It takes every ounce of willpower not to slip my hand across the milky white skin on her throat, grasp the back of her neck, pull her towards me, and claim her mouth. "This isn't even me talking right now. I don't feel these things, Rook. Ever. When did I become capable of jealousy?" I huff out some air. "Well, it's not really a mystery. It was the day I met you, that's when. You've changed me, Rook. You make me weak, you make me stumble, you make me fall, and even though I know you'll pick me up if I ask you to, it's not enough. I want you to make me stronger, just like I made you. I want it all or I want nothing. And since I can't have it all, I'll take nothing."

She stares up at me in silence, the shock of my words displayed on her face.

I can't stand to see the hurt in her eyes. I can't stand to see her fear and sadness as the realization of what's happening finally sinks in.

So I do what I have to do. I make it worse.

So she's left with no more doubts about what kind of man I am. So she will release her hold on me. So she will stop looking at me like she cares.

So I can let go and move on.

I turn away.

I walk out.

And I never look back.

ONE

lick. Click. Click.

That's my shoes on the stone steps in the Chaput Building. I listen for a call. Or maybe even an echo, telling me that another pair of shoes are behind me.

But I get nothing. Not even sounds from the New Year's Eve party up on the fourth floor leak out. Just nothing. My steps are quick when I begin, but now that I'm nearing the door to the basement they are slow. I finish my escape more confused than I've ever been in my life.

I told her.

I want her.

But she belongs to Ronin.

You will not look back, you will not look back.

That's what I tell myself the entire way down. But of course, when I'm a few paces from the garage door, I do look up. All the way up to the fourth floor where that dark princess is leaning over the railing, her hair spilling over and shrouding her face in a blue shadow that must be a reflection of her dress or a play of the light.

"Ford," she whispers.

It's so soft it stops me cold and I just stare at her. She is the most tragically beautiful creature on this entire planet. And even though I know it's impossible to see her blue eyes in this hazy darkness and from such a distance, I see them.

"Rook," I whisper back. "I can't."

I turn away and this time she yells, "Ford!"

I force myself to keep walking.

"Ford! Wait!" Her feet are flying down the stairs now, so I push through the door and walk quickly to the Bronco. The air is frigid. Steam blasts from my mouth as I breathe heavy, a cloud of evidence that betrays my rapidly beating heart and announces my agitation to the world. I walk to the far end of the parking garage and I'm shoving my key in the truck lock when she bursts through the door.

I climb in and start the engine. I haven't been here that long, it's only nine o'clock, so there's no protest—it turns over immediately. Rook lifts her long skirts, her feet scurrying underneath as she frantically tries to catch me.

I wait. Because I'm weak. She makes me so fucking weak. I am nothing. I am a mess.

She knocks on the window. "Please, Ford," she begs from the other side. "Pleases stop for a moment. Please, talk to me, please."

I shake my head no, but she pulls on the door handle and opens the door. "No. No, no, no. You're not leaving like this, Ford. No."

I can't say anything.

I have so much to say, but I cannot say *anything*. Because if I talk to her, if I utter her name, I will break and I will take her, right here in her boyfriend's parking garage. I'll pick her up, slide my hands up her thighs as I lift her skirts, crash her against the cinder block wall, and fuck the shit out of her.

"Ford, please. Talk to me. Please."

I push in the clutch and ease it into first.

"Please, Ford. Just tell me where you're going, OK? Just don't leave me like this."

I ease up off the clutch and roll forward. She walks alongside, still holding the door open.

"Goddammit! Talk to me, please!"

I grab the door and try to close it but she reaches in and tries to take my keys. "No," she says in a huff. I press on the brakes and grab her wrist, squeezing it until she squeals. "You won't hurt me, I know you won't hurt me."

I squeeze tighter and she whimpers.

"I *will* hurt you, Rook," I say evenly as I stare into her soul. "I'm hurting you right now. And it feels good. Because you've been hurting me since the day we met. You're selfish. You take. That's all you do—take. You're a Taker, Rook. And I've got nothing left to give you. You took it all."

Her jaw drops as she processes my words.

I told her. I warned her.

She yanks her wrist free and steps back, shaking her head. "You're saying that on purpose. To make me go away. And fine. Leave, then. You *Runner*. You're a Runner, Ford. Who's running away now? Huh?"

I slam the door closed and she pounds on the window. I roll forward, looking out my window to make sure not to run over her feet. I tune out her pleas and press down on the accelerator, shift into second, and then blow past the parking attendants standing guard at the exit. I turn left onto Blake Street until I hit 19th, then take that all the way down to Broadway. I fully intend to go home, but when my building appears a few blocks later, I just keep driving past.

The streets have been cleared of yesterday's snow but another storm has already arrived. The flakes are small and scattered now, but soon they will blanket the entire Front Range in white. I have a flight out to LA tomorrow afternoon but suddenly the thought of going home to my high-rise condo, with the massive four-bedroom, three-thousand-square-foot floor plan—empty save for me and all the impersonal things that came with it when the Biker Channel people rented it—it just… I just…

Can't.

I can't do it. I can't live like this for another second. I can't pretend like this is working for me. I'm…

My phone buzzes in my pants. I turn right on Colfax and check the incoming call. Ronin.

"Yes."

"Ford, what the hell is going on? Rook is hysterical. She said you're leaving or something."

"Oh, I'm sorry. I should've explained better, I suppose. I have a flight to LA, a new show. That series I told you about a few months ago. I got the call, so I'm going."

Silence. He knows I'm lying—not about the show, I did get that show. And it's an HBO candidate, so I'd be a fool to pass it up. But I think everyone knows that what Rook and I have, our friendship, is not all that's going on. And really, what's Ronin going to say? 'My girlfriend sorta loves you, but she never wants to be with you, so she knows this is your way of leaving her behind and moving on and I think you should come back and continue this… thing you two have to make her happy?'

No, of course he's not. Because then he'd have to admit Rook is not completely his. She is half mine.

She has always been half mine.

And maybe Ronin is content with the arrangement. I huff a little air at this. Why wouldn't he be? He gets to sleep with her every night. He gets to share dinners with her and take her on vacation. He gets to watch her brush her hair in the morning, and mope about their apartment in her sweats, perfectly comfortable and sighing with contentment as they watch TV, or plan their fucking grocery list. Because even if a part of her belongs to me, he knows. He knows I'd never steal her. I would never do that.

"That's all that's going on here, Ford?"

"Of course," I say. "Listen, it's starting to snow pretty hard now, I'll give you guys a call the next time I'm in town." I end the call, turn the phone off and throw it on the seat next to me as I cross over I-25, pass the stadium and leave downtown. And I just drive.

I have no idea what I'm doing.

I just drive.

I could go home. Not my condo, but my mother's house in Park Hill. She's having a party like she does every year. I never go, but I *could*. I should. I should just go home and pass the night with her in all those familiar rooms, with all those familiar faces.

But then I'd just be reminded of the other person I lost. And I can't do that tonight. Not tonight.

I'll turn around at the next light, I tell myself. And then the next one.

But I keep going and the next thing I know, I'm getting on the I-70 in Golden, heading up towards Lookout Mountain.

But I blow past that exit too, the Bronco straining with the steep ascent that will take me up into the Rocky Mountains. It's a long climb. Denver might be a mile up, but the altitude in these mountains is a whole other level of high.

The transmission whines at me, reminding me that it's old and vulnerable.

But I do not care.

Where are you going, Ford?

I don't answer the voice. Partly because I have no idea and partly because it's not good to encourage the internal monologue. My flight out of DIA tomorrow is too far away. Tomorrow is just way too far away. I'm not going to survive the night if I stay here in Denver. I need to get out of this state right the fuck now.

The snow builds with each vertical mile, the sky nothing but white everywhere I look. No stars above and just dark forest on either side. There aren't even many cars on the road. Hardly any coming towards me from the west, and only slightly more traveling from the east like me. Locals know when to stay off the mountain passes and not many tourists are driving on New Year's Eve.

TAUT

The snow grows thicker as I finally make it to Genesee. The perfect curtain to keep my thoughts at bay. Because they are filled with longing and aching. With self-loathing and hatred for what I am. For what I can't be. For letting her get away. For letting Ronin take her. For wanting something I can't have.

For caring.

And I vow to myself as I push the accelerator to the floor to make the steep grade that will pluck me from civilization and pour me out into the wilds where I can be alone with myself, I swear, I will never—ever—care for another woman for as long as I live.

I will never allow myself to be weak like this again. I will never learn their names or buy them presents or plot out a way to help them reach their full potential.

Never.

TWO

The drive is more and more tedious as I move west. The climb seems endless, with a few reprieves every now and then as I reach a flat stretch of road on a summit, then plunge a little, only to be reminded there is nothing for hundreds of miles but these mountains, and begin the ascent all over again.

It's a stupid idea to drive the Bronco up here. I've had this truck since high school—worked my ass off at the Science and Nature Museum for three years saving for it. I started working there—unofficially, of course—when I was twelve. My childhood neighborhood is across Colorado Boulevard from City Park, and the museum was right there all growing up. I spent so much time there I started giving tours. Except they were unauthorized and there's just something a little intimidating about a pre-teen leading a group of tourists through the exhibits that tends to piss off the higher-ups. But they couldn't stop me. I had a clipboard and a sign-up sheet out in back of the museum near the kids' fountain.

It's a public park. I was a member of the public. My prices

were cheap. Five dollars a person, a family of four for fifteen dollars. It was a niche waiting to be filled, so I filled it.

And the day I turned sixteen my dad took me to buy the Bronco. Of course, we're filthy rich so I could've had any car I wanted. Our house is the largest in Park Hill. It's an old foursquare, has seven bedrooms, a brick wall, and a gated driveway. No small feat in such a congested neighborhood. But I wanted to earn my first vehicle, to make it worth something to me. I wanted to be invested in it and I didn't want it to be perfect. I wanted it to be flawed. I wanted it to be a work in progress. I wanted to rescue it.

It was not in bad shape when I bought it, but these older cars need constant work. And this transmission is not happy with me at the moment. If I was smart I'd get off on the next exit and turn around. Go back home to my mom's, drink a shitload of Jack, and pass out until my flight takes off tomorrow.

But I'm wounded. And, I admit, sad. I see her face in everything. Even now, I wonder what she thinks of the mountains. Ronin has a penchant for gambling, so I know they go to Black Hawk and Central City, but did he take her to see the aspens when they changed color in the fall? Does he take her skiing? I've never heard them talk about skiing, but I haven't been around them on the weekends in months.

Do they go to Grand Lake? Or Granby? Or Pikes Peak?

I want to know every thought in her head.

It's a weakness I have, this longing to understand the thoughts of others. And I had limited coping abilities as a child, so I had to assign labels to wrap my head around people's thoughts and actions. I came up with a system. The Leaver, that's what I called Rook last fall. But she proved me wrong. Oh, she left all right. But she didn't *leave*. She put her life on the line to save Ronin. And then Spencer and I put our lives on the line to save her.

And then we all came back and things moved forward. It was stressful at first, watching Rook be publicly massacred by all sorts of people who judged her to be a fraud, a liar, a whore, any number of terrible things that just made me want to tuck her under my arm and never let her out of my sight.

But she's not mine to protect.

What is she thinking now? I pick up the phone and turn it on. Seven messages. I press voice mail and her messages start.

"Ford? Please, call me back, OK?"

"Ford?"

"Ford, come on. Don't do this to me. To us," she corrects. And I want to correct *her*. Because there is no *us*. There is only them. Her and Ronin. "Ford." She lowers her voice to a whisper for this part. "Please, come back. I need you."

"I need you too," I say softly to the snowy mountain highway. "I need you so bad." I'd give anything to have her alone, free of Ronin's claim, so I could tell her all the things I've been holding in since the day I met her. So I could get her honest answer without her guilt of wanting two men at the same time getting in the way.

So I could get the truth out of her.

She almost said it, back in the CSU stadium when I crossed her line and let her know I saw through her walls. She admitted to having feelings for me. But then she said I'd ruin her.

That's what she thinks. That I'd suffocate her, take away all the parts I love. All the parts that make her so desirable. Because she sees me as some sick and twisted fuck who gets off on submissive woman and that couldn't be farther from the truth. I like the power, yes, because I need the control, because I cannot stand to be touched by anyone. I like to be the one who does the touching during sex, so I bind them. Hands off only. I take them from behind, I blindfold them so they can't look at me.

But I do this because it's the only way I know how to cope with the intimacy I want, but cannot allow myself to accept.

And Rook missed the point I was trying to make last summer. I'm not interested in a submissive woman. They're interested in *me* because I require this control. Why deny them? I like what they offer, but only as a diversion. Why does she think I never get their names? Because I could give a fuck about those women.

I want a strong one.

TAUT

I want one who will keep up, challenge me, help me reach my full potential.

And yes, I'd like to tie her up and slap her ass during sex, make her beg for me, have her submit herself fully—let me own her in private.

But Rook misunderstood me completely. Because I *want* a woman to touch me. So very, very badly. And she is the only one I've ever considered giving that privilege to. Ever.

The highway dips again and then gets twisty as I pass by Idaho Springs. They have a good pizza place there. Whenever we'd come home from skiing in Vail when I was a kid my dad would pull the car over in Idaho Springs and we'd get a mountain pie from Beau Jo's before heading down the mountain.

It brings back memories of being tired from a weekend of strenuous activity, sore muscles, and an overwhelming feeling of being well-loved by my family, even though I was the epitome of a parent's nightmare.

My childhood couldn't be more different than Rook's. Yes, I'm odd. I've got a lot of emotional issues that I've been working on my entire life. I refused to communicate with my parents in anything other than sign language until I was four. Then I started speaking Russian instead of English and that threw them for a while. But my dad—I have to stop and smile at his memory. Well, let's just say I got my intellect from him. He caught onto me and learned Russian to spite me.

We sparred in four other languages before I settled on English at age six.

And by seven they had a diagnosis. Asperger's syndrome with some savant tendencies. Mostly numbers and math, but spatial things as well because of my photographic memory.

I rebelled against that label—defective, the books said. Defective in communication and emotion. I read everything I could find on it in my dad's psychiatry books in his office, but the information was sadly inadequate. So I started secretly taking the bus to the public library when I was eight to do research.

And finally, after months of reading, I decided I did not have this syndrome and I did everything I could to prove it to myself, and others, that I was *normal*.

I stopped doing well on my tests. It was too late, of course. My IQ was firmly established to be in the neighborhood of 190 by the time I started speaking English. But my parents, even though they knew I was a full-fledged freak, treated me like just another kid.

They used that phrase often whenever I started getting weird. 'Ford,' my mom would say in that mom voice when I was about to blow a blood vessel over the rule against reading under my covers past midnight. Or when I got a little older, researching any of the hundreds of obsessions I had as a teen on the internet. I only require a few hours of sleep a night, why should I have to go to bed at midnight? It never made sense. But she'd never give in. 'Ford,' she'd say. 'You are just another kid. And kids have rules. So you will follow the kid rules, or else.'

'Or else what?' I'd ask with my chin tipped up in defiance.

'Or else I'll kiss you. And not only that, I'll kiss you in public.'

I'd recoil every time at the horror. Because even though I love my parents, and they love me and I *know* they love me, they were not allowed to touch me. Not when I was a toddler, not now that I am a man. And I'm sure this is what ticked me off as a baby. The fact that they were constantly touching me. I suspect it's the reason I refused to talk to them.

Ronin might have a penchant for gambling, but I have a penchant for holding grudges. Even as an infant, apparently.

I laugh at this. I know I'm odd. I do, I admit it. I understand this, I own it. What can I say. I was just born this way. But Rook never seemed to mind. She barely noticed—in fact, she said she didn't believe that I was incapable of emotion. And I guess she was right. I love her. I had feelings for Mardee. I have strong attachments to Ronin and Spencer. Strong enough to stop me from pursuing the only woman I've ever wanted so bad I had to run away from her to control myself.

TAUT

So I guess I was right after all. I'm not defective. I want to be touched. I've denied myself this most basic of human comforts my whole life and I'm ready to move on.

But the only woman I want to move on with is the only one I can't have.

THREE

The transmission whines as I climb up out of the canyon and hit the curve that takes me into Georgetown. The signs on the highway are flashing the winter storm warning and I only hope the Eisenhower Tunnel is open, or else all this driving will be fruitless. If they close the tunnel, and they do this often in the winter when there are accidents, then there's nothing to do but go back. It's pointless to spend the night up here in the mountains. Pointless, unless I can make a clean escape. Otherwise I might as well just go home and suck it up until my flight tomorrow.

The snow builds as I climb. I pass through Georgetown and then climb again until the tunnel warnings become common. There wasn't too much traffic for the entire drive, but there is now. And that can only mean one thing. The tunnel is either closed or they are stopping everyone going forward to see what their destination is.

We slow to a crawl and all of a sudden I notice that the heater is no longer blowing hot air. I flip the switch to the off position and stew in my tuxedo.

TAUT

"What the hell are you doing, Ford?"

This is not the internal monologue. This is me talking to myself.

Of course, I don't answer. I know what I'm doing. I'm running the fuck away, just like Rook accused me of back in the garage.

My phone buzzes and it surprises me. I thought I turned it off.

I check the screen. *Rook.*

Ignoring it, I take my attention back to the traffic as the pace picks up. That's good news from my point of view. It means the tunnel isn't closed. At least, not for everyone. As I get closer to the entrance more and more trucks are on the side of the road. Some of them putting on chains, some of them just sitting there.

I wait my turn in the dark until finally the car in front of me is waved through the tunnel and I pull up to the state trooper and roll down my window. He eyes my suit, then smiles. "Where ya heading tonight?"

"Party in Frisco," I lie. Frisco is in the valley just on the other side of the tunnel. It's a safe destination. Close.

"Cutting it pretty close," he says, squinting at me either in suspicion, or maybe just trying to keep the blowing snow out of his eyes.

I look down at the clock on the dash. Eleven thirty-two. "Yeah," I huff. "Fucking hate parties. Girlfriends," I say, sighing at him.

"Yeah," he says back in a conspiratorial tone. "Totally. I got out of it this year." He points to the sky. "Storm duty. OK, well, go on ahead, but be careful, we just got word that the other side of the Divide is getting it pretty bad. And"—he stops to sniff—"you should check your fluids before you head back down the mountain. Smells like antifreeze." He stoops down to check under the car, but straightens just as fast and shakes his head. "Can't see shit. Too dark, too much snow."

"Yeah, I just lost heat, so you're probably right. I'll check it tomorrow before I head home."

He pops off a little two-finger salute and waves the car behind me forward as I move into the tunnel. The whole world is wiped away in here. I always loved this part of the trip when I was a kid. We have a house in Vail and before my dad died a couple years back, it was a pretty regular thing to spend a few weeks up there at Christmas and a couple months over the summer. When I was a teen it was every single weekend year round. But...

My thought trails off. I'm not in the mood to think about that tonight.

The tunnel ends abruptly and from here it's all downhill for a good while as I head into Silverthorne and then Frisco. I don't stop. I have no intention of stopping. Heat or not, I'm all in now. I just need to get the fuck out of this state. I'll check the fluid levels the next time I need gas, but right now I still have half a tank. So I'm good. Heat is nice, especially when it's the dead of winter and I'm in the mountains, but I'm not gonna die from exposure inside the truck. I've got an emergency kit in the back anyway. I'll live for another half a tank.

Besides, the Bronco loves me right now. We're going downhill. And I feel better already. Crossing the Great Divide is sorta cleansing. Like Rook is on the other side of something. She's east now. And I am west. She's far away. Even though it's barely an hour's drive in good weather from the tunnel to Denver, it feels... significant.

My pensive mood lasts for like three minutes, because that's how long I get to enjoy the flat stretch of highway before I am climbing again.

The transmission whines, it's a steep grade, but I downshift, give it some gas, and then pick up enough speed near the next summit to shift back into fourth. The trooper wasn't lying, this side of the Divide is much worse off as far as the snow goes. It's thick and wet, sticking to the windshield even though I have the wipers on full.

Copper Mountain comes into view and I briefly entertain the thought of stopping. But I can't make myself do it. If I can get to Vail, well, then at least I can be on some familiar territory. Spending a cold night in a Copper parking lot does not sound fun. The mountain house is not somewhere I'd like to be right now, but it's doable.

A few miles past Copper cars start to appear on the side of the road, but it's clear they are not just stopping to put on chains like the trucks on the eastern side. They are stuck. Or broken down.

I shift down as the grade levels, then give it some gas to pick up enough speed to get back into fourth gear. It complies, but not without protest. Blowing by Copper might be a mistake I come to regret because there are no more towns between here and Vail. But I'm almost there and the drive evens out over Vail Pass.

The snow grows heavier, falling in a thick blanket of white, just like I wanted. Only it does nothing for my mind, which is still hopelessly wrapped around Rook and the last memory I now have of her.

Not the picture my mind took of her flashing blue eyes and cardboard crown back in Antoine's office.

No. Her face, screwed up in anger and hurt, as she called me a Runner.

And she's right, isn't she? I'm running. I'm running so fast I'm in the middle of a snowstorm—*blizzard, Ford,* the internal monologue corrects me—up in the mountains, driving a truck that is almost thirty years old and is working on three gears. It whines and I downshift. *Two gears,* I'm corrected again.

I can see the first lights of the Village off in the distance. It's a miracle I can see anything in this weather, so that means it must be very close. I squint out the front window, trying to get my bearings. Our house is on the east side of the village, thank God for small favors, so I'm gonna make it.

I believe this even as I coast down the off-ramp in first gear, the engine protesting each time I step on the gas. Because no matter how hard I wish it, the tranny is shot.

I pull off to the side of the road as far as I can get without actually plowing through a snowdrift, and then the Bronco just stops.

Fuck.

After all that, I'm stuck in a blizzard on the fucking off-ramp, two miles from my family's mountain home. If I had a coat, I could probably walk there. But I'm in a tuxedo and that's it.

I laugh a little and pick up my phone from the seat next to me.

No fucking service. Awesome.

I rest my head on the steering wheel and then jerk up when a horn honks at me from outside. Squinting through the snow I can see a truck, so I roll the window down and some guy is yelling at me.

It's hard to hear him over the wind, and at first I figure he's pissed because I'm still kind of in the middle of the road. But then the wind dies and his words are more clear.

"—a tow?"

"What?" I ask.

"I said…" He jerks his thumb behind him and I look at what he's pointing at. A car on a flatbed truck. "You need a tow?"

I look back at the man and this is when I notice there's another person in the cab with him. A girl who is doing her best to shield herself from the wind and snow. "Yeah," I reply back. "But—"

"OK, look. Let me drop her off at Jason's, then I'll come back for you. It's just right there." He points up ahead on the frontage road where there's a small strip mall-type building. Or as close to a strip mall as you can get in Vail. I know the place well. Hell, I even know Jason—we took skateboarding lessons in the same fucking summer camp one year.

Real asshole. He bullied me a little, thinking I was weak just because I was quiet and smart and no one was allowed to touch me. But then I electrified the urinal flusher in the boys' bathroom at camp, watched him go inside, and then proceeded to laugh my ass off when the ambulance came.

TAUT

I never officially got caught, but everyone knew I did it. And my dad was not happy about that. Not one bit. He made me clear a fifty-foot radius of brush and pine needles around our house that summer. Forest fire precaution duty, he said. But it was really no-electrocuting-kids-at-camp duty.

The garage's a family-owned place, Jason is really Jason Junior, and there's a Travel Saver Motel next door with a blinking vacancy light that they own as well.

Wonderful.

Before I can answer the tow truck is gone, so I have two choices. Get out and walk the two miles up to my house in a raging blizzard, or wait for the driver to come back and tow me over to Jason's and see if he'll swing me across the freeway to the bottom of my driveway after he drops the Bronco.

It doesn't take a genius. And the wait is not that bad, since I can practically see him dropping the car he had on the back of the truck. It must belong to the girl who was in the front seat with him.

I get out, painfully aware of how underdressed I am for the mountains in January, and then catch the exasperated look from the driver that he probably reserves for stupid tourists from the Tropics.

"Nice coat," he says as he grabs his chains from the flatbed and lowers himself down onto the snow to hook up the Bronco. "You can wait inside the truck if you want. I don't need help, ya know."

He's an asshole. And he looks familiar so I study his face when he comes back up from the ground and goes over to the controls on the truck. Dakota. Dillon. Dickhead.

"Dallas," he says like he's reading my mind. "I'm surprised you don't remember me. Jason's cousin. I fingered you right away. Of course, who can forget this hunk of shit." He points to my dilapidated truck. The drive train whines as the chain tightens and starts to pull the Bronco onto the bed. Snow is coming down so hard now, it might be piling up on my head.

"Right. Dallas. I think I almost blew you up on the golf course with an exploding golf ball." I laugh.

He doesn't.

"Sorry about that," I continue. "My antisocial and psychotic tendencies have mellowed over the years."

He glares at me.

There is no way this guy is taking me any further than the fucking garage five hundred yards away, so I resign myself to getting a room at the Travel Saver. I'm not walking into the Village and I highly doubt a cab is available. This is Vail, not Denver. There are no public safe driver programs to keep the drunks off the road on New Year's. Besides, almost everywhere you need to go is within walking distance here.

Of course, there's that little detail about the blizzard. But that's why hotels have ballrooms. So partygoers can stay the night at the party. I doubt there are any rooms available in the Village anyway.

This whole thought exercise is pointless. I have a fucking house two miles away that I can't get to. Why the hell would I walk the opposite direction to get a room?

I jump in the cab and scare the shit out of myself when I sit on something that squeaks. I brush the seat off and a little yellow duck toy goes flying onto the floor.

"Oh, shit," Dallas says as he gets into the cab with me. "I bet that belongs to that chick's baby. Pick it up, will ya?" He pulls out onto the road as I pick up the toy. It's all muddy from my wet shoes now, so I stick it in my pocket. We drive down the frontage road, pass the hotel, and then turn into the parking lot. The girl is still in her car, the interior light on as she fumbles around with something. I see the baby now, tucked inside a seat, bundled up with blankets. Dallas backs up the truck and positions it so he can drop the Bronco off in a snow-covered space not quite next to, but near, the girl's brown Honda.

I jump out and walk over to Dallas as he works the truck's bed controls. "How much?"

"Two-fifty," he says with a straight face.

I shrug it off and grab three hundred-dollar bills from my wallet. Who cares. He saved my ass. He deserves it. "Here you are. And Dallas?" I wait for his eyes to find mine. "Thank you. I appreciate it. Maybe I'll see you tomorrow when Jason opens and we can grab a beer or something."

This is my new thing, since I met Rook. I'm trying to make amends for any and all weird past behavior. I figure trying to blow him up on the golf course counts as something that requires an effort.

"Jason's probably not gonna show up tomorrow. And he's always closed on the weekends, so Monday, huh? If you're still around." He takes the money and goes back to his business so I take that as my cue to leave.

I stuff my hands in my pockets and make for the motel office, my head ducking into the wind and snow.

FOUR

The bell on the door jingles as I enter the hotel, the faint sound of a TV coming from the back room. An older woman appears and sighs heavily when she sees me, like I'm interrupting her *Jeopardy* game show and walking up front to wait on a customer is the last straw.

"Help you?" she asks curtly as she punches some keys on her computer.

I put on my *I'm not a psycho* smile and remind myself that this place was once my home, but she doesn't look at me, so it makes no difference. I try for directness instead. "Room?"

"One left," she mumbles. "But you gotta be out by ten, because there's a tourist bus coming in tomorrow and all our rooms are booked for the weekend."

"I can manage that. How much?"

"Two-fifty plus tax."

"Hmmm, everything tonight seems to cost two-fifty."

"It's New Year's Eve. Prime season for us. You want the room or not?"

TAUT

"Yes," I say through my smile. "Thank you." She passes me a form to fill out and give her all my details. When I hand it back she stares at it for a moment, then looks up at me with the same squinting eyes that Dallas perfected back at the tow truck.

"Rutherford Aston."

"Mrs. Pearson," I deadpan back at her. "How's the library treating you?"

"Retired. We manage this place now. Can't complain."

And that's it. That's all she has to say to me, even though if you add up all the time I spent at the library when I lived here as a kid, it would total in the years.

It's my turn to sigh heavily and I turn away as she finishes the job of checking me in. She doesn't inquire why I'm staying here at the crappiest hotel in Vail when I live down the street. She doesn't inquire why I left the make and model of my car blank on the registration form. She doesn't say *here you go, have a nice night* when she slides the key across the counter. The only other thing she says is, "Room 24, last door."

I nod and smile once more, but it's futile. She's already got her back to me, heading into the room where her game show awaits.

I push through the door, the bell jingling my exit, and the snow assaults me as I make my way under the covered breezeway that at least attempts to block out the raging elements. I walk all the way to the end of the building, slip my key into the door and glance over at my Bronco.

It's not my truck that I'm looking at though. Dallas and the flatbed are gone. Probably more cars to rescue from the storm. It's the car next to the Bronco that catches my attention. I can still see the girl inside, still fussing around under the dome light.

I twist the key, open the door, find the lights on the wall and flip them on before closing the door behind me.

It's fucking freezing in here. Like they have no heat at all. I hit up the unit under the window that acts as a heater and air conditioner and turn it to full-blast hot.

Now what?

There's two queen-sized beds, a table and chairs, a long low dresser with a mirror, and a TV mounted on the wall. I grab the remote and switch it on. The time flashes on the screen for a moment. One-thirty AM. Shit, time has flown by. Last I looked it was eleven-thirty.

Well, happy New Year, Ford. Yet another one spent alone.

I watch a repeat of the ball dropping in Times Square, and then realize the room is not much warmer. I fuck with the controls on the under-window unit for a few minutes, trying to see if the dials are just lined up wrong and another setting will deliver the heat I'm badly craving. But it's no use. I take out my phone and check the thermometer app. Twelve degrees outside. I calculate the probable temperature in this room and come up with fifty-three.

Fifty-fucking-three degrees. For two hundred and fifty dollars a night.

I can go complain to Mrs. Pearson. Or I can suck it up, go sift through my winter survival bag from the back of the Bronco, and grab the self-heating blizzard blankets.

I opt for the blizzard blankets because Mrs. Pearson is just... *no.*

The snow is still coming down hard, maybe even harder than before. I can barely make out the garage parking lot and it's only about a hundred yards away. I jog over and open the back of the Bronco, yanking the tub of gear towards me. The blankets are down at the bottom, so I just dump all the shit out on the bed of the truck and take out the flat packages. I slam the door and a baby's cry almost gives me a heart attack.

I look carefully at the girl's car and realize it's steamed up from breath. They're still inside.

I knock on the back seat window and see some blurry movement inside, but no one answers. "Hey," I call. "Do you have a ride coming?"

The baby answers with a small complaint, then some gurgled

noises. And nothing.

Even though I'm freezing my ass off now, I try again. A softer knock this time. "Hello? It's too cold to be in a parked car with no heat."

Nothing.

I get the hint and walk away. Hey, if she wants to stay in the car, it's none of my business. I get all the way back to my room door before I realize I could at least give her a blanket. I look at the door. Then the car. Then the door.

And walk back over to the car. I'm fully wet now, so I stop by the Bronco again and pull out my gym bag that at least has a pair of running shorts and a dry shirt.

I knock on the window again. "Hello—"

"Go away!" the girl yells. Then the baby starts crying for real and she starts swearing inside. Like she's reached the end of her coping capability and is about to lose it.

I'm familiar with this feeling. I used to get it often.

I scrub my hand down my face and decide to switch tactics. "If you do not answer me, I will call the police and report you for child abuse."

There's a brief pause, then the window cranks down a single inch and the girl inside peers up at me from dark eyes. She is young. No older than twenty if I guess right. The snow swirls in the small opening, chilling the baby out of its temporary acquiescence. It straight-out bawls.

"Report me? Are you serious? I have no money for a room, OK? I didn't plan on getting stuck here in this blizzard, there's nothing I can do about it. So go ahead, call whoever you want!" She rolls the window back up and I knock again. It rolls back down, a half an inch this time. "What?" she snaps.

I look down at the blanket, then up at the snow illuminated in the street light. It's so thick the light comes across as a dull gray. I am fully planning on just handing the blanket over and telling her that it will self-heat once she opens the package and exposes it to oxygen. But instead my mouth says, "I have two beds in the room. You could sleep there. It's the last room they have or I'd just buy you your own."

"What?" she says, rolling the window down another half an inch.

"I, ah… I'm offering you a place to sleep for the night."

She stares up at me, blinking.

And then I can't stand her attention anymore and I pivot and walk away.

What the fuck am I thinking? Stupid. What the fuck?

I push my key into the door and slam it closed behind me. I throw the gym bag on the bed and rip open one of the blanket packages. It takes about fifteen minutes to fully heat up once the bag is open, so I set it on the bed and go start the shower. The water gets hot immediately and this is the first stroke of luck I've had all night.

Luck. We are not on speaking terms, luck and I. Because my name is not Ronin Flynn. Luck loves him. Shit, if Ronin was in this predicament, he'd have broken down across from the Four Seasons, they'd tell him they only had the penthouse available, and he could have it for half price since it was sitting empty anyway. They'd send up complimentary fruit baskets and give him free spa passes to ease his worried brow.

I laugh. The sad thing is that it's closer to the truth than I'd like to admit. Ronin is like… walking magic when it comes to life. Everything he wants, he gets. People love him immediately. They don't scowl at him because he conjures up memories of almost blowing people up on the golf course or electrocuting boys in the skate park bathroom, or for being the town freak who read every book in the library, even the dictionary and the encyclopedias.

I have had my share of women, albeit on my own very strict no-touching terms. But Ronin has women throwing themselves at him everywhere he goes.

It's… it's infuriating. He's literally a professional liar, for fuck's sake, and all they see is sweet perfection. But when they look at me they see freak.

TAUT

I'm a goddamned movie producer. I know famous people. I have a mountain home in Vail, a luxury condo in Denver, and a five-million-dollar monstrosity on Mulholland Drive in Bel Air. I take care of myself, I'm well educated, I'm not bad-looking. I'm sorta hot, actually. I know this, I have no trouble finding sex when I want it.

And yet I get sluts. I swear. Sluts who don't even blink when I tell them they can't touch me.

And Ronin? He gets Rook.

She does not give one fancy fuck what Ronin's part in our business is. Her exact words. Not one fancy fuck. She loves him, no matter what. Unconditionally. She rode a thousand miles on a motorcycle back to the place where the most horrific things happened to her, stole secret files, and almost got her legs burned off in a house fire to save his professionally lying ass.

And I get no-name pets who want me to bend them over a couch and smack their pussy to make them come.

It's just… what the fuck? Why? It's like I have a sign on my fucking head that says I like the weird ones.

I might like to try a nice girl, or at the very least, a semi-nice one with a little freak to her.

I admit, I'm not wholly dissatisfied with the naughty ones. But just once, just fucking once, I'd like the Sandy instead of the Rizzo.

Holy fuck. I just used a *Grease* Rookism to illustrate my point.

That makes me smile. But then I remember that Rook's not mine and I just walked away for good. That action—walking away from her, slamming that door and driving off—that was the most painful thing I've ever done. And it still hurts. Like… in my chest. I'm not sure what it is, really. This feeling. It's a little bit like when my dad died a couple years ago. But not really. It's different.

That was just… unreal. Like I was watching a movie of everyone around me going through the motions of mourning.

I did not cry. Not once. But my dad would not take it

personally, because as far as I can remember, I've never cried. Not for a stubbed toe, not for being called names in elementary school, not when my dog died when I was ten. And not when my dad died when I was twenty-three even though I did out-luck Ronin in the dad department and I miss him this very moment.

I came to the conclusion a long time ago that I don't have tears. I'm deformed.

This is not logical reasoning and I realize this. If I had no tears I'd need eye drops. I'd have all kinds of eye problems, and my vision is perfect. So of course, I *make* tears. I just don't cry tears. This gets me through the introspection required to understand why I have never felt the deep sadness that others experience.

I look at myself in the mirror as the steam floats out of the bathroom. People who know me see the imperfect weirdo. They see the anti-social freak. They see nothing about me that's real. And the people who *don't* know me are instinctively suspicious. I have a vibe, or something. A vibe that says *stay away*.

And yet when people look at Ronin they see honesty. Even though he's a fucking professional liar.

I scrub my hands over my stubbly chin. I'm gonna grow it out. I'm gonna be someone different. I'm going to do things different from this second on. I'm not going to look for happiness anymore. I'm going to eschew happiness and seek out the glum. The broken and doomed. The dark and the dirty.

Why not? It's where I belong anyway.

I'm New Ford. Fuck happiness. Fuck the nice girls. Fuck everyone. I'm all about me now.

I take off my suit coat and hang it up using the pathetic hangers in the makeshift closet next to the bathroom vanity, then strip off my shirt and do the same thing with that. Like it or not, I'll have to wear it tomorrow. Even New Ford realizes gym shorts will not do in the aftermath of a blizzard. I check the water temperature in the bathroom one more time and I'm unbuttoning my pants to strip down when there's a small knock at the door.

TAUT

I peek around the corner and stare at it.

The knock comes again.

I walk over and open the door, expecting Mrs. Pearson. But it's the girl with the baby.

She swallows hard, like it's taking an incredible amount of willpower just to stand here at the door. "I'd like to take you up on your offer. I'm sorry I was rude."

I don't even know what to say. She sways back and forth a little, like she's trying to comfort her baby who must be hidden under the blankets covering the carrier, but the child is silent so it comes off as nerves.

And then she decides my silence is a message and she hears it loud and clear. She turns and starts walking back towards her car.

"Stop." I find my voice. "You can stay."

Her shoulders stiffen, but she stops walking and the snow just pours down on her like blobs of white rain. Her dark hair is soaking wet and dotted with sparkling flakes. It takes another second for her to turn and then she nods at me. I open the door wider, letting in the blizzard and freezing cold air, and she brushes past my bare chest when she enters my room.

I shiver, but not from the cold.

So much for New Ford.

FIVE

I close the door with a whoosh and my heart beats erratically for a few seconds before it calms down. We stand still, her looking at the room, not turning to face me. And me looking at her.

The distressed cry from beneath a blanket covering a baby carrier snaps me out of my surreal funk and brings her focus back. "I'm sorry," she says as she sets the carrier down on the floor and kneels. "I just…" She pulls the pink blanket away and snow falls onto the floor. The baby is trying its best to sleep, but there's too much going on and its little fists flail as it winds up to wail.

I grab the remote and flip the TV and the lights off at the same moment. The girl gasps.

"Sorry." It's my turn to apologize. The bathroom light is still on, so it's not completely dark, but the baby quiets down. "It was too bright and I don't mean anything derogatory by this remark, but crying babies are not my thing."

She finally turns to face me. Her eyes are brown and so is her hair. It's soaking wet, and now that I have a good chance to look her over, so are her clothes. Her skin has olive undertones, but maybe she's tired, or maybe she's scared, because she's very pale at the moment. "I was just saying that I'm sorry to have to ask for help. I'm just... stranded with no other options."

"Of course," I say, waving my hand at the beds. "This is out of character for me as well. I do my best to ignore society as a whole. I just happened upon you in a vulnerable moment. I was just going to take a shower, so—"

So what?

"So just do whatever you need to do."

I go back into the bathroom and close the door. What the fuck did I just get myself into? I shake it off as I undress then get in the shower. Luckily the water is still hot, otherwise I'd be pissed. When I'm done I realize my gym bag is still out on the bed so I wrap a towel around my waist and go to retrieve it.

She's lying down with the baby, huddled under the blanket. She might even be asleep, although that is not a very smart move. I could be a serial killer for all she knows. My bag is on the bed closest to the door, so she's sleeping in the one nearest the bathroom. I grab the bag off the bed and when I turn she's staring right at me. Her eyes take in my bare chest for a few seconds— not in a seductive way, either, more of a *do you mind putting on some fucking clothes* way.

I ignore her and go back to the bathroom and change into my gym shorts, then flip the light off and walk back over to the bed.

"It's freezing in here," she says softly. "I tried to change the setting on the heater, but it's just cold air so I turned it off."

"Oh, yeah, I forgot." I switch the bedside light on and grab the heat blanket on my bed and offer it to her. "It's a blizzard blanket. Self-heating. It should last all night."

"What about you?"

I offer her a small smile and hold up the other bag. "I have two. But takes like fifteen minutes for them to heat up, and this one's already warm." I wait a few seconds as she studies my face. "Want it?" She still says nothing. "Well—" I throw it over the top of her and then sit back down on my bed. "I'll have to insist. You're still wet." I rip open the other blanket bag and her reply is so small I almost miss her, "Thank you."

"No problem." I throw the other blanket over my bed, turn the light off, and let out a long sigh as I get under the covers. What a fucking day.

"Good night," she says. And then there's some rustling as she turns over.

"Night," I say back to the darkness. I expect to stare at the ceiling for a good long while, since I'm not a big sleeper on the best of days and having a strange girl with a baby in my room is pretty out of the ordinary for me. But I'm drifting off before I can even close my eyes.

I sit up in bed, confused, and then instinctively reach over and switch on the light. "What's that fucking sound?" *And where the hell am I*, I don't add out loud. My heart slows as I remember. I turn to the girl in the bed next to me and her expression is nearing fearful. "Sorry," I say.

"She's hungry, that's all. I'm trying to be quiet."

It's only then that I notice the sound that woke me is a baby suckling. On a breast. That's partly exposed right now. I'm not sure what comes over me but it takes quite a few seconds to pull my eyes away. When I find her gaze she's not afraid anymore, she's mad. I laugh a little as I switch the light off and lie back on the bed, my hands behind my head.

"What's funny?" she asks, annoyed.

"That look. Like you'd punch me in the face if you didn't have a baby attached to you."

"I'm going to ignore you."

And she does. The baby slurps away happily and I can make out the girl's face in a stray beam of light that filters through an opening in the curtains from the parking lot. Her eyes are closed and she appears utterly content.

My dick twitches a little and I laugh again.

"Do you mind?"

"I actually do not mind. Not one bit." And then it's my turn to turn away and ignore *her*. But the smile is still on my face and even though I'm almost embarrassed to admit it, I think that breastfeeding a baby not six feet away from me—a man she knows nothing about but seems ready to trust completely—is just about the sexiest fucking thing I've ever encountered.

SIX

A knock at the door pulls me back from my dreamless slumber. I open my eyes and stare at the door. "Now what?" I look over at the girl but she's still asleep. I wrap the blanket around me and check the time on my phone. Seven AM. Who the fuck is up at seven AM on New Year's Day?

I pull it open, ready to bitch out whoever's on the other side, but stop short when I realize it's Mrs. Pearson.

"Rutherford, sorry to bother you…"

I wait.

"Do you mind if I come in? It's six degrees out here."

"Oh, sure." I step aside and let her in.

She pushes past me and then stops short as I close the door. "Oh, I just assumed you were alone last night. I only charged you for a single."

"So bill me," I reply dryly.

"No, no, that's fine. You know we were all so disappointed when you never came for your father's funeral. The whole village turned out. Everyone wanted to see you."

TAUT

I have nothing for that.

"At any rate, I'm happy you're back. I'm sure everyone will be glad to talk to you."

"I'm not back. I broke down and I'm passing through, that's all."

Her gaze remains on the girl in the bed and I have to clear my throat to get her attention back. "Right," she says, finally turning back to me. "Dallas called Jason last night and told him of your… situation." Her eyes linger on the girl again, like she just can't accept the fact that she's there. "Anyway, Jason said he'll be in at eleven to take a look at your truck. You still have that thing, huh?"

"Yes, Mrs. Pearson, it's a classic."

"Oh, well… I hope it has seatbelts. You know, for the *baby*."

I look over at the girl, who now has her eyes open and is starting to pull herself up from the bed. She's stripped down to a t-shirt and her legs are bare when she swings them out from under the covers in a half-dazed state. The baby is sleeping next to her and shifts a little as she maneuvers, enough to make Mrs. Pearson jump into action to prevent a potential roll-off.

"Thanks," the girl mumbles groggily. She's clearly not awake yet.

I look over at Mrs. Pearson and she's frowning. "Why is it so cold in here?" she asks.

"The heater's broke, so we had to use blizzard blankets," the girl replies as she rubs her eyes.

"Oh, dear. Why didn't you ask Rutherford to come tell me?" Mrs. Pearson goes back over to the heater unit under the window and messes with the switch for a few seconds. "The dials on this one are off, you have to put it halfway between hot and cold to make the heat work."

"Wonderful, thanks," I reply. "Now that the fucking night is over and we have to leave, I'm so glad we have heat."

"Rutherford, your mouth!" Mrs. Pearson chastises. I feel like I'm ten again.

"Rutherford?" the girl asks, looking up at me, confused.

"Ford, I suppose you know him by, right?" Mrs. Pearson nods to me and my eyebrows raise at the girl's stare. "I was the village librarian when he was little, so naturally I stick to given names." She walks over to the girl's bed, pushing me right out of the way as she does this. "Blizzard blankets," she says, her fingertips gliding across the blanket, testing for heat. "He always was resourceful. Did he tell you he was an Eagle Scout?"

The girl laughs and suddenly I feel like I'm just scenery, something to be talked about, but not talked *to*. I shake my head and then stare at the two of them as they discuss me.

"Was he?" the girl asks, interested.

"He never told you about how he electrocuted Jason in the boys' bathroom and then used that apparatus for the sixth-grade science fair and got his electricity badge out of it at the same time? Rutherford is not one to waste an opportunity." The girl laughs a little at this image and Mrs. Pearson is encouraged. "Honey, I have some stories—"

"OK, that's enough." I snap out of my daze and grab Mrs. Pearson by the arm and start pulling her towards the door. "And for the record, I was not charged for that small mishap in the skate park bathroom that year, so technically I never did it. Thank you for delivering the message, Mrs. Pearson. If Jason calls back, tell him I'll meet him over there at eleven."

"OK, but your wife can come visit with me while you figure out the mechanical stuff. I'd love to talk to her—"

"I'm sure you would. Thanks!" I shove her out the door and close it before she can open her mouth again. I look over at the girl and she's smiling at me. "What?"

"Rutherford?" she snickers as the baby squirms in her arms. "You look nothing like one now, but I can totally see you as a nerdy little prankster."

"A what?" I'm not sure if that was a compliment or an insult. "And please, only my parents call me Rutherford."

She hugs the baby to her chest and coos at it for a few seconds, then gets back under the covers and lifts her shirt and slides the baby in next to her bare skin.

I want to look away.

That's a lie. Not only do I not want to look away, I *can't* look away, so the girl catches me staring again.

"The librarian thinks I'm your wife," she says, closing her eyes as the baby begins to suckle.

"Yes, sorry about that. I'll set her straight next time I see her." I climb back into my bed, hoping all my chance encounters with Mrs. Pearson are over. I'll just leave the key in the room and not check out. The heat's blasting out of the unit now, and the room is warming up nicely. "We have a couple more hours, might as well enjoy it."

I get no reply and at first I think she's ignoring me, but when I open my eyes and drag my stare over to her, she's already breathing heavy with her mouth open. Her dark hair spills over her shoulders in a long cascade and for a moment I imagine she's Rook.

Would I want a wife and a child if it was with Rook?

Yes. Unequivocally, yes. I would like that. I'd like that very much. I take the daydream a little further and imagine Rook's body pressed up against mine as she feeds our baby. How warm her skin would be. I allow the slurping noises the baby is making in the next bed to lull me further.

If that girl was Rook, she would be naked, tucked up into my chest as she nursed. I'd rest my cheek against her and pull her as close to my body as I could.

I'd touch her all over. Every bit of her body would get my attention. I'd explore her daily. Take her as often as I could get away with it. And not from behind, either. From below. So I could watch her move on top of me, watch her breasts as she arches her back when I make her come.

I could make her happy and she knows it.

She is the only woman I've ever wanted.

She is the one woman I cannot have.

The daydream fades and the baby sounds jerk me back to my reality. I'm with a strange girl and her child in the cheapest motel in Vail—a town I've avoided successfully for two-plus years. My vehicle is fucked and even though I could just rent a car and be on my way right now, that hunk of shit means far too much to leave behind.

SEVEN

I sit up straight in bed, confused as fuck again. "What is that *smell*?"

I get baby noises as a response.

"And why the fuck is it so cold?" I manage to locate the source of the noise—the baby is cooing in her carrier seat on the floor. Then the cold—the door is propped open with one of my shoes. The girl bursts through a second later, shivering from the frigid alpine air, and shuts the door. When she turns around she jumps and puts her hand on her chest.

"Oh, crap, you scared me! I thought you were asleep."

I lie back and put my hand over my eyes to block out the light. "I was, until that smell woke me up."

"Sorry," she says quietly. Everything she does seems quiet to me. Slow. "She had a stinky diaper. I took it to the dumpster. That librarian lady said we have to be out by ten and it's almost nine-thirty. So if it's OK, I'm going to take a shower."

I don't even move my hand from my eyes. "Fine with me."

"Um, I hate to ask, but… do you mind just keeping an eye on

the baby for like five minutes? I promise to be—"

"Absolutely not." I do take my hand away from my eyes for this, because I want to look her in the eyes. "No," I repeat, shaking my head. "I do not do babies."

She shoots me a dirty look, scoops up the baby carrier, and walks into the bathroom.

I do not care how angry she is. I do not do babies and I especially do not do babies belonging to strangers. And, I add to boost my reasoning, she should not want a stranger watching her baby, anyway.

The shower starts a minute later and I can hear her talking to the infant. I get up and get dressed in last night's tuxedo, leaving off the tie. I button up the shirt without tucking it in and lay my suit coat on the bed. I don't even have a winter coat because the last thing on my mind when I got dressed for the Chaput party last night was trying to drive the Bronco over the motherfucking Rocky Mountains and ending up stranded in Vail after a blizzard.

I stuff the bow tie into my suit coat pocket and find the little rubber duck I picked up in the tow truck. I set it on the dresser and try and flatten my hair down with some water. It's bad enough I look like a leftover New Year's Eve drunk in this fucking suit, but I refuse to look like an unkempt one.

By the time I'm putting on my shoes, the girl comes out dressed in yesterday's clothes. Her hair is wet but she smells fresh. The baby is still wearing her yellow footied sleeper.

"How old?" I ask the girl as I point to the baby.

The girl ignores me and I suppose she's upset at my lack of showering assistance.

"I found this toy in the tow truck last night. The driver said it was yours." I point to the duck and the girl's face contorts into something strange. An expression of relief. She picks it up tenderly and then smiles as she slips it into the diaper bag on the floor.

OK. Whatever. I gather up my keys and my phone and wait for her to get all her baby crap together. She's got a bag and the carrier and her purse. I didn't notice she had all this last night, so maybe she went to her car and got it. I hold the door open for her and she mumbles out a thank you.

"They have breakfast in the hotel office—"

"Yes," she says immediately, and when I stop to look at her, she's studying the office door with longing. "I'm so hungry. I haven't eaten since yesterday morning."

"Well, Jason won't be here for another—"

"Yo! Ford!" I turn and Jason is getting out of a tow truck in the garage parking lot. "Long time, dude!"

"Oh," the girl moans. "He's already here."

"Give me your keys, I'll take care of your car while you eat." Her whole face changes, like I just promised her a million dollars. I give her a smile in return for that little vote of confidence and offer up one better. "In fact, just stay in the office. It's too cold for a baby out here anyway. I'll come get you when it's sorted."

"Oh, thank you," she says shuffling through her purse for her keys. She hands them over and sighs. Her hand rests on my arm. I pull away instinctively, but she's too busy telling me how hungry she is and how I'm literally saving her life to notice my minor freakout. And then before I can fully come to terms with the fact that she just touched me, she turns and starts walking to the office.

I look down at my suit coat where I can still feel her hand. Then at her keys. The key chain is a military dog tag and says, *Proud Marine Wife—Ashleigh and Tony Forever* with a little heart stamped on it.

"Hey, what the fuck you doing, dude?" Jason asks from behind me. "You know that girl? Dallas said he picked her up on the freeway, her engine blew going up the mountain or something."

I turn and take him in. He hasn't changed since he was fourteen. Same reddish-blond hair, so short it might as well be shaved, same dull gray eyes, and same football build that put him squarely into the jock category at all the childhood functions we were forced into together simply because we were the same age. Not much changes around here. "We shared a room. You only had one left and I had it. She was trying to sleep in her car during the blizzard."

"That's a pretty efficient death wish. Well, come on, we gotta dig out your piece of shit before I can check it."

It's only then that I notice how much snow fell overnight. At least three feet. The parking lots and roads are mostly cleared though. That's one thing you can count on in Vail. Plowed streets and lots. Gotta keep the golden roads clear so tourists can ski on the mountain and everyone can make money.

"Where's your coat, Ford?"

I look down at myself and shake my head. "I didn't bring one. I had no plans on stopping here, believe me. I was on my fucking way to LA."

He laughs. "Well, you two dumbasses make the perfect pair then, right?"

"Ha ha, yeah, you're funny. It's the transmission, by the way," I tell him as we walk up to the Bronco. Another kid comes out of the garage with a snow blower and walks up to us.

"My brother Jimmy, remember him?"

I nod to Jimmy, but he's already starting up the blower. "You need to dig her out too," I say, pointing to the girl's old Honda Civic hatchback as I hand him the keys. "Let me know what's wrong with it and I'll pay. She's broke."

"Yeah, OK." Jason goes over to Jimmy and talks close to his ear so he can hear over the machine, then hands him the keys. "Come on, we'll go inside and catch up."

"Well," Jason says an hour of *A Christmas Story* and five cups of coffee later. "You're right. Your tranny's blown and your coolant system isn't much better. You need a rebuild and some hoses. Gonna be about a week to get this one done." He eyeballs me and I know what that means. It's a week if you want it done at regular rates.

"Well, let me guess, Jason. I can get her back in three days if I just pay you double, right?"

He shrugs. "Us little guys gotta make a living somehow."

"Please. You are not starving. You own a frontage road garage and the only cheap motel in Vail. And I've seen your fucking family compound. So spare me the theatrics. I don't care how much it costs, just get it done by Monday."

"Well, that means I gotta start today, though, Ford. And not only is today the Friday after a big fucking blizzard, which means I should be out on the mountain instead of in here working on that piece of shit you've been driving since high school, but it's also a national holiday. So that's like mandatory triple time, I figure."

I add up the cost of a transmission rebuild and triple it. "You want six grand to fix the transmission on a truck that probably costs four when she's running?"

He shoots me a *paybacks are a bitch, aren't they* look. "You can junk it, leave it with me. I'll take care of her for ya."

I take out my card and flick it at him. "What's the damage on the girl's car? Add it in."

He grunts. "She blew her engine, probably trying to force it up the mountain. But I know a guy down in Copper who specializes in these old Hondas, he's got a used one. Hundred and two thousand miles on it, fourteen hundred plus tax for him, seven hundred for me, and a hundred-dollar delivery fee. Jimmy's gotta make some money out of it too. That will not be done by Monday, so she's stuck here for at least a week."

"Just ring it up."

EIGHT

I make calls while Jason does the paperwork.

Vail. For an entire weekend. It's like my bad luck is smiling down on me, saying that's all I'll ever have, so get used to it.

The shop door opens and a strong burst of wind throws it backwards, slamming it into the building. The frazzled high-school kid grabs at the door frantically and then pulls it closed behind him. He stomps his boots on the rug near the door and calls over to Jason, "Another storm's coming and all these fucking tourists will be stuck, whining and complaining that they have no fucking this or no fucking that." It's only then that he notices me. "Oh, sorry."

"I'm not a tourist."

"Right."

"You have my car?"

"Yeah," he says with a wince. "I know you ordered a truck or SUV, but sorry, man, this is all we got." He pans his hand behind him and I strain to see the vehicle through the blowing snow. "My coworker even had to follow me over here in that stupid

Ford Focus."

Jason grunts out a laugh at that, but I ignore him and get up so I can see the vehicle properly.

"A minivan? I said four-wheel drive. I live on fucking Goat Hill."

"It's all-wheel drive. Same thing."

"A lot of good those fucking wheels will do me when it bottoms out in the driveway."

He shrugs and I drop it. It's not his fault I'm stuck here. It's mine. "Fine." He hands me the keys and I hand him my card, which he runs in a portable device on his phone, and then hands back to me. "You get double bonus points for renting—"

"Yes, thank you," I say as I take the keys he's offering. "Jason, we're on for Monday, then? What time?"

He doesn't even look up at me, just continues punching something into the computer. "I'll call you Monday AM and let you know. Do you know where that girl is? I need her to sign the paperwork."

I grab the pen and sign for her and then push it back across the counter.

Jason gives me a weird look. "OK. Well, tell her I won't even start working on her new engine until next week sometime, and it'll take at least a week after that. So, I'm not sure what she's gonna do—"

"I'll take care of it."

I head out, pulling my suit coat around me as a gust of wind barrels across the parking lot, then jog over to the minivan which is, thank God, still warm when I get in.

"Fuck," I say out loud once I close the door.

I've got snow. I've got Vail. I've got a girl and her baby. I've got a past that's doing its best to catch up with me. I've got Rook, who I want to talk to so desperately it actually makes my chest feel funny. And I've got a house that's been winterized for two fucking years, being de-winterized at this very moment, and who the fuck knows if anything works. Hell, maybe all the pipes burst and we have no plumbing.

I rev the engine then put the van in gear and drive forward down the parking lot towards the motel office. I park right in front, leave the van running, and then get out quickly and make for the door. The heat assaults me as soon as I enter and the first thing I hear is Mrs. Pearson trying to gossip over a very fussy and unhappy baby. The girl looks at me, her body swaying slightly to soothe the child and her eyes wide as she subtly motions at the incessant chatter of Mrs. Pearson—like she's pleading with me to make her shut up. Mrs. Pearson simply continues to talk, directing the conversation to me. I tune her out completely.

"Put the baby in the car," I tell the girl in a low voice that rumbles under Mrs. Pearson's high-pitched one. She doesn't even balk, just nods, puts the baby in the carrier, and heads to the door.

I did not have to tell her twice.

He obedience gives me more pleasure than it should and I'm trying to figure out why when Mrs. Pearson appears next to me cackling about how I should trade my Bronco in for a minivan like my rental. "It's not my child, Mrs. Pearson. She's some girl I'm helping out, that's all."

But Mrs. Pearson's not listening. She just goes on and on about the safety rating on a Bronco. "I'm fairly certain a 1986 Bronco has no safety rating," I tell her absently as I walk around the office lobby picking up the baby crap, shoving it into a diaper bag decorated with pink teddy bears. I make my way to the door as quickly as possible, barking out a loud, "Thank you," as I go back out into the blizzard. The girl is still struggling with the seat in the back of the van so I stand and wait for her to be finished, the snow beating down on both of us. It seems rude to get in when she's about to be blown across the parking lot.

She finishes with the baby and turns into me, her hands pushing on my chest and her eyes wide in surprise. I grab her wrists to remove her hands and she yelps. "Sorry," she says softly, then snags the diaper bag and throws it on the floor. I back away as she whooshes the van door closed and runs to the other side to get in.

Mrs. Pearson is watching us from the door with a concerned look on her face and I get in hurriedly to prevent her from coming out to help. I slam the door and the girl lets out a long groan.

"Oh. My. God. I did not know it was possible for people to talk so—oh, shit! She's coming! Go, go, go!"

I put the van in drive and give Mrs. Pearson a small wave as we pull away. "Yeah, she's something, that woman." I look over at the girl and she's shaking her head, but also smiling. It's the first time I've seen the smile. It's nice.

She looks very different when she smiles. Softer.

Her eyes are wide and dark, excited. She looks back over her shoulder as we leave the motel behind and then her gaze rests on me. "Sorry. You're probably wondering why I'm in your car."

"I know exactly why you're in the car."

Her smile fades slowly. "Why? Why am I here? Why didn't you tell me you were paying for my car to be fixed? Mrs. Pearson called over to the garage and that guy told her you were gonna take care of it. It's a big bill. More than two thousand dollars. I—" She stops to study my face intently. "I don't even know you. Why are you helping me?"

"I thought you needed it."

She stares at me for a long time. I'm busy navigating my way across I-70 towards my house, but I can see her out of the corner of my eye. Hesitating. Like she's got a choice in front of her and she's not sure which way to go. "I do need it," she finally says.

"That's a nice change."

"What is?"

"Admitting you need help. Most people refuse on principle."

She grunts out a laugh. "I left my principles behind a while back."

This piques my interest. "How so?"

"Never mind." She turns in her seat to check the baby as I veer left onto Sunburst. "Not that I'm in the position to be picky, but where are we going?" She sits back down and suddenly realizes she has no seatbelt on and we're driving through a blizzard. She drags it across her chest and snaps it in the other end.

"I have a family home here. We can stay there. I would've gone last night, but we're at the very end of this road, up on a hill. Plus the house has been empty for two years, so it would not have been much comfort with no heat or hot water. It should be working now, though."

She accepts that answer without comment, but a few seconds later she's back. "How can you even see where you're going?"

"This is Vail. It's a small village situated in a very narrow valley between two giant mountains alongside a major highway. There's really nowhere to go."

"Oh. Well, I'm not a local, so pardon me."

I ignore that and stop the van at the security gate that leads to our driveway. I open the window and the baby bellows out a wail when the wind blows snow in. I key in the code and the gate slides open. "If I had come last night, I'd never have made it past the gate with the snow. So good thing I didn't try, I guess."

She says nothing to that, just looks back at the baby with a concerned expression.

I close the window but the infant is not so easily consoled. At least the property management people plowed the driveway. Otherwise this stupid van really would've bottomed out on the way up. We climb slowly, the girl letting out a few gasps as we slip around, the all-wheel drive kicking in just in time. And then it flattens out and I pull around the side of the house to the garage. "Stay here, I have no garage door opener so I have to key it open with a code."

I jump out and pick my way over to the door, minding the slick covering of ice under my dress shoes, then open the garage. The girl has jumped into the driver's seat and she pulls the van in, looking like she's trying hard to concentrate on doing a good job parking.

TAUT

What have I started here? I'm not sure, but yesterday and today seem like two different lifetimes. Unrelated in almost every way.

The girl jumps out and swings the back seat door open. The baby is sprinkled with snow, her eyes closed, but her little mouth is scrunched up like she's ready to lose it. "Oh no!" The girl bites her lip and looks back at me.

"What?" I ask.

"All our clothes and stuff are back in my car. I have a few diapers and a clean t-shirt for her, but not much else." She looks at me like she's afraid I'll bite her head off over this.

"What?" I ask, annoyed with that expression.

"You'll have to take me back. I'm sorry. Really, I know I'm a major pain in your ass right now—"

"Save it." I hold up a hand and grab her bag from the floor and then move out of the way so she can unhook that baby contraption from the seat belts. "We have to go back out anyway. I just wanted to come check on things before I went to the store. There's nothing in this house to eat, and aside from tap water coming through pipes that have been sitting for two years, and some very fucking expensive Scotch whiskey, nothing to drink either. So there's no way we're not going back out. And since the Safeway is on the west side of the village, we have to go past the garage again anyway."

"Oh, good." She lets out a long breath of relief as she lifts the carrier out of the back seat and we walk over to the door that leads to the house. "OK. Thanks so much for your help. The room, the car. I'll pay you back."

I wave her through the door, then flip on the lights. "There's no need, really. And I'm not trying to have a polite argument about it, I seriously don't want or need your money. So drop it."

I catch the dirty look from the corner of my eye, but she holds her response back.

I do not care at this moment because I am back in our family home. I walk through the kitchen, drop the baby stuff on the granite island, and then walk into the middle of the living room and look around.

Dark hardwood floors. Everything is shades of black, white, and gray. It's got a minimalist feel.

"It's nice," the girls says as she looks around. "Not how I expected a house in Vail to look—I figured ski lodge people would have rustic homes. But still, it's nice."

"It's horrible." And it is. Ultra-modern—just like my downtown Denver condo. My parents hated this look, but they redid this house and let me pick the designer. And my designer picked all this cold furniture with the chrome and glass. All these sharp lines and contrasting colors.

That was right before my dad died.

I used to like the minimalist look, but I'd give anything to have our old stuff back right now. The sagging brown couches instead of these gray ones. The dark walnut coffee and end tables instead of these glass ones. The family photos on the walls instead of this pretentious shit they call art around here.

The girl tries to bounce a little on the long gray couch, then gives up. "Huh."

"Huh what?"

She looks up at me with a sly smirk. "Yeah, it's horrible."

"The basement is nicer. More casual. At least the couches are overstuffed leather. I'm gonna sleep down there."

"Why? Don't you have more than one bedroom?"

"Yeah, I have a room and my parents have a room. But I'm not sleeping in either of those beds, so I'll take the downstairs couch."

She looks down the hallway towards the bedrooms and for a second it feels like she's gonna say something, but then she closes her mouth and looks back up at me with a smile. "OK."

I walk to the bathroom and turn the water on. It runs clear and after about a minute or so, it's warm too. "Well," I say, coming back out to the living room. "Looks like we have hot water, so that's good." The girl is slumped against the back of the couch looking exhausted. "Do you want to stay here while I go into town?" She shakes her head and drags herself up. The baby is already sleeping. "She sure does sleep well."

"Yeah," the girl says a little wistfully. "People think new babies are hard, but the new ones sleep." She turns her face up to me and smiles. "A couple weeks from now she'll keep me up all hours of the night, but for now, all she wants is milk and rest."

"How old?" I try again since she's not pissed at me right now.

"Three and a half months."

"And you're driving a piece-of-shit car over a snowy mountain with a three-month-old, all alone… why?"

She gets up and grabs the baby carrier, her jaw tense and her posture stiff. "I'm ready if you are."

I wave her back the way we came, but I'm not satisfied. Not at all. Because this girl has a ring on her finger, a new baby, and she's alone in a strange place with no money. Crossing the mountains unprepared in the dead of winter is stupid. And in spite of the fact that I did the same thing, it's not even remotely comparable. I'm a man, I'm rich, I have a house along the way. I'm from here. I, at the very least, have a survival kit in my truck with very expensive blankets that will keep you warm in subzero temperatures even if you sit your ass outside in the snow.

She has nothing and she's not the least bit bothered by it beyond keeping it to herself.

And I don't like that one bit.

Because this girl is starting to remind me a little too much of the old Rook.

NINE

"The car is locked inside."

I feel a little bad for her as I fool with my phone web browser. She's genuinely distraught at having all her things locked away inside Jason's garage. "He won't come open it so you can get your stuff, so we'll just get what you need at the store."

She turns away from the window she's fogging up with her breath and stares at me. Silent.

"What?" I ask absently, still paying attention to the search results on my phone.

"Nothing," she sighs. "If you say so." She turns back to the window and I put my phone away. I pull out of Jason's and make our way back onto I-70 to get to the west side of the village, and then she turns back to me. "Thank you. I'm sorry I'm not more appreciative. I'm just…"

I wait. The car is silent except for the blast of hot air coming from the heater vents. But she's dropped it and I hate that. "You're just what?" I prod.

She waits again. And then, just when I think she's ignoring

me, she says very softly, "I'm just not sure what's happening."

I slow the van down so we don't slide into the car in front of us when we get off the freeway, but as soon as I turn right to go to Safeway, I can't wait anymore, so I ask. "You're not sure about what? I don't understand your confusion." I figure she's gonna ask me what my intentions are. Hell, if I was a girl with a new baby traveling alone, and some guy picked me up and wanted to pay for everything, that's the first fucking thing I would've asked.

But she's done talking about it because she changes the subject. "Do they have a Wal-Mart here?"

I laugh.

"What?"

I laugh again. "This is Vail. We have a Patagonia, a Sports Authority, a million ski and board shops, several survival gear stores, one 7-11, and a Safeway. Unless you count the boutiques in Vail Village, but I do not. We can go there tomorrow and get you more clothes if you need it, but not today. You have to walk in from the parking garage, and even though the sidewalks are heated so snow is not a problem, I'm not in the mood to boutique shop in Vail Village during a blizzard. So I'll hit the Safeway for groceries and you can shop for clothes in the consignment store next door."

"What if it's not open?"

"I already checked, they're open until four."

"Well," she says with a little sigh that might be relief. "I guess you've got it all figured out, then."

"I do," I say as I pull up in front of the consignment shop. She gets out and opens the back door and the wind whips snow inside. She grabs that pain-in-the-ass baby carrier and I get out some cash from my wallet and thrust it at her. "Here, get whatever you need."

She stares at the bills in my outstretched hand for a moment, then looks up to my eyes. "Did he send you?"

"What? Who?"

She shakes her head and mutters, "Nothing." And then she

grabs the cash and the baby carrier and whooshes the door closed.

"Did who send me?" I have a paranoid vision of her being some mob boss' daughter on the run after witnessing a triple murder of some important politician's family… and then I laugh myself out of it. *Fuck, Ford. You have some imagination. Not everyone is a criminal.* I'm not sure who this girl is or what that remark just meant, but right now I do not care. The snow is getting worse and I just want to get this shopping crap over with and go home.

Home.

That word in association with Vail evokes feelings in me that I'm not sure how to identify. I've lived here on and off my entire life. In that house. In that bedroom. But now this place feels… empty for me. It's missing something.

No, that's not right. It's missing everything.

I park the van and jog towards the entrance before the snow drenches me.

The Safeway doors slide open when I approach and I'm bombarded with leftover Christmas shit. I skirt around an employee trying to hand me samples of corned beef, and then grab a cart. I hit the alcohol first. I grab a few local brew six-packs and then head to the meat department.

I can cook. Regardless of what Spencer thinks, I have no problem cooking. I might not push a vacuum around, but that's only because I have maids who do that for me. But eating is something I have to do a few times a day so cooking is a survival skill.

I grab a few pounds of boneless chicken, some rice, and other small things to make it taste a little better. I wander around the produce department and pick up some vegetables for a salad. I'm perusing the drinks aisle when I hear the baby behind me.

"Hey," the girl says as she comes up laden with bags and the carrier.

"That was fast."

TAUT

"Yeah, the shop girl practically kicked me out. I was her only customer all day and she was just thinking she could close early when I walked in. I got a few things real fast. I didn't spend much."

I take the bags and put them in the grocery cart and she balances the baby carrier on the front seat and takes over the driving.

I shake my head at that. Fucking girls. "I got a few things, but you can get whatever you want."

"I have to get diapers." She looks back at me. "If that's OK?"

I wave her on. "Whatever you need."

She leads the way after that and I follow, feeling a bit uncomfortable to be doing something so personal as grocery shopping with a total stranger and her child. But then, I spent last night with her, she's staying with me this weekend, and I paid for her car to get a new engine. So I guess grocery shopping is not so strange after all.

She whips the cart around the corner and looks up at the aisle signs as she walks, then takes a hard right into the baby stuff. She barely stops, just grabs things off the shelf as she walks. Tosses in diapers, a bib, and a box of something. "I have a bowl and spoon, so I don't need that," she explains when she notices me watching her intently.

"OK," I reply. She stops at the end of the aisle. "You done?"

"I think so."

"Do you need anything specific? Milk?" She glances down at her breasts and I let out a small chuckle. "For you, I mean."

"Oh, I'll eat whatever, but thank you."

"OK." And that's that. Shopping is over. We stand in the checkout line, which is long since there's a threat of another storm coming and people are reactionary when they think they might be snowed in for a day. I pay and the girl talks to the baby as the bagger loads our cart back up. And then we go back out and brave the snow. It's really coming down and the parking lot hasn't been cleared since earlier in the day, so I have to fight the cart through the slush.

We load the kid and the crap, then climb back into the van. Our doors slam at the same time and we let out a collective sigh. She looks over at me and gives me a smile again. "Thank you so much."

"No problem. Jason will be at the shop tomorrow, so we can go by and get your stuff if you need it. The Bronco will be done on Monday, but he won't be able to start your car until later in the week, so you'll have to stay up here in Vail until it's done."

"Oh." She seems disappointed and that's all she says as I drive carefully through the snow, the tires making that crunching noise as we go.

"Don't worry," I say, looking at her frown. "You can stay at my house. Just call the property managers when you leave and they'll come lock it all up again. I'll leave you some cash for food, and you can use this rental if you want."

She nods and looks out the window.

"What?" I ask as I get back on the freeway.

"Thanks," she says with an almost too cheerful smile. "It's very nice of you to help me out like this. You don't even know me." And then she snorts a little. "You don't even know my name."

"Ashleigh," I say quietly. "You're Ashleigh." She gives me a quizzical look. "Your key chain. It said Ashleigh and Tony Forever or something like that."

"Oh, right." The smile disappears.

"But yeah, I'm not usually so nice. You caught me on a bad day."

"This is a bad day? What are you like on a good day? A saint?" This brings the smile back, at least partly.

"No, on a good day I'm myself. On a good day I would've left you in your car all night."

She looks over at me quickly. "Would not've."

"Yes, I would. On a good day I would never've knocked on your window when I went to get the blizzard blankets. I would've pretended I never heard you and your baby. And then I would've walked back to my hotel and gone to sleep. I'd have forgotten you before I even reached the motel door."

I get off the freeway at our exit and turn right onto Starburst. The snow is even thicker over here and I start to worry about the driveway. I punch in the gate code once we make it to the house, and then hold my breath as we climb the steep hill. We slide even more this time and it's freaking her out.

"I don't like this. Drop me off, I'll walk up."

"I'm not dropping you off. Just relax."

She looks nervously behind us. "I'm afraid we're gonna slide backwards and—"

"Stop it. I'm not going to let us slide backwards."

"But what if you can't control it?"

I shoot her an annoyed look and she turns away as I accelerate a little, making the tires spin. She makes a few indescribable noises and grips the seat, but after a few seconds of sliding sideways, we get traction and continue upwards. When I finally pull around to the garage she lets out a long breath like she was holding it in the entire time. "Told ya," I say smugly as I put the car in park so I can go open the garage door.

"Yeah, you did, didn't you?"

I glance up at her as I get out to see if this was sarcasm, but she's already scooting over into my seat. We've got this down to a routine, I guess.

She smiles at me again. Like she trusts me completely even though three seconds ago she thought I was gonna let us slide backwards down a steep hill. I open the garage and she pulls forward with the same careful attention she did earlier, and then I close the door behind her. I start grabbing bags and she messes with the baby.

I set all the bags down on the kitchen island and start taking things out to put away.

"Nope," she says in a light tone. She walks over to me and puts her hand on my chest to push me away, and then grabs the bag with her other hand at the same time. "You paid, so I'll put it all away and cook us dinner."

I try to remove her hand from my chest, but she whirls around before I can even come to grips with the fact that she touched me *again*.

Fucking girl. That's three times now.

"Go," she says. "Shoo. I'll take care of it."

"Shoo?" I chuckle. It feels good to laugh after all this bullshit that's been rattling around in my brain these past few months. "I can cook. I don't need you to take care of me."

She stops what she's doing and looks over her shoulder at me. "Just go, OK? I got this. It's my way of paying you back. Don't ruin it for me."

She goes back to the bags and leaves me to decide. I watch her from behind for a moment. Her small body is busy as she takes things out and sets them on the counter. And then the baby whines and it breaks the hold this girl has on me.

I don't exactly hate babies, they just freak me out. They're all needy with the feeding and the diapers. Plus, most of them like to be touched.

I shiver at the thought and make a quick escape before she asks me to do her a baby favor.

TEN

I head downstairs immediately. This is the front of the house and it's not your typical dark basement. For one, it's got a whole wall of windows on the far end of the lower floor great room, and for two, it's a walk-out basement, so it's built into the side of the mountain. If it wasn't dark I'd be enjoying a spectacular view of the mountain peeking out from the tall pine trees. There's no skiing on the mountain we face, it's just wilderness. I prefer it. I can imagine nothing worse than looking out the window and seeing tourists.

I drag my gaze away from the dark window and look to the left at my dad's office door. I haven't been back here since the day he died. And as Mrs. Pearson pointed out to me this morning, I even missed the funeral.

I don't do funerals. I don't do weddings, or baby showers, or anniversaries.

I did one birthday. For Rook. I did Ronin's get-out-of-jail-free party. Again, for Rook. And I've been to Antoine's New Year's party twice, including yesterday. The first was to get drunk with

TAUT

Spencer and Ronin after Mardee died. A formal goodbye from the three of us. And last night was to say goodbye to Rook. A last-ditch attempt to disconnect whatever it is we have between us.

I flick the light on in my dad's office and take it in. Books on shelves, of course. We are alike in that respect. A large mahogany desk, spotless. I huff out a puff of air at that. Because his desk was never cleared off when he was alive. I walk around the desk and sink into the burgundy leather chair. It's soft. It probably cost more than that girl's car.

I slide open the top drawer and take out the key, twirling it between my fingers before inserting it into the bottom drawer and pulling it open. The light oak color of Macallan 1939 is apparent even in the shadow of the desk. Farther inside the drawer are two copita nosing glasses tucked inside some dark purple cloth.

My dad was a whiskey man and I bought him this bottle at auction after I completed my first job producing a two-week reality show in Japan. I spent my entire salary on this bottle of liquid gold. I told my dad to just drink it, shit, that's why I bought it. But he said he was saving it for something special.

That's a hard lesson to learn. You should never save anything for something special. Because something special might never come and that ten-thousand-dollar bottle of Scotch you admired in a desk drawer will just to go to waste on your piece-of-shit son as he mopes about losing yet another girl to Ronin fucking Flynn.

I open the bottle and grab both glasses. I pour a little whiskey into each glass, then walk over to the window, open it up, and toss it outside.

I pour again.

Apparently I'm secretly hoping the girl will wander down here and join me. Save me from my wallowing. Or maybe just get drunk with me. I smell the whiskey in my glass, then do the unthinkable with such a fine grade of drink. I guzzle it.

It burns like fuck as it goes down, but after that's over I'm left with a rather pleasant taste.

I drink the girl's glass too, and then pour us another.

Those two go down a lot easier and the coldness that has permeated my body all day is gone. In fact, my body is so warm I open the window back up.

Courage, that's what I'm drinking. It's not liquid gold, it's liquid courage.

I reach into my pocket and take out my phone and turn it on. I'm almost afraid to see what's waiting for me since I turned it on earlier in the day to make calls. It takes its time powering up and then the damage stares me in the face. Seventeen messages in all since last night.

I page to the list of missed calls. Rook, Ronin, Rook, Rook, Rook, Ronin... I study them for a moment, then realize she's got a pattern. She calls on the hour. Ronin's calls are random.

Just like him. He has no pattern—he's random. That's why luck likes him.

I hate it. I hate it because Rook does have a pattern. She's symmetrical, she's even, she's... perfect. And he's... not. I check the time real quick—ten minutes to seven—and then press the number for the other missed calls on my screen.

"Ford?" my mother asks as she picks up. She knows it's me, she's got caller ID, so asking this as a question is irritating.

"Yeah," I say.

"Are you... OK?"

"I'm in Vail."

"Oh."

"I was driving to LA and I broke down in Vail, so I'm at the house."

"Oh."

"I'm fine, I saw that you called, so..."

"Ronin has been calling. He says you left the party unexpectedly last night."

"I was only there for the exit interviews."

"Your assistant in LA called, she said you missed your flight."

TAUT

"I said I'm driving. It's no big deal. I'm just letting you know, since…"

She waits. She's not a Pusher. She's a Waiter. I smile at this. I really do love my mom. She's kinda flaky and her whole life is wrapped around her charity things, but she's cute and even if I didn't love her for being my mom, I'd *like* her for being someone interesting. "Since there's a blizzard. Anyway, I'll be leaving on Monday, so I'll call you when I get back to LA. OK?"

She does some small talk before we hang up. She's always like that. Trying to get me interested in having a long conversation. But I'm just not into it.

The phone buzzes an incoming call almost as soon as I hang up with my mother. It's Rook, right on time. I press speaker for this one. I need both hands—one to hold the glass as I drink and one to pour the whiskey when I finish. "How can I help you, Miss Corvus?" I answer.

"Oh my fucking God! You finally picked up! What the fuck, Ford! What the fuck?"

She's almost hysterical and I have a moment of guilt. But it passes.

"Ford? You better talk to me, goddammit! I swear to God, I'm so not in the mood for your weird shit! I'm pissed off!" She's huffing on the other end of the phone and then I briefly hear Ronin talking to her in the background. There's a shuffling of the phone and then he comes on.

"Ford? You OK, man?"

I take a sip of whiskey and enjoy it. "Why wouldn't I be?"

Rook is going crazy in the background now. I can hear her losing control. "Well, Rook says you broke up with her…" He stops as she snaps at Ronin and I enjoy that a little too much. "Rook, those were your words, OK? Ford, what the fuck is going on?"

"I'm just done with her, Ronin. That's all. I've used her all up and I don't require her friendship anymore, so please, apologize—"

The line goes dead. I smile a little as I take a sip. That's one way to stop the calls and get my phone back.

"Wow," the girl says, standing in the door to my dad's office.

"Wow what?" I answer back, instantly annoyed that she overheard that conversation.

"That was harsh."

"You think?" I point to the chair in front of the desk and pour some whiskey in her glass, then scoot it in that direction. "Try this."

"No," she says, but she's moving towards the chair I just pointed to, like she thinks she's gonna sit down and have a conversation with me. "I'm breastfeeding. I can't drink."

"I'm not asking you to get *drunk*. It's a fucking bottle of 1939 Macallan. Take a fucking sip and form an opinion. You might never get another chance in your lifetime to drink a whiskey this fine. Live a little, *Ashleigh and Tony Forever, Proud Marine Wife*."

She's still crossing the room when the last of my words come out, but they make her physically recoil mid-stride. She looks hard at me for a moment. Just staring.

"What?" I snarl. "You've never seen a man be a dick to a woman before?" I laugh. "Well, you're in for a real treat then, because I'm at my peak tonight."

She never says a word. Just turns and walks out.

I'm not sure how long I sit there drinking my dead father's ten-thousand-dollar bottle of Scotch, but I am good and drunk before I finally figure out she came down to tell me dinner was ready.

My life sucks.

I'm still wearing my New Year's tux, I haven't eaten since yesterday, and I have almost two days' worth of stubble on my chin that's annoying the hell out of me and the only person in this fucking world who gives a shit about me is my mother. And she has to care about me. It's like, the law.

I cap the bottle and slip my phone into my pants pocket. I leave the fucking suit coat on the chair. I've seen the last of this tux, and I could care less what happens to it. Rook and Ronin never called back. My phone went from secretly-ringing-off-the-hook to might-as-well-be-dead. I climb the stairs with some difficulty, and then remember the fucking girl is probably still here.

Where else would she be, Ford? She's totally dependent on you.

"Don't start with me right now, internal monologue." I laugh a little at that. The house is mostly dark. Only the small light over the stove is on. I go to the kitchen looking for signs of dinner, but it's spotless. I open the fridge and squint at what's in there.

Next to the microbrews I bought at Safeway, in front of the bowl of leftover salad, is a plate. It's got a little sticky note on it that says, *Ford.*

Fuck. She's one of those *considerate* people.

I take out the plate. It's got clear Saran wrap over it, so I slip it into the microwave, then scarf down the salad while I wait. By the time the microwave beeps I've eaten half the bowl. I put it aside and dig into the meal.

It's good. Chicken and rice is chicken and rice, and maybe I'm just half-starved, but it's fucking better than good. It's delicious.

I eat standing up and then put all my crap into the sink.

The drunk feeling is subsiding and now all I can think about is a shower. I find my way to the bathroom in the dark hallway and lock myself in there, the steam and calming white noise echoing through the bathroom, momentarily taking my mind off Rook.

She told Ronin I broke up with her.

I laugh out loud at that. Fucking Rook. She's so adorable. What kind of girl tells her boyfriend that his best friend broke up with her?

My laugh dies. Because only a girl who has nothing to hide would say that to her boyfriend. And that's what hurts right now. I'm so off her radar she can tell Ronin that and not even blink. She wasn't worried about what *he* thought of that statement, she was worried about what *I* thought of that statement. That's why she snapped at Ronin when he repeated it.

I lean against the tiled wall and let the water beat down on my head as the full impact of her words suddenly hit me. She's not worried about what Ronin thinks because she knows nothing will ever come of her and me. Nothing. Ever.

I shut the shower down and dry off, then wrap the towel around my waist and go hunting for a toothbrush in the medicine cabinet. The girl already has hers out, sticking up out of a cup next to the sink. I open a new one for me, then some toothpaste and brush my teeth to chase away the whiskey.

I leave the bathroom and cross the hall to my room and flick on the light so I can find some clothes.

And stop dead.

That fucking girl is sleeping in my bed. Her shirt—actually, my shirt, it says *CU Buffs* on the sleeve—is pulled up to her neck, exposing her swollen breasts. Her nipples are large and a shade or two darker than her slightly olive skin. The baby is lying next to her, right up against her belly, but she's also sleeping.

I flick the light off and stand in the doorway, backlit by the hall light.

"I'm awake," Ashleigh says. "If you need clothes, just go ahead and turn on the light. I'm awake."

I flick it back on and notice the shirt has been pulled down. "Sorry, I just assumed you'd be in the other room."

"You said you were gonna sleep downstairs. Did you change your mind?"

I can't speak for a moment, because it almost sounds like an invitation. I look at her. I mean, really look at her. She's pretty, but not in any way beautiful or striking. More cute than anything. She has a curvy shape about her. Not so much her body, but her face, her features. They're not angular and hard, they're round and soft. Her eyes are large and brown, like her long hair, and they have a slight almond shape, like she has some Asian heritage. She's small. Tiny really, for a girl who just gave birth a few months ago. She was probably one of those pregnant girls who are all belly and breasts.

"No, I didn't change my mind. I just… need some clothes."

"OK," she says and then clutches the baby to her chest and turns over, exposing her pink panty-covered ass. It's a stark contrast to the dark blue comforter as it peeks out. I have an urge to slap it.

I laugh at this and she turns back, this time without the baby. "What's funny?"

I surrender with my hands up. "You wanted me to notice your ass when you turned? Mission accomplished. But I don't like a tease, so don't start something you can't finish."

She stares hard at me and I feel a little nervous about what kind of reaction she might have. "I'm sure I can handle it."

I raise my eyebrows but I'm not sure what to say back. I might be at a loss for words. *I'm sure I can handle it.* "Is that a challenge? Or an offer?"

"Take it however you want." She closes her eyes and then slips her hand between her legs. I'm not sure she's doing anything naughty with it, but it's provocative all the same. "Why are you still standing there?" she asks with her eyes still closed.

"I'm having trouble controlling myself, to be honest. I might just think of it as both an offer and a challenge."

Her eyes open at my response and then she throws the covers off, baring her legs all the way up to her panties. She gets up and then walks out the door, shutting the light off as she goes.

I don't let her get more than a few paces before I grab her around the middle and push her face first against the wall. I drop my towel and jam my thigh between her legs. "Open," I growl into her ear.

She obeys without words and my dick expands to its full thickness as she presses her ass into me.

"What do you like, Ashleigh? You like it slow and tender? Because if so, you're out of luck. I'm not that kind of guy." I press my chest into her back and I can almost feel her rapidly beating heart.

"I like what you like, *Rutherford.*"

She says my name like she knows me intimately. It almost puts me off my game, because I'm not used to the women I fuck speaking, let alone addressing me by my given name. "You have no idea what I like and if I were you, I'd be careful what you agree to. Because I like it dirty and if I decide to fuck you, I'll expect compliance."

"Just get me off," she says in a low whisper. I push my legs up against her thighs and feel my dick press up against her ass. She moans but I pull back and slip my hand in there instead. The same place where *her* hand was just a few seconds ago.

I rub her clit through her panties. She moans again. "I like that. Keep doing it," she says in a breathy whisper.

I lean into her neck and nip her earlobe. "I will, because I'm tired and I want to go to bed, but if there's a next time, I won't be taking requests."

My left hand slides up to her full breasts and I palm one. Her nipple bunches up under my fingertip and she lets out a moan. My right hand grabs under her knee and lifts her leg up to bring her ass even with my cock. She goes up on her tiptoes and whines a little as I take control. "Do you want me to stop, Ashleigh?"

She says nothing so I push her panties aside and slide my fingers around her pussy, not touching her clit at all. I get close and her ass presses up against me so I return the gesture, pushing her hips into the wall forcefully, pinning her with my legs. "Put your hands above your head and keep them there," I command in a low throaty voice.

She obeys and at the same time I press against her sweet spot, then dip inside and rub her. Her juices coat my finger and if I wasn't still a little drunk I'd throw her down on the floor and eat the shit out of her from behind. But I am drunk, so I move along so I can get her warm, wet mouth on my cock.

I pump her hard and press one finger into her asshole. "You may come, Ashleigh." As soon as her name comes out of my mouth she moans and I feel the gush of wetness as her pussy and ass clench around my fingers. She must've been primed before I ever walked into the room. She presses back against my chest and instead of moving away like I normally would, I push back, pinning her fully beneath me against the wall and dipping my mouth down to bite her on the shoulder. Her body is less resistant now and this is the part I like. When they just give in. I'm just about to push her down on her knees so she can take me in her mouth when I glance up and see her hand pressed up against the wall.

I forgot she was wearing a fucking ring. I pull away and she almost falls down. "Fuck!"

"What?" she asks, getting her balance back after her orgasm. I just stare at her finger. "What?" she asks again.

"You're married. Fuck!"

I go back into the room, grab a pair of sweats from the dresser, and walk back out into the hallway. I stop in front of her—so fucking hard I almost poke her with my dick—and shake my head. "You're fucking married. I do not, *do not*, fuck around with married woman. I'm sorry. The whiskey…"

"I'm not married," she says softly. And then she looks down at her ring. It's not a huge diamond, but it's respectable. "I was… I'm just engaged."

I belt out a little laugh. "Close e-fucking-nough for me, Ashleigh."

I pull the sweats on right in front of her and walk away.

ELEVEN

"Ford." A hand is touching me.

I shrug it off, roll over and go back to sleep.

"Ford," the fucking hand that should not be touching me but is, says again.

"Stop touching me," I growl. The hand pulls back from my shoulder.

"It's like, afternoon. You've been sleeping all day. I just wanted to make sure you're not dead."

"Clearly I am not dead."

"Yes, OK." She stands up and it's only then that I realize she was sitting down next to me.

I lift my head up and watch her walk to the stairs. Her ass was touching me. And it didn't even wake me up. "Wait." She hesitates but does not stop. She climbs the stairs instead. I listen for a few minutes as she walks all over the place. To the kitchen. Down by the bedrooms. Then back to the kitchen. And finally to the living room where she stops. She must've sat down.

I let out a long breath and pinch the bridge of my nose with

177

my fingertips. I am not hungover. I do not get hungover. I swing my feet off the side of the couch and get dizzy.

Maybe I'm a little hungover.

I lie down and fall back asleep.

feel her this time. She sits next to me again, her ass pressed up against my lower leg. "Ford?"

"Ashleigh, I'm sleeping."

"No," she says. "You're doing something, but sleeping is not it. Maybe you did drink a lot last night. The bottle is only half full, so I guess that's a lot of whiskey. But you went to bed early. Before midnight. And right now it's four in the afternoon. So that's a lot of fucking sleep."

Her swearing makes me look up because so far she's kept her language clean.

She smiles as she shrugs. "It got your attention."

I lay my head back down but I smile into the soft leather cushion. "You've got my attention. The question now is…" I lift my head again and turn so I can see her reaction clearly. "What do you want to do with it?" She looks down and I follow her gaze to her left hand. The ring is gone. "You took off your ring. Is that what you want me to know?"

She nods.

"Speak."

"Yes."

"Why? Why do you want me to know that, Ashleigh?" Her name comes out a lot softer than I mean it to and that evokes a feeling of desire in me. I want her, I realize. Maybe just the blow job I didn't get last night, or maybe even an actual fuck. But either way, I'm not done with her yet.

My softening attitude gives her some courage and she meets my gaze.

"Because I'm sorry about last night. And I don't want you to feel bad about it. I'm not engaged."

"Any longer, you mean. You're not engaged any longer."

"Right."

I twist my body so I'm lying on my back and I can see her clearly. I'm not one for conversation with strangers, but she's interested in something. Me. She's interested in me. I put my hands behind my neck and enjoy her squirming. "And you want me to understand this, the fact that you are not promised to another man… why?"

She hesitates, opens her mouth, closes it again, looks at me, looks away.

I laugh. "Speak, Ashleigh. Or this conversation is over and you can go back upstairs."

"Because you felt good last night."

"You didn't even touch me. I touched you. So what you really mean is that I made you feel good last night, correct?"

"Yes," she says. A quick learner, too. Not nodding her head but using words as I asked. "And I'd like a next time."

I smile. The first real smile in… fuck, I have no idea how long. And then she blushes and I have to pretend to scratch the stubble on my chin to hide my pleasure.

"Even," she adds, "if you won't take requests."

This remark makes me laugh. "Is that so?"

She bites her lip and nods, then catches her mistake and whispers, "Yes."

I kick off the blanket, forcing her to rise, then sit up on the couch properly and look up at her. She's got on some dark gray leggings, another t-shirt from my closet—it says *You can have my ski poles when you pry them from my cold, dead hands*—and some of my white sport socks. I'm sure they're mine, they're huge on her and they're all bunched up near her ankles. "Tell me, Ashleigh, what do you think I meant when I said I don't take requests?"

Her chest rises and falls under my t-shirt, a little bit quicker than it was a few seconds ago. Like my question makes her nervous. "You like to be in control," she finally says.

TAUT

That's a nice answer. Sometimes the girls say I like to give orders, but that's not entirely true. Sometimes they say I want to force them, but that's not even close. I get rid of those girls immediately. But control, that's a good answer. Control is right on the money. "Yes, that's what it means. Tell me what you see. What do you imagine it would be like? Having sex with me?"

"What?" she almost chokes.

"Describe it, Ashleigh." Finally, she is uncomfortable. I don't want to bother with girls who want to call the shots. I'd rather know now if she's acceptable, otherwise I won't waste my time.

She takes a deep breath and then blushes a bright pink.

Yes.

She lets out a long breath of air. "I don't know, Ford. I don't. You're way out of my league. But I think it would be fun. Last night was..." She stops to swallow and look away and then shakes her head like she can't believe she's gonna go there. "Just what I needed."

Oh God. If I wasn't doing my best to keep her off guard I'd laugh right now. "Do you like to be controlled?"

She looks at the couch and then at me. "May I sit?"

My dick gets hard at her polite and formal question. "Where's the baby?"

"Sleeping. Up in your room. I piled up a bunch of pillows around the edge of the bed so she won't roll over and fall off."

I glance up at her. "Do they *roll over*?"

She laughs at me and nods her head. "They can. She doesn't yet. But if I turn my back for a second, you know, she'll decide that will be her first time and off the bed she goes."

I let out a breath at that. Too true. "Fucking Murphy's Law, right?"

"Exactly," she replies, her shyness at bay for a moment as she talks about something she's more comfortable with.

I bring her attention back to me, because fuck that. I didn't get her all red for nothing. "You may sit because you asked nicely." She steps towards the couch and lowers herself, not quite on the opposite side of the couch, but not so she's touching me either. "So tell me, Ashleigh, what are you hoping for?"

She stares at her hands for a moment, then looks me in the eye. I'm almost stunned, that's how surprised I am that she can meet my gaze after that question. "Just your brand of dirty fun."

I want to keep it serious, because that's what I do. I do not allow the girls to have the upper hand, ever. So I'd really like to keep this professional. But I can't help it, I have to snicker. That was not the answer I was expecting.

"You're... laughing at me?" Her confidence falters for a moment.

"I'm not," I tell her. I rather like her directness because it's real. It comes out a little bit desperate maybe, but it's still real. "I'm not. It's just, you threw me for a moment. Your honesty. I like it."

She nods her head and smooths down her—*my*—t-shirt and her fingertips pass over her nipples. I'm not sure if this was a deliberate attempt to seduce me or just a nervous gesture, but either way, it turns me on. "I could tell," she replies.

"You could tell what?" I ask, still staring at her nipples that are pushing against the thin cotton fabric.

"You don't put up with much. And I'm already a big inconvenience for you. I'm trying to be what you want so—"

"Wait." I have to stop her here because I'm not sure what she's alluding to. "What do you think I want?"

"No one. I think you want no one around, and I'm someone. And I have a baby, and no money, and no car. And you're helping me for some reason. You're feeling—" She stops to look up at me here. "Obligated, I guess. And I'm... I just don't want you to get tired of me."

"Tired of you?" I'm not following.

"Come to your senses and stop caring."

I laugh. It hurts her, I can tell that much. I might not be the most emotional guy, but I'm not oblivious. "I never cared, Ashleigh. Not that night I invited you in. Not yesterday when

TAUT

I paid your bill or gave you cash to shop. Not last night when I got you off. And if you want me to do it again, I won't care today either. So what do you want from me? Because I won't be keeping you around, if that's what you're after. I can get any girl I want to suck my dick or let me finger her in a hallway. I don't need you for that. You're just *here*."

She thinks about this for a few seconds and then stands up. "OK." She smiles. "I'll leave you alone then."

"What?"

She walks to the stairs, puts one hand on the banister, and then turns and speaks calmly. "You're nice-looking. You're smart and wealthy, well-bred, maybe. And I feel indebted to you. But you're also very rude. And I'm not a worthless person. Maybe I've got a lot of problems and pretty much everything is going wrong for me right now, but I'm not worthless. So I won't stay and allow you make yourself feel better by making me feel worse. I can dig myself out of whatever I'm into without you. It might not be as easy and it definitely won't come with any promise of sexual fun. But I don't mind. I probably deserve the hard road anyway. So if you want me to shut up and go away, I'm happy to do that for you."

And then she does shut up and go away.

I sit here thinking it over for several minutes before I come to the conclusion that I have just been word-slapped by a girl who never raised her voice or used profanity.

TWELVE

After about half an hour I hear her upstairs in the kitchen. She doesn't make any unnecessary noise, not like she's banging pots and pans on purpose, but somehow her movements sound different. And I know that it's because she's still upset with me. Occasionally she talks to the baby, or the baby fusses and cries. But that's all I hear from above. No TV or music. Which is understandable, because all the entertainment things are hidden behind panels. She'd have no idea where to even look for them.

I'm still sitting on the couch thinking about this when I see her shadow standing at the top of the basement stairs. Our stairs are wide and open, so she casts a shadow all the way down the steps. I wait for her to descend, but she stands still, like she's listening.

"Dinner's ready," she finally says in a normal and even tone. Like she knows I'm waiting for her to say something and she doesn't need to raise her voice in order for me to hear.

Or maybe she's hoping I don't hear her and I just stay down here and let her eat in peace. I don't answer her and she waits there for a few seconds before going back to the kitchen.

I force myself to get up and climb the stairs, because fuck her. This is my fucking house. She catches my eye as I come up but I turn right into the hallway instead of walking directly into the kitchen. I clean up a little in the bathroom, then go into my bedroom and stand there and take it in. Modern, again. A low slat bed makes for an easy fall if the baby actually did roll off. It's not quite futon height, but not much taller either. The bedding is dark blue, as are the walls. There's a desk, a couple dressers, and some nightstands on either side of the bed. I have nothing on my walls. Nothing. I was very into emptiness as a teen. Minimalism. And this room is large, so all this furniture is not even close to being enough to fill it up. The floors are dark hardwood like the living room, but there's a navy blue room-sized rug that covers almost the entire bare space.

Normally my room is spotless. I'm not a freak about neatness, but I like my things orderly.

Right now my room looks like a completely disheveled person lives here. And her name is Ashleigh. All her baby crap is everywhere, her bag of used clothes strewn about the floor, and a few of my things are thrown in there for good measure. I go to my closet and pull down a faded blue t-shirt that says *What happens on the mountain stays on the mountain* and a pair of faded jeans. They are a few years old and all these clothes smell a little dusty, but they are clean enough for me at the moment. Better than a crunchy tux. I don't bother with socks, just make my way to the kitchen.

Ashleigh's sitting on the living room floor, spooning something into the baby's mouth and making noises that might trick her into thinking that crap on the spoon is delicious. I check the dinner—it's chicken and rice again. But what did I expect? That's all I bought.

"Come sit at the table," I say as I load up my plate and grab a beer.

"I'm feeding the baby some cereal," she calls back.

"I'm not sure how that matters. Come sit at the table."

"It matters because she's not big enough to sit in a chair and I don't want her carrier on the table."

Round one to Ashleigh. I guess that makes sense. I take my plate and drink to the coffee table and sit on the couch next to her. Her plate of food is on the coffee table as well, but it's not been touched. "Tired of chicken and rice already?" I take a bit of mine and then point to her plate with my fork.

She ignores me and just continues to offer the baby some of that goop she's calling food.

"Want to watch TV?" I ask.

"There is no TV."

I knew that would get an answer. I get up and open a drawer on the far side of the living room built-ins and remove the remote, then sit back down and mess with a few buttons. The wall panel in front of us slides up and the flat-screen turns on.

"Well, that's ostentatious," she says dryly.

I point the remote at her. "Love that word, and the TV panel is a bit flashy, but still cool." I hand the remote over to her. "I'll put on hockey, so if you like hockey, I'm happy to man the remote. If not, you better choose."

She finally looks over at me, confused. "Since when does a man give up control of the remote?"

I study her for a moment, wondering how old she really is. I pegged her at twenty back at the hotel, but she acts more mature than that. She's small, so that makes her look young, and she's stranded with pretty much nothing in the way of resources, so that makes her appear vulnerable. But she's got a worldliness about her. Like she's seen things. Like she's seen things that change people overnight. She doesn't seem to be worried about her predicament with me. She's not acting afraid of me or upset at being stuck here with a stranger, instead of on her way to wherever it was she was headed. She's pretty much made herself at home. "I hate TV," I finally reply. "I only watch hockey and an occasional stock report. The Market's closed and the Aves aren't playing tonight, so I really don't give a fuck what I watch."

"Oh, do you play or something?"

"I *can* play, if that's what you're asking. But I don't play regularly. No." I take another bite and chew. She accepts the remote, flips through the guide, and then turns on a hockey game.

"I like hockey too, and I have a soft spot for the Stars. They are good enough for me."

Ashleigh is not what I expected. At all. One minute she's shy and blushing, the next she's confident and strong. I'm not sure which is the real her. "I'll watch, but only out of pity. We're kicking their asses this year."

The baby starts coughing on the crap Ashleigh is still absently spooning into her mouth and then it all becomes too much and the cough turns into a full-fledged wail. Ashleigh takes her out of her carrier and hugs her to her chest, patting her firmly on the back and telling her sweet things in her ear. Then she lifts up her shirt and slips the baby right up to her breast.

I don't know what it is, but this baby-feeding shit almost... turns me on. She's not flaunting her tits at me, she's just barely lifting her shirt so the baby can get access, but fuck. It's provocative for some reason.

"Sorry for dirtying up all your t-shirts. Mine are too small to do this," she says as she leans her head back against the couch and closes her eyes. Like breastfeeding exhausts her.

"Take what you need, I don't mind."

"That's weird, you know." Her eyes are still closed.

"What's weird?"

"That you're so easy-going about certain things and yet so uptight about others."

I grunt out a laugh. "I'm gonna need examples."

"You pay for things like money means nothing. You take care of the car and let me sit in that hotel office, and then come to pick me up and bring me here. You let me practically take over your house, you hand over the remote. I think you're easy-going about these things because they're outside of you. But then you seem to be obsessively controlling about anything that has to do with the inside of you. And then there's that whole no-touching thing. You almost freaked out about it back when I was putting the baby in the van at the hotel."

I actually huff at her assessment. Who the hell is *she*? "You don't know me well enough to even form those opinions."

"So you're saying I'm wrong?" She doesn't open her eyes. In fact, she looks like she's about to go to sleep. That's how slow and even her breathing is.

"I'm not saying anything. You just don't know me."

She stays silent, just tilts her head to the side so she's not facing me. Her neck stretches, exposing her throat.

I have a thing for throats. Maybe some guys like tits and pussy. I like tits and pussy. But throats. Fuck. That shit turns me on. I imagine my hand sliding up to her throat, palming it gently. I do not squeeze them. But I like to apply a little pressure to make the girl come.

I've never had a pet complain about the throat thing. Not that they're allowed to complain per the rules. But if it freaks them out, they'd probably say so on their way out when they're busy calling me an emotionless freak. And they never do. They all like it. It's like an orgasm button when used properly and I've perfected the technique.

Ashleigh becomes still and begins to breathe deeply. "Does it make you tired, Ashleigh?" I'm not sure why I ask, it's just weird how she changes when the baby is nursing.

"Yes, you make me tired," she says softly.

"No," I laugh. "Breastfeeding."

"Oh." She turns her head back to me, opens her eyes, blinking a few times to shake off her drowsiness. "Yes, it's like a drug. It relaxes me."

"So it feels good?" My dirty mind is wandering.

Ashleigh smirks a little. But she doesn't answer. I change the subject and point to her plate with my fork since she's shut me down. "You're not eating anything."

She pulls herself fully awake and then stands up, removing the baby from her breast and adjusting her shirt. "Be right back." She wanders down the hallway talking quietly to the baby, then disappears into my room.

THIRTEEN

finish eating and then grab another beer from the fridge and sit back down on the couch. Her plate sits on the coffee table untouched and regardless of what she said, she does not come back. I try to concentrate on the hockey game but my mind is racing with curiosity and after about thirty minutes I get up and walk down the hall to the bedroom. I stop and listen at the closed door.

"Ashleigh?"

I knock. Nothing. I open the door and she's sprawled out on the bed topless, the baby tucked up against her belly, their mouths open, their breath soft and even.

God, that is just sexy. She's all sideways on the bed, not using a pillow, and her hair is spilling out on one side of her body like it was positioned that way for a photoshoot.

I watch her for a few seconds and then give myself the creeps and back away, closing the door behind me. It's only about eight o'clock, and I just woke up a few hours ago, so I'm not even remotely tired. I wander back to the basement and glance over at

189

the bottle of Scotch on my dad's desk, and then, before I can stop myself, I'm sitting down in front of it.

I put the bottle away. I'm not in the mood to drink alone. But I do take a better look around the office. All the shelves are filled with books. Mostly medical books because my dad was a psychiatrist. He specialized in autistic spectrum disorders because I was diagnosed with Asperger's syndrome when I was a kid.

My dad was a great man and the awards and certificates on his office wall in here are just the beginning of how special he was. He was my biggest champion. He made me stronger. He kept up with me in every respect. He pushed me to be better, learn more, try harder. And he never did it in a mean way like some fathers. His reprimands were always calm, his urges to do better always came with just the right level of excitement and assurance.

One of the characteristics of Asperger's is uncoordinated motor skills, so my dad compensated by enrolling me in every sport available. I did baseball, basketball, track, football, skiing, boarding, hockey... not all at the same time of course, he was just looking for my sweet spot. The sport I might excel in.

And like the language skills that I shouldn't have, I had physical skills as well. I excelled in skiing, baseball, and track. But it was the skiing that captivated me. If you're a skier and you live in Vail, that's like heaven. I was the reason we came here every weekend in the winter. And everything I did, my dad did with me. He pitched to me, he threw the football, he put on all the smelly hockey gear and got up at five AM to get rink time. He ran with me. Every day. In Denver we ran in City Park and then later we did the steps at Coors Field. But when I spent my summers here in Vail, we did the bike trail just down the hill from our house. It runs from Vail to Frisco. Twelve miles down, twelve miles back up. We did that whole run at least once a month in the summers.

He skied insane runs with me. We did more than our share

of double black diamond runs all over the world.

He never said no. He always had time. No matter how crazy my plan.

I grab the bottle from the bottom drawer and I'm shuffling through the back of it, searching for the rocks glass I know is in here, when I hear the knock.

I look up and Ashleigh is standing in the doorway. "Sorry, I guess I drifted off."

I look at the bottle, then her. She's all disheveled, just like the bedroom. Her hair is tousled and a little bit sweaty from being asleep and her cheeks are pink against her pale skin. I picture her topless like she was up in my bed and it renders me silent for a moment.

"I'll drink it with you, if you want," she says to break the awkward moment. "One drink won't hurt. Besides, I already fed her, so she's good for a while."

I nod and grab two glasses from the drawer. When I look back up she's got the bottle. "Not in here, though. Let's sit out there."

I just stare at her, trying to figure out what that means.

"I think this room…" She looks around at the pictures of my dad and me. "Depresses you." I can't even move, that's how much these words affect me. "Maybe depress is the wrong word." She offers me a small smile. "Maybe it just… makes you think too much."

"Yeah," I grumble out, then clear my throat and try again. "Yeah, it does. My dad died a couple years ago." I look up at the closest picture and the memories flood in. "We did everything together."

"I can tell. Lots of good times on these walls. Let's drink out there."

She doesn't wait for me, just turns and walks over to the couch, sits down and sets the bottle on the coffee table. I walk over and sit down next to her, but not close enough to touch. I pour us each a drink and she clinks her glass to mine. "To dads."

"To dads," I repeat. "Drink it slow," I say softly. "It's very special. It should be enjoyed, not consumed in a rush the way I did it last night." She nods and takes a small sip, makes a face, and takes another one. She holds in a cough and that makes me happy for some reason. It satisfies me in a way I can't explain.

"I'm not a whiskey girl," she says after taking one more sip and setting the glass down. "But it does seem special." I smile big at that. She catches it and scowls. "You're a weird guy, Ford."

I take a bigger sip this time. "Tell me something new, Ashleigh."

"New, as in you want to know something about me? Or new as in you already know you're weird?"

"Both," I say, leaning back and slumping down a little, my drink perched on my thigh, my bare feet kicked up on the coffee table. I pick at the strings from a hole in my jeans and she leans back too, but then the largeness of the couch clashes with the smallness of her body and she has to tuck her feet underneath her to get comfortable. I take another drink of my Scotch as she begins to talk.

"Hmmm. Something new about me... I'm in Colorado with a very attractive jerk. I've thought about him almost constantly since he appeared at my car window, and I'm not sure why he's doing all this, so I've spent the entire day imagining him as a serial killer trying to lower my keen defenses so I'll fall for his unorthodox charm and then beg him to kill me during kinky sex."

I spit out my fucking whiskey, that's how funny that is. "Oh, shit." I just shake my head. "You're the strange one, Ashleigh, not me."

"Sorry," she says as she takes another sip, grimacing as she forces it down. "Sometimes I say things I should bury deep inside."

"So, you think I'm a hot serial killer? And you're still here because... it's OK to be a serial killer as long as I'm eye-candy?"

She smiles, but looks down like she's embarrassed.

"Or you know I'm not a serial killer and you trust me?"

"That," she says, swallowing more alcohol. "I know you're not a serial killer because you called your mom last night to let her know you were OK. You're drinking because you miss your dad. You have friends who are worried about you because you ran away from some bizarre love triangle. And you're not a guy who likes to talk about his feelings, so you were very mean to them when they wanted answers." She lets out a long breath. "Serial killers are loners. And Dexter doesn't count, he's fake. So you're not a serial killer, just a very attractive jerk who wants to be left alone so you can deal with your relationship issues in private."

"Hmmm. Well, I guess you nailed it. Now it's my turn." She gives me a sideways glance that says bring it, so I don't hold back. "You're running from something, too. Maybe someone, but not the guy who gave you that ring. You love him, even if it is over, because you have it stamped on a dog tag. And maybe some people think a dog tag is just a cool piece of industrialized jewelry, but a woman who calls herself a Marine wife doesn't. She takes that shit to heart. So you're still in love with him, you might even want to see him again." She looks up at this and I smile. "That right there just confirmed it. But you can use some attention right now, so you're into the one-night stand while I'm around."

She stares at her feet.

"How'd I do?"

"Close."

"Which part did I get wrong?"

"You got enough right that I don't want to talk about it anymore." And then she gets up and smiles a very polite and very fake smile. "Thanks for the drink. I'm super tired, so I'll see you tomorrow." Then she walks away.

"Ashleigh." I laugh out her name a little. "Come back here." She shakes her head and treks up the stairs. "Ashleigh!"

But she's serious. She never looks back or slows her retreat.

I hit her button and she is done.

Nice going, Ford. You're a real fucking people person.

FOURTEEN

When I was a kid I knew I was a genius. No one had to tell me, and maybe that sounds… what? Egotistical? Conceited? Boastful? Arrogant? Prideful? And if I extrapolate out a little bit, it probably borders on selfish and indifferent as well. But it is what it is. I'm fucking smart. I'm way beyond fucking smart. I'm an intellectual anomaly.

And this did make me a little bit of a brat as a child. For one, I figured since I was so smart, I was a superhero and my superpower was mind-reading. Because that's kinda what I thought my dad did. Before he knew the full extent of my intellect, he talked to me like any other kid. So when I asked him what he did for a living, he said he figured out what people are thinking. And to me that translated into mind-reading.

From that second on, because I was just as smart as my dad and I wanted to be like him, I decided my superpower was mind-reading.

My mind-reading *faux pas* with Ashleigh and her internal motivations for being where she is right now is something I do often. Most of the time I get the same result from my efforts, so I tend to ignore my superpower. But she started it. She dug into my mind, and she was cheating as far as I'm concerned. She heard my phone calls. Anyone could figure that stuff out from those telling phone calls. So she got what she asked for.

But let's face it. I'm not your average guy. I've been to dozens of doctors over the years. More when I was small than when I got older, since I didn't yet realize that admitting to what I could do and the issues I faced would lead to more doctors. But none of the doctors who examined me were very interested in *helping* me. No, they were only interested in *understanding* me. And they always asked the same question first. How did I learn Russian?

I have always said I didn't know, it just came out. And that's true, because I didn't understand my photographic memory until I was a teen and I wanted to pass tests without studying. That's when I realized that everything I've ever read and heard was imprinted on my brain. Almost catalogued in there like a library with a reference number that could bring it back to me if I ever needed it.

It's like my brain is a museum and my consciousness is the curator of everything I've ever experienced. So if I were asked the Russian question again today, and I felt like telling the truth, I'd say, *I heard Mikhail Gorbachev giving a speech on TV. I watched it for about ten minutes and that was it. I decided I'd like to speak Russian.*

How? That would be their next question. They never got this far with me because I never admitted to learning Russian from the TV. If I had, I could tell them *why* it happened—that was the speech. But I wouldn't be able to tell them *how* it happened. I don't understand what I am, I just deal with it. And I do that by turning it off ninety-nine percent of the time. So most of my life is spent trying to be something I'm not.

The real me is filled with curiosity. I want to know everything. I want to understand everything. It pisses me off that there are things in this physical world that are unknowable. Just plain pisses me off..

So I have to turn me off. I have to be something else. I am forced to exist in a state of half-truths.

I try to not over-analyze things. I try to accept the things people say and not question them. I try not to assign motivations to actions and then make predictions.

But I'm not very good at being normal. For one, I typically just say what's on my mind. Like all that stuff I said to Rook.

I wish I could go back. I'd like to take it back. I planned for that night for months. Ever since we got Ronin out of jail, I was planning my getaway. Because I knew the moment she said she wanted to save him that it was over for me. She belongs to him.

And I miss her. I miss our friendship. I miss our runs. I miss it all so, *so* much.

Those morning runs with Rook made life bearable for me. And I let myself be deluded up in Fort Collins. I wanted to believe so badly that Rook and I could just be friends, that I'd be OK with it.

But I'm not OK with it. I'm... crushed. Devastated. Hurt. Sad. Maybe even depressed. And I realize looking back that my window of opportunity with Rook was very narrow. Those first few days of the Shrike Bikes pilot, back when Ronin was busy with Clare and Rook was still deciding on what she wanted. That was the only chance I ever had and I blew it. I was a dick to her. She had no reason to trust me, let alone like me.

Why am I always surprised when the same fucking actions give me the same fucking results?

I want to change. I want to allow people to get close. But it's difficult to just accept things. I'm not Zen. I have trouble simply existing and yet that's the only way I know to survive. To assign motivations and insight to every possible movement, conversation, and change is to invite madness. But to ignore all those parts of me is to invite delusion. I am in a constant state of dynamic dichotomy. So I cope with the stress of who and what I am with physical activity.

TAUT

The way I used to deal with things was through skiing, but I don't ski anymore. Now it's just running. I like solitary sports even though I'm pretty good at the team sports too. I only ever played baseball after I figured all this shit out. Because baseball is about as solitary a team sport as you can get.

But running. Running is the ultimate solitary sport. And for most people it's them against their mind when they run marathons and stuff. Can they talk themselves out of the pain? Can they fool their tired muscles? Can they turn around their negative thoughts that tell them they will fail? Will they suffer to achieve the reward of completion? That's the runner's battle.

But for me, I *am* my mind. So I don't compete with anyone. There's no voice in my head saying I can't do it. It's the opposite in fact. If there is a voice in my head, then it's my dad, and he only ever gave me encouragement. He only ever told me, *You can.*

So I just run, because I can.

I'm not sure how far I could run if I never stopped. That run down to Frisco and back is pretty intense. Twenty-four miles and half of it is uphill. But the thought that I'd have to stop before I got home—that has never entered my mind. Because my mind has no room for silly things such as failure when I run.

My mind is free when I run. Free to think about things I normally partition off to the deep recesses of my subconscious.

So that's what I do now. I run. I pull out an old running outfit from my dad's closet so I don't wake Ash and the baby, and I run the fuck out of Vail. The bike trail is out, it's covered in like six feet of snow. But the streets are clear and it's the middle of the night so they are empty.

So I run.

And I love every fucking second of it. Because the only sound I hear is myself. Breathing into the frigid night air, a stream of steam coming from my mouth in a controlled regular rhythm. I let my mind wander out of the cage I keep it in, I forget about Rook, and I think about shapes, and equations, and the sound of my feet as they pound the wet pavement.

The freak goes away and the real me emerges.

That's what running gives me. And when Rook ran with me, she filled a gaping hole in my life. She was my partner. She was mine. I love my team. I can't picture my life without Ronin and Spencer. We had a falling out a while back and we spent years apart. And even though life went on and I was fine, the minute we were all back together for the Shrike Bikes pilot, our bonds realigned. Like it was meant to be. Like we were charged molecules, pulled together by a force of nature.

But I'd like to be more than one third of a team—one fourth if I include Rook. I'd like to be *half* of something. I'd like that emptiness to go away. And that's what it felt like to have Rook. She filled me up.

But now that hole is back and it's deeper than ever. I am just one man, alone.

I get back to the house around five AM and sneak quietly into the shower. I pull on the sweats I've been sleeping in so I don't disturb anyone, and then I go downstairs and crash on the couch, my muscles aching with fatigue, my mind at bay for another day.

The crying baby is what wakes me. And even though she's upstairs, she is *loud*. I take the steps two at a time and find the screaming infant in her carrier in the middle of the living room. "Ashleigh?" I walk down to my bedroom and peek in, but it's empty. Bathroom is empty. Parents' bedroom also empty. "Ashleigh?"

The baby is wailing so hard she's shaking and it's starting to freak me out. I walk through the kitchen and open the door to the garage. Ashleigh is sorting through the van looking for something. "What're you doing?"

Her head pops up in surprise. "What?"

"Can't you hear that fucking screaming?"

"Sorry, did she wake you?" Ashleigh doesn't look sorry. She

barely notices me in fact. Just keeps searching for something on the floor of the backseat.

"Yes, she did wake me, but I'm more concerned about why she's fucking screaming her head off and you're out here doing… what the fuck are you doing?"

"I can't find that yellow ducky." She pops up again, her face all blotchy and her eyes red. "Have you seen it?"

"Yeah, I gave it back to you at the motel, remember?"

"I know, but it's gone!" She dives back down into the van.

I walk over and take her by the arm. "Ashleigh. Stop." She pulls away and starts to climb over the seat to the third row. I grab her by the waist and haul her out, then push her against the van and hold her there by the shoulders. "What. The fuck. Are you doing?" The tears start to roll and then she just looks down and hides her face from me. "Answer me, dammit."

She wipes her face and drags her sleeve across her nose. "I just need that ducky, that's all. I need it."

OK—I take a deep breath because I know mania when I see it. "You put it in the diaper bag, Ash," I say softly. "I saw you. Did you take it out?"

She shakes her head.

"OK, then let's go look inside. It's cold out here and the baby is crying. Can't you hear her?"

Ash tilts her head like she's listening and then she looks up at me with her watery eyes. "I can hear her."

"Good, you go take care of her and I'll check the diaper bag. Where is it?"

I pull her inside with me and catch her answer between screams. "The bedroom."

She picks up the baby and I watch her for a second, just to make sure. But she seems fine as she slides the baby up to her breast and sits on the couch to feed her. The screaming lessens as the baby latches on and then everything goes silent except for Ashleigh's sniffles.

Fuck. Women and their drama. Over a stupid toy.

I go into the bedroom and it's a total catastrophe. Clothes are everywhere, diapers are spilling out of the package, a few toys are scattered around. And that diaper bag is upside down in the middle of the floor. I kneel down and shuffle through it, but there's no yellow duck. I don't know how the fuck she can find anything in here, and now that I think of it, I'm wondering if she's not having some trouble holding things together. She's a single mom for whatever reason. I'm not sure what's going on there, but it's got to be tough to handle an infant alone. Plus she's stuck here in a strange place with a guy who's been fucking with her head. And all those post-baby making hormones are probably still in her system.

It's a miracle she's not batshit crazy already.

I stuff all the clothes on the floor into the hamper in the closet, then pick up all the diapers and stack them on the dresser. I sort through her diaper bag and nope, that duck is not in there. So I fill that up with baby toys and straighten out the bed a little. That's a huge improvement. I pick up her winter coat and the yellow duck is lying underneath. I hang the coat up on the hook near the bedroom door. I walk back to the living room holding out the duck as I come towards her.

She bursts into tears and takes it from me.

Oh, fuck. Manic tears I can handle, but I don't do *I'm crazy-depressed-sad-happy-worried* tears. I really don't. But I'm pretty good at making girls shut up when they're crying. So I try that route. "Ashleigh," I say firmly. She looks up, muttering out some *thank yous*. "You're not allowed to cry around me, I hate it. It bugs the shit out of me. If you don't stop, I'll bend you over my knee and smack your ass so I can give you a good reason to cry. At least then I'll get some pleasure out of it."

She stares up at me, speechless. Then she blinks. "What?"

I laugh. "That got your attention."

Her chest hitches a few times as she takes a deep breath. "Sorry," she mumbles.

I take a seat on the couch and watch her watch me as she

feeds the baby. "Where were you headed, Ashleigh? When you broke down?" She makes a face and shakes her head. "What? Why are you shaking your head at me?"

She ignores me.

"Ashleigh, where are you going? And for that matter, where the hell did you come from?" I wish I had looked at her car closer, to see the plates. But either I was too distracted by my own circumstances or the snow was covering it up, so I never noticed.

She cuddles the baby and whispers in her ear for a few seconds and then she looks up at me with that smile she smiles when she's being overly polite. "Look, I understand you might be freaked out about my little... emotional display... but I'm fine. OK? I'm fine. I'm just..." She stops and takes a deep breath. "Exhausted. I'm tired. I'm running on no sleep, I'm stressed, I'm hungry, I'm desperately in need of a shower, I smell like spit-up, and that stupid toy means a lot to me. OK?" She stares at me, calm but frowning.

I wait for her to look away before I speak and bring her attention back to me. "Got it. Now, answer my questions."

"Or what?" she challenges.

"Or nothing. You can choose not to answer, it's your decision. But if you refuse, I'm going to call Jason, get your plate number, hack into every fucking DMV in the US, and figure out who the fuck you are."

She snorts out a laugh. "Good luck with that."

"I'll let that pass, since you don't know who I am. And I would have to go back to Denver and grab my own laptop to make sure the connection is secure. I'll take you with me, by the way. So if you think I'm gonna leave you here alone, you're wrong. And then I'll fucking get that data right in front of you. Or I can just call up Mrs. fucking Pearson and have her tell you some more stories about how I fucked with the virtual lives of anyone who crossed me as a teenager." I wait a few beats as she tries to decide if I'm telling the truth. "But either way, it's a two-hour drive to Denver, tops. I'll know who you are in three hours or less, because I already have code written for the DMV search. I can do that shit with my eyes closed."

Now she gets angry and plucks the baby from her breast, making her squeal, as clearly five minutes of feeding is not enough. She starts to get up and I grab her by the waist and force her to stay. "Let go," she snarls over the baby's wails.

"No." I say calmly. "Feed her, Ashleigh. And tell me which way you'd like to do this. Answer my question, or I call Jason and figure out who you are myself."

"Fine," she says as she positions the baby over her breast again. "I'm coming from Texas and going to LA."

She said she was a Stars fan, so that makes sense. But then again… "That makes no sense. Why not just go across New Mexico and into Arizona? Why come north?"

She bites her lip and scrunches up her face as she thinks. Is this a lying pause? Ronin would know, but I'm not as good at this lie-detector shit as he is, so I'm not sure. "I just needed more time. That's all." She looks me in the eye and repeats it. "I just wasn't ready to face things yet, I just wanted a little more time, so I took the scenic route."

I sit back and laugh. "The scenic route? Through the fucking Rocky Mountains in the dead of winter? Are you crazy?"

"I didn't know it was so…"

"Cold? Dangerous? Wild? It's the fucking mountains!"

"I get it now, obviously. But I'm more of a beach person, so I didn't understand it might be dangerous."

"What part of LA are you going to?" She might actually be from Texas, but I think her destination is a lie. She heard me tell my mother I was driving to LA on the phone. I think she's just telling me what I want to hear.

"Westwood. I'm going to Westwood. Satisfied?" she asks with a sneer.

"Hardly. Why are you going there? What's in LA?"

She takes a deep breath like she's about to say something

important, and then she looks me in the eye. "Tell me why you're going to LA and then I'll tell you why I'm going."

I smile. "You think that's cute?"

"I think you're running away. At least I'm running *to* something."

Ouch. "Tell me why right now, or I get the car warmed up for a nice drive to Denver."

She shakes her head and tries to stop the tears, but they roll down her face anyway. A few seconds later I realize she's holding her breath to stop the sobs, but it starts coming out in ugly gasps.

I sigh and lean back into the uncomfortable modern piece-of-shit couch. "OK, stop. Please." She doesn't stop and the baby starts fussing. "Ashleigh—"

"I need to talk to him one more time, OK?" She looks up at me and she is a fucking mess—her eyes are wild and bloodshot, her face is all contorted as she tries to hold it together but simply fails, her skin is pale like she hasn't slept in weeks, and that coupled with the crying baby makes her look like some poor teen mom from a bad MTV reality show. "Is that a good enough answer for you? I just need to talk to him one more time." And then she gets up and bolts towards the bedroom before I can grab her.

FIFTEEN

I sit in the living room listening to Ashleigh as she concentrates on the baby in the bedroom. She calms her down pretty fast, but her own loud erratic breathing is hard to miss. I lean over and hold my head in my hands as I think this through.

She's probably insane. Total nutjob. She might be stalking her ex, who knows.

I sit like this for a while, just thinking, and then I hear her playing games in there. "Peek-a-boo."

The baby squeals, but not in a bad way. She's laughing.

Ashleigh says it again. More squealing laughter—and then Ash is laughing too. Hell, even I smile.

OK, maybe she's not nuts. She's just sad. She has a new baby. The father—for whatever reason—is gone. That's gotta hurt. She's got herself into some whackjob of a road trip and maybe she really is going to LA. Maybe she can save whatever it is she's missing right now. If I were her, wouldn't I try?

I definitely would. Yeah. I'd give it a shot.

I scrub my hands down my face, get up, and get to the open

bedroom door just in time to see the baby laugh. That's a cure for just about anything. Ashleigh looks a thousand times better already, just because she's smiling. They're lying down on the bed. She leans over the baby, her long hair falling over to cover her face. And then they giggle like girls. I reach into my pocket and take a phone picture of them because it's sorta cute.

The shutter sound gives me away and Ash sits up real fast. "Look," she says with a hitch in her breath from crying. "I'm sorry, I'm just hormonal, OK? I can't help it. I miss him." She has to stop and pull it together here, but she manages and that makes me feel better. She's just sad.

"I understand, Ashleigh, I do. But if you really are going to LA and not lying to me, then I'm gonna have to take you with me. I'll have your car delivered to wherever you want when it's done. But I can't leave you here alone. I don't think it's a good idea."

I half expect a little fight over my perceived opinion of her state of mind, but she just nods. "That is where I'm going, Ford. So thank you. And for what it's worth, I realize it's over. That life is over. I get it." She stops to wait for a response, so I give her a nod. "It's over," she says again, trying to talk herself into it. "It's over. And I just have to accept it." For a second I think she's about to cry again but she swallows hard and wipes the tears. "And once I talk to him, I swear, I'll let it go." It takes her a few seconds to meet my gaze, but she does it. "I'll let him go, I just have so much to say." Her chin starts quivering and shit, it sorta tugs at my heart, all this sadness from her.

"Do you want to tell me about it?"

She shakes her head. "No, I can't. I just can't. I would, but it's—"

"OK. That's OK. But are you two still together? Because to me, it doesn't look like it's over."

She sniffs and looks over at the baby. "It's over."

"You just have to have your say, that's all?"

She nods. "Yes, I just have so much to say to him. I just need to say it to *him*, ya know?"

"OK." I can deal with this. She just needs closure. It's totally normal to take some time to figure things out after a big change. I'm no relationship expert, I've never actually had a relationship, but it doesn't take a genius to understand the psychology of a one-sided breakup. "Let's go get some breakfast. You hungry?" She nods. "I'll take a shower downstairs so you can use the bathroom up here. If you need me to watch the baby so you can relax a little, I will."

"No," she says softly. "I got it. I'm OK, I swear. I just needed to vent. I feel better." And then she looks up at me and smiles. "But thank you for offering."

I pull into Jason's parking lot half expecting the place to be closed, but one bay is open and his brother Jimmy is pulling in a car as I park. "Stay here," I tell Ashleigh. "I'll grab your stuff."

She nods out a yes and says nothing. I'm not convinced she's OK, but she's not the least bit argumentative, so I'm enjoying that part of her right now. I leave the van running to keep them warm and then go inside the shop. No one's at the front desk, so I walk around it and open the door to the garage. Music is blaring and Jason is talking to Jimmy in the far bay where the new car is.

"Hey," I call out. "I need some stuff out of this car."

Jason looks and waves to Ash's car. "It's open."

I check the license plate as I walk up to the car—it's Texas, so that makes me feel better—then pop the hatchback and go around to grab her shit. When Ashleigh said she had a bag of clothes I didn't expect it to be a plastic grocery bag with one outfit in it for her and yet another footied sleeper for the baby. That's all the kid's been wearing since I met her. There's some stray diapers so I stuff those in the bag, and a stroller. That's what she really wanted.

"You marrying this girl now or what, Ford? Playing daddy?"

TAUT

I turn to Jason and he's laughing, like this is some fun joke. "I'm helping her out, you moron. How's my Bronco coming?"

"She'll be done tomorrow, probably around noon. I'm almost done but I'm gonna knock off early today. My nephew's skiing slalom at Loveland in a couple hours. You wanna come?"

"Fuck you." I grab the bag and the stroller and walk away.

"Just kidding, Ford," he calls back.

"Just have my truck ready by noon." I exit through the mechanic's door and throw the shit in the back of the van. "You said you had clothes. All I found was a grocery bag with some baby t-shirts, a sleeper, and a pair of jeans."

"Yeah, clothes," she says.

"Well, we can pick stuff up in the Village after we eat."

"My stuff's not good enough for you?"

I pull away from Jason's still irritated about his remark, so I say nothing more about it—just head over to the Village, park the van, and get the stroller out for Ashleigh. It's like a modern marvel of engineering, that thing, but she presses levers and flips it open, and then lies the baby down inside.

"She looks cold. Doesn't she have a coat?"

"She's three months old, Ford. Her wardrobe's a little short on Alpine gear."

"We'll get her a snow suit on the way to the restaurant. There's a baby store."

"It's your money," she mutters as we walk down the sidewalk to the village. "Wow," she says as we enter the shopping district. "This is pretty swanky. I don't ski, hate it in fact. So I've never been here before."

"Swanky, yes." I laugh a little at that. Vail Village is surrounded by five-star hotels built to look like the Bavarian Alps. Why? I have no idea. It's the fucking Rockies, they should just own it. If I was planning this place I'd make it look like *Deadwood*. "Here's a baby store right here."

"They play on your guilt, that's why the baby store is near the entrance. She's got like six blankets, Ford. She's not cold."

I ignore her and open the door. Ashleigh scoops the baby up and leaves the stroller outside, since the boutiques here are pretty cramped and small.

"Can I help you?" the saleswoman says.

"Yes, I need snow gear for an infant."

"Oh sure, we have—hey, Ford? Ford Aston?" The woman smiles at me, her eyes picking up interest now that she's recognized a familiar face. "It's me, Stacylynn." She gives me a little wink. "Remember me? Senior year at CU? The Hairy Buffalo New Year's Party?"

"I never went to that party, but yes, I do remember you, Stacylynn. How have you been?"

"I know, we never made it inside—believe me, I've never forgotten that night." She sways her hips a little as she stares up at me.

"Eh-hemmm," Ashleigh says. "Do you mind? We're shopping for baby snowsuits."

Stacylynn barely acknowledges Ash and if we were together that might piss me off. In fact, it does piss me off. "That part was rather forgettable for me, sorry, Stacy."

She scowls at me. "All the infant wear is over against the back wall. Let me know if you need help."

Ash and I walk to the back and she picks up the first one she sees. "This one's good. Let's go."

"What about a hat? And mittens?"

She waves her hand at me and takes the suit up to the counter. I grab a hat and mittens and join her, pay Stacylynn, and then we head back out. Ashleigh slips he baby into the snow suit, which is more like a down-filled cocoon, and pushes the stroller. "So did you live here your whole life? In Vail, I mean? It's pretty nice."

"No, I lived in Denver most of the time. I went to school in Denver. But we came here on the weekends, for winter break, and summers. I guess it adds up to about half the year. So it's home for me."

"Did you really not remember your tryst with that girl back

there?"

I have a photographic memory, I forget nothing. And Stacylynn was what I'd call adventurous. But I know what Ashleigh wants to hear, so I say that instead. "She's one of many, nothing more. Completely forgettable."

"Are you gonna forget me?" She keeps walking even though this is a pretty big question. "When we stop hanging out. Will I be just another forgettable girl?"

We walk past a large group of drunk skiers, so I wait until they are behind us before I answer. "I guess that depends."

"On what?"

"On whether or not you let me forget you."

"So it's up to me to hold your attention? What if I forget you? Will you care?"

Normally I'd never participate in a conversation like this, so the fact that I'm even considering it tells me that no, I won't forget her. She's different. She's nice, for one. She's calm—mostly. And even though she had me pretty wound up this morning with the crying stuff, she's not being difficult on purpose. But I'm not gonna give in so easily. "I'll think about you every time I break out a blizzard blanket, that's for sure."

"Oh."

"Or see a pretty woman breastfeeding," I add before I can stop myself.

She laughs at that. "Perv." I know my limits, so I say nothing. "You want to watch me, don't you?"

I look over at her and I swear, my dick does a little jump at her words. "No." I think about it for a second. "Maybe a little." She snickers this time. "OK, I'd like to explore my options."

She has to bite her lip to hold down the smile, but it leaks out anyway.

We reach the diner and I hold the door open and wait for her to push the stroller in. It's not crowded since breakfast is over and lunch hasn't started yet. The hostess bends down to coo at the baby, and then Ashleigh asks if they have a booth that might be more private so she can breastfeed. She shoots me a look and I raise my eyebrows and smile. They don't, not really, it's a diner. But the waitress takes us to the back where there are only a few other tables.

The baby's asleep, so she's not going to be nursing. But the innuendo lingers in my mind. She's playing with me now. Maybe because of Stacylynn, maybe because I saw her in a vulnerable spot earlier. Maybe because she knows we're gonna spend the next few days together on the road. I'm not quite sure what she's thinking, but she's laughing at me right fucking now. "What?" I ask.

She shakes her head and looks at her menu. "What's good here?"

Your tits, I think. *Take them out for me.* They are hard and swollen under her—*my*—t-shirt. "Maybe I should just give you all the shirts in my closet, since you seem to like them so much."

"I think it's interesting that you just now noticed I was wearing it."

"You two ready to order?"

I glance up at the waitress and thank God that it's not someone I know. "Number seven, scrambled, toast, and turkey bacon."

"Number eleven, strawberries on top, hash browns and real bacon."

"And coffee," we both say at the same time. "Decaf," Ashleigh adds quickly.

She smiles at us and leaves.

My phone buzzes in my pants and I take it out and check the screen. "Fuck."

"Who is it?"

"Rook."

"Who's Rook?"

I hold up a finger at Ashleigh. "Yes, Miss Corvus."

"Ford," she starts calmly. "I'm sorry for yelling at you. OK? Don't say mean things to make me hang up. I can't take it."

"Where's Ronin?"

"Downstairs. I'm at home."

"So you're calling when he's not around. Why?"

"Ford—"

"Rook, I'm done. I've walked away. When I walk away I mean it. I'm not coming back. It's over."

"Ford, you don't end friendships that way. That's not how you end a friendship. I know we're still friends. I know we are. You're just… I dunno. You're just… *Help me.* Say something, Ford. Help me understand this. You know I love you, you know I do. I just…"

"You just don't love me like you love Ronin."

She says nothing to this but Ashleigh's eyebrows go up. She puts her napkin on the table and starts to rise, but I grab her wrist and shake my head. "Stay here."

"It sounds private, Ford."

"Who's that?" Rook asks.

"My new friend, Ashleigh. We're driving to LA together. I have to go, Rook. Tell Ronin I said hi." I press end on the phone and set it down. I'm still holding Ashleigh by the wrist. "It wasn't private. It's over."

Ashleigh sits back against the seat. "I don't want to be used like that. Whatever you have going on with this girl, don't make me the reason you hurt her."

"I'm not. She's my best friend's girlfriend. She made her choice, and now I'm over it."

"And this is why you left Denver and were driving in the mountains on New Year's Eve?"

"Yes, I had to leave or I'd betray my friend. She and I would both regret it after."

"So it was the friendship with her boyfriend that had you upset, and not really your relationship with her?"

"Mostly. He and I go way back. We have business together, but beyond that, I'm not interested in betraying him. I'm not a cheater." At least when it comes to relationships. But I keep that shit tucked away.

Ashleigh thinks about this for a moment, pretending to fuss with the baby's blankets in the stroller. "So why are you mad at her? If you know it's best for both of you?"

"I'm not mad, I just don't want to be a part of her life anymore. I—" I look away and think it through for a second before speaking. "I still want her, I just can't have her. And she doesn't want me, not enough, anyway. So what's the point of continuing to torture myself? It's better this way."

"So you're punishing her. Because she loves you in a way that doesn't satisfy you?" Ashleigh shakes her head. "That's fucked up."

I scowl at her swearing.

"Sorry," she apologizes. "It just is."

"She made her choice. She could've chosen me, she didn't. That's the end of it."

"So you have a line and if someone crosses it, you just cut them off? Walk away?"

"Doesn't everyone have a line like that?"

She studies me for a moment. Forming an opinion, maybe. "Well, there's lines, and then there's *lines*. Some have a line as thick as the Great Divide. Others the width of a hair. Your line might be microscopic. Do you at least explain your expectations? So people who get close to you understand? Or do you just take what you want and then move on like this all the time?"

I stare at her, angry at that accusation. But I control it before I speak. "For the record, I gave Rook more than anyone else in my entire life. I did everything for her. She only had to ask and I was there. So I did not take anything from her, she took from me."

"And now you're pissed and feel used?"

"Are you asking me because you want to sleep with me, Ashleigh? Are you trying to nail down what you can expect from me should that happen?"

"How the hell did you go from what I said to that?"

"Because that's what people do when they're thinking about sleeping with someone new. They test the waters by asking questions about the inner workings of previous relationships. Now answer my question. Do you want to know these things so we can push our relationship a little further?"

She gives me a nervous laugh and plays with her earlobe. "Maybe. But I'm not going to let myself be used, Ford. I'm not a piece of trash. I think you're"—she thinks about her word choice for a moment—"nice-looking. But I'm not interested in being thrown away after you're *done*, to quote your words. Especially if I don't know where that line is drawn."

"What about the ex—whatever he is?"

She takes a deep breath and stares at her hands in her lap. "I need to let go. I need to accept that it's over. So"—she looks up at me—"maybe starting something new will help."

"If you think what I have in mind is the beginning of something new, then we definitely need rules."

She scowls at me. "I didn't mean it like that. And if we make rules, then we're playing a game. I'm not in the mood for games."

"Are you afraid of losing?"

"Aren't you?"

"I never lose."

She laughs. "So that means I'm already the loser. How's that fair?"

She's got a valid point. "I'm interested in having sex with you. What do you want?"

She looks down, then catches her gesture of doubt and corrects herself by staring me in the eyes. "The same. But I don't want to be treated like shit."

I laugh a little at that. "You want me to respect you? But you're negotiating the terms of a no-strings sexual relationship in a diner?"

"Take it or leave it," she deadpans.

"How about one fifteen-minute interlude and then we revisit our expectations. To keep things open."

"Fifteen minutes?" she snorts. "You're pretty confident."

"It only took two the other night."

"I'd been thinking about sex all day before you came in. Besides, you're weird with the no-touching stuff. I like it to be personal. I imagine it's cold with you. Fifteen minutes would not be satisfying."

"An orgasm isn't enough?"

She looks around nervously to see if anyone heard me, then lowers her voice, probably hoping I'll lower mine. "No. I can do that myself. I want more."

I squint at her. "Like what?"

She turns her head away, like she's hiding from me. But when she turns back, her eyes have a little gleam in them and she's biting her lip to tuck away her smile. "Conversation. Answers to my questions about you."

"No."

"Yes," she counters quickly. "You get fifteen minutes with me and I get one question—answered to my *satisfaction*."

"I get fifteen minutes of *total control* over you and you get one satisfactorily answered question from me."

She smiles but looks down again. I'm already imagining her ass up in the air and her swollen breasts bouncing so badly, she has to hold them to her chest as I fuck her from behind.

"That's the deal. You want in or not?"

"Deal," she whispers as the waitress comes with our coffee. And then, like luck is spitting in my face, the baby wakes up. Ash rocks her in the stroller, cuddles her for a few seconds, and then lifts up her shirt to nurse.

She looks right at me and smirks.

I look away, mostly to stop the hard-on, but also to see if any men are checking her out. Nope. I'm the only perv in here. I look back at her and smile. "I think we should skip breakfast." She laughs and I can't help myself. I laugh too. Because I just negotiated a sex deal with a girl who will probably blush so hard the first time I smack her ass I might not be able to control myself.

SIXTEEN

We manage to keep our minds off the potential dirty sex we might have tonight and talk about mundane things during breakfast, then head out to the Village to hit the shops. "What do you need here? Clothes?"

"I don't need any clothes, Ford. Besides…" She tears her gaze away from the architecture and finds my face so she can let out a smile. "I enjoy wearing your clothes. I might wear your jeans tomorrow."

I look down at her body. "They'd fall off you."

She shrugs. "It's called a belt. I like them loose."

I can definitely picture it, in fact, I almost get lost in the picture and slam right into a family cutting across the street to get to a chocolate store.

"Sorry, man," the guy says. Then he turns back. "Ford? Is that you, dude?"

Shit. *Deny, deny, deny.*

"Ford!" The man's wife comes up. "Wow, it's been a while. We haven't seen you since—"

"How are you"—I search my memory for a moment— "Angela and"—I stare at the guy—"Paul."

Paul grins at my recollection. I do remember them, but not because I know them well. Paul moved to the Valley when I was in high school, Angela was never on my radar. I know her face, but we never had conversations or anything like that. They are just faces.

"Hey!" Paul says. "I heard you guys sold after the accident with your dad."

"No," I say, glancing at Ashleigh. She's staring hard at me. Looking like she has lots of questions. "No, we didn't sell. We just never came back."

"Ah." He claps me on the shoulder and I pull away and stick my hand up. "Fucking Ford. You never change, dude. Got it, stay out of your *sphere*." He laughs again and now Ash is enjoying this whole interaction a little too much.

"Well, it's been nice to catch up. See you next time." I tap Ashleigh on the shoulder and she walks forward with me. I can hear them laughing as we leave.

"What the hell was that?"

"Nothing."

"Stay out of your sphere?"

"Ford?" Another voice comes off to my left. "Yes! I knew that was you!"

Aww, fuck. "Lacy, how are you?"

"Oh my gah! I can't believe you're here for Locals' Day! What a great surprise! Did you ride the new gondola up at Lionshead yet? They have it open for us today, no charge."

As if any locals need a free ride on the fucking gondola.

"Mike and I just got back. Mike!" she yells over to a line of people waiting for hot chocolate at a kiosk in the middle of the street. "Mike! It's Ford Aston! Come here, quick, before he ditches me!"

Mike leaves his place in line and jogs over. "Fucking Ford! Hey, man, haven't seen you in forever! I read a story about you a few months back"—I look over at Ashleigh and she's all ears now—"you, Spencer and Ronin were in some shit again, yeah?"

"Are you Ford's wife? Ford, your baby is adorable!" Lacy squeals.

"So you got a project these days? I heard you and Spencer did a show? What channel's that on? I wanna watch."

I put the hand up. Both hands, actually, since Lacy is on one side and Mike is on the other. "Sphere of privacy, people. Now."

Lacy laughs and turns to Ashleigh. "He was always doing that sphere stuff when we were kids. *Keep out of my sphere, back off my sphere.* No one was allowed in his *sphere.*"

She laughs again and this time Ashleigh joins in. "He's cute like that, isn't he. All weird about his sphere. It's like his Jedi power!"

"OK, we're done here."

"Wait, Ford, I'd like to chat with your old friends," Ashleigh says with a fake innocence.

"Ashleigh?" the voice calls her from across the street near a Bavarian pretzel shop.

"Oh, shit." Ash winces. "Mrs. fucking Pearson. Let's get the hell out of here." She holds her hand up like I just did. "Sphere of privacy, Mrs. Pearson. We're in the *sphere.*"

I laugh and pull on her. "Not so fun when you're the target, is it? Just start walking. They'll leave us alone, I've perfected the detached getaway. It's my signature move."

"I guess it is. Can we ride that gondola? I'd like that. To see the mountain."

"Sure, we need to drop the stroller off at the van and take a bus over to Lionshead though."

"Is it far?"

"No, a few minutes' ride. We can go. Might as well see the place since you're here."

We get on the bus after dropping off all the excess crap and I look at Ashleigh with her bundled baby in her arms as we ride over to Lionshead. "See, that snowsuit was a good idea.

Otherwise you'd have to bring all those stupid blankets."

She sighs. "What would I do without you, Ford. You're a genius."

I smile. "Damn right."

The walk to the gondola is short—this place is not big. And when we get there I have no Vail ID to prove I'm local and no one I recognize is working the lift, so I end up having to pay anyway. Our car is packed, the full capacity of ten people.

Ash sits by the window facing backward and I sit across from her facing forward. We're squished by some rowdy teen boarders. "You look tired," I say. "This ride might make you fall asleep."

"It just might, because the baby's getting fussy and she needs to eat. And that's like my sleep button."

"It's a seven-minute ride up, and then these guys will get off and we'll have the car to ourselves on the way down. The baby can eat then." No way is Ashleigh nursing with these assholes in here.

She rests her head against the cool window and I turn to look down at the mountain. We've gotten a lot of snow this year, so it's nothing but white and green.

"It's beautiful," she says softly.

"Very," I say back. Her cheeks are flushed red from the cold and her eyes are heavy. She's prettier than I first thought. And she's smart. I like smart girls. I'll fuck a dumb one, but I prefer them smart. Her hair is very dark, almost black. But unlike Rook, she has dark eyes to match. I like that too. Her lids slowly close and I stare at her until we get to the top. She jolts awake when the doors whoosh open and the boarders get off. The baby is sleeping again, so even though we have the car to ourselves for the ride down, the privacy is not necessary.

"You're missing the view, Ashleigh," I tell her when the doors close again and we start the descent. "Come sit on my side so you can see it going down."

She hugs the baby and settles on the bench next to me, totally within my sphere. "I like it here. I bet it was fun growing up in such a beautiful place."

"It was. Where'd you grow up?"

"Hong Kong."

"No shit?"

She laughs. "Yeah. My dad is half Chinese and he worked there until I was twelve. Then we came back to the US and lived in a bunch of different places."

I chew on that for a few minutes and the next time I look, her eyes are closed again. Her head slumps over on my shoulder and instead of freaking out and pushing her away, I let her stay.

She's warm.

And it feels kinda nice.

By the time we walk back to the van and she gets the baby belted in and is settled in her seat, she looks completely wiped.

"Too much excitement for you today?"

"I'm boring, I know," she says with her eyes closed.

I pull out of the parking lot and get on the freeway and then get off a few seconds later at our exit. When we get to the house she's already asleep but the baby is just starting to realize she's hungry. Ashleigh pulls herself awake and grabs the baby. She heads straight to the bedroom when we get inside, not even a *see you later* for me. I stand in the kitchen for a few minutes, just listening. She talks in a low voice to the baby as she does something that is not well-received. Changing a diaper maybe. Then I hear the bed creak and everything goes silent. Must be nice to have someone with you at all times like that. I see the toll it's taking on her, but still. That baby just loves her. No questions asked.

I grab a beer and go downstairs and stretch out on the couch. I wonder what Rook is doing. I wonder what Ronin thinks? I take out my phone and press Spencer's ugly face.

"Yeah."

"Spencer," I say.

"I'm sorry, do I know you?"

I roll my eyes. He is such a child. "What's going on?"

"You mean besides the fact that you broke my Blackbird's heart? What was that, Ford? I mean that was low, even for you. So she's not interested in you. Get over it."

"She *is* interested in me, Spencer. That's the problem. If I stick around I might—"

"Whatever. She's upset and I don't like it. You handled it all wrong, dude. There are better ways to get your point across. You could've just said, *Hey, we need to take a break. I can't handle this right now. But I'm still your friend and I'll be back when I figure this mess out.* I mean, what the fuck, Ford? You just talk shit to her and leave?"

"That's not what happened."

"No? Well, those words came out of her mouth. So that's what *she* thinks happened, regardless if it did or not. She said you told her hurtful things to make her go away. And it's fucked up. You don't do that to her, of all people. And now she's worried you're not gonna be around for the trials. If you leave us hanging, Ford, I swear—"

"I won't. You know me better than that."

"I get that you're Mr. I don't-give-a-shit with everyone else, but that's not who you are to us. You understand? We are tight. We don't fuck each other over. We stand together. And Ronin is not happy. He might never say anything, but you've lost a lot of credibility in his eyes. And it's not because you *want* her, Ford. It's because you *hurt* her. And you did it on purpose."

I sigh.

"That's it? That's all you have to say, Ford? A long, pitiful breath of air that tells me you're feeling sorry for yourself? Well, get the fuck over it, asshole."

And then the line goes dead.

SEVENTEEN

It seems like hours pass until I finally hear Ashleigh moving around upstairs. It's dark now. I grab my phone off the coffee table and check the time. Past seven. I've been down here all fucking day thinking about Rook and I just don't get it. How do I get the blame when she's the one who's driving *me* crazy? I mean, what the hell is wrong with Ronin? He should be mad at her, not me. He should be asking *her* why she cares so much. Because if the situation was reversed, I'd sure as hell want to know how she felt about him. Doesn't he ask her? Doesn't he care that she has feelings for me? If I was Ronin, I'd be happy I was out of the picture.

I pick up my phone and press Ronin's face. He picks up on the fourth ring, just before it goes to voice mail.

"What?" he barks into the phone.

"How is this my fault? I left. Why do you even care?"

"Because, Ford—" I can hear Rook in the background talking in a low voice. "We're friends. You never did understand that. And I get that you have trouble in the relationship department, but this—*this*, Ford? I'm not sure who the hell you are right now."

"I just can't do it, Ronin."

"Fine, we get that. Obviously. But dude, you're almost twenty-six fucking years old. You can't manage a fucking friendship? I'm sorry you're infatuated with her. Sucks to be you, right? But you're the one who *wanted* her to depend on you. And you got your wish. She depends on you. She cares about you. Maybe not in the exact way you want, but she fucking cares, Ford. And you just shit all over her. She's worried about you—even after all those things you said, she still wants me to make sure you're OK."

"Put her on the phone then."

"Fuck you. You don't call up here and say put her on the phone. If you want to talk to her, show the fuck up and talk to her."

"I can't, I'm on my way to LA."

"Yeah, with some girl you just met. So this new pet is more important than us?"

I ignore the derogatory remark about my women, because he's baiting me and I don't take bait. "I'm not coming back and that's the end of it."

He hangs up on me and I pull the phone away and just stare at it.

"Wow, you're on a roll with these people."

Ash is standing at the bottom of the stairs in a t-shirt that says '*I'm not a ski addict, sometimes I have sex too*' and nothing else as far as I can tell. The shirt hits her mid-thigh so she may or may not have panties on. I'd like to find that out right now. "Ready?" I ask her before she can comment further.

"I'm ready," she says with a sly smile.

"Where's the baby?"

"Finally sleeping."

"Finally?" She walks over to me slowly and I stand up. "You've been up in the fucking bedroom all damn day."

"Yeah, but she wasn't sleeping. I was." Ash laughs at that. "Well, I was trying anyway. She was babbling almost the entire time. I'm surprised you didn't hear her."

I find the timer function on my phone and set it for fifteen minutes. Ashleigh glances down at it then looks back up at me. "So, fifteen minutes?"

I don't smile, on the outside anyway, but I do on the inside. "That was the deal."

"And I'm gonna be satisfied?"

"Well, that's up to you, I guess. I promised you a satisfying answer to your one question. You turned down the promise of an orgasm if I recall correctly."

"Hmmm…"

I want to laugh because she just has no idea how I work. But I don't laugh, because she's about to find out and I want to watch her reaction when it hits her. I like to read their minds as they try to figure shit out.

"Well, what do I have to do to get satisfaction?"

"Follow directions."

"Sounds easy."

"Then you should be wildly satisfied in fifteen minutes, Ashleigh." She shivers when I say her name and I know she's been thinking about this all day. I press start on the timer. "Take your clothes off and don't talk. I'll be right back."

She's got the shirt off before I can even turn away. It stops me dead for a moment, because even though I've seen her breasts on several occasions, I'm just not ready for how spectacular they are when bared specifically for me. They almost look fake.

"They're not fake," she says. Like she's reading *my* mind.

"No talking." I point to the pink panties. "Remove those and present yourself to me, I'll be right back."

"Timer's running, Ford. So chop chop."

I look back at her as I get to the stairs and shake my head. "I own you right now, Ashleigh. I'd be careful."

I'm quiet when I enter the bedroom. The baby is lying on her back, arms out, mouth open and breathing deep with sleep. I fish around in my dresser drawer until I find the black silk scarves, then quietly leave the room and go back downstairs.

Ashleigh is standing naked all right. She's shaved clean down below and she's got her hands behind her back, her chest out. She's wearing a big smile and she's swaying back and forth a little, like she's the one in control here.

I smile too. "Well, you've almost got the position down, but your form is a little off. So I'll correct that later."

"With those?" she says, looking down at the scarves.

"Shhh. That's three now. You're gonna be sorry if you keep this up."

"You just wasted four minutes, Ford—"

I cup my hand over her mouth and put my other hand firmly on the back of her head to hold her still. Her eyes widen and look up at me. "I don't like to repeat myself. When I tell you to be quiet, I expect compliance. I own you, Ashleigh. That was the deal. And if I want you to open your mouth, believe me, I'll let you know when to do it and where to place it."

I remove my hand from her mouth and take my attention back to the scarves.

"Yes, *sir*," she quips softly.

I smack her on the ass. Hard. She yelps and tries to move away, but I have her wrists and I bind them up behind her back with one of the scarves. "I warned you. Now stop."

She looks up at me, her brow crinkled, but I just slip the other scarf around her eyes and that takes care of that. "Follow me." I take her by the elbow and lead her over to the far side of the room. I hold her at the waist, then put my hand on her forehead so she doesn't crash it on the window as she bends. "Lean forward."

"Am I facing the windows? With the lights on?"

I smack her ass and it makes a nice loud crack sound.

"Ow!"

Another smack and now her entire ass is bright red. "Stop talking, Ashleigh. And then I'll stop the spankings."

"What if I like the spankings?" she purrs.

"Lean forward and press your head up against the window," I growl into her ear. This time she obeys and I rub her ass a little. "Good girl."

She lets out a grunt, but it doesn't really qualify as speech, so I let that one pass.

Her ass is beautiful and has just the right amount of firmness. I hate girls who are all muscle and Ashleigh, whether built this way naturally or carrying a few extra pounds from the baby, has a nice round ass.

I continue caressing the red handprint on her cheek, then let my fingers slip between her legs briefly, but pull them back the second she reacts. I lean down into her neck, breathing in her ear until she shivers before I start to whisper. "You're a very good girl when you behave, Ashleigh. You please me when you comply. You make me hard. You make me want to stick my fingers in you and make you come." She moans again and I pull my fingers out. "Now let's talk about what's happening. I asked for control, you agreed. I told you to be quiet, you disobeyed. When you disobey, I have to punish you. Do you like the spankings, Ashleigh?" She says nothing and I smile a little. "You may answer."

"Some of them."

I reach around to her breast with my other hand and cup it gently. It's hard and full. "Have you ever been spanked before?"

"Yes."

"Have you ever been tied up before?"

"Yes."

Well. I'm a little surprised. "Did you obey your master, Ashleigh?"

"Sometimes."

"Will you obey me?"

"Maybe."

At least she's honest. But I'm not looking for honesty now, I'm looking for submission.

"Let's see if you want to play nice tonight, shall we? Spread your legs." She complies and I smack her on the cheek, not as hard as before. She groans but doesn't complain. I rub her ass with my full palm and let it tease her folds for a moment before pulling back. "That's one. I owe you two more." She stiffens but I don't smack her again. I lean into her neck, breathing into her ear again. Then I let my mouth dip down to her shoulder and I bite her. She whimpers at this act. "I don't kiss, Ashleigh. I bite. I don't like to kiss, but I do like to bite. So when I bite you, pretend it's a kiss. Can you do that?"

"Ye—"

I bite her again and her word cuts off.

I thrust my thigh between her legs and raise it so she's off balance and teetering on one set of tip toes like she was last night. I grab her waist to steady her and she moans as my leg pushes against her bare pussy. I remove my leg and let her regain her balance. "Open wider, Ash." She obeys. "I'm going to go outside so I can see what the neighbors see right now. Stay still for me now."

I study her from the side for a moment. Her breathing picks up and this makes her chest heave. Her tits hang, not freely, they are far too full to dangle. Her nipples are hard, her areolas are wide and dark. I move around to the back and look at her ass. I was wrong about her blushing. She's into it. But I wasn't wrong about how her ass in the air would make me feel. "Stay," I command her as I open the basement door that leads out to the front of the house. I walk down the driveway a little and then turn.

Fuck. She is like a sexy little goddess up in that window.

The neighbors can't see her. There's a shitload of pine trees in the way. But she doesn't know that, so the threat serves its purpose. She thinks people can see her all spread out against the window. And she's still doing it. So she likes the thought of being watched.

I take out my camera and snap a picture, then walk back inside. She's shivering with cold since I left the door open. I grab her arm at the elbow and tug her back towards me. "Stand up straight now, keep your legs open."

She does and then I pull her back into my chest and put my arms around her. "Sorry for leaving the door open. Now you're cold." She sinks into me as I rub her tits and then her stomach. I breathe into her neck, trying to make her warm. My hand drifts around her body, and these light, feather touches make her shiver more instead of heating her up. Her nipples are incredibly hard and bunched. I twist one and she cries out, her whole body doubling over and recoiling as she tries to pull away from me.

Too hard. "Sorry," I murmur. "They're sensitive?" She nods her head against my chest and I catch her holding back a potential sob. That's it for her. She's about done with this. "Come with me." I lead her over to the back of the couch and push on her shoulders a little. "Bend over the couch, Ashleigh." Her ass goes up and her bound hands are clasped tightly together near her waist. I slap her left cheek. Hard.

"Ow!"

I slap her again, not so hard. "No talking." I slip my fingers between her legs and cut off her words with my attention. "I owe you one more. I warned you not to talk. You promised me total control, yet you disobeyed, so I have to punish you. Do you understand, Ashleigh?"

She nods her head and just as she starts I smack her hard again. She whimpers but holds in her cry. I can tell this is not what she expected, so I rub her ass gently. First the one red cheek, then the other. My touch calms her and then I slip my fingers inside her and pump a little. "I hadn't planned on you being so naughty, Ash." And just as my last word is out, the timer beeps. "We're done."

I stand her back up, unbind her wrists, remove her blindfold, and walk away. "You want a beer?" I call out as I go up the steps.

She doesn't answer me.

I grab two anyway and go back down. She's just pulling on her shirt and I can tell by the look on her face that she's angry. I offer her a beer and to my surprise she takes it and plops down on the couch. I sit down on the other end. "Thoughts?"

TAUT

She takes a sip of her beer. Breathes deeply for a moment. "Well, I guess I wasn't expecting *that*."

"What were you expecting?"

"To be fucked hard and left satisfied."

"Do you wish I'd fucked you hard and left you satisfied instead?"

She takes another drink and gives this some thought. "I'm not sure," she finally says.

"Do you want to do it again?"

"Tonight?"

I laugh. "No. You need to think about what happened before we try again. It took you a while to give in and for me, that's not a good sign. I asked for control, you fought me. You were rude."

"Rude?" She shoots me an incredulous look, like I have some nerve.

"You promised me control, then you were a smartass. I think that was rude."

"So you punished me by not getting me off."

"I didn't get off either. We're even. You said you've done this before."

"Yeah, but your spankings *hurt*."

"They're punishment, to let you know I'm unhappy with your behavior. If I made them pleasant you'd never care if you displeased me. We never got past the initial control. Who is in charge and who is not. If we had, you'd be a lot happier right now, I guarantee it."

She grunts and leans back against the couch. "Well, whatever. It's my turn now. I get one question, fully answered to my satisfaction."

"Shoot."

She looks me in the eye, her frown gone and a sly grin replacing it. Her eyes almost gleam in the light. "Why didn't you go to your father's funeral?"

And this is when I realize I might've underestimated Ashleigh. Because this question was just as planned and plotted as me having her ass up in the air in front of the window.

EIGHTEEN

"How do you know I didn't go?" I ask. I already know the answer to that, because it's only been brought up once.

"Mrs. Pearson, that morning in the motel. She said everyone wanted to see you there and you never showed."

I study her expression for clues to what she's thinking. It's not very telling. She might in fact, be some kind of pokerface expert, because I'm not seeing anything beyond her almost stoic, flat glare.

"I guess," she says in a low voice, her chin tipping up in superiority as she talks, "I'll have to find my own satisfaction tonight."

"With this question."

"Yes."

"Why?" My eyes are squinting down into slits, I just know it.

"Because you don't want to talk about it."

"So you're mad because of the spanking and now you want to get even."

"Maybe. You want to use your power over me, and that

seems to be fine. Yet when I do it, I'm some sort of conniving bitch. Is that how this works?"

"I don't do funerals."

"Ha!" she belts out. "OK, first, *Ford*." She says my name with a snarl. And now I know I really pissed her off with the spankings. "Do not insult me with your answers by assuming I'm stupid. Second, even if I accepted that as a plausible answer, and I don't, but even if I did, I'd need every detail on why you *don't do funerals*. And then I'd like to know exactly why you couldn't muster up some courage and just attend a function for a few hours to honor the father you say you loved."

I might like to turn her over and slap her ass for that remark. Luckily she continues and doesn't wait for an answer, because I'm very close to leaning over and doing it.

"You had your way with me in front of the window, now it's my turn." She gets up and walks over to the office and grabs the Scotch out of the drawer and the nosing glasses from the desk. She sets the bottle on the coffee table in front of me and goes to the basement bathroom to wash the glasses. I have a full two minutes to seethe properly before I have to tuck that shit down and pretend she's not pissing me off.

"Pour," she says as she sets the glasses down.

"I'll make it a double, how's that?" I ask her with fake amusement.

She takes her glass and sits on the far side of the couch. As far away from me as she can get. It's only then I notice she's still only in her pink panties under that t-shirt. It's hard to miss, she's flashing them at me. "Cute," I say, tilting my glass in the direction of her open legs.

She laughs. "You think I'm going to give in and let you win this game, Ford? I won't. I don't like to lose either."

"So you've been hiding this cut-throat fem-Nazi behind some demure broken-hearted wife routine for what purpose?"

"Fuck you. Don't speak about my—" She stops mid-sentence and takes a deep breath and this sets off a small alarm bell in my head. "Don't talk about him."

"Then don't talk about my father."

"I'm allowed. You wanted me to submit to you for this game. I wanted you to answer my question. That's the deal we made, and from what I can tell, you're being disrespectful to me right now. Rude, even. Because you're not doing what you promised."

Wow. I might regret ever meeting this girl.

"Fine, you want to know why I don't go to funerals? I'll tell you. I was diagnosed with Asperger's syndrome as a child. I've seen more than forty specialists over the course of my life—"

"Wait. Why? Asperger's doesn't require that many doctors, especially if you're high-functioning. And if you do have Asperger's then you're definitely high-functioning. So you left something out."

I squint at her again. Who the fuck *is* this chick? "I've left a lot out. But you only get one question. You want to know why I didn't go to my father's funeral. I don't do funerals because I don't experience emotions like most people. Funerals, celebrations like birthdays, that sort of thing… New Year's parties—none of these things have meaning to me. And my father would've understood my decision not to go to the funeral. So don't pretend like you know enough about me, or him, to even form an opinion about that."

She stares at me.

"Are we done? Are you satisfied?"

She downs her double shot of whiskey and sets her glass down on the coffee table. Then lets out a long breath. "OK."

"OK?"

"I guess that's the only satisfaction I'm getting tonight, so I'll take it." And just like that the other Ashleigh is back. The pit bull has been collared and leashed.

I huff out a laugh and then drink my whiskey as well. "*You* decided you didn't want me to satisfy you, so don't blame your disappointment on me."

"You hit me!"

"You disobeyed. I told you I would spank you if you disobeyed. You admitted to liking it. You pushed me on purpose."

"It fucking *hurt.*"

And this is not an exaggeration. I did hurt her and she's mad. Mad enough to have tears building, so I ease up a little. "Believe me, I'm not into hurting girls. I'd rather make you squeal my name in pleasure."

She shakes her head but a reluctant smile comes forth. "I thought it would be"—she shrugs—"fake. Playful. I didn't expect it to hurt like that." She palms her breast through the t-shirt and pauses on the nipple I pinched. "And it still hurts now. I won't be able to nurse."

"Sorry. I didn't know they were so sensitive. And for the record, if you were just some one-night girl I'd never touch you again after your behavior. I'm not looking to punish people. I just like to be in control. I don't want to hurt you. I'm not into whips, I don't want to humiliate you or piss on you for fuck's sake. I just like to call the shots and I like to fuck girls who let me do that."

"And that's why you have the sphere of privacy?" She laughs as the words come out. "You're so stupid, Ford."

"What can I say, it's my Jedi power." I smile and she sighs, then leans back into the couch, tucking her legs up close to her chest. "Come here, Ashleigh."

"Why?" She's scowling at me with suspicion. "So you can pinch me again? Or smack me? Or something else equally stupid? No, thank you. I might be in a tight spot but I'm not a slow learner."

This girl, I swear. She is kinda cute with her silly superiority complex. "Because I'm sorry I hurt you. I know better, so this was all my fault. It *can* be playful, but for me it's serious. Now, come over here and I'll make it up to you."

"I thought you don't like to be close to people."

"I don't like people touching me. But I can touch them if I want. And right now I want to touch you, so come here." I beckon her with a finger. "Come on." She crawls slowly across the couch to my side and I open my legs to make room for her. "Turn around and lean back." She obeys and when her back rests against my chest I feel a bit of satisfaction. She did not submit to me tonight for the fight, but she does for the make-up. I lean down and whisper softly in her ear. "Thank you. Now put your hands in your lap and don't move them, OK?"

"OK."

I put my arms around her shoulders and squeeze her a little, then nip her ear until she sucks in a breath. "I *am* sorry. If we do it again, I'll be more careful. But you have to obey."

"I'm not sure I want to do it again."

"I'm not gonna force you. I won't even bring it up."

"I might, but I'm just not sure yet."

"If we do it again, then no more questions about my dad. Don't take this personally, but I don't want to share that with you. I don't want to share that with anyone." She stays silent, just calmly breathing. "Oh, and one more thing." I get my phone out of my pocket and find the picture. "Here," I say as I hand it to her.

"Oh my God! You took a picture of me like that?"

"It's sexy, huh?"

She giggles and it vibrates through to my chest.

"You can delete it. I just wanted to show you how fucking hot you looked."

The phone makes a few noises as she deletes the picture and then she lets out a little gasp. "You have a picture of me and the baby on here."

"I took that this morning, remember? You looked pretty cute with her when she was laughing." Ashleigh squirms in my embrace and I hug her tighter to keep her from turning around. "Stay put, Ash."

"Ford?" she asks softly as she stops wiggling.

"What?"

"Thank you. For helping me. For talking to me this morning. I just freaked about the duck thing. It was a gift. A very special gift. I'm sorta sorry for making you worry, but then again, I'm not. Not really."

"Why's that?"

"Because you said you'll take me to LA and honestly, that makes me really, really happy. I thought I'd be OK by myself when I left Texas, but I don't think I can do this alone. It's not good to have too much time to think about things, ya know? It's not good. And I know you're only in it for yourself, but I'll take any help I can get."

I sigh and internalize this. I can relate to that, for sure. Thinking too much about Rook is getting me nowhere. "I can use the company on the drive. And you're pretty, so what the fuck, right?'

She leans into me a little more and for a moment my heart rate jacks up. I don't usually embrace the pets, hell, I don't even talk to them beyond barking commands and handing out the occasional praise when they're exceptionally good. So I'm not all that skilled at this comforting stuff.

"You're like crazy sexy, Ford. And all this weird shit you do, that just adds to it. I'm not sure why, but I like your strangeness. It's real. And it drives me a little wild."

It's my turn to laugh and my heart calms down as I let it out.

"I better go back upstairs. I can hear the baby fussing."

"You can*not*. She's fine." The truth is I don't want Ash to leave. I kinda like this.

"No, listen."

And sure enough, when I listen very carefully I can hear small cries. Not anything urgent like she was this morning when Ashleigh was in the van looking for that duck. But she's definitely about to become demanding. I let go and Ashleigh sits up and turns a little to look at me. "I'm tired anyway, and I need some alone time to satisfy myself."

I pull her back and poke her ribs until she laughs. "Don't. If we do it again, then there are rules. One is you obey me. The other is no cheating. And *that* is cheating."

"I was kidding."

"You were not."

She laughs and wiggles free and gets up. "You're right, I wasn't. But I'll be nice and give you one more chance to pleasure me. Then I'm on my own." And then she runs to the stairs, her pink panties blinking at me as my t-shirt bounces along her ass to the rhythm of her climbing.

I think about those panties and her bare ass spanked red for hours before I finally fall asleep.

NINETEEN

A squealing baby wakes me, but I'm getting used to it, so I just try and let it go. She sounds happy, not upset like yesterday. And I can hear splashing, so I figure Ash has her in the tub down here for a bath.

I close my eyes again and drift off until the spin-cycle of the washer wakes me back up. Laundry room is downstairs too. Babies make lots of things dirty, so… right.

The smell comes next. "Fuck, Ashleigh! You have the whole upstairs to do that shit. Come on!"

I open my eyes and see the baby, sitting in her carrier on the floor next to the couch, presumably content with her warm and stinky diaper because she is fast asleep. The shower's going this time, so I guess I'm sorta doing babysitting duty.

"Fucking moms. They are sneaky shits."

I drag myself up and go to the bathroom to see what the fuck Ashleigh's gonna do about this diaper, because I'm sure as hell not taking care of that. The door is wide open so I just walk in. This bathroom is not modern and updated like the ones upstairs. It's the only tub in the house, and it just has a shower curtain instead of glass doors. Ash is not singing or anything stupid like that, but I can imagine her washing her hair under the water because it makes various splashing sounds like she's moving around a lot.

I have an urge to pull the curtain back.

Normally I do not give in to impulses, but today I want to. I'm shirtless already, so I just slip off my sweats and peek my head inside. She's got her eyes closed as she rinses her hair. Water drips down her face, her mouth opens a little and catches some, spitting it out. But my gaze follows the stream that runs down her front, right over her nipples on those absolutely perfect breasts, one of which is actually bruised from me squeezing it last night.

"Sorry about that bruise," I say in a low voice.

Her eyes pop open and I expect a little flash of protest, some squeal telling me to get out. Or a scowl at the very least. But she smiles.

I pull the curtain back and step in with her. She takes in my body. Like, *thoroughly* takes in my body. She checks me out for way longer than I did her. "Turn around," I tell her.

"Why? Then I can't look at you and you'll get a good view of my ass."

"You catch on fast. Now do what I asked."

"Wait," she says, putting a hand up as I try and turn her around. "Are we playing? I need to understand what you're asking first."

I am instantly hard and it is impossible for her to miss this. "Do you want to play?"

"We have no timer."

"I have an internal timer, trust me. Now answer my question."

"Yes, but I need some satisfaction this time. I can't take it, Ford. I won't last."

"Satisfaction is yours to be had. All you have to do is comply."

"OK, I will. And then I get satisfaction *and* another question."

"But not about my dad."

"Deal." She lets out a low cackle. "I'm totally winning."

"How the hell do you figure?"

"I get two things, and you only get one."

"Yeah, but I get you, so *I'm* winning."

She just stares at me, confused. "That was… almost… nice."

"I can be nice," I growl into her neck as I turn her around and bite her ear. My hands glide down her arms and then settle on her hips. "Now bend over."

Her whole body shivers even though the water is hot and it's still blasting down her front. My grip on her hips tightens as she leans forward, her ass bumps up against my hard-on, and then she lowers her hands to the floor of the tub. I reach up and adjust the water so it's spraying down her ass and then lean back a little to take a peek. Her pussy is fully exposed and even if we weren't in the shower, she'd still be sopping wet.

"Put your hands behind your back, Ashleigh."

"But I might fall over."

"I have you, I won't let you fall over."

"But—"

"And no talking."

Her hands come behind her back and they are flashing signs at me. *This fucking girl!* I smack her ass, not hard, but the water makes it echo and the handprint appears immediately because of the heat. "How the hell did you know I understand sign language?"

She signs something else. *May I speak?* she asks sloppily with her hands.

"Speak."

"I went through all your shit and found a crapload of sign language stuff. You even had a Boy Scout badge for it, you little over-achieving nerd. And for the record"—she tries to look over her shoulder at me but she can't see much bending over like that—"you should not trust a girl alone in your bedroom. We're nosy." I smack her again, this time a little harder. She moans a little, like she enjoyed this one. "What was that for?"

"Fun, mostly. But also for snooping. I'll get your sign

language story later, but for now, what did you need to say that you had to break the rules and talk?"

"I'm not on the pill, just so you know."

"I'm not gonna fuck you, so it won't matter." She almost stands up when I say this but I push hard on her back and force her down. "But I'll take care of you if you're good." She says nothing to this but I can tell she's unhappy. "What's wrong now?"

She says nothing.

"You can talk, I won't spank you."

"Nothing's wrong."

I smack her hard on the ass, but not as hard as I did last night. It still makes her gasp but she says nothing.

She's learning fast.

"If I ask a question, Ashleigh, I want an answer, not a lie. You want me to fuck you? And you may speak."

"Well, yeah. The whole point of me bending over and baring my ass to you is so I can get fucked, right? How is this rocket science?"

She is trying to drive me crazy with her silliness, I swear. "I can get you off without fucking you, so what's the problem?"

"It's just not…" She tries to look up at me again, but she can't. "As much fun, that's all. And I don't see what you get out of it."

"I like the game. Now you've wasted almost five minutes so far. We can keep it up or you can give in, be quiet, and trust me."

I get a long sigh from her and I almost laugh. "Poor, poor Ashleigh." My right hand glides over her hip and my fingers slip between her legs. She lets out a small moan. "Her empathy for me"—I slip one finger in and stroke her—"is almost overwhelming." I pump her a few times and she responds, but not as well as she did the other night in the hallway. "Stand up."

She obeys immediately this time but she doesn't try and look at me, and that's what I really like. Ashleigh is not submissive. I can tell. She gives in when she has to and she's vulnerable right now because she's in a tight spot with her car and money, but she's not easily subdued. So getting her to obey is a big deal and brings me a lot of satisfaction.

Not like Rook, who would do things so willingly if I approached the request the right way. Rook needed very little prodding when I was asking her for compliance. She was extremely submissive and responded to firm and gentle guidance. Rook responds to kindness the way some subs respond to punishment. That stupid fuck Jon had no idea how precious she was. He abused her and that still pisses me the fuck off. I'd never smack Rook on the ass. I could never correct her physically. Ever. Not even if we were playing. But I liked that about her. I liked that she could be controlled with kind words instead of harsh actions.

She was the perfect girl for me. Totally willing, yet so gentle and innocent.

Ashleigh breaks my little daydream about Rook and peeks around her shoulder, like she's waiting for me to do something. I grab a bottle of baby wash that she must've put in here. It smells like baby powder. I squeeze some on her back and begin washing her. Rook would like a gentle shower, I bet—

"OK, I quit." Ashleigh flips the shower head back to its normal position and turns so she can wash the soap off her back.

"What the hell are you doing now?"

"Forget it. I don't need a question answered that bad." The water rolls down her face and she flicks the wet hair out of her eyes.

"What are you talking about?"

"I'm not sure who you were just thinking about taking a shower with, but it wasn't me. And you know what?" She points her finger up at my face. "Fuck you." She throws open the curtain and steps out of the tub. "Just—*fuck you.*" She grabs a towel and wraps it around her and walks out. Leaving me standing there with a hard-on.

I chuckle a little at her defiance but I'm glad she can't hear me. Because I get the feeling Ashleigh might punch me in the teeth if she heard me laughing at her right now.

Fucking girls. No, not fucking girls. This fucking girl. She's trying to push me over the edge with her antics.

But I have all day in the truck to cool her off, and maybe if I drive straight through we can make it to Vegas and stop for a day of fun tomorrow. I'll even get us a nice suite at The Four Seasons.

So I could care less that she's off pouting—and changing a dirty diaper, I add with a smug smile. Because I have her undivided attention for two more days and I plan on making the most of them. Mrs. Pearson was right, I'm not one to let an opportunity go to waste.

TWENTY

I pull into Jason's parking lot a few hours later. He called me around nine and said he was done, but fucking Ashleigh had to get all her crap together, so right now it's almost noon. She's not talking to me either. In fact, she's sitting in the back of the van with the baby so she's not tempted.

I let her do her thing. She'll crack after an hour in the Bronco with no radio.

"OK," I tell her as I turn the van off. "You get all your shit together and put it in the Bronco, buckle the kid in, and I'll be right back."

I get no answer, but I don't wait for one anyway. I push through the door of the garage and Jason is talking on the phone. He chats about the ski contest yesterday in Loveland, then something about family dinner and then pops off with an *I love you*. Must be his wife.

"OK, Ford, you're all set," he says after hanging up the phone. "Transmission's good as new. I gave you a few new hoses, got the heater running, changed the oil, rotated the tires, and put on new wipers. I figured you deserved the red carpet treatment since I overcharged you by almost five thousand dollars." He smiles broadly.

"You're a dick."

"I'm not gonna start the girl's car until Thursday at the earliest, since you're taking care of her. So tell her it'll be about two weeks. Just call me with an address and I'll set up the haul for you." He slides the keys over the counter and grabs the printout of my services and holds it out. "Don't be a stranger, Ford. Everyone is talking about you. You're like the biggest news this fucking town has seen in months."

"Everyone who?"

"All the poker buddies. We still have poker nights on Saturdays at the community center. Sandy Ralston was there, too. She's the local reporter these days. Gonna do a big story on you and your criminal past and put it in the Vail Daily tomorrow."

"What criminal past?"

We both look over at the door and Ashleigh is standing there with the baby in her arms.

"I told you to put the stuff in the truck."

She rolls her eyes and walks up next to us. "Door's locked, genius. Now what's this about a criminal past?"

"Oh, Ford here is a colorful fellow—"

"I have no criminal record, Ashleigh. Jason, thanks for taking care of the Bronco and here's the keys to the rental. Call them for me and tell them to pick it up." I grab the receipt and turn Ashleigh around. "Let's go." I have to push her to get her started but once her feet are moving she skips a little to keep up with my long strides across the parking lot.

"Ford?"

I ignore her, just unlock the Bronco and then go around to the van to grab the baby seat.

"Ford, wait."

The seatbelt clicks as I release it and pull the seat out, push past her and stick the seat in the back of the Bronco. "I have seatbelts back here, I know I do. I just need to find them." My hand sweeps under the back cushion searching and I find the webbed strap and pull it out, then go looking for the lock. "OK, I'm not sure how to buckle that seat in, so you do that and I'll get the stroller and stuff." I push her out of my way, not roughly, just move her aside, and go back to the van to get the rest of the stuff. When I look back she's just standing there by the open door.

"What?"

She's got that look on her face. The look pretty much everyone gets after they realize I'm either a genuine freak or a psychotic criminal.

"What?" I ask again, because she's just staring at me.

"OK. I'll wait you out on this one, but I'm not done." And then the look is gone and she turns back to the baby seat and gets busy.

I grab the stroller first and put it in the cargo area of the Bronco, then go back for the bags. She's using grocery bags again. This time she's got a bunch of my clothes in the bags with her meager wardrobe.

"I packed for you since you never bothered."

I look at her and she's got her hands out, asking for me to load her up with bags. "It's not a long drive to LA, I'll buy what I need. And I figured you were stealing my t-shirts."

"I am," she says with a smile and I relax a little. She's not gonna push it and I'm grateful. I'm feeling the need to get the fuck out of Vail all of a sudden. I hand her a couple bags and I grab the rest. "Can we stop and get some snacks and stuff?"

"Yeah, but not here. We'll stop in Grand Junction." I look over at her and smile as she packs the truck. "They have your favorite store there." She flashes me a funny look over her shoulder. "Wal-Mart."

She laughs. "Have you ever been in a Wal-Mart, Ford?"

"I have people shop for me."

"We shopped yesterday."

"I made an exception. I figured you needed stuff but you

decided to be a cheap date."

I close up the back of the Bronco and Ashleigh keeps the diaper bag with her and gets in the passenger side. Front seat this time, so I figure she's over her tantrum from this morning.

"I'm still mad at you," she says, slamming her door.

I close mine as well and start up the Bronco. She rumbles alive and I smile. "Fuck, I missed you, baby." I look over at Ash because I know she's waiting for me to say something. "What?" I play dumb.

"I'm done with your games. I'm not playing anymore. I can't do it. You win. So let's just be friendly until we get to LA and I swear, I'll pay you back for all your help."

I back out of the space, honk at Jason who's waving from the door as he talks to some guy who just pulled up, and we are off. "I don't want your money," I reply to her statement once we're on I-70 heading west. "I'm fucking rich. I have way more than I need."

"Your loss, then." And then she settles into her seat and stares out the window and stays silent.

We drive past the rest of the village and a few miles later I see the turn-off for Minturn. "That's where my dad is buried," I say as I nod my head to the road sign for Highway 24.

"Oh, really? I bet it's beautiful. There are definitely worse places to be laid to rest."

"I wouldn't know. I've never been up there to see it."

"What?" She looks over at me with an incredulous look. "You need to go *now*."

"Yeah, right," I laugh.

"You're a few miles away, how often do you come up here?"

"Never anymore. I wouldn't be here now if the fucking truck hadn't broken down. Or if I'd stayed put in Denver on New Year's Eve and flown out to LA the next day like I planned." I blow past the exit for Minturn and Ashleigh physically turns around in her seat to watch it disappear.

"Go back."

"No, I'm not going back. Just turn around."

"Go back, Ford. I'm not kidding."

"Why do you care, anyway?"

"Because it's a cowardly move, that's why. I've lost all respect for you."

I grunt. "As if you had any."

"Actually," she says, glaring over at me, "I respect you quite a bit. You're not a creep, you seem to be honest, and even though you might be some famous criminal in these parts, I trust you. And I'm telling you, if you don't go see that grave and get over this thing with your dad, then you're a coward. You're running away from this too. Just add the cemetery to your list of things to avoid along with those friends of yours back in Denver." I stay silent and she huffs out some air. "Coward," she repeats, crossing her arms across her chest as she crosses her legs. A gesture that practically screams *I'm done with you.*

For some reason this graveyard bullshit might be her line. And I might've crossed it.

I sigh and take the next exit, get off the fucking freeway, get back on going east, and head back towards Minturn. I look over at her and she's smug and smiling. "Happy?"

She swings the foot of her crossed leg and her hands are in her lap again. She's absolutely triumphant.

I backtrack few miles, then get off the Interstate and take 24 towards Minturn.

"Do you know where the cemetery is?"

"It's Minturn, Ashleigh. It's like Vail. You can't get lost. It's a strip of places along a road. I'm pretty sure the cemetery won't be hard to find."

"You small-town people are sorta stuck-up. *It's Vail, Ashleigh,*" she says in a mocking voice. "I'm from the city. We have loads of cemeteries and if you take a wrong turn, you might end up dead in one before your time. So excuse me for asking."

I like smartass Ashleigh, she's entertaining. So I let her stew in her anger and defiance until I see the cemetery sign. "OK, I've had enough of your mouth. Just be quiet."

I'm nervous, I think. It's not like my dad is really here, but it's meaningful to me. And I didn't have a chance to prepare for it, so it's all sorta rushing up at me at once. I turn the truck into the lot and read the signs real fast to see if there are rules. There are—*no one after dark* and that kinda shit. But nothing I need to know since it's midday. "I don't even know where he is." The words are already out of my mouth before I realize how bad that sounds. My own father, laid to rest two years ago, and I have no idea where he's buried.

"I can help you look if you want. What's his name?"

I look over at her to see how serious she is, but her mood has gone from smartass to somber in a few seconds. "Rutherford Aston."

"You're a Junior?" she asks smiling.

"No, he was the third, I'm the fourth."

She stares at me and then nods her head. "It's a great name. I bet if you have a boy you'll name him Ford too, huh?"

Would I? I have no idea. I don't answer, just open the door and get out. "You can help look if you want."

She grabs the baby and we take off in different directions. I head to the headstones that look new, but Ashleigh goes off towards the old ones. I wander around aimlessly for about five minutes and then give up and call my mom.

"Ford?" she asks when she answers.

"You know it's me, the caller ID says Ford. Why do you always ask?"

"It's possible you just did a butt-dial, Ford. Your calls are so sporadic, how should I know."

I laugh. My fucking mom is such a freak. "I only did that once, like six years ago. Anyway, I'm up at the cemetery in Minturn looking for Dad's grave, and I don't know where it is."

Total silence on the other end.

"Mom?"

"Sorry," she says softly. "I'm just a little stunned."

"I'm standing next to a giant angel with a trumpet in the center. Where do I go from there?"

She gives me directions and I find the grave a few minutes later and hang up before she starts crying. My mom misses him too and I bet she's sorry she's not here with me.

His headstone is not huge like you might expect for a man who was the heir to a massive manufacturing empire. It's a medium-sized upright slab of polished black granite that is gray on the inside, so the lettering has a high contrast to it. It says *Husband, Friend, Advocate* on the top line, then *FATHER* in much bigger letters on the second.

My heart swells a little at this. Because I'm an only child so the stone was lettered this way specifically for me. Why didn't I come for the funeral?

"Dad," I say softly. "God, I'm so sorry." I look up and Ash is watching me from the other side of the cemetery. She gives me a little wave and then turns away and walks back to the truck. "I'm so fucking sorry," I say it again. These are the only words I've ever said to him since the accident. I used to say it a lot, but it's been a while so it feels necessary.

"What would you say back to me, Dad? If you were here?" I try and picture him, standing in front of me. What he'd think about how it all ended. What he'd think about me not coming to say goodbye. I try to read his mind from across the vast emptiness of death and I'm not doing too well.

"Do you blame me?" I'd ask him that question first if he was here. "Because I blame me." I stand there as the cold wind picks up and then bend down to look closely at the various things people have left at the grave. There's a red and green wreath leftover from Christmas that says *I miss you*. The card is plastic and written in waterproof marker. It's in my mom's handwriting. She comes all the time, from the looks of it. How sad to lose the one person in life you loved the most. How does she get through her days?

How can she even look at me knowing that I was the one

who killed him?

I let out a long breath and turn away. There are no answers in this graveyard. Just me and my guilt and my sadness. I walk slowly back to the Bronco with my hands stuffed in my jeans and my head ducked into the wind. Ashleigh is in the backseat nursing. I smile at her as I get in, trying to push down the feelings that threaten to overwhelm me. "Someone's hungry?"

"Yeah," Ash says softly. "Me. I feel the need for gas station food. Can you wait a few more minutes while I finish up? Then I'll put her back in her seat and we can go."

"Yeah, sure." All I really want to do is get the fuck out of here, but babies have to take priority over my guilt, so I busy myself looking for music on my phone. "What bands do you like? I have no radio but I can make this hunk of shit play Spotify."

Ashleigh laughs. "You have a cassette player, Ford."

I reach over and open the glove box and pull out one of those contraptions you stick in the cassette deck so you can hook modern shit up to an old-ass car. "I'm an Eagle Scout, remember? I'm always prepared."

"Play something soft then. So she'll fall asleep." Soft. I do a quick search on my phone and come up with a playlist of classical music for babies. When it starts playing Brahms' *Lullaby* Ashleigh lets out a little sigh. "That's perfect."

"Yeah. It sorta is." I turn around and look at the baby. She's pink and a little bit sweaty in all her clothes and blankets. Her hair is very dark, like Ashleigh's, and I know her eyes are dark and not blue because I've seen them, but they are closed now as she suckles for a few seconds, then stops and just when I think she's really asleep, she suckles again. "What's her name? You never told me her name."

"You never asked," Ash says as she peeks up at me through her hair.

"I'm a dick, I know."

"Yeah, well, I'll cut you some slack because I get the feeling you're used to being on your own. Her name is Katelynn, like the two names put together and not the trendy spelling. But I call her Kate. Like the Duchess."

"Kate," I say as I turn back to pick out my dad's headstone in the small sea of markers popping up from the snow. "It's perfect. Very classic."

"Like the music," Ashleigh replies.

"Yeah," I say, looking back at Ash. She's got her eyes closed now—the baby's pushing her sleep button. I laugh a little at that and she opens her eyes for a moment, then they get heavy and drop again. "You want me to go? Or you need to put her back in the seat?"

"No," she says with her eyes still closed. "I'll put her back." And then she gently removes the baby from her breast and whispers soft things in her ear so she'll stay asleep when Ashleigh buckles her up. She climbs over the console, resting her hand on my shoulder for support, and plops down in the passenger seat. "Sorry, I forgot I can't touch you. It won't happen again."

I squint my eyes at that remark, wondering if it was a dig, but she just busies herself with her seatbelt and ignores me.

"OK, I hope you're happy. We're officially an hour behind schedule."

"Are we on a schedule?"

I look over at her as I start the engine. "Are *you* on a schedule?"

"Nope."

"Well, I have meetings every day this week, but fuck it. I missed today and I'll miss the rest most likely. But I'm not worried about it so we'll just do our thing and we'll get there when we get there."

Ashleigh smiles at me. "Sounds good to me." She turns her head to the window and tucks her legs up near her chest, like she's trying to curl up into a ball. And before I can get back onto the highway that will take us back to I-70, she's asleep.

I have to admit, I might like Ashleigh. She's assertive with me, and she was pretty pissed off this morning, but she's not a grudge-holder. She might be the opposite of me, actually. She's almost easy-going. And that's something considering how much stress she's probably under. She's small. She can't be any more than five foot two. And she's very blunt. She doesn't offer much, but every time I've asked, she's given me more than I'd give her. And she's not pushy. She did try to insist I come out here to the cemetery, but I doubt she'd have been mad for long if I refused. And whenever she gets the back-off vibe from me, she does exactly that. She gives me space. It almost makes me want her more when she pulls away like that.

So what is she? She might be a Complier. With conditions. Because she's kind of a Fighter too. But not a Grudge-holder. And she likes me, that I know for sure. She would not travel across four states with her infant baby if she didn't at least *like* me. And she's a Mother. I'm sorta digging that part of her. How she talks to the baby in that low whisper and the way she falls asleep when she's nursing. I like it.

Plus she keeps my mind off Rook.

And maybe it's wrong to use her like that, but I'm having a hard time feeling bad about it right now.

TWENTY-ONE

The girls sleep all the way to Grand Junction. I almost want to wake Ashleigh so she can see the drive because it's really breathtaking, but I guess if she was interested in it, she'd try to stay awake.

"I can't believe you're still listening to this music, Ford," she says as she tries to pull herself out of her slumber in the Wal-Mart parking lot.

"I barely noticed it. My mother played this kind of stuff for me all growing up. Said it was calming." I look over at her and I can tell she likes it when I talk about personal things because her mouth forms this half-smile and her eyes open a little wider. "And it is. Put the two of you to sleep."

She stares are me with that half-smile for a moment longer, probably waiting to see if I'll elaborate. Then decides I won't and sits up straight. "You were messing with me earlier, right? About never being in a Wal-Mart before?"

"I grew up in Denver, Ash. Not Beverly Hills. We shopped at the Wal-Mart every week."

"Well, sometimes you're so serious, it's hard to tell when you're joking. What are we getting, anyway? Snacks or something?"

"Yes, and baby things. I'm sick of looking at her stupid footied sleepers." I open my door and get out and Ashleigh does the same, then unbuckles and grabs the carrier from the back seat. "And what's the deal with that thing anyway? It's such a pain in the ass to buckle that seat in every time we get back in the truck."

"I have two at home, but I only brought one."

She blows out a long breath of air and looks up at the sky as we walk towards the store entrance together. It's snowing a little but it looks like the storm's coming from the southeast this time, which means it'll swirl around once the tail end hits the mountains and head east again, so we should be fine heading west. "Were you in a hurry when you left?" We grab a cart and she puts the carrier in the back this time.

"Sorta."

And that's all I get. Just *sorta*.

She heads over to the baby clothes, doing her best to ignore me.

"Are people missing you? I mean, you have family, right?"

"What's with all the questions? I'm not prying into your personal problems." She sorts through some baby clothes and then gravitates to the footied sleeper and starts flipping through the rack.

I look at the stuff nearest me. Car seats. "We should get another car seat. Then we won't need to keep taking this one in and out."

She stops looking through the clothes and stares at me.

"What?"

"What's with this *we* stuff all of a sudden?"

Her words are like a slap. "Just thought you could use another one to make life easier, Ashleigh. Believe me, I'm not about to start playing daddy to your kid. So relax."

She throws some sleepers in the cart and I grab a few other

articles of clothing the same size that do not have built-in socks, and follow her over to the diapers. She puts two large packages on the bottom of the cart, and then wheels us into the next aisle where she grabs a few small toys, a bib, and some baby wipes. There is like a shitload of crap you can buy for babies and if I was the one shopping, I'd be stuck in this aisle forever trying to decide what to get.

"OK, I'm done," she says in a curt manner.

"Are you mad?"

"No, I'm just done." She turns the cart and begins walking up towards the front to check out.

"Done with me apparently."

I get silence. And she stays that way as we check out. I grab a handful of snacks and drinks in the line, then pay for everything and we head out to the truck.

"I'll pay you back for all this stuff, Ford. But thanks for taking care of it right now."

"Do you have money?"

"Not on me, which is why I'll have to pay you back."

"Do you normally have money?"

"Wow, that was rude. Of course I have money. Do I look like some sort of homeless trash? I'm not, OK? I just needed to figure some stuff out and I couldn't do it from home."

"Where's home? Texas?"

"No, I said I came from Texas. And I did. Because I had to see someone there before I could go to LA."

"To see your ex?" I say as I unlock the truck and start piling things in.

"Just stop." She grabs my arm and waits for me to turn and look at her. "Stop prying. I'm not talking about it. You have your problems and I have mine. Let's just leave it at that."

She puts the baby in the back and I get in and wait for her to finish. It's snowing a little more now. "Hurry, we need to move west quick before this storm catches up with us and we get stuck somewhere else."

She climbs in the backseat and closes the door. "I'm gonna sit back here in case she wakes up and needs to nurse."

"We'll have to pull over for that anyway, though, right? So why sit in back?" She doesn't answer but I don't need one either. She's avoiding me. "I'll try and drive through to Vegas, then we can stop there and rest."

"Sounds good to me."

I get back on the freeway but I was right. We just need to pull over a half hour later so she can nurse when the baby wakes up. There's nothing out here in the way of services, but there's a turn-out near the sign that says *Welcome to Utah*. I mess with the music playlist on my phone and try to pretend that her ignoring me isn't an issue. But it is.

"You know," I say once she's settled with the feeding, "I'm not sure why you're mad at me, but it's childish. All I did was ask a question about who might be missing you. Believe me, Ashleigh, I'm not into prying into the personal lives of others. So you can stop worrying that I give a shit. OK? I don't. It was fucking small talk." I flip through Spotify on my phone and look for some music. "Who do you like to listen to? I'll put something on so we don't have to sit in silence."

"Here," she says with her hand out. "I'll find something."

I unplug the phone from the wires that connect it to the cassette player and hand it back to her. "Then will you get in the front with me again? I cross my heart, I won't be interested in you at all."

She grunts a little at that but doesn't say anything. Her expression is almost sad as she looks through the music. Her fingers fly around the touch screen and then she hands it back. "There, that's a good playlist."

I plug it back in and look over her selection as the music starts. "The Naked and Famous. Never heard of them."

"I'm not sure you count, Ford. No offense, but you're sorta on the outskirts of fringe as far as pop culture goes."

"Why would I possibly be offended?" I turn back in my seat

and just look outside. "We've wasted the whole fucking day. It's almost dark now." She's still in a mood so I get the silent treatment as the music plays. "This stuff is sorta sad, don't you think?"

More silence. More sad music. More baby slurping noses. More darkness creeps in as the sun sets to the west. I'm about to lose my mind and insist that she come up front when I hear the sniffling. Like she's trying to cover up sobs.

Fucking girls.

I wait it out and then the baby cries a little as she's put back into the seat and I let out a long sigh of relief when the back door opens.

"Come to your senses?" But when I turn to watch her get in the front with me all I see is her back, walking off into the wilds of fucking Utah. I lower the window on the passenger side and yell, "Ashleigh! What the fuck are you doing?"

The baby does not care for my screaming one bit and decides she's having none of it. I lean back and rock her seat a little. "Shhhh," I tell her, like I've seen Ash do it. That fucking girl. What the hell is going on?

I turn the music off and start the engine. Ash has stopped walking away, and that's a good sign, but she's on her knees now, like she can't take it anymore. I put the truck in four-wheel drive and plow down the small embankment, then drive slowly out towards Ashleigh. I keep the engine running and turn the heat on a little higher since the sun's about to set and that means a sudden drop in temperature up here at this altitude.

I check Kate real fast, but she's got her eyes closed, so I get out and close the door quietly. I walk a few paces towards Ashleigh and stop. "You OK?"

Dumb question. Obviously, she is not OK.

I walk a few more paces and shove my freezing hands into my pockets. Ash is only wearing one of my zippered hoodies— her winter coat was discarded when she started nursing. She's got to be fucking cold. I cross the distance between us and I can hear small muffled sobs.

TAUT

"Ash," I say when I get directly behind her. "Come on, it's cold out here. We can talk about it in the truck if you want."

"I don't," she snaps. "I do not want to talk about it." And then a full-fledged sob erupts and she bends over at the waist and presses her head to the frozen ground as she cries.

Fuck. I have no idea what to do.

"Ashleigh, get up. We don't have time for this."

She shakes her head and sobs harder.

I kneel down behind her and pull her up off the ground. "You're freezing." I wrap my arms around her upper body and pull her against my chest. She's trying very hard to stop crying because she's holding her breath, but that just makes it worse because her sobs escape eventually, only now she's on the verge of hyperventilating. I can't ask her what's the matter because she's not interested in talking about it. And she's clearly not ready to get up off the ground.

So now what?

My mind races for an answer as her cries become more and more desperate-sounding. She is in full-on life-sucks mode.

"Ashleigh, I don't know what to do for you. Just get in the truck with me."

She shakes her head. "It can't be fixed, Ford. Nothing will ever be better again."

I guess she's talking about her ex, but fuck, I have zero information on this girl beyond the fact that she's not anywhere close to home and she's got nothing but a baby going for her right now.

"I don't know what's going on with you. You've told me nothing. Is it bad?" I get a nod this time. That's something. "The kind of bad that just makes you want to move away and never talk to anyone again?"

She's silent for a moment, then she lifts her head a little. "No, Ford. The kind of bad that makes you want to curl up and die."

I'm not an emotional guy. I mean, I get what she's saying, but even after my dad died, I never wanted to like, kill myself

260

or anything. I have a strong sense of self-preservation. And I suppose that's why I don't always put others first. I don't really know how to put others first, but I'm good at manipulating people, so I figure I need to distract her. Take her mind off her fucked-up life and redirect her somewhere else.

"I have never been to that place, Ashleigh. But I have had my share of fucked-up times. A couple years ago I tried to fall off the face of the Earth and lose myself in work that took me as far away from Colorado as I could get. But the shit always catches up with you. In my case I lost a girl I liked, she died of an overdose. I almost got in a lot of trouble for something I did with some friends of mine, and then my dad..." She leans into me a little as soon as that word leaves my mouth. "My dad was killed in a..." I laugh for a second. "I was gonna lie and say a terrible accident, but it wasn't an accident and everyone knows it."

"What happened?" she asks, turning a little so she can try and look at me.

Mission accomplished. I should just get her in the truck right now and stop this conversation before it starts.

But the trip to the cemetery has opened up something inside of me. Something that says I made a lot of mistakes after my dad's death and it's time to get over it. "Stay still now. I'm trying to keep you warm since you insist on falling to pieces outside in the dead of winter." She doesn't stay still, in fact she turns all the way around and presses her face to my chest. I unzip my jacket and try and wrap it around her as best I can. Her arms reach under my coat and circle my waist. Her hands are cold, but it makes me feel warm.

And then, before I even have time to reconsider... that shit just comes pouring out.

"I loved skiing. Fucking loved it. It's like, fuck. That sport consumed me. Every weekend in the winter I was in Vail skiing. When I bought this Bronco in tenth grade, I'd ditch school early on Friday so I could get in some afternoon runs. My parents never really cared about that, they encouraged me in pretty much everything I did. And my dad and I, we were so much alike. I was definitely less socially astute—he had a ton of friends and I've never had any, not really. Just Ronin and Spencer, the guys I keep calling back in Denver. But most of it was business and that was college.

"But my dad and I were like brothers born a generation apart. He was smart, not freaky smart like me, but just so intelligent. And he was good at all the stuff I liked to do. Skiing, running… all of it. So one day we were gonna hit the slopes in Vail. But I needed some new gear and we always get it from a shop in Copper. A friend of the family owns it. My dad and I went in there to get me some poles and I bumped into a couple of guys I knew from competition days back in high school. And they were gonna ski some backcountry nearby, just up Loveland Pass."

I stop to lean down and whisper into her neck. "It was fucking Loveland, Ashleigh. It's like our back fucking yard. It's less than an hour from Denver. I've been skiing these slopes since I was seven. It was fucking *Loveland*. My dad and I did that backcountry run a few times in my teens. This wasn't some virgin cliff in Alaska. It wasn't some run you gotta sign a fatality release form for up in the Tetons. I could see the goddamned highway when we started."

She looks up at me with her red face, chapped and dry from the cold and wind. "Tell me the rest."

I stare out at the setting sun, a bright orange outlining the mountains off in the distance. "I saw it. We *all* saw it. There was a crack in the snow near the summit. But the accumulation the night before wasn't heavy, just a few inches, so we took a vote and it was a go. We hiked up, put on our skis, and I went first.

"I can see it clearly in my mind. Pulling my goggles over my eyes, looking back at my dad as he gave me a thumbs up. And then the rush of taking off in that fresh powder. Everyone followed me, my dad second, then the other guys, but I was way out in front—just hitting that shit hard.

"I triggered the avalanche. My route is what did it. I loosened the slab, heard the crack as it pulled away from the base. And then everyone I came up that mountain with was dead. I was the only one who lived. I didn't even get buried. I skied off to the side and watched the whole fucking thing happen right in front of my eyes. I saw the look on their faces as they tumbled, then there was nothing but white."

The only noise I hear is the idling engine of the truck behind us. Ashleigh says nothing.

"We all had beacons. Hell, we all know the dangers—we were all very experienced skiers. So we all had beacons and packs with probes and shovels. Just in case. That's like famous last words, right? Just in case."

I stop and take a deep breath as I picture it all in my head again. "And if you're in an avalanche and you're not buried, you switch your beacon from transmit to receive. So I switched it to receive and I got my dad's signal. We had a high-end system with W-link. The other guys had regular beacons, no W-link. There's a big difference in how you read these signals. So I knew which signal was my dad and I hauled ass down to where it was emitting and started probing and digging.

"We both know how it ends, obviously. But I watched him die on my transceiver." I look down at Ashleigh and she's staring up at my face, all thoughts of whatever it was that was bothering her gone as she listens to my story. "W-link detects the movement created by a beating heart." Her face crumples a little. "He was buried seven feet deep. I got about four feet of snow removed when his heart stopped."

She climbs up my lap and wraps her arms around me and pushes her face into my neck.

And I let her, because fuck it. I like it. She's warm and her body is soft. She feels good to me and I probably feel good to her too.

"I'm so sorry, Ford."

"That's not the worst of it."

I stop again, because I've never talked about the accident

afterward. Not even to rescue officials. I'm trained to say nothing if I'm questioned by authorities because of all the jobs I did with Spencer and Ronin. So when it came time to talk to the ski patrol I just shut the fuck up because I had no Ronin to talk for me. We weren't even on speaking terms back then.

"I knew where all the other guys were in that group. I could see all their signals on my transceiver. Their beacons didn't transmit movement, and my dad's did. So I clearly knew which signal belonged to my dad and which ones belonged to them. And even though I was a lot closer to every one of those guys, and the signals were stronger so they were probably closer to the surface, I decided to dig out my dad instead."

"Ford—"

I squeeze her a little to make her stop. "Don't bother. My mom has already said it multiple times. Everyone said it over and over. But none of them were there. If I could dig down four feet, I could've dug down three and saved Rob. Or four feet and saved Steve. He was practically right next to Rob. I could've saved two people that day if I was rational, but instead I let everyone die because I decided to try and save my dad instead. Hell, I'm the one who caused the fucking slide in the first place. So you can tell yourself I didn't kill them, but I absolutely did. Maybe it wasn't intentional, but it hardly matters to the families left behind, does it?"

Ashleigh has nothing to say to that. And I don't blame her. There's nothing to say.

She starts shivering uncontrollably and I haul both our asses up off the frozen ground and lead her back to the truck by the hand. When I open her door the heat rushes out and I check Kate real fast. She's still asleep so I go around to my side and get in.

"I'm sorry," Ashleigh whispers. "It sucks. And there's really nothing anyone can say to make it better. It just… sucks."

I navigate us back onto the highway. It's fully dark now, just the headlights out in front to break the black that surrounds us. There are no streetlights here. There are no cars behind us and several minutes can go by before another car comes from the west heading towards us.

"I'm lonely," Ashleigh says with a sigh. "It's dark and empty here and that's exactly how I feel right now."

"You have Kate," I offer up. But it's a half-hearted attempt because I feel the exact same way. Everything sucks right now. I have nothing. At least she has a baby that needs her, depends on her for everything and loves her back.

Ashleigh rubs her eyes to stop the new tears. "I know, and I should be thankful about that. Things can always get worse, so I should just shut the fuck up and be happy with what I have." She looks back at her daughter and I know she's crying again, just silently this time. "But I'm so far from satisfied I just want to curl up in a dark corner and die. Because part of making a family is getting to experience life with the person you love. You know?" She looks over at me but I have nothing to say. What do I say? "And I don't have that anymore. So who gives a shit about her but me? Who do I celebrate all her firsts with?"

"Your parents? His parents?"

"My mom's dead and my father—" She snorts a little at the mention of her dad. "He's ashamed of me. And Tony's parents absolutely hate me. They've never even seen her."

"What? Haven't they seen a picture?" I don't get this.

Ashleigh shakes her head. "No, nothing. It's like…" She stops and looks out into the darkness for a few seconds. "It's like no one even cares about me. And I think…" She stops again to try and swallow down whatever it is she's feeling. "I think I'd be OK with that, if I just had *him*, ya know? I could live with all the rest of it if we were in it together. Is that how you feel about Rook? Like, you could give it all another shot and live through the next day if she was with you?"

Is that how I feel? "No," I conclude. "No, actually, that's not how I feel about her at all. I just want her around. I like her company. I want to try normal things with her, like—well, just normal things."

"Oh." This defeats Ash and she turns away from me and faces the darkness again. But I can still see her reflection in the window from the dim dashboard lights.

"She's pretty though, she's a model."

"Figures," Ashleigh snorts. "You're handsome, Ford, I'm sure your girlfriends are all beautiful, so I'm not surprised."

I'm not even sure what to say in response. I've never had an actual girlfriend and I've never had a conversation with a girl about this kind of stuff. Hell, I might never've had this kind of conversation with *anyone* about this stuff. "Well, she used to be a model, now she's an out-of-work reality show receptionist. But she doesn't need the money. Ronin has enough to keep her happy forever, I suppose."

"What's Ronin do?"

"He's a model too."

Ash snorts loudly this time. "You're totally fucking with me."

I laugh a little. "No, really. He lives this life straight out of Cinderella, only he's the fucking long lost princess. I don't get it. It's not fair to get handed things so easily."

"My sister's like that. She's got everything. My father gave her a position in the company a few years ago. She's older than me. Taller, skinnier, prettier, smarter, *politer*. And she's got this perfect husband." Ashleigh stops to stick her finger in her mouth and pretend to gag. "And she never got pregnant out of wedlock, so that's like the golden ticket to everything as far as my father's concerned."

"Yeah, but you have Kate, so you win."

She looks over to me and smiles through her tears. "I do have her, so I do win."

A sign for an upcoming town passes by on the road. "We should just stop for the night. It's not late, but I'm ready to get the fuck out of this truck, how about you?"

"I don't care what we do, Ford. I'm happy to put off the inevitable forever, I think. I'm not even sure I want to go see him now anyway. It's not like anything will change. Nothing will change. I'll still be alone in the end."

"Let's forget about LA for tonight." I pull off at Green River and turn into the first decent-looking hotel they have. There's not much to choose from, but it will have to do because life just needs to stop for a little while. Just be still and let us breathe.

TWENTY-TWO

The hotel lobby is large and clean. That's always a plus. It's locally owned, not a chain. And that's not always a plus.

Ashleigh and the baby are standing next to me at the counter. "Single or double?" the clerk asks.

"Single," I say. I look at Ashleigh from the corner of my eye to see if she's gonna contradict me, but she doesn't.

"Do you need a crib?"

Now I do have to look at her. "Do we need a crib?"

"You seem to be the one calling the shots, why stop now?"

I squint at her, trying to decide if this is her way of being mad, but I can't tell. "No," I say to the clerk. "We've gotten by without one so far, why change what's working."

"We've gotten by on separate beds too."

The clerk raises her eyebrows at us. "Do you want two beds? We have a room available."

"No," I say before Ashleigh can. "We're fine with the single."

Ashleigh wanders off after that and after the clerk hands us the key card, I grab her numerous shopping bags filled with clothing and crap. We meet up again at the elevator, get in, and she presses the button for the fourth floor.

"So…" she starts as we ascend. "One bed. What's up with that?"

I look right at her. "Exactly what you think is up with that, Ashleigh."

"You mean you might actually fuck me tonight?" She's got a devious grin on her face.

"Probably not."

"*What?*"

The doors open and I wave her through. "That's it," she says as we walk down the hall to our room. "I'm done with you. I'm drawing a line down the middle of the bed and if you so much as put your big toe over on my side, I'll kiss you on the lips."

I use the card to open our room, then flick the lights on and wave her in. "If your lips come in contact with mine, I'll bite. I'm warning you now."

She puts the baby down and starts taking off her snowsuit. "I might take my chances anyway."

I set the clothes on the little table. "Let's go out to eat. Don't undress her."

"No, I need to feed her." She rubs her breasts and winces a little. "They hurt because I didn't give her enough time when we were on the road. I need to nurse or they'll start leaking."

Holy fucking shit. I just got insta-hard. "*Leaking?*"

"Mmmm-hmmm," she says seductively as she squishes them together a little. Little wet spots appear through her t-shirt. "Oops." She looks up at me, smiling. "I leaked."

"Leaked?" My eyes are still on her hands as she plays with herself.

"I guess I'll have to change my shirt." She whips it over her head and throws it across the room. Her pink bra also has little wet spots on it. "Oh, darn. My bra's wet too." She unhooks the clasp between her breasts and they fall free as she takes it off.

She's fucking leaking all right. That shit is practically

dripping.

She grabs the baby, takes her over to a chair and plops down. Kate is half-asleep but she accepts the nipple and begins to eat. "I'm sorry, Ford. Were you saying something about going out for dinner? I'd love to actually. I'll be done in a minute."

"You're *evil*."

She laughs.

"I'm not sure it's funny. I might have a fetish."

"Oh, you mean like tying girls up and posing them in front of windows? That kind of fetish? Or spanking them until they cry? You have quite the assortment of fetishes, Ford. I'm not sure leaking breasts even qualify."

"You enjoyed all of that. You let me pose you in front of the window and you admitted to enjoying the spankings."

"I did like it. The exhibitionism more than the swats, just FYI. In fact, I think you should pose me in front of this window right now." She grins an *I win* smile. Because right now I realize she *did* know that no one could see her in the window up at the Vail house. Maybe she didn't realize it at that moment, but she's on to me now.

"Maybe I will."

"Go for it. But I'll get another question."

Now it's my turn to grin. "I paid you forward today. I told you how my dad died. I've never told anyone that story."

Her smile falters at this revelation. "No one?"

I shake my head. "Not even my mother. Not even the lawyers. I'm not allowed to talk to the police. Only Ronin is allowed to talk to the police, this is part of the business we have together. So I never gave a statement."

"Can't they *make* you give a statement?"

"Nope. They could arrest me if they suspected foul play, but they didn't. It was a tragedy and no one wanted to make it worse. Besides, we were all locals. There was too much pain to worry about me. They know I'm a freak. My weird behavior afterward just confirmed it."

TAUT

She's quiet for a few seconds and then she lifts her eyes and stares at me with a small smile. I can't believe I didn't think she was beautiful when I first met her, because right now, I've never seen a more stunning girl. Sitting here with her baby like that. I just… fuck. I don't know. I like it. And it's not the nursing, although I suspect that's part of it. She's got some sort of glow to her.

"I think that town loves you, Ford. I think they care about you and were happy to see you come home. I think they worried about you. I didn't hear anyone call you a freak. They thought you were adorable. Even Mrs. Pearson. She told me all about your childhood up on the mountain. You were quite the troublemaker, and she had this feigned annoyance to all her stories, but to me, she relived your antics like she was fond of you. Like you gave that town life when you were there."

I just stare at her. For like half a minute at least. Because Ashleigh just told me something I've been dying to hear my whole life. "I got one bed because I want you next to me tonight. Touching me. Not sexually, I'd never do that with the baby in the room. But just… give it a try."

"Well." She giggles a little. "I was not expecting that. I'm up for some sixth-grade heavy petting if you are. I'll walk you through it, step by step. From knee-rubbing to hand-holding, I'll be your teacher."

Fucking Ashleigh. "Knee-rubbing?"

"Yeah, you know, when you sit next to a girl and you bump your leg against hers and then you both get all tingly."

I shake my head. "That has never happened."

"Why? Because you had them bent over with their asses in the air? Or because you never felt that shocking excitement with a girl before?"

"Am I really having this conversation?"

"Yes. So tell me. Was it because you never got the chance or because you've just never found a girl who makes you excited like that? And I'm not talking hard-ons," she says, nodding to my dick. This makes me laugh. "I'm talking that spark that says *this one's different*. You said you were into this Rook girl, if that's true, then you should've felt that feeling."

I think about this for a moment. "I liked her. I wanted to kiss her."

"Oh, you might fatally wound me with that admission!"

"I would've kissed her if she let me. But not when she's with Ronin. I can't do that. He's too important."

"Well, maybe that's as close as you get then?" She shrugs and then notices the baby is asleep. She stands up and gently puts her in the middle of the bed. "I have to express this one," she says pointing to the breast that got no baby attention. "I'm dying here. Be right back."

And then she walks off to the bathroom topless to *express*.

I'm insta-hard again. I want to go in there and give her a helping hand, but I stay put and breathe. Fucking Ashleigh.

"Ford?" she calls from the bathroom.

"Yeah," I answer back.

"That was your cue to get your ass in here and fuck me."

I laugh and get up and go stand in the doorway. "I'm not fucking you, Ashleigh. I don't even have condoms with me. Besides, I like watching you, so I'll enjoy the view and you go ahead."

She raises her eyebrows at me. "You want me to get myself off in front of you?"

"Why are you talking to me like this? You were so sweet when we met and now you're all into the dirty talk."

She leans over the sink and squeezes until the milk shoots out. It even makes a squirting sound. "I'm just trying my best to make you interested, that's all. If you want me to stop, I will."

I walk up behind her and lean down so I can talk in her ear. "Just slow down and be patient."

She turns around so she can look up at my face. "I think once you figure me out, you won't like me anymore. So I want to rush into it and then maybe you won't run away when we get to LA."

"Why would I run away?"

She swallows and looks down, like she feels defeated. "Because I'm a mess, Ford."

I pull her towards me and put my arms around her bare back dragging a single finger up and down her spine "You seem pretty together to me, Ashleigh." She shivers from my touch and I stop.

"No," she says softly. "Don't stop. I like it."

I use two fingers this time, tracing the vertebrae of her spine. Her back buckles slightly and she gasps. "Does it hurt?" I ask.

She pulls back and looks up at me. "Hurt? No, it feels so good I almost can't stand it."

I squint my eyes as I try to imagine how she interprets these sensations, and then I flinch when her finger traces a line down my arm.

"Does it hurt *you*?" Ashleigh asks, her eyes trained on mine.

Do I want her to know me like this? Do I want her to know that I'm a freak, in the strictest definition of the word? Is this what intimacy entails? Baring your weaknesses to someone who might take advantage, but trusting them not to?

I let out a long breath. "Yeah. It fucking hurts." Her finger pulls back but I catch her tiny wrist in my hand and study her face for a reaction. She's listening, that's all. Just listening. "I can stop it from hurting. It only takes a second, but my brain is wired wrong. Everything hurts until I tell it not to."

"Oh shit, Ford. I'm sorry. I didn't understand that."

I shrug. "You wanted to know why I had to see so many doctors? It wasn't for the Asperger's, it was for this whole no touching thing. It took a really long time for someone to believe me. I'd tell them over and over again, *just stop fucking touching me and I'll be fine.* But they never believed me because they could never find the cause of it. My dad was the only one who thought it was an actual physical response and not just some strange psychosis. And those fucking doctors all just wanted to poke me over and over again. It was like torture."

"But it's better now?" Ashleigh asks.

"Mostly," I say impassively. "I didn't really understand myself until high school. That's when things started to make sense. I caught up with my mind and was able to take control. The touching is not a big deal these days. I'm good at turning off the pain. I only feel it briefly if I'm touched unexpectedly. If I see it coming, I process it just fine."

"And then it feels good?" She's watching me, very carefully. I can almost see her mind working, putting the pieces of me together in a way that makes sense.

"Well, it's a fine line between pain and pleasure and as you know, my line might be microscopic."

She smirks out a laugh between her lips. "Well, that kind of explains a lot about you Ford."

"Yeah, this pain pleasure thing has consumed me my whole life. It's the only thing I thought about as a kid. And I wasn't bullied or anything, I'm far too vicious and devious to put up with that shit, but I walked through childhood afraid of people finding out how easy it was to hurt me."

"So how do you tell the difference? Doesn't it get all mixed up in there? Inside your brain?"

"I just choose to experience one sensation and not the other." I turn her around until she's facing the mirror and then I grasp her nipple between my thumb and forefinger. I don't squeeze, just hold it gently. "Let me show you." My other hand follows the curve of her hip, unbuttons her pants, and then slides down her lower belly. "Tell me what you feel, OK?" She nods as my fingertips dip down between her legs and find her folds. I press against her, but at the same time I squeeze her nipple hard and then release.

"Ow!" She laughs out the word. "Well, that was painful."

I smile at myself in the mirror and she catches me and makes a face. "Let's try it again," I whisper down into her ear. Her pussy floods with wetness and becomes slick around my fingers. I play with her a little more forcefully and this time she moans. I rub it faster, then dip my mouth down, nip her earlobe, and then squeeze her nipple.

This time she actually comes. Whimpering, and moaning, and pressing herself into my chest.

Fucking Ashleigh.

"You need to learn how to play hard to get, Ash. You're perpetually on the cusp of explosion."

She slumps against me, languishing in her moment. "Ford, the promise of your full sexual attention is just about the highlight of my life right now, why pretend?"

Holy shit, this fucking girl!

"I pinched it much harder that time but all you felt was the pleasure. I'm pretty good at that. I hardly ever hurt the girls when I'm paying attention, so I'm sorry I hurt you the other night. I was off my game." She's still relaxed against my chest, her legs a little wobbly, so I turn her around, lift her up, and set her on the bathroom counter. "Will that hold you over for a while? And you can stop pestering me for a fuck?"

She looks up, watching me intently. "It's a good start."

TWENTY-THREE

Green River, Utah is not known for its varied selection of restaurants, so we settle on a tavern that looks like Billy the Kid might've eaten here back in the day. It's either this or Arby's. It's quiet since it's Monday night, but you can just tell it's the local hangout on the weekends. There's fliers on the wall advertising a band called Scuffed Boots and a jukebox playing some kind of pop country music.

"Does she sit up yet?" I ask Ashleigh of Kate as she wedges the car seat between the table and the back of the booth. "When do they sit in real chairs?"

She looks at me like I'm an idiot. "Real chairs? Like in a booth and not a high chair? Maybe three years if she has a booster seat."

"Years?" Man, I have no clue and thankfully I get ignored. We order the burgers when the waitress comes since that's the only thing this place serves. "I could go for some sushi. When we get to Vegas, we're going out for sushi."

"I have to admit, it was kinda fun being in the middle of nowhere at first. But it's getting old. How long to get to Vegas from here?"

I pull up my map app and punch it in the phone. "Says six hours with light traffic. If we leave early we'll be there a little after noon, then we can go out and have some fun."

She points to Kate. "I'm with her, sorry."

"We can get a sitter at the hotel."

"Hmmm, I'm not sure. How do we know they're trustworthy?"

I flash her a sideways glance as I look out the window. "Let me take care of that. I'll make sure. Won't be too hard, and I don't even need my own computer to dig for that shit."

Her mouth makes a little O shape and she squints her eyes. "I forgot about that."

"What?"

"Your comment about hacking into the DMV and the Vail people talking about your criminal past."

"I told you, I have no criminal record."

"Yeah, but criminal record and criminal past aren't the same thing."

Yeah, this girl—she misses *nothing*. "I was a troublemaker as a kid, I already told you."

"And the DMV hacking? That was childhood pranks too?"

I chuckle a little. She's not gonna let it go, so screw it. "I have some skills."

"So that's what you do huh? You're some kind of computer expert?"

"No—I mean, yes. I do do that. But that's not what I *do*. I'm a film producer."

"What? No. You're an inside trader, surely?" She smirks at me and I kick her under the table until she giggles.

"I just finished a reality show that starred Rook and my other best friend Spencer. He owns Shrike Bikes, ever heard of them?"

Her mouth gapes open. "Wait, your best friends are Ronin the model and Spencer fucking Shrike, the hot-ass biker whose show will be on TV next month? The one the Biker Channel's been advertising non-stop since November?"

"What? He's not hot. I'm hot. He's lame. He paints Elvis costumes on naked girls. I make films. I produced that show. In fact, I'm in most of the episodes in Season One."

She smiles coyly as she sighs. "I'm wet, Ford."

I beam at her.

"I can't believe you know Spencer Shrike. You should introduce me."

"What?"

"Kidding, you jealous nerd. That's pretty cool though. I pegged you as a banker when I saw you in that suit on New Year's. But since then you've only wore jeans and t-shirts. And after you talked about skiing, I conjured up an image of you as some kind of X-Gamer. But now... I'm not sure anymore. Who are you, Ford Aston?"

The waitress comes with our food so I wait to answer her question until she's gone and we're both eating. "Maybe I'm both of those guys. I do normally wear suits. I like to look professional. People treat you differently when you wear a suit. When I wear casual clothes the weirdness seems to stick out. Or maybe people just make quick judgments instead of giving me the benefit of the doubt because I appear wealthy."

"That's very rational, Ford. But if I were you, I'd wear the shit that makes your package look big." She takes a big bite of burger to hide her smile.

"I hope you realize I'm gonna get even with you for all this dirty talk."

"Oh, I'm counting on it," she says with her mouth full. "I'll agree to a background-checked babysitter in Vegas if you stop by the drug store and buy some condoms. How's that?" She flashes me an exaggerated wink.

"Wink all you want, Miss—wait, what's your last name?"

"Li," she says with her mouth full again.

"Li? Your name is Ashleigh Li?" I laugh a little at her expense. Serves her right. "Whose bright idea was that?"

"I know, tell me about it. My name was originally Ash Li in

Hong Kong, it was like a cute play on the spelling—of course, it's not Chinese at all and now that I think about it, it kinda made me sound like a porn star. Plus everyone still knew I was American, so stupid, right? And then when we moved back to the US my parents changed it so it was less Chinese, and maybe less porn star. And now I'm Ashleigh Li." She rolls her eyes and bites into a French fry. "I can't wait to get married."

We sit and eat in silence for a while, maybe both of us thinking about how nice Ashleigh would sound in front of Aston.

"So anyway, back to the condoms."

Or maybe that's not what we were thinking after all. I grin at her. "I'm still in control and as long as you keep asking for it, I'll never give in. So keep it to yourself and let me handle things."

"But you're slow."

"You owe me so big for all this unladylike behavior, your ass cheeks will be bright red when I'm done. Don't think I'm not adding it all up. I have a photographic memory."

"Wait. We never had an agreement about unladylike behavior. I have *no* spankings coming."

I laugh. "Miss Li, you have no idea what you've been begging for. And if you want it, then you owe me an entire night of submission." She bites her lip and tries not to smile. "You're smiling now, but just wait."

She just takes another bite of her food and then leans in to coo at Kate when she starts to fuss in her seat.

"When do they crawl?" I ask.

She leans down and kisses Kate on the nose and gets a smile and some feet kicking for her effort. "Crawl?" She looks up and thinks. "Six months maybe. Why?"

I lean back in the booth and stretch my arms out as I study them together. Ashleigh might be a mess. And this road trip of hers was probably a monumentally bad idea. But she's not neglectful of her daughter. "I guess I never thought about how needy babies are."

She shoots me a dirty look.

"Not in a bad way, just a literal way."

Ash puts her hand gently over Kate's head. "They are the most helpless creatures on the whole planet when they're born." And then Ash looks up at me and smiles. "She changed my whole life. You might not realize this, but I was a little bit on the wild side a year and a half ago." She gently tickles Kate's little chin and gets some arm-flailing this time.

"Yeah, I can see it."

Ashleigh straightens up and grabs some fries. I'm not sure if she wants to be wild or calm, so I prod. "But you can be calm when you want to."

"Which do you like better?" She watches me, studies me almost. Her eyes go to my hand draped casually across the top of the booth, then traverse my arm, my chest. Finally her heated gaze stops on my face. Like she's seeing me in a different light right this very moment.

"Calm," I say softly.

"I like you wild."

I laugh. "You are a silly shit."

"No, really though," she says. "I like you when you've got the walls down. When you're just you."

"When have you seen me without walls?"

"When you told me about your dad."

"I told you the story, but not how it felt. So I still had all the walls up."

Her smile falters and her eyes get a little sad. "I don't need to be told how that feels. Your walls are transparent, so even if you still have them up, I can see through them. And a glimpse is all I need. I know that feeling."

"You done eating?"

"Yes, but that's a deflection. I don't mind, don't get me wrong. You can deflect all you want because deflection is my friend these days as well. And to pay you back for telling me that story when I was outside losing my shit, I'll be calm tonight just for you." And then she smiles. It's not big, but it's genuine. It's warm and it says a lot of things. It says *I trust you tonight. I might not trust you tomorrow, but tonight I'll be good because you want me to.*

"Then I win."

She smiles bigger this time and looks down at Kate. "You do win, because you've got *both* of us."

TWENTY-FOUR

I play her words back in my mind as we drive down the road to the hotel. I have them both.

I do. For now. I have their complete undivided attention. But as soon as we get to LA, she's going back to her ex. I can feel it. She loves him. She wants her baby's father to be a part of her life. She wants it so bad she falls apart just thinking about raising this child alone.

And I don't think she's afraid of that. I'm getting the impression Ashleigh comes from money. Maybe some serious money. Your father doesn't do business in Hong Kong for a dozen years without having a significant position. And she said straight out he gave her sister a job in his company.

No. Ashleigh isn't worried about money. She's not stressing out about babysitters and health care. She's lonely. She wants a partner. She wants to share the joys of parenting with someone who loves that baby just as much as her. And I'm not sure what's going on with the ex. Maybe he's an asshole. Maybe he cheated. Maybe he did all sorts of stuff. But if he takes her back—there's just no way I can compete with that.

Why the fuck am I thinking about this? I'm not even interested in being with her like that. I want to fuck her, under certain conditions. But she's very vulnerable and she might jump to conclusions. I'm not looking for a girlfriend, let alone a partner. No. The only girl I've ever wanted that with is Rook.

We don't talk on the way up to the room. The baby babbles a little and Ashleigh whispers to her about things. Lights, potted plants in the corners, the music in the lobby. The slamming of a door and the ding of the elevator. She explains each stimulus with soft words and a smile.

I turn on the bedside lamps instead of the overhead light and then Ash takes off Kate's snow gear and settles herself in the chair again. Gone is the teasing about sex. Now she's exactly like she promised me she would be. Calm.

"Thanks for packing me some stuff," I say as I grab my toothbrush. "I'm gonna jump in the shower."

"I'm gonna fall asleep," she says without opening her eyes.

I watch her for a second. Her body is totally relaxed and I envy her a little because I don't think I've ever been that comfortable in a strange place. Hell, maybe not even in my own home. But she's here, in a hotel, in Middle of Nowhere, Utah… and it's like home to her. It's almost like everywhere is home for her, because home is Kate.

I take my shower and then put on the cut-off sweats Ashleigh must've found in my dresser. I wonder what the hell else she found. I have no idea what's in that room anymore. I haven't thought about it in years.

I go back out and the lights are all off. The bathroom light lingers outside the doorway a few feet and I can make out Ashleigh's body under the covers. The baby is breathing loud and even, sleeping. I turn out the light and climb in next to them. I've slept with women, of course. But never *slept* with them. Like sleeping. That's not something I like to do. In fact, I'm not so sure about this right now, and my rash decision during check-in might be a mistake. But there's nowhere else to sleep other than that miniature love seat or the floor. And I'd be a fucking idiot to give up these two for those options.

I lie there, flat on my back, my hands behind my head, looking up at the ceiling.

"Ford?"

"Yes."

"Want to play a game?"

"What kind of game?"

"A silly junior high one." She sits up a little and takes her shirt off, then throws it across the room and lies down facing away from me. "You trace a word on my back and I try to guess what it is. If I guess, I get to trace one on yours."

She stops to see if I'll protest, but I don't. My heart beats a little faster at the thought of her behind me, touching my back. "What do I get if you don't guess?"

"Anything you want that doesn't involve me getting up from this bed." She laughs a little. "Because I'm too damn tired to bend over and put my ass in the air right now."

"What if I don't guess, then you get to ask me for something?"

"Yes, but I promise not to ask for anything that makes you uncomfortable. How's that?"

"Then this game has very little risk for either of us."

"Exactly. It's a *let's be nice and go to sleep together* game."

I smile. "I think I can handle that. In fact, I'm pretty sure I'm gonna win."

I feel her body shake a little with a silent laugh. "I might just let you win, just to see what it is you want from me tonight."

"You say that now to compensate for your sub-par performance, but it won't work. Now hold still so I can write. How many words can it be?"

"One. Just one word."

"OK." I think for a moment. "Does it have to be in English?"

She snorts. "Oh, God. I should've expected this from you. What language do you want it to be in? I can guess letters."

"What languages do you know?"

"Some Chinese, but I'm not fluent. And Japanese. I'm better at Japanese."

"Then Russian's out, I guess."

She snorts again. "Definitely."

"Let's do hiragana to English for five hundred, please, Alex. Ready?"

"Are you serious? What the hell? Only you can turn a lover's bedtime game into the SAT's!"

"You're gonna miss it, now be still."

I trace the two Japanese characters very slowly. Hiragana is not intricate like kanji, the shapes are pretty simple. But Ashleigh doesn't move at all. She's trying very hard. Or maybe she fell asleep. "OK, what is it?"

"What is *mizu*, water?"

"You're smart, Miss Li. I like that. And you phrased your answer in the form of a question, so you're a *Jeopardy* watcher. I like you more now."

She turns over with the baby, who is miraculously still asleep. "My turn. Face the other way. And since you think you're so smart, let's do kanji to English for one thousand, please, Alex. I'll even repeat the pattern three times for you, just so you're not at a disadvantage."

I smile and turn over.

"Ready?"

"Ready."

She traces the lines on my back and I shudder before I can stop the reaction. "You OK?" she asks.

"Yes. Keep going."

She starts again. "This is the first character." She draws a lot of lines. One is slanted and almost connected to a vertical one. The rest are horizontal with a box at the bottom. "OK, second one."

"I've already guessed it."

"You have not, now quiet." She traces the second character,

which is much more complicated than the first. I know the answer, but I want to see what she'll make me do if she wins, so when she finishes, I lie.

"What is *shinkou*, faith?"

"Ha! I got you! It's *shinrai*, trust."

"Your characters are sloppy, it's not my fault."

She puts her hand on my shoulder and squeezes. "I think you knew it was trust and you're lying. But I don't care. I'm gonna take the win because cheating means you forfeit."

"You got me. Now how can I please you?"

"You have to turn around first."

"No kissing," I say as I change positions.

"No, no kissing. I'm not gonna force a man to kiss me, that's ridiculous. I want to ask a question, but it's an easy one, is that OK?"

She stares at me in the dim light. She's not pretty—she's beautiful. I'm appalled that I didn't see it immediately. Her dark hair is straight and long, even in the front. So it hangs over her eyes a little and she is constantly brushing it out of her face. Even now, she does this with a gentle sweep of her fingertip. Her nose is small and has a little upturn to it. And her lips. Fuck, her lips are plump in the center and then thin towards the corners of her mouth. I want to bite them, to see if they are as soft as they look, but I take a breath instead. "It's your win, you can ask away."

She smiles, but it's not the devious one like when she ambushed me back in Vail. It makes her eyes lift up a little and the stray light catches them with a glint that makes it impossible for me to look away. "Why do you think you're weird?" she asks in a whisper. Like it's a secret.

"I am weird. Everyone knows this."

Her eyes dart back and forth, watching me like I'm watching her. What does she see? My unshaven jaw? My dark eyes? My thoughts? Is she a mind-reader too? "You're very handsome," she says in that low voice. "You're strong and confident. You're smart, like super-smart, I think. I found a journal with equations in your closet."

We're still watching each other, on the verge of something. A new opinion. A new direction. Something. "You really are a snoop."

She takes a deep breath. "I'm sorry, did I cross a line?"

"No. Equations are not personal." She's visibly relieved. "Are you afraid of me?" I'm not even sure where that came from, the words just fall out of my mouth.

Her head moves, just the slightest shake. "No." Her voice is so soft, like our lives depend on this perfect discretion in the darkness.

"Even after I spanked you?"

She looks away at the mention of the spankings. She did not like it. Not the way I did it. "We talked about that afterward. It was a game."

"It's not a game, Ashleigh. I like that stuff."

"You don't like me, do you?" Her lips are frowning now and I hate it. I want more than anything to make that frown go away.

"That's not true at all. I like you. I've told you things over the past few days that I've never told anyone." Her frown remains. "Why are you asking me that?"

"I'm not the girl for you."

"Is that a question or an answer?"

"Did he send you?"

"What?" That question again. "Did who send me?"

"Never mind. Obviously that's a no." She lets out a long breath like she's disappointed. For a moment I think she'll turn away and we'll end the night confused and sad. But then she looks back at me and meets my gaze. "You're not strange. You're nice, Ford."

"Nice?" I shake my head. "Nice? I'm certain no one has ever called me *nice* before. I'm a dick. Asshole. Emotionless freak is what most sexual partners end up calling me. But never nice. I think I've given you the wrong impression, Ashleigh."

"No, Ford," she sighs. "I think you're trying to make the

world believe you're something you're not."

"Now why would I do that?"

That little bit of light filtering in through the sheer curtains is just barely enough to make out the brown of her eyes in the darkness. "I'm not sure. But I think you're trying to keep people away. Mrs. Pearson said you got in a lot of trouble, but she never said you were weird. She said you were"—Ash stops for a moment, like she's trying to remember the exact words— "unnaturally bright and curious."

"I think that was her very diplomatic way of telling a woman who might be in a relationship with me that I'm weird."

"I think it was a compliment. And you said you have trouble with emotions, but you feel all kinds of things. You were upset with Rook. Mad, maybe sad. Maybe lonely, like me. But you're loyal to your friend, Ronin. So loyal that you refused to allow yourself to be tempted and you left town in a blizzard on New Year's Eve. So I think you should give yourself another chance. Stop seeing yourself as Weird Ford and start seeing yourself as Nice Ford."

"I'm not Nice Ford, Ashleigh."

"OK," Compliant Ashleigh says. The girl I saw the first two nights we were together is back. She did promise me she'd be calm, after all. "I like you either way, so it doesn't matter to me. It's just a suggestion." She smiles and then hugs the baby to her bare chest and turns back over. "I'll sleep facing this way so you're not uncomfortable. Night, Ford."

"You're not even gonna give me a chance to win a round in our game?"

"Nope. You let me win you tonight." She turns her head a little, but I can make out her profile in the dark. "I'll let you win me tomorrow."

I'm glad it's dark, because I'm grinning big and I don't feel like hiding it. "I look forward to it, Ashleigh."

TWENTY_FIVE

I'm the first one up the next day, mostly because I'm horny as fuck and I need to take my mind off the fact that Ashleigh's ass is right up next to my dick, but also because I'm in a hurry to get the hell back to civilization. Ash was right yesterday—being lost in the wilds is cool for a while. But then things start closing in on you. And for me, it's my erratic feelings towards this girl and her baby.

I like them.

There. I admitted it.

I like them. I could get used to them. I'd like to see Kate crawl and throw a tantrum in the store because she wants a toy. I want to watch her develop a personality and learn new things. It's got a certain appeal. I'd like to watch Ashleigh cook me dinner and the three of us sitting at a table that is not in a restaurant. I'd like to try this.

But I sure the fuck know how to pick them. First Rook and now Ash. Why can't I fucking find a girl who is not taken? Although I have no trouble stealing Ashleigh away from this

TAUT

Tony fuck. None at all. If he left her with a newborn baby, that's just wrong.

I'm safe. I never fuck without protection. Never. It's not difficult putting Ashleigh off because I know I can't have sex with her until I get some condoms. It's not even an issue for me, that's how firm I am in this doctrine.

So I would never get a girl pregnant by mistake. Ever.

But this guy did get her pregnant and she kept the baby. Which says a lot of things about her. And they never married. Which says a lot of things about him.

Or maybe these two planned this baby and things didn't work out?

Regardless. If I did get a girl pregnant I'd never—*never*—walk out. I have a very solid image of what a family is. Mine. The one I was raised in. That's a family. And if I create a child, it's going to be with a woman I'm married to and plan to grow old with.

That's naive, maybe. Whatever. I don't care. Because I'm patient. I want it all or I want nothing. I was not just saying that to Rook to make her feel guilty. I meant it. I've got the slutty girls, the ones who want me to use them any way I want. I have them to keep me satisfied—because I'd rather be alone than be in a relationship with a woman I don't love or who doesn't love me back.

And if Ashleigh wants to get back with her ex, then I'll just have to step aside and go back to my old life—the life before Rook and girls in blizzards who need saving. Concentrate on work. We're filming on location in New Zealand for six weeks starting in nine days. I've missed a shitload of meetings, my email is probably going off, and I'm definitely running out of text excuses. My assistant has been fielding all calls since last week, but pretty soon life is gonna catch up to me.

And Ashleigh's life will catch up to her at the same time.

As soon as we get to LA in fact. We could make it there today if we wanted to. Ten hours, give or take. But I'm not ready to let this go just yet. Maybe her ex is a total dick. Maybe she just needs to see more of Nice Ford and less of Asshole Ford and she'll change her mind about Tony?

But then I'd constantly be in his shadow. He'd probably get partial custody of Kate. I'd have to share them.

I picture what that might look like. The weekends that Kate would be away from us. The phone calls when Tony wanted something from Ashleigh. The split holidays and dealing with Kate's paternal grandparents. Knowing Kate's bond with her father is stronger than her bond with me.

I'd be crazy jealous.

But I'd do it. I'd share if Ashleigh loved me. I'd do it to make her happy, make Kate's life less confusing. I'd be nice to Tony. Shake his hand maybe. Be a graceful winner.

I get out of bed as quietly as I can and get dressed. I'm putting on the clean socks that Ashleigh packed when she wakes. "You're up early today."

"Yeah." I grin at her from across the room. "We have a date in Vegas tonight." That makes her smile and my whole body floods with warmth. "We need to get there, you need some fancy clothes, Kate needs a babysitter. We have a big day ahead, so let's get on it." Ashleigh actually sighs and I laugh. "What's got you sighing?"

"I think this is going to be a good day. Maybe a great day. Maybe the first great day I've had in a long time." She throws the cover off and Kate stirs. "She's not hungry, I just fed her like an hour ago. So I'll feed her on the road if she needs it."

"I didn't hear you all night. How many times did she feed?"

"Like four." Ash snorts. "I was half asleep for most of it. Except the last one. I watched you sleep." She gives me a seductive smile as she tugs on a white t-shirt of mine that has a black diamond on it and says *I'm difficult* across her chest. "Stop staring at me."

"Why?"

"Why?" she giggles. "Because it makes me feel weird."

Life gets a little more interesting. "Weird how?"

"Like you're looking at me naked."

"You just rolled out of bed topless. And you just admitted that you were watching me sleep, so that's the weird shit."

"I know. But you don't just look nice when you're sleeping, you're like…" Her words trail off and she shakes her head.

"I'm what?"

"I can't say it. I'm not allowed to talk dirty to you anymore or you'll spank me."

I stand up and walk over to her, pull her hair aside and lean down into her neck. "Miss Li? Your ass will be red no matter how many good deeds you perform today to try and make up for your unladylike behavior. So you might as well get your dirty talk over with so you can concentrate on behaving tonight when I have your ankles tied to your thighs and your pussy open for inspection. Because I'm going to have a lot of rules, Ashleigh. And a lot of commands you'll have to follow. I'm going to touch you in places that will make you scream. I'm going to let you please me in ways you've only dreamed of, and then I'm going to fuck you sore."

Her body stiffens and her head goes back a little as she looks up at me. "I think I just came, I swear to God, I'm not even joking."

My laugh is so loud the baby startles and starts crying. Ashleigh takes a step to go after Kate but I pull her back and rub my hand along the crease of her pussy. She's sopping wet even through her panties. "You are in a lot of trouble for cheating."

"Cheating?" she exclaims and Kate is getting ready to wail now. "You talked me into it! It's your fault, Ford. I should get to spank you for *making* me come!"

I push her away gently and laugh. "I think someone needs a rule book."

"Yeah, you!" She picks up the baby and rocks her a little before turning back to me. "You need rules, Ford. Not me. How come you're allowed to call all the shots anyway? How come I can't make *you* do things? How come I can't tie you up and parade you in front of a window? You've got a nice package. I bet

I could charge money to see that shit."

I have no words for this girl, that's how fucking cute I think she is right now. But I tuck down my amusement and put on the serious face. "I like control, remember?"

She thinks about this for a minute. "So I have to do everything you say? It just makes no sense. I might need that rule book. Do they sell it online? I could read up on the way to Vegas because I found an old eReader of yours in your room and I plan on using it today."

"You can read it out loud, so we're both on the same page."

She sighs. "I'm gonna come again if you don't stop making me think about sex. And it's not even my fault, you've been teasing and denying me for days!"

"Welcome to my world, Ashleigh. Tease and deny is my MO."

She lays Kate down on the bed and grabs a diaper. "It's not fair, you know. You get to make all the decisions and I just have to follow orders."

"What's not fair about it?"

"You get to have all the fun." She cleans Kate's bottom with a wipe and rolls up the old diaper. "Here, put this in the trash, it's not a stinky one." I take the diaper and toss it in the bathroom trashcan. "I'm not sure what I get out of it if I give in to you like this."

"You said you've done it before." She takes a deep breath like she has a lot to say, then changes her mind and lets it out. "What?" I ask.

"It was… pretend, you know? He'd smack me a bit but it was never a consequence for an action. That's different. It was just for fun."

"Ah, I see."

"You see what?" she asks as she grabs a new outfit from the diaper bag. I smile when I see it's not a footied sleeper but the little pink sweat suit I picked out from the store yesterday. It's got a silver princess crown on the shirt and leaping unicorns on the pant legs. Then Ash fishes through the bag until she comes up with some tiny white socks and a little bitty pair of pink sneakers.

"You don't understand. So I'll explain what you get. When you let me take control, you get to forget about everything but the ways in which I please you. You simply get to enjoy yourself."

"Enjoy—? How is getting smacked fun?"

I laugh. "You're supposed to be good and then you don't get smacked, Ash. You wanted to be spanked that night, so I gave you what you asked for."

"It sorta hurt. I did not enjoy that part. I like the soft spankings."

"Then that's a reward and to get those you have to be good."

"Oh." She Velcros the miniature sneakers onto Kate's feet and the baby is actually content. I think it's because she knows she looks cute. I take my phone out and snap a picture. Ashleigh glances over at me with a weird look on her face. "I want a picture of you wearing my t-shirt and panties, and her in the outfit I chose, because you two are adorable." She picks Kate up and hugs her close, but she's looking me straight in the eyes so I continue. "If you trust me to take care of you and do everything I ask, then it's a very special experience." She frowns at me. "*Now what*?"

"Do you have these special experiences with all the girls you control during sex?"

I shake my head. "I told you, Ashleigh. I do not care about them."

"Yeah, but you said you didn't care about me, either."

I scratch my chin. I did say that. And I was mean about it.

"Do you care?" she asks.

"I like you, so I think I care."

"I'm not sure *think* is good enough for me to trust you not to hurt me during sex—even if it's just mentally. You asked me last night if I'm afraid of you and the answer is yes and no. Do I think you're one of those asshole woman-beaters? No. But you're asking me to give up who I am to make you happy. And I'm not saying I'm unwilling to do that for certain people under certain circumstances. But I'm not about to make you happy at my own expense and get nothing in return but an orgasm. It's too small of a thing. Too fleeting. Too insignificant. I'm not one of those girls who follows orders, Ford. I like the sexy spankings. I don't mind posing for you in front of a window. I like some of this stuff. But I only like it when the person who is asking me to do these things actually cares about me."

"Who did you do this with before? Tony?"

She swallows hard and for a moment I think she'll cry, but she presses her lips together and tilts her chin up. "Yes, Tony."

"And he loved you?"

This time she can't speak. She only nods.

"Well, how can I compete with him? I'm not him."

"I know," she chokes out as her chin quivers.

"Why are you crying?"

She hugs Kate close and it's like the baby knows she needs comfort and rests her head on her shoulder.

"Why, Ashleigh?"

"I can't talk about it. I just can't. It hurts."

"Why are you on this road trip?"

She sniffles and sits down at the little dining table. Kate's eyes are closed now. "I just need to see him, Ford. I told you, I'll let it go once I get all this stuff off my chest. But—"

She cries now. Real tears, not holding it in. They are silent, but even sadder than if she was actually sobbing. I give her a few moments to pull it together and then I prod again. "But what?"

"None of this is fair to me. Nothing is fair. I'm the one who got shit on in every way. I had everything and now I have nothing."

"You have Kate."

She rolls her eyes at me and sniffs again. "I know that. Believe me, I realize how significant that is. But I still want *him*, Ford. It's like my insides have been ripped out. Like I'm empty. Life has no meaning. And I'm tired of hearing that I have to let it go and move on. I'm tired of it. I'm just not ready to let it all go and give up on that dream we had."

"So this trip is what? A break from reality?"

TAUT

She thinks about this for a few moments, sniffs. I grab a tissue from a box on the dresser and hand it to her. "Yes. That's a good way to look at it. A break. A pause. I just needed things to stop for a while. Does that makes sense? I just need to think."

"Maybe you're thinking too much?"

She rolls her eyes again and snorts.

"Like I was, back in my dad's office with the Scotch. Surrounded by all those pictures of us living life."

She looks up at this. She's paying attention to me.

"Maybe you just need to feel and stop thinking, Ashleigh?"

"But it feels bad, Ford. I'm OK if I think of other things. You really help, actually. You take my mind off him."

"Then let me take control so you can stop thinking. Let me make it feel better. Just trust me, Ashleigh."

"I don't want to be hit. I don't want to follow orders just because someone tells me to."

"I'm not talking about that now."

"Then what?"

"Just give yourself to me. Trust me. For one day. I'll take care of you." She exhales and stares up at me. She looks lost and broken. She looks sad and defeated. And I hate it. "One day of trust, Ashleigh. Just one day. And then tomorrow we can drive to LA and life can start again. But don't let your pause end up meaningless. Make it count. Give me control. I'll show you life goes on."

She starts crying again. "I want life to go on, Ford. I do. I want to get over it. I just can't find my way right now. I can't see past this pain. It shuts me down completely."

"Listen to what I'm offering, Ashleigh. You're not listening. You keep repeating yourself. I get it, it sucks. You got shit on. You don't know what to do, you're lost, you're wandering aimlessly looking for answers. And I'm the answer, Ash. I'm the answer and I'm offering you relief. I don't want you to give up, I just want you to give in."

She takes a deep breath and I can physically see the mental

shift she goes through. One second she's defeated and closed off, the next she's—open. Not quite hopeful, but there's a spark of acceptance in there. "OK," she finally says as she wipes the tears from her eyes. "For today then. I'll give it a try."

My smile is immediate and all the hurt I was just feeling over her sadness melts away.

One day.

I have one day to wipe her mind of Tony.

TWENTY-SIX

"Eat in Green River or next town we come to with a restaurant?"

"I thought you were calling the shots?"

"Ashleigh, I'm not trying to take away your freedom, I'm trying to take away your pain."

She smiles at that and then relaxes into the seat. "Next town then." She looks back at Kate and then to me. "Why wake her up if we don't have to." I like how she uses *we* in that sentence. Like we're in this together. "This state is weird-looking," she says as she looks out the window. "I've never seen this kind of landscape. It's a little like New Mexico with the red rocks and the sandstone, but it's even more desolate, if that's even possible."

"I like Utah. I used to take the Bronco out to Moab in college and rock crawl." We're both silent as we look around. Utah is unique. It does look like New Mexico, but with real mountains.

"You're like one of those outdoorsy guys, aren't you Ford?"

"I guess. I like to keep busy, that's all."

"And you like to compete."

"No, I like to win."

TAUT

"But you can't always win."

I grin over at her. "Depends on how you look at it. I always win."

"But some things have definite winners and losers. Like in a hockey game. One team wins and the other team loses."

"True, but maybe one player wins on the losing team? Then it's still a win."

She huffs out a breath. "So you're a half-full kind of person? Figures. You know I first pegged you as a mopey emo guy, but it turns out you're sorta goody-two-shoes."

Oh, fuck. "What? How the hell do you figure?"

"*It's all in how you look at it,*" she says in a false voice. "That is annoying. It's all upbeat and positive. I'm gonna put the Naked and Famous back on, that'll cure your optimism."

I grab the phone in the center console before she does. "No way. I'm not chasing your ass across Utah again just because these songs make you think about *Tony.*" I sneer his name this time and she gasps at that. "Today is all about Ford. No more sad music. Get that reader out, read to me."

"Pfffft. They have audiobooks for that, Ford, I'm not your personal narrator."

"Yes, Miss Li, you are. Get the reader and do as you're told. You can choose the book—wait, are there even books on that thing? It's like a few years old."

"Oh, yeah, it has books all right. I made the mistake of turning it on and it synced all your freaking books since the last time you used it. It said three hundred and forty-five. I had to leave it on all night to get all those stupid books on there."

"My choice in books is very classic. They are not stupid."

"You're right, they're not stupid, they're boring." She cackles at that as she stares out the window.

"You can choose the book, just get it and start reading."

She climbs into the back seat and reaches over into the cargo area to fish around. She comes back a few minutes later with the old reader and turns it on. "God, it's even in black and white."

"You have one minute to find a book and then I'm pulling over and finding one myself."

"Hold your horses, I'm looking... oh, what? You like Odd Thomas? I love him."

"Good, read one of those."

"No, I've read them all. You like them because he's weird, right? You can relate to his oddballness? I mean, his name is Odd, that's strange right off the bat. And then the whole I see dead Elvis thing? Yeah. Ford and Odd are like blood brothers."

"You know why I really like him?"

She lets out a long breath and looks over at me, serious now. "Why?"

"Because I lost a girl a few years ago when I started reading this series. I always thought they sounded stupid, sorta supernatural, and sappy. But Odd Thomas had that girl, what was her name?"

"Stormy."

"Yeah, great name. Stormy. Odd had Stormy and the ending on that first book had a twist that made me—well, feel bad for him, frankly. It was a new thing for me. I've never really identified with a character before. I read them for the plot. I like thrillers because they hide secrets and you have to figure them out along the way. But I never saw that ending coming in the first Odd book."

"What was *her* name?"

I know who Ash is talking about even though it's a vague question. "Mardee. Ronin stole her from me. She got involved in drugs, overdosed in his family's studio building. In fact, it was the anniversary of her death last month. Four years."

Ash is silent and I wonder what she makes of this.

"I didn't love her. I know that now. I mean, I might've thought I loved her back then. I wanted her. Ronin used her. He liked her well enough for business deals, and they even did some modeling contracts together. But he wasn't into her. I miss her, I liked her, I spent a lot of time with her. But she was never going to be with a guy like me."

"What's that mean? What kind of guy are you?"

"The kind who likes to call the shots." I grin over at her. "Now pick a book and enough stalling."

Ash looks back down at the reader. "It's all boring. I mean what is this? *The Count of Monte Cristo*? Seriously?"

"I love that book. It's about delayed gratification. Something I wholeheartedly believe in."

She snorts and pushes the tabs on the front of the reader, scrolling for books. "You proved my point. Delayed gratification. You just want me to suffer, constantly wanting your hot body but only ever offering me a small sample of it."

I shake my head. *Fucking Ashleigh.*

She falls silent as she searches for a book, then huffs out a sigh. "I'm never gonna find—whoa, whoa, whoa! What is this little gem? *Spelunk Me*? You have *Spelunk Me* on your eReader? Bahahahaha. Oh my God, I might die, that's how funny this is."

"I've never heard of that book, perhaps it's a promotional freebie?" I bought that book for Rook, back when she was modeling nude for Spencer's body art painting and needed a distraction. But I'm not about to admit that to Ashleigh. If she's not allowed to talk about Tony then it's only fair I leave Rook behind as well.

"*Ashley*—the little tart has my name! Which, by the way, is spelled wrong. *Ashley, the only virgin in her freshman dorm, is desperate to be deflowered by long-time crush Eaton Fuller. But that's before hot and dangerous Rowdy Breaker saves her from a spelunking adventure gone wrong.* Oh, my fucking God—"

"I'm gonna spank you for that."

"What? What'd I do?"

She's got the most bewildered innocent look on her face and it takes a monumental effort on my part not to give in and laugh. "Unladylike behavior?" I say seriously.

"When?"

"Ashleigh."

She smirks at me. "Fine, I'll take it because this is too fucking funny and we are totally reading this book right the fuck now."

"That's three new ones."

"OK, hold on. Just let me be unladylike for one moment, can I?"

I squint at her. "Ten seconds."

"I'd like to request a fun spanking and I promise to follow all your other orders especially when it comes to *pleasing you in ways I've only dreamed of* ." She smiles. "Deal?"

"No deal. I get that no matter what."

"Yeah, because I agreed. But I'll do more than agree. I'll be"—she stops to lick her lips and I almost swerve off the road—"*enthusiastic*." And then she waggles her eyebrows at me.

I could love this girl.

I could love her and look forward to all her silly antics every single day. I just need to be strong and tell her no. But I'm competing with her ex right now. So I do the unthinkable. I give in. "Maybe I'll give you one fun spanking for every two meaningful ones. How's that?"

"Mmmmmm." She hums as her eyes go to half-mast like she's picturing it in her head. I almost want to pull the Bronco over and fuck her on the side of the road. "I totally agree, Ford. I'm all yours if you do the fun ones."

"Read."

"*The freshman dorm was nothing like I imagined. It was hot, and not because of the heat, even though it was August. It was hot because it was co-ed and the boy across from me was standing in his room, with the door open, wearing nothing but a smile.*

"*I smiled back.*

"*And that was when I knew. Rowdy Breaker was dangerous.*

"*Just then a girl's face peeked out from behind the door. She stepped out in full view, wearing nothing but a scowl, and slammed it closed.*

"*So much for a free peep show. But I had that boy's body burned into my brain and I would use that image to satisfy myself later.* She *is* a tart."

"Hold the commentary, it ruins the mood."

Ash busts out a laugh. "The mood?"

"Yes, and when you speak in Rowdy's voice, make it deeper, you know, like the professional narrators they have doing the audiobooks."

"Ford?" she says in an overly sweet voice.

"Yes, Ashleigh?" I look over at her with a dimpled grin.

"I'm gonna get you back for all this control, you do realize that, right?"

I reach over and grab her thigh. She jumps a little and lets out a gasp. "I never lose, Ash. Never. So if you think you can get me back by playing nasty with me tonight, then by all means, show me what a loser I am." And then I slip my hand down her thigh and pinch her skin until she yelps. Before her hand can even move to swat mine off, I'm caressing her pussy through her jeans. "Do not come or I will tease you and withhold orgasms later."

She holds her breath and nods.

I let up on the pressure. "Unbutton and unzip your pants."

She breathes. But she obeys. She pops the button and the zipper makes a soft ripping sound.

"Stick your hand inside your panties."

She doesn't even hesitate and this makes me so fucking hard. I can feel her fingers through her jeans. "I can feel everything you do, Ashleigh. I'll let you come right now, but you have to do all the work. Are you ready?"

"I'm ready," she whispers. When I look over at her she's looking right back at me. Her stare never wavers.

I look back to the road. This highway is deserted. No one is traveling I-70 west with us. There are cars every now and then going east, but very few.

"Begin," I command.

She shudders before she even starts and I almost die thinking she already came. But it was just an excited shudder, not an orgasm. She begins in slow circles over her clit. I press down a little and her breathing becomes heavier. She continues this a few more times but then she scoots her butt down more towards the edge of the seat and slips in farther. I can feel the back of her hand on my palm through the thick fabric, and then it dips. "Tell me what you just did, Ash."

"Put my fingers inside me," she says in a low, breathy voice.

"Does it feel good?"

"Not as good as yours would. But I'll make do."

I say nothing to her joking, just cup her hand with mine and increase her movements. Her other hand hovers over mine. "Can I touch you, Ford?"

"Yes," I say, because I want her. I want her more than I don't want to be touched. Her hand rests on top of mine. It's very small, and I chance a look over to compare sizes. "Keep on task."

She pumps into herself and then she takes my hand and places it over her belly, where the opening in her jeans is. "I want you to touch my skin."

"You'll get your wish," I tell her with my eyes still on the road. "But for now—" I withdraw my hand and put it back on the steering wheel. "For now, you will pleasure yourself to satisfy me."

"I'm going to imagine you doing it, then."

"That's against the rules, you should be thinking only of how much you will please me by following my instructions."

"I don't care, it's my mind and I'll picture you fingering me if I want." And then she opens her eyes all the way and stares at me. I look away and concentrate on the road. "And you will never know, Ford. Because you're not a mind-reader."

I want to thump my head against the steering wheel repeatedly, that's how crazy she's driving me with this rebellion. That's how bad she's being. If she was one of my pets I'd have her strapped face first to a wall, gagged and blindfolded right now— she'd be getting the spanking of her life. And I wouldn't feel bad about it at all. I'd enjoy it.

TAUT

But she's not a pet. She's Ashleigh. And she's a little more like Rook than I previously thought. She wants to be loved, not punished, commanded, or manipulated. Just loved.

Maybe that's why Rook rejected me? Ronin just loves her, no questions asked. He just accepts her. Lets her make mistakes, always careful to watch and make sure she doesn't get hurt. Protecting her from a distance if necessary. Close by, but unseen at times. That's what Rook was trying to tell me back in the stadium that day when she was describing how different we were. How we treat her differently. If she stayed with me, I'd make her do things she'd rather not, just because she's been trained to please. Just because I can.

I'd ruin her drive to be herself.

I don't want to ruin Rook. And I don't want to ruin Ashleigh, either. I like her the way she is, I want her to be herself. Small and vulnerable, yet brave and willing. Caring and honest, yet suspicious and hopeless. I've laughed more times with Ashleigh than I have in years. I like that she can do this, that being herself is so damn desirable to me.

But I want to be *my*self, as well. I want her to find me desirable the way I am.

The moaning interrupts my internal thoughts and then Ash buckles her back against the seat and releases a long breath. "I can't wait to get to Vegas," she says as she rests against the headrest, her eyes closed. "I hope I can satisfy you, Ford. I really do want to please you but I have this recessive wild side that I can't control. It just pops into existence every now and then."

"Ashleigh." I wait for her to open her eyes and look over at me. "You're perfect. I like the way you are. Don't change for me."

She puts the seat back and curls herself up in a little ball facing me. Like she's a little cat getting ready to nap. "But what about the spankings?"

"I'm still going to spank you, *koneko*."

She blushes and lowers her eyes.

"You can't get out of that."

"That's cute. Kitten. It's one of those erotic pet names, right?"

"I don't care for pet names, but the way you curl up in the seat—you're tiny, Ashleigh. So small."

"Mmmmm. Yeah, I've always been the little one. I'm nothing like anyone else in my family at all. My mom was very tall, so's my dad actually. He's half German, so he's bulky for an Asian-looking man. And my mom had blonde hair and blue eyes. My sister takes after her. Everyone in Asia loved my mom and sister because of how pretty they were, how they both had perfect Chinese accents. But me, I was the little quiet one who sat in the corner and drew. The one who refused to talk to the important people who would come to our house for business parties. They tried to make me speak Chinese and I just didn't want to."

I'm captivated by her story. I want to hear so much more so I stay quiet and let her think.

"My dad might not look Chinese—he's very tall for one. And his eyes are this weird green color. But he's very serious about the culture. And I was always a little bit wild when it came to discipline. When we moved back to America I found so many ways to rebel. It was too easy. So when I moved to Japan I kinda liked the fact that I had to rein it in a little. Not too much, but just a little. It was good for me to give in to a new culture and think about things differently. Give the old me a rest and try something new. I've always felt a little out of place, ya know?" She looks over at me and I nod, because yes. Yes, I do know. I've always felt a little out of place as well. "Have you ever heard the story of *The Boy Who Drew Cats*, Ford? It's a Japanese folk tale."

"No, but I'd like to hear it. Tell it."

She takes a deep breath, like she's preparing for something. Building up her courage. I'm not sure why a folk tale would require courage, but she must need it for something. So I turn on the mind-reading skills and pay attention.

"This story is about a boy who refuses to do anything but draw cats. His family is patient, but they insist he try to be productive, so they send him out to learn trades. But the poor

TAUT

boy has an obsession. He only wants to draw cats. So one night, after drawing a massive cat on a long room-sized rice paper screen, he falls asleep in a cozy closet and hears a monster come in the night. There's a battle outside his door, but he's too afraid to go out and look. So he waits until morning and finds a giant dead rat and the cat he drew on the rice paper screen is facing the wrong direction. He puts all the clues together and decides that his huge cat drawing came to life and killed the giant rat that's been terrorizing the village. From that day on, all the villagers celebrated his cat-drawing skills."

She stops to giggle. "It's absurd, but that's Japanese tales for you. I like them though, and this one especially. Japan always felt like home to me, from the moment I stepped off the plane it was home. And this story speaks to me. It says, *Be yourself, Ashleigh.* You can be appreciated for who you are, even if your only talent is a little bit strange and seems to have no value. Because everyone is valuable. That's what the moral is. So maybe I am a *koneko* and I'm part of this story in a way. I'm on a quest to try and be my true self but I have no idea who I am, Ford. My identity has been taken away. Maybe a kitten is my true self? Maybe I am something small and delicate that needs to be taken care of. Not something strong and determined that finds a way to appreciate her own strange place in the world."

"Maybe you're both. Maybe you can be independent and delicate at the same time?"

"Single mothers don't have the luxury of being delicate. Single mothers have to do everything alone. So even if I wanted to be a kitten, I'm not allowed."

That's it. I need this girl. She's so lost. She's looking for someone to help her and I'd like to be that person. She's got a hold of my heart and I can't let her go back to Tony. She's practically begging someone to take care of her and that fuck left her. "When did you live in Japan, Ashleigh?"

She turns away and looks out the window, still curled up in the seat. "Kate and I just got back, actually. Christmas Eve." She

310

looks over at me. "I've been in Japan since I was eighteen. I ran away and I had no intention of returning to the US ever again."

"Why did you come back? Because of Tony?" She nods but I can feel her sadness like it's a thick fog. This conversation is reminding her of him even as I sit here falling in love. "How old are you now?"

"Twenty-three."

"You look very young."

"I know," she tells the window instead of me. "Because I'm small. But I feel so old. Like life has passed me over. He said we'd grow old together but then he left me. And I feel like in the time since then, I got old without him. I feel like my life is over."

There's a pull-out up ahead on the side of the road. A spot for travelers to stop and take in the view. It's an odd view, that's for sure. Most of Utah is odd with the strange rock formations and the colors. But I'm not stopping for the view, so I just pull the fuck over.

"What're we doing?" she asks, sitting up and flipping her seat back into its normal upright position.

I put the truck in neutral and pull the e-brake. "Ashleigh—" And suddenly I can't say it. I want to. I want to tell her so many things. How I feel about her. How much I like Kate. How she makes me laugh. How desperate I am to stop her falling into a sad depression. Because I see it coming. If she's not clinically depressed right now, she's on the verge. She's teetering on the edge.

I want to say so many things, but her word-slap in Wal-Mart comes back to me. She sees me as a distraction until she gets to LA to talk to her ex. To possibly beg him to reconsider and take her back. And I can't take another slap like that. So I protect these new feelings and hide them away. I pull up the *I'm in charge* routine instead. "Ashleigh, I'm making a rule. You agreed to do what I asked—for one day. You agreed to this. So my rule is, no more talking about Tony."

Her eyes squint down into slits immediately, but she holds

her tongue.

"I don't care if it makes you angry, I've heard enough. I won't put up with it. You're mine today. I won you. And I say fuck Tony. OK? My rules. No more Tony."

She stares at me, her face hardened.

"Agreed?"

"Agreed," she replies. But she turns her back to me and stares out at the window.

She stays silent for the entire two-hour ride to Richfield.

TWENTY-SEVEN

We hit up another diner because it's not even nine AM yet, so that's pretty much all that's open. Ashleigh is feeding Kate in the backseat before we head in. "So what should we do in Vegas tonight? You like to gamble?"

"No, not really," she replies absently.

I check a website for what's playing in Vegas right now. "Shows?"

"You said sushi."

"We can do sushi. But that's like an hour of time. What else?"

"I'm not sure I want to leave Kate with a sitter, she—"

"Ashleigh."

"No, listen. I have to feed her every few hours so I can't be gone long anyway. It's stupid to get a sitter when I have to pop in every four hours."

"Give her a bottle." I get an angry sneer at that comment. It almost shuts me down, that's how snide it is. "What?"

"She breastfeeds. I'm not giving her a bottle so I can have sex with you tonight."

"So you're mad about my Tony rule."

"What's that got to do with breastfeeding?"

"You were dying to have sex with me a couple hours ago. And now you're mad because I told you to stop moping."

"No, you told me to stop thinking about Tony. Like I can just turn it off and forget. I think it's incredibly insensitive for you to make that rule. He's all I think about. Ever."

"It's insensitive to me that you're distracted."

"We're not even dating, Ford. We're—we're—"

"We're what?"

She just shakes her head.

"We're what, Ashleigh?"

"We're temporary. I like you—you're handsome and rich and actually a nice catch for someone else. But not for me. OK?"

"It's just fun."

"Yeah, it's just fun. I appreciate all the help you've given me, but I'm a mess, Ford. I have no room right now for most of life. *Existing* is difficult. I need to make things slow and simple and you are the definition of complicated. You have rules and expectations, and you play these mind games with me. You don't know anything about me or my life. Or Tony. You don't know anything about him, so when you make a rule that says I'm not allowed to think about him, I don't like it."

"I know he's not here and I am."

She clutches the baby to her chest and starts to cry.

Fuck.

"Ashleigh, come on." I sigh. "Ashleigh. I'm sorry, OK? I can see that you love him, I'm sorry."

I reach back and touch her knee and she swats my hand away. "You're mean. Just don't touch me."

I get out of the truck and get inside the backseat with her. We're pretty squished since the carrier is buckled in on the passenger side and Ashleigh's in the middle with the baby. She's crying hard now and Kate is getting upset along with her. I reach down and grab the baby. "Here, I'll take her for you." I'm actually stunned that she hands the baby over to me. If I was her, I'd probably tell me to fuck off.

Kate makes some distressed sounds but I hold her up at almost arm's length and smile at her. She just stares at me, blinking her big brown eyes and kicking her dangling feet.

"Hi, Kate."

Ashleigh laughs through her sniffles.

"What?" I ask, looking over at her.

"You look ridiculous, Ford. Holding her out like you want to hand her off. You're supposed to hold babies close."

"I've never held a baby before."

She wipes the tears away and laughs again. "Obviously."

I bring Kate into my chest and she's so soft it's easy to want to hold her tight. She squirms a little in my arms and I pat her on the back the way Ashleigh does when she's trying to calm her. She relaxes her heavy head on my shoulder and that's it.

It's over.

I'm done.

I'm a Kate lover. "I'd like a Kate," I whisper down to her. Ashleigh snickers, and that makes me feel better. At least she's not crying over Tony or mad at me for being an asshole. "Did Tony ever hold her?" I figure why fight it. Can't beat 'em, join 'em, right?

"No," Ash says softly. "He never did."

"I'd make a horrible father, I think."

"Why?" she asks, scrunching up her face.

It's probably a bad idea to admit my care-giving limitations when I'm trying to get her to reevaluate her feelings about my partner potential. But fuck it. I'm already losing, what's it matter? "My father was so good at it. He did everything right. He was patient, he was encouraging, he was firm when I needed discipline, but never angry or abusive. He never hit me, not even a swat. And"—I stop to laugh here—"as I'm sure Mrs. Pearson made you well aware, I was not an easy kid to raise. I did all sorts of really bad stuff. Electrocuting Jason was the least of my crimes. But my dad, he protected me no matter what because I just didn't have much capacity for empathy back then. When I got older I finally realized that I was hurting people, that just because I *could* make golf balls into mini-explosives didn't mean I *should* make golf balls into mini-explosives."

I look over at her and she's smiling. Very big, in fact. I look down at Kate and she's sleeping. I slump down in the seat a little so she can be more horizontal. "Anyway, my dad played innocent whenever the suspicion fell on me"—I look down at Ash again—"as it often did. But he covered for me and I never got caught. I was too smart and too well-protected. He always told me, 'Ford, I am always on your side. No matter what you do, no matter how much I disagree with it, I'm always on your side.' But whenever I got home from whatever meeting my dad was called to about my atrocious behavior, he always handed out the most clever punishments. Except he never called them punishments."

"Like what?" Ash interrupts. "How did he punish you?"

"One time I had to cook the meals for a month and I wasn't allowed to use the same recipe twice. It had to be the perfect balance of protein, carbs, and vegetables. I had to shop for all the ingredients, learn the recipe, and serve it at dinner. I'm a fantastic cook when I want to be. All because of some practical joke I played on a nun in school."

"You did not go to Catholic school."

I smile. "I did. They were the only private school that would take me. And while our neighborhood was nice and close to lots of city amenities, it was not a place you sent your kids to public school if you could help it. So I went to Saint Margaret's. That's where I met Spencer Shrike."

She busts out laughing at that. "*He* went to Catholic school too?"

I nod. "He did. So did Ronin, but that was much later. I didn't meet Ronin until high school, he was already modeling for major clothing designers by then."

She tilts her head and smiles. "Damn, I wish I'd gone to that school. I could rock a tartan skirt and some knee socks. I went to a private school too, but it was all girls." She makes a face at that.

"What color was your uniform?"

"Burgundy with gold accents."

I take a moment to picture her like this. "I'm gonna need the name of that school so I can hack into their records and get a picture of you."

She chuckles. "So it sounds like you had the perfect father. You'd probably make a great one because you had such a good example."

"Yeah, but I'm not my father. He was a lot like me, but I'm not a lot like him."

Her eyes squint together and she pauses her smile, like she's thinking really hard about that statement. "I'm not following."

I shrug. "He and I shared a lot of characteristics. Looks, speech, a love for foreign languages. He played all the same sports that I excelled in. He was super smart, but not in a freaky way like I am. He was the perfect me, if that makes sense. He had all the good things but none of the bad. I'm like Bizarro Rutherford Aston III. The mirror-image of him. I look like him. But I'm lacking in all his altruistic qualities. I'm not generous. I'm not understanding. I'm not a Giver." I look over at her and her attention is rapt. "I'm a Taker, Ashleigh."

She leans her head against my shoulder, right next to Kate's face. "You haven't taken anything from me, Ford."

"Yeah, but I want to. You have no idea how bad I want to take things from you."

She sits up and looks me in the eyes. "Like what?"

"Your body, for one. Just because I haven't had sex with you doesn't mean I don't want to. And—" I almost stop myself, but fuck it. I'm on a roll, might as well just keep going. "I'd like to take Tony from you too. I'd like to make you forget all about Tony."

She sighs and rests her head back against my shoulder, wrapping her hands around my upper arm like she's holding on for dear life. It takes me several seconds to realize how much of her body is pressed against mine. I've never let another woman touch me like this. Ever.

"But I realize it's not going to happen. It's OK, I get it. You love Tony. I was wrong to make that rule and I take it back."

She thinks about this for a little while, then lets out a loud sigh. A resigned sigh that speaks volumes. That sigh says, *I give up*. "I'd like to go for a quiet walk on our date tonight. And hold hands."

I should be worried that she's giving up. If I was a good person, one who cared about what's best for her, I'd be worried about this. I'd tell her to forget about me, be with Tony. He must love her. There has to be some misunderstanding. Give it another try.

But I'm not a good person. So I lead her away from Tony and towards me. "You'd like me to take you on a quiet hand-holding walk in the biggest party city on Earth?"

"Yeah. Something slow. Where we can just be still, and look around, and think. Where we can watch life, and not participate in it."

"I'm not sure Vegas is the right place for a slow and quiet walk, but I'll give it my best shot."

"You're an overachiever, Ford. I'm one hundred percent confident you'll pull it off flawlessly."

I smile at that assessment. "Ready to go in and eat? Kate's out, we should take advantage while we can."

Ashleigh reluctantly untangles herself from my arm and nods her head. I open the door and she unbuckles the car seat and scoots out after me. I lay little Kate in her seat and Ash covers her with a blanket because it's pretty damn cold out here, and then we walk into the diner like we're a team in this baby thing.

TWENTY-EIGHT

"Stop texting, Ford. It's rude."

Ashleigh and the baby are on the other side of the booth from me and I'm typing on my phone frantically. "This is the first good signal I've had in days. I'm not wasting it. I have work, you know. I've missed a shitload of meetings, my assistant is going out of her mind, and I need to make plans for a quiet date in Las Vegas for tonight." I look up at her and she's grinning. "What?"

"You look very serious. Very determined. Very... professional. Even though you're the one wearing the *I'm not a ski addict, sometimes I have sex too* t-shirt today."

I look down at my shirt and smile. She was wearing this the other day and just knowing that makes me feel connected to her in some small possessive way. "I got this shirt after completing a double black in Jackson." Her face is blank. "Wyoming? Jackson Hole? Ever heard of it?"

"It's a lake?"

I laugh. "A lake? Shit, they have Corbet's Couloir in Jackson

Hole, Ash. *Corbet's Couloir.*"

"No idea what that is," she says shrugging.

"Like one of the scariest double black diamond runs in the world, that's what. My dad and I did it once." I stop to smile at her. "Just once. I mean, if I had fucked it up I might've tried it again to get it right—if I was still alive. But it was one and done for both of us on the first jump and that was enough."

She clicks her tongue in disapproval and scowls. "Why would you do that? If I was your mom I'd have said no way."

"I was twenty," I reply, laughing.

"No, I mean, I'd have told my husband if he wanted to go do dangerous shit like that he can be single again. That's bullshit."

"Yeah, I don't blame you. And don't think I didn't just notice those unladylike words you just used. But my Corbet's days are definitely over. It was a once-in-a-lifetime thing."

"Because your dad's gone now and he was your bucket-list partner?"

I look up from my phone and study her face. It's contemplative. Normally when someone asks about my dad—and normally they don't, but if they do—I shut it down. I don't like to think about it. But I've already told Ashleigh about him, so what the fuck. It takes less energy to just answer the question honestly than it does to fight about why I refuse to discuss it. "Yeah," I say after a few seconds. "That's why. He and I did it all. I don't want to do it with anyone else. It's over." I hold her gaze for a few more seconds and then go back to my phone.

"That's how I feel, Ford." I look up again and she's got that sad look on her face. "About Tony. That's why it's so sad for me." She looks over at Kate and smiles. "I'm gonna get over him. I will. But right now, that's exactly how I feel. Like it's over, why bother with anything."

"Maybe you need to talk to someone. My dad was a psychiatrist, and I'm not saying you need that level of help or anything, Ashleigh, but maybe just a counselor. To talk things through."

Her laugh comes off a little sarcastic, if that's even possible. "Right."

I drop it because one thing I learned from being a kid who required a lot of counseling is that people generally do not like to discuss their mental health status. And Ashleigh is not interested in letting me in on the state of her mind at the moment.

But it doesn't take a genius. She's definitely depressed. All the crying, and then the abrupt back-to-normal mood changes. It's very obvious she's struggling with this breakup. "Anyway," I say to bring us out of this funk. "I have my assistant, Pam, on it for tonight." I tilt my head a little and unleash some dimple charm on Ash when my smile gets big. She giggles, like I'm obvious. "And I have the perfect quiet place to have a hand-holding walk in Vegas all set up."

She raises her eyebrows at me. "In fifteen minutes? They should call you the Fifteen-Minute Master."

"I might make you call me that tonight, thanks for the idea."

She makes a face at me.

"I know people. Famous people. Important people. People who I've provided certain favors to in the past. And I've called in a return. You're gonna have a great time with me tonight."

Her whole chest expands as she takes a deep breath, but before she can say what's on her mind, the waitress comes to our table. "Ready, folks?"

I take over since Ash is still daydreaming about our date. "We'll both have the number six. Pancakes, real bacon for her, turkey for me, scrambled and coffee. One regular, one decaf."

The waitress writes it down on her pad, takes our menus, and walks away.

"Back in control then, are you?" Ash says with a crooked sideways grin.

"I was never out of control, Ashleigh. But I know when to give a person space and when to make my move."

"Your move is breakfast?" She giggles again.

"This whole day is my move. Tomorrow you can let me know

how I did."

She looks away, a little embarrassed. "You just made my stomach flutter."

"Just one of many flutters I'll make you feel today, so get ready."

This time she laughs out loud. Several people actually turn to look at us. "Oh, shit—"

"I'll add that on to your count."

"What?"

I tilt my head at her and wait for her fight, but she gives in and that gives me a little thrill.

"What's my count up to anyway? Ten?"

"Ten? OK, if you say so."

"No!" she laughs. "I was asking, not telling!"

"Ten it is. Ten good ones, Ashleigh. Ten spankings that will change your life. Are you ready?"

She does that unconscious gesture where she puts her hands between her legs. I can't really see her do it, but I know from her posture and movement. I almost want to bend her over the table right now, that's how much it turns me on. "I'll just warn you. A night with me, my undivided attention, that's not something you'll ever forget. I might ruin you for life. I might make it impossible for you to ever be with another man again. I might—"

"Ford?"

"Yes, Ashleigh," I answer, smiling.

"I can't wait."

I'm about to reach under the table and grab her, but the waitress returns with our coffee and by the time she leaves, I'm back in control.

"I like this part," Ashleigh says as she takes a sip of her coffee.

"What part?"

"When everything is new and interesting. When you meet someone and you just have to know everything."

"Then tell me something new, Ash."

She takes another sip of her coffee. "You have to ask specifics, otherwise I don't know where to start."

Everyone likes guidance once in a while. And she basically just asked me to guide her. So I do. "Why did you go to Japan? Why did you run away?"

"Well, it's not quite as dramatic as I made it out to be. I call it running away because for me, it was. But everyone knew I was going to Japan. I went for college. I have a nice trust fund for education, but not much else."

I nod at this. My educational fund worked the same way. School was always paid for, but I only had so much discretionary income for expenses. I got the house in LA when my dad died. It was one of his last wishes. And I get money from another trust that matured when I turned twenty-five, so I'm far from broke now. But college wasn't an endless stream of money like most people think.

"And I wanted to get as far away from my family as I could, so I chose a school in Japan. I knew Chinese, some anyway. And I took Japanese in school for a few years. Mostly to piss off my dad, who wanted me to be fluent in Chinese. So I picked a school in Japan and left."

"Did you graduate?"

"Yeah, I graduated," she says a little defensively. "I'm in grad school. Well"—she sighs—"I *was* in grad school. I'm sure they've kicked me out by now. I haven't even bothered to call in and explain what the fuck—oops." She covers her mouth with her hand and looks hesitantly at me. I smile and she continues. "I never told them what was going on, and then I was very pregnant and was put on bed rest last fall. Kate was born a little early, there were some complications, and they have very different ways of delivering babies compared to the US, so I had to stay in the hospital for almost a month. I had to stay another two weeks after Kate was born because they wanted to monitor her. There was this whole breastfeeding debacle. They were pro-formula in the little hospital I was at. And I'm not against that, I just really wanted to breastfeed. I just needed it, that... *closeness* with someone, you know? So I figured it out. But it was not easy and it was painful for a while. None of that was easy." She stops to let out a long sad sigh. "In fact, I think looking back, even though I did get Kate out of all of it... the past six months have been hell for me. I'm not even sure why I'm still here."

She takes a moment to steady herself and I try to imagine what it must've been like, to be all alone in another country and going through all this. "Did your family come? Your father or sister?"

Her head shakes out a no. "They never knew I was even pregnant. Not until I came home, and even then I never intended for my father to find out. It was an accident. I only wanted to come back, talk to Tony one last time, and then go home to Japan and be left alone."

"Friends?"

"I have some friends, but I'm sort of a loner. My grad school friends were just co-workers, really. I was the only American in the program and even though I look a little bit Asian and I speak Japanese pretty well, I'm not Japanese. I enjoy the culture, I fit in, I guess. But Tony was my life. So when he was gone, I got very lonely."

We're both silent for a few seconds and then she huffs out a laugh. "I'm sorry for being such a downer. I bet I make your head spin with my mood swings."

"I like hearing about it."

"I like hearing about you, too, Ford." She peeks up at me from under her hair.

"Well, then I have a confession to make." She waits for a moment to see what I'll say and I enjoy her attention. Her eyes sparkle a little and I look for that now. I crave it. It means she's happy and I like seeing her happy. I'm looking for ways, words, things that will make that sparkle appear in her eyes. "I didn't tell you the whole truth back in Vail. About why I never went to the funeral."

"Are you going to tell me now?"

"Do you still want to know? It's not a big deal. I'm not even sure why I left it out, other than I would've had to admit that my dad died in the avalanche and I didn't want to do that with you right then."

She nods enthusiastically. "I still want to know. I really do."

"OK." I take a deep breath and let it out slowly. "Well, Minturn is the town where he was laid to rest, you already know that because we went there. But there's this out-of-bounds run on the backside of Vail Mountain, it leads to Minturn and it's called the Minturn Mile. It's three miles long, so don't let the name fool you. It's no Corbet's Couloir, it's a baby trail compared to that shit, but you know, it's got its own set of challenges."

I picture the ride up on the lift and the sign that says you're leaving the in-bounds run and if you need a rescue, you better have a lot of money because there will be a bill. That memory is a little funny, but knowing that part of my life is over, that's not fun at all. I suddenly know how Ashleigh just felt admitting that having her baby alone in a foreign country hurts. It's hard. It's hard to admit this stuff hurts.

"My dad and I did the Minturn Mile at least once a year. We'd take the lift up, hike over to the trail, and ski down to Minturn, then take our skis off and walk into town and have lunch at the local tavern. My mom always picked us up later. It's kind of a Vail thing, right? A tradition. Something we do as locals, something people come and do when they want to pretend they're local. So when the lawyers gave us his final wishes it said he wanted to be cremated and then buried in Minturn and he wanted to go down the trail one last time. It was a pretty big deal to set it all up, and like Mrs. Pearson said, everyone turned out for it. Everyone but me. The whole town was disappointed I didn't come."

I stop because I'm suddenly overwhelmed with shame that I missed it. My dad made his final request something special for me. Something we could share together, something that might give me a bit of pleasure. Something that might ease my pain.

TAUT

And I missed it.

I ran.

"But you couldn't bring yourself to do it, could you?" Ashleigh asks quietly.

My throat feels like it's closing up on me and I have to clear it several times to make that tight constricting feeling go away before I answer. "I never skied again. I never went back to Vail. I just… left. I left my mom to clean it all up and took a job producing a game show in Japan."

"When were you in Japan?" she asks, her eyes squinting down a little.

"On and off for the past few years. I started out there after graduation and they liked me. My weirdness never rubbed them the wrong way. I almost fit in there, if you can believe it."

"So you and I were living in the same foreign country at the same time. And yet we met on a freeway in Colorado. Do you think that's weird?"

That conversation I had with Rook at Coors Field comes barreling back to me. She got off the bus in Denver on a whim, so she could go to CU Boulder and study film like the guys who made *South Park*. The same school I went to.

I said *fate* and she said *weird*.

But I'm done with fate. "Yeah, it's weird all right."

We're silent for a few moments. And then Ash kicks me under the table. "You know what's really weird? The game shows in Japan! I can't believe some of the strange stuff they do on TV there. What was your show called?"

I go from sad and ashamed to embarrassed as fuck in two seconds flat. "I can't tell you," I say, laughing.

She knows why because she's laughing too. "Let me guess, it was Kiss Ass Roulette? And saying ass isn't a spankable offense, because it's a real show!"

"Oh, I know. Believe me, I know all the game shows in Japan. But no, that wasn't it." I have to lower my eyes and shake my head a little, that's how funny this moment is. "I can't even think about

326

Japan without remembering those shows. When people look at my resume they think I'm making this shit up. But when they realize they're real productions, they give me the job out of pity, I think. When I got the call for the HBO show in LA I almost couldn't believe it. I really thought my career would end up being one long string of Japanese game shows or Shrike fucking Bikes reality TV."

She laughs with me and then the food arrives and we sit back and wait for the plates to be served.

"Ford—" she says after the waitress leaves.

"Yes, Ashleigh."

"You are a nice guy."

Any other moment and I'd probably brush her off, but today I feel like a nice guy, so I just accept the compliment. "Thanks. I don't try to be nice all that often, but it's good to know I can put in an effort and it makes a difference."

"You've made a difference to me, Ford. And even if we never see each other again after we get to LA, I'll never forget you."

Her words hit me hard. The fact that she can say that so easily and not be bothered by it. So I shut down again and don't answer. Just dig into my food. Because I can't even go there yet. I can't. I'm not gonna let her get away. I'm not gonna stand aside so this guy can take her back and probably throw her away the first chance he gets. I let Ronin keep Rook, but Ashleigh is mine. And I'm not giving her up without a fight.

TWENTY-NINE

I **I**haven't been here in ages," Ashleigh says as Vegas shimmers off in the distance. She's got the windows down and the breeze whips her hair around as we finish the final leg of our journey today. "And I've never come from this direction. We come from the west, so it looks so different. Where are we staying?"

I don't answer her, I want it to be a surprise.

She sits up a little so she can tuck her feet underneath her. Her socks and shoes were discarded as soon as the climate changed about an hour ago. It's not hot, but compared to the frigid temperatures we just left behind in the mountains, this feels like August. She had to climb in the back and relieve Kate of all her blankets and her pink sweat suit. Thank God for a little bit of sun. At least the child can wear a dress now.

"We need to hit the stores for So Cal clothes."

"I say we shop for all our clothes in the gift shops."

I look at her like she's crazy.

"Yeah, we can be walking Vegas billboards!"

"Get my phone and look for Pam in my contacts."

For once she doesn't even ask why, she just finds Pam on the phone and then looks at me for directions.

"Tell her what kind of clothes you want for Kate. I've already got an infant gift basket in the room, so we don't need any of that essential stuff. Tell her what size and she'll have the hotel shoppers send some stuff up."

"I love this," she says as she types out the message.

"Love what?"

"Being taken care of for a day." She stops typing and looks at me. "It's been a while and ya know, sometimes you just want a gorgeous man to take you out to eat and buy you stuff."

I want to say a thousand things back to her. Things like, *I'll be getting my payback later* or *just wait until you see what I'm really going to do with you tonight.*

But I keep my mouth shut. Because I don't want to cheapen the experience for her. I want her to feel taken care of. I want this to be the best night of her life.

"You have an appointment with the fashion consultant at six, but you'll be busy all afternoon. I'll be watching Kate."

"I'll be doing what?"

"So eager," I say with a hint of innuendo. "Be patient. Slow down, enjoy this, Ashleigh. Make it count."

"You smell that, Ford?" Ashleigh sticks her head out the window and her hair whips past her face. "That's called pollution." I laugh. "I've missed it!"

It takes another forty-five minutes to get to the Four Seasons and by this time the novelty of traffic has worn off, the baby is cranky, and Ashleigh is looking sleepy. But as soon as we pull up to the valet everyone perks up, even Kate. She's quiet and still as she lets us bustle her out of the Bronco.

Everyone looks at us like we are vagrants who drifted in off the desert like tumbleweeds, but as soon as I hand over my credit card, they change their attitude. Maybe this bothers some people, but I could give a fuck. I stand there in my *I'm not a ski addict* t-shirt and hand the keys over to the valet. "This vehicle is very special, do not get a scratch on her."

He looks at me with a very serious face and says, "Yes, sir."

Money does this. The fucking Bronco is nothing but scratches from top to bottom because the two-toned brown and tan paint is original. Ashleigh just shakes her head at me and we walk through the lobby doors together.

The concierge approaches us immediately and I bark out, "Aston family."

"Yes, sir. You have the Presidential Strip-View Suite on the thirty-ninth floor. Can I have someone help you with your bags?" He looks around, noticing we have no luggage. Ash has a purse and the diaper bag and I have the baby in the car seat and that's it.

"There should be clothes upstairs?"

"Yes, everything you asked for has been provided."

"Thank you. And have the staff come find Miss Li for her spa and dressing appointment in thirty minutes."

"Yes, sir." He hands the key card to the bellboy and we follow him to the elevators.

Ashleigh squeals again and kisses Kate on her head.

"You act like a resort virgin, Miss Li."

"I'm a resort slut, Ford."

I shake my head at her.

"But it's been a pretty long time since I've been pampered, so if it's all the same to you, I'm gonna be a silly virgin today."

I take it Tony is not loaded. But I'm not gonna bring him up at all. She doesn't need me to point out the financial differences between the two of us so I hold in any and all snide remarks I feel like making and concentrate on keeping her on her toes. "I love silly virgins who are really sluts so I do not mind one bit."

The bellboy laughs, then pretends to cough as Ashleigh kicks me and shoots him a dirty look.

I wink and hand her a dimpled smile in return, and before she can decide if she's really upset or not, the elevator opens. The bellboy walks us to our door and presents it to us like he's Vanna White. I set Kate's carrier down in the room, then stuff some cash in the bellboy's palm and shove him down the hall.

"OK, let's see what they left us."

"Baskets filled with baby stuff." She sorts through it and then looks over at me with a questioning smile. "Breast pump and bottles?"

"Hey," I say, opening my arms up wide. "It's what all the moms do."

"Says who?"

"Says Pam, my assistant. I asked her how I'm supposed to sweep you off your feet if I have to bring you back to feed Kate, and she said pump."

"I think you have a thing for Pam."

"She's fifty-two, Ashleigh. I do not have a thing for her. Now get pumping. I want it stored in the fridge before you leave. And I rented the room across the hall for the babysitter. When we're done, the baby can come sleep with us. But I get you alone until I say we're done."

I wait for the fight but she tips her head up and smiles. "Deal." Then she grabs the pump and the bottles and settles on the couch. The room is boomerang-shaped, like it's got two wings. One side has the master bedroom and bath, the middle is the sitting area, and the far side has the dining room. Our dining room has been transformed into a nursery complete with crib, baby swing, changing table, a supply of diapers and so much other shit I can't identify, I start to feel a little apprehensive. "Should I put Kate in the swing? Does she use one of these?"

The pump is making noise in the other room so I walk back out and pick up Kate and ask again. "Can I put her in the swing, Ashleigh? We have a whole room filled with baby stuff back there."

"Yeah, she might like that," Ash says with her sleepy eyes. Shit, I guess pumping makes her just as tired as nursing.

"Come on, Kate, let's check out the rides." I carry Kate over to the dining room and set her down inside the swing. I lower the tray that locks her in place so she can't slip out, and then turn the thing on and press start. It begins slowly, gently swaying back and forth and each time Kate comes forward she closes her eyes. Each time she goes back, she tries to open them again, and after about ten swings, she's out.

I go back to find Ash and she's sleeping too.

Fucking girls.

I'd like to just stare at her, but the bottle is almost full so I tap her on the shoulder. "Ashleigh. You need to change the bottle."

She reluctantly opens her eyes, switches the pump to the other breast and gets a new bottle. "This thing is the shit, Ford."

I laugh. "Is that right?"

"Yes, I like the nursing, but bottles of breast milk, that's like revolutionary. I should've done this a long time ago."

I grab the remote and turn the TV on for some background noise, then go back to my phone to check messages. Pam is handling things—Pam always handles things. I've been living in Denver for the past seven months, taking a few trips here and there trying to secure this producer job for the sci-fi thing, so Pam had to keep everything in check. I'm not worried about what's going on in LA professionally, but I am getting nervous about what Ashleigh might do once we get there. If I knew Tony's last name I'd look him up, check his shit out and see what his deal is. But now that Ash knows I can hack, I'm pretty sure she'd see through any prying questions.

A little while later Ashleigh is packing the bottles away in the pantry fridge and Kate is sending off stink signals. I get up and get her out of the swing, just as Ashleigh comes out of the pantry.

"She needs a new diaper, Ford. I got this."

There's a knock at the door and Ashleigh looks conflicted.

"I'm not helpless. Besides, it's just Kate and me while you're getting all spa-ed up. I'm gonna have to do it eventually, might as well give it a try now."

"Ford—"

"Go. That's an order."

She hesitates a little longer but then lets out a long sigh. "OK, thank you. I totally owe you for all this."

I smile big and if she could read my mind right now, she'd be wet and blushing.

I wait until she's gone, then lay Kate on the changing table near the window. It's got a mobile toy thing over top of it, and even though Kate is a little bit upset at first, she's attracted to the bright-colored things dangling above her. I take off her t-shirt and open the diaper carefully.

"Yeah," I say to Kate, my captive audience. "That's some shit right there." She throws me a gummy grin and I laugh. I manage the diaper duty, toss that thing in a bag, and then put it in the diaper pail in the corner.

I grab a diaper that has Elmo on it and slip it under her butt, then close it up with the sticky tabs. Any man who cannot figure this out is a moron. I get busy dressing her in a new outfit next and this is a little more challenging, but I'm not called a genius for nothing.

THIRTY

I answer the knock at the door a little while later. "Can I help you?" I ask.

The messenger holds out a slip of paper. "The name of the babysitter procured for this evening, sir."

I get some cash out of my pocket and hand it over as he passes me the envelope. "Thanks," I say as he smiles and walks off. I close the door and go back to the couch. Kate is in the swing again. She's a pretty good baby. Not that I have a lot of experience, but from what I can tell, she's not anything like those babies you see in movies that make fun of clueless dads.

I take out my phone and start with the first name in my professional contacts. It's Adam. His name's not Adam, he's just my number one. I don't usually call him for easy shit like this, but I know he'll do it while I'm waiting if he's available.

If. He's iffy. And the last time I talked to him over Christmas, he had a huge mess on his hands, so he might be holing up, trying to stay out of sight. Which means he might actually be available. I press the generic avatar used for his name and listen to it ring.

One. Two. Three. I'm just about to hang up and call the next guy on the list when he picks up. "Yeah."

"Can you vet for me while I wait?" I can hear a girl panting on the other end. Fucking Merc.

"Is it absolutely necessary?" Now the girl is grunting, then a slap and a squeal.

"I don't call unless it's necessary."

"Hold on," he says as I listen to shuffling, the girl protesting in Spanish, and then, "Get off me, I gotta work for a minute. Stay put, though. Don't move. OK, dickhead, give me the name." I can hear his keystrokes as he gets online.

"Dee Vasquez, birthday 10-27-62, born in Jacksonville, Florida."

"One sec, let me pull it up. Why don't you just do this shit yourself?"

"I'm on vacation and I left the rig at home."

"OK, coming up." He snorts a little. "She's got two traffic tickets for speeding back in the Nineties. Lives in… Vegas. You in Vegas? I'm in Palm Springs. You should stop by."

"Negative. What else you got?"

"Nothing. This bitch is boring. Who is she? She fuck you over or something?"

"No, babysitter for tonight."

He laughs. He laughs so hard I have to hold the phone away from my ear. *"Baby-fucking-sitter?"*

"Nice talking to ya, Merc. I owe you a small."

He's still laughing when I hang up. I walk over at Kate and she's got her eyes open, staring up at me. "Fuck him, huh, Kate. He has no clue." She smiles at me and I melt a little and pick her up. She flings her little fists around in agreement. I take her back over to the couch and sit down. She's got her head on my shoulder, just kicking it, so I flip through channels until I get to the news.

We relax together listening to the stock report.

Merc's laughter comes back to me. If he saw me right now

he'd never let me live it down. We met at a recruitment weekend for MIT back in high school. He was from Boston, not the nice parts, so he took me on a memorable one-night bender through numerous back-alley bars. I think they stuck us together to avoid corrupting the normal students. Or maybe they hoped we'd both go to jail together before the weekend was over. That's a toss-up.

Merc and I both got offers—they couldn't *not* give us offers. We're fucking geniuses and MIT likes to hoard the country's geniuses, keep us all neatly contained in the socially accepted bubble of serving the nation.

I went to film school—and I'm pretty sure my recruitment adviser from MIT threw up on the other end of the phone when I told her that. And Merc went into the army, but only so they'd train him how to kill. He never wanted to be a SEAL or a Ranger. He just wanted some hard and fast training so he could slip underground and not get himself offed when he completed his more hands-on jobs. He never had a team like I did. He's a solo guy.

But he's good at what he does, so if he says Dee Vasquez is clean, then she's clean.

Pam had one of my suits driven up from LA and the staff delivers it at six. Kate's asleep now, so I take the suit into the bedroom and get dressed. I don't mind the jeans, but I love the suits. This one's black, has a short coat, the sleeves are tailored just right so it shows some of my crisp white shirt at the cuff, and my broad shoulders are accentuated by a taper from the waist of the jacket all the way down the slim-fit trousers. The white pocket square and the black tie sets the whole thing off.

I comb my hair back and leave the one-day stubble on my chin.

Even I know that shit looks sexy.

The sitter arrives at six fifty and takes Kate and the bottles of breast milk across the hall to the second room I reserved that is stocked with everything she'll need for the evening.

And at exactly seven o'clock Ashleigh walks through the door.

THIRTY-ONE

unleash the dimple on her. "I love it."

"Well." She blows some hair out of her eyes. It's piled high on top of her head but she's got those cute bangs that are too long to stay out of her eyes and too short to put up with the rest of her hair. "You *should* love it, they tell me you picked it out."

The dress is very revealing, but only in the back—and that's because there is no back. But her front is covered from neck to toes as it drapes down in a triangle shape and then fastens at each hip. The top is attached to a delicate red ribbon that circles her neck like a collar and the flowing fabric is snug at her waist, and then falls to the ground like a red waterfall. Her matching red toenails peek out from black strappy heels. "I have no bra on, Ford. If I leak through this dress in public—"

"Relax, Miss Li." I hold my arm out to her and she smiles.

"It's nice. Thank you. I haven't dressed up in forever and I haven't been on a real date in, God, I have no idea."

I have a million questions and I want to ask them all this very second. I want to know why he left her. Did she do something?

TAUT

Is Kate not his baby? I admit, that question has popped into my head more than once. Maybe that's why his parents haven't seen her. Maybe that's why he left? I secretly hope that's the case. In fact, I'm in full-on fantasy mode right now, picturing all the ways in which Ashleigh might've fucked up and ruined her chances with this guy. I want to ask so fucking bad. What the hell kind of relationship was she in that he never took her out? But this is her night and the last person we're gonna spend our time talking about is Tony. "You look spectacular in red. Are you ready?"

She looks around the room, trying to see into the dining room-turned-nursery. "Where's Kate?"

"Across the hall in the other room." She opens her mouth to say something, probably about checking on her, but I put up a hand. "Ashleigh, stop. She's fine. I'll bring her back at the end of the night, she'll sleep with us tonight. I had the babysitter checked out, she's got the milk, she's perfectly safe."

"OK, sorry. I'm kinda nervous."

"Why?" I ask as I touch her elbow and lead through the door and down the hallway to the elevators.

"I don't know what to expect." The elevator doors open and I put a hand on her bare back and guide her inside. "What are we doing?"

"We're having a night out. A slow, quiet night out."

She looks up at me and her eyes are wide and uncertain. "What about after?"

I think this through for a moment because I'm starting to understand what has her so edgy. She's scared of me. Of what I might do to her tonight. Of what I might expect of her tomorrow. I pull her in front of me and put my arms around her waist, then lean down into her neck. She's a few inches taller in her heels so she's easily accessible. "You can say no anytime you want. *Stop. Enough. No more.* All these are words you can use if you want to. I would like it if you trusted me to take care of you, but you're not my prisoner. You can sleep in the room across the hall if you'd like. I won't be mad."

"You won't?" She looks over her shoulder at me and I impulsively bite her earlobe.

"I'll be disappointed, but not mad. If it's not fun, there's no point in doing it."

"So those ten spankings—"

"Will make you scream my name five times, I promise you."

She lets out a long breath as the elevator doors open. There's a crowd of people waiting but she doesn't move and neither do I. The other guests stare at us as Ashleigh tilts her head up and says so everyone can hear. "So for every two spankings I get an orgasm? It's a two-to-one ratio?"

Snickers from the audience and I guide her forward. "For that outburst, Miss Li, you'll get an extra swat."

She laughs and takes my hand. "I can do that, you know. Hold your hand. I requested it and even though you said you don't take requests, you lied."

I pull her towards the valet area and chuckle. "You're working on number twelve now, Ashleigh." Our car is waiting and I open her door. She slides in and I get in after her.

"So where are we going?"

"Patience." I put my arm around her and the driver pulls out, but we don't exit onto the Strip, instead he turns right and we take the hotel access road around the property. "Are you excited?" I ask, leaning down to bite her ear again. I'm having a hard time keeping my mouth off her body right now.

"A bite is a kiss, right?"

"Yes."

"What if I want a real kiss when the night is over?"

"What if I want a promise when the night is over?"

"What kind of promise?" She looks up at me and her nerves are back. I can feel her heart thrumming inside her chest as she leans into me.

"What kind of kiss do you want? A small peck to say thank you? A romantic one that says I care? Or a passionate one with some bite mixed in that will make you come in the hallway?"

She inhales and swallows. I'm really making her nervous now. "I'm not sure yet."

"I'm not sure what kind of promise I want either. Something small, maybe—a phone number? A little more serious perhaps—another date tomorrow night at my house in Bel Air? Or maybe you just never leave and we give it a real try?"

The car stops before she can answer, but she takes those few seconds before the driver opens the door to steal a look at me. "I can't think about tomorrow."

"Then don't. Forget about tomorrow. Tonight it's only you and me and no one else exists until this date is officially over."

The door opens. I get out and reach for her hand, pulling her gently to her feet. She looks past me into the lobby and smiles. "OK. I'm all yours."

Damn right, I muse.

I lead her inside to the elevators and we take it up to the top floor where the restaurant is. Our table is waiting when we arrive and the maître d' guides us to a private semi-circle booth that faces the Strip and has an absolutely stunning view. "I said sushi, but the sushi bars in Vegas are not intimate, so we'll have to make do with this tonight."

She hunches her shoulders a little and gets excited as she looks over the menu. "Wow, fuck the sushi—I'm getting lobster."

I close my eyes and shake my head slowly. *Oh, dear lord.* She's going to drive me insane with her antics. "Why must you try me like this?" I ask as I open my eyes.

She laughs. "Ford, you think I'm adorable, you said so. How much fun would I be if I just did everything you said and behaved myself?" She looks up at me and bats her eyelashes. "You'd never have your dirty way with me if I was compliant. And by the way, your package looks so good in that suit." She looks down and then up and waggles her eyebrows.

"I take it you've settled into the date, then? Your nervousness has passed?"

She sighs and nods. "Yes. You're too wily for me, Ford. You

think of everything. Why fight it?"

I slip my hand behind her neck and fist her hair as I whisper in her ear. "I do like the fight, but not tonight. Tonight you're mine. Tonight I own you. I get to take care of you. I get to make you feel things for the first time. Tonight I promise you perfection. So just give in, Ashleigh. Give yourself to me and let it happen."

She turns her head, just slightly, just so her lips are against my rough cheek. My free hand involuntarily comes up to her neck and presses against her throat. She moans a little before I loosen my hold. "Ford," she says seductively into my ear. "I'm going to kiss you right now. In public." And then I feel the stretch of her neck under my palm and her soft lips touch my earlobe, just skim across the sensitive skin before pulling away.

It actually makes me close my eyes for a second.

"See," she breathes. "It's nice. I trust you. But I like soft kisses. So in between the rough stuff you like, be careful with me. Give me something soft, because I really need it."

I'm speechless. I'm still thinking about her kiss, so I have to play catch up with her words.

This confession from her unlocks something deep inside. Something that makes me want to hold her close and protect her. To wipe away all the things that have her worried and make her world perfect.

I want her. I'd let her sloppy-kiss me right here in front of everyone if she asked right now.

But the waiter arrives and we both turn our attention to food for enough moments that the insane attraction I have to this girl is checked. She gets the lobster and I get the prime rib. But my appetite is gone and my mind is only on one thing right now.

How the fuck do I keep her from leaving me tomorrow?

When we're done ordering we sit in silence and enjoy our drinks. This place is over-the-top yet subdued at the same time. Our booth has a high back that curves around the plush bench so we can't see the diners on either side of us. It's just Ashleigh, me, and the nighttime Vegas skyline.

"Tell me something new, Ford."

I smile at her request. "That's what started it, you know. Your confession that you thought I was a hot serial killer."

"A hot serial killer who would beat back my keen defenses with his unorthodox charm so that I'd beg him to kill me during kinky sex."

"Hmmm…"

She laughs. "Yeah, seems like your diabolical plan is working. Please don't make me beg you to kill me tonight."

"I'll make you beg for something, but death will be the last thing on your list. More, that's what you'll be begging for. More."

She smiles and shakes her head a little, like I'm such a cocky bastard. "Let's play a game."

"You have a game for everything, it seems." I have my arm around her shoulder and I trace the curve of her small muscles in her upper arm, thinking of her shivering touch on my back last night. "What kind of game?"

She turns her body a little so she can see my face. "It's called Lie, Lie, Truth. You tell me three things about you, two of them lies, one not. And I have to guess which one is true."

"What do you get if you guess?"

"A favor. To be claimed at some time in the future."

"I've never heard of this game, I think you make these games up."

"It was something my friends and I played in school. We had no boys, remember? We had to keep ourselves occupied somehow."

"Were you a Sandy or a Rizzo when you were in school?" She bursts out laughing and I have to shush her because it's so loud. "Stop."

"A Sandy—are you talking about *Grease*?"

Even I laugh now. "Sorry, I'm a film producer, remember? Now tell me, Sandy or Rizzo?"

"You tell me. Ready?" I nod. "OK." She stops, to think up

her lies presumably, and then turns to me grinning. "In tenth grade I won a contest for selling the most candy bars for our school orchestra. I can play four instruments. I got kicked out of the orchestra in eleventh grade because I stood up and yelled, *Play ball* after we performed the Star-Spangled Banner for a competition."

"No contest, number two. You're a Sandy who thinks she wants to be a Rizzo."

She squirms and huffs out a small laugh. "Yes, that's true. I liked being smart as a kid. I was an overachiever. But why do you think that? I mean, how did you know that was the truth?"

"It's pretty difficult for foreigners to get into a Japanese university. I might not know much about you, but I know you're exceptional. Selling the most candy bars is not exceptional and I don't think you'd ever ruin someone else's special moment just to be a brat. You play four instruments was the only logical answer. So I win a future favor and now it's my turn. Ready?"

"Yes, I'm ready," she says, her eyes locked on mine.

"I've never had a girlfriend. I've never wanted a girlfriend. I wish I'd never met you." I look down at her and her mouth is open, gaping at me.

"Um…"

"Should I say them again?"

She stares at me. "You've never had a girlfriend? How is that possible?"

I shrug a little. "I've never had a girlfriend and I've never wanted one… until you. I've had lots of sex. And I've been on dates. But the girls I'm usually with have strict rules and no talking or touching were two of them."

"What did you do on the dates, if you didn't talk?"

"I fucked them in the limo on the drive to the restaurant. I bought them dinner and drank some expensive Scotch. I fucked them in the limo on the drive back to their place. I dropped them off."

She looks away, a little bit stunned, I think. "Why do they let

TAUT

you treat them that way?"

"Because they can't stop themselves. Because finding a man who will love and cherish them is too much trouble. Because I was offering a physical encounter only. Because I was unavailable except in this very specific way. Because they're unable to see the benefits of nothing, and instead settle for something."

"Do you want to treat me like that?"

"Never. And now I owe you a future favor too."

Before she can say anything else the wait staff delivers our salads. When they leave I change the subject and we talk about ridiculous things like Japanese game shows and the character development of Odd Thomas. But the entire time I'm really dying to ask her what she thinks of me. I need to know, but not yet. She needs to see all of me first. She needs to experience me and I her. We need to experience what us together looks like.

We'll do that tonight.

When dinner is over we take the elevator downstairs and she leans into me as we wait for the car to be brought around. "Are we going back to the hotel?"

"You didn't get your long quiet walk yet." The car pulls up and we get in. I take the silk scarf out of my pocket and hold it out in front of her. She looks up at me with a sly smile and I chuckle. "Ready?"

"I thought we were talking a walk?"

"Trust me."

She rolls her eyes. "I do." And then she takes a deep steadying breath as I tie it around her eyes and knock on the window that separates us from the driver so the car can move forward.

"Do you like being blindfolded?"

"Yes," she breathes.

"Good, because after our long quiet walk is over and I have you back up in our bedroom, I'm going to do it again." She smiles but I can practically feel her nervousness. The car stops and we wait for the driver to open our door.

"That was fast."

"We didn't go very far." I step out and take her hand, pull her into my chest, and then put one arm around her shoulder and the other on her waist as we walk forward. An attendant opens the door to the building and we're accosted by the smell of the ocean.

"Where are we?" she asks.

The subdued bluish light from the tanks ripples across her face, making her look like an underwater sea goddess. "Guess."

"An aquarium?"

"Very good guess."

I slip her blindfold off and she actually claps her hands and squeals. "The Shark Reef! Are we the only people here?"

"They closed an hour ago. You can't have a quiet walk when there are throngs of tourists around, now can you?" I offer her my arm and she wraps her hands around it and leans her head on me. "Ready?"

She simply nods and we walk forward. Slowly. Looking and thinking about life, but not our lives. We go in the tunnel and look at the reef first. "You wanted to watch life and not participate in it, right?"

"You're amazing. That's exactly what this is. A glimpse at life from the outside looking in. It's perfect."

"Yes, I think it is." We watch the fish for a while, a part of their world, but yet not.

"I want to cash in my favor now, if that's OK."

"Ask away, Ash."

"Promise you won't forget me."

I get this immediate pang in my chest. Like a twisting knife. Fuck, that hurts.

"You're not promising, Ford."

I huff out some air. "Of course not, Ashleigh. I'm never going to forget you. But I won't have a chance to forget you either. I'm not letting you out of my sight." She squeezes my upper arm and

TAUT

I turn her around so she's facing me. I tip her chin up with my fingers and lean down, closer, keeping eye contact the entire time. My lips hover over hers. Almost no space separates us.

"Will you kiss me?" she breathes into me.

"No, Ashleigh. I need a promise first."

"Then what are you doing?" Her gaze never wavers from mine.

"Teasing you."

She laughs and starts to pull away but my hand slips up to her neck and my thumb traces the line of her jaw. I lean in again and she actually sighs at my small touches. "I won't give up. And this is my night," I say so softly that the words almost escape even my detection. It elicits a moan and I pull back.

She draws in a long breath. "I don't want to be teased, I want to be kissed."

"Miss Li, we have all night for that. But this part of the date is for being slow and quiet. Just like you asked. And if I kissed you now I'd end up ripping your clothes off and bending you over so I could take you from behind. And I might still do that when we go back to the hotel, but I have so many, many other things I'd like to do first."

She looks up at me as she absently chews on her lower lip. She notices me noticing and she smiles. "You made me tingle."

I laugh. "Did I?"

She nods, holding back her smile. "What favor will you ask of me?"

"Are you nervous about it?"

She nods again.

"Do you think I'd ask for sex?"

She shakes her head. "No. That's the last thing you'd ask for. Either I give it willingly or you don't want it."

"How do you know me so well?"

She puts her hands on my shoulders and then rests her head on my chest, like we're slow-dancing to the music of a captured sea. "We're complements, you and I. Aren't we?"

"Yes, you bring me to perfection."

"I love my date."

"It's not over yet. We're still in the first tunnel. Should we keep going?"

"Yes, but I'm afraid of what comes after."

"Of me?"

"No."

And that's all she says as she pulls back and takes my hand. I let it go because she was referring to tomorrow. She walks forward, leading me away from our moment and back into our date.

We marvel at the fish. We walk through the tunnel and stop at all the tanks, and we look up at the sharks swimming above us with our mouths gaping open like children. We talk about the ocean and beaches we've visited and how many gallons of water are in these tanks. I hold her hand the entire time. She points at sea turtles. She makes a face at the Komodo dragon and quakes a bit when I point out the golden crocodile and the giant snake swimming in the water. She sits in front of the luminescent jellyfish for so long I have to pull her away. She lies on her stomach over the concrete bench around the stingrays and reaches down to touch them and then squeals and pulls back exclaiming they are slimy. I get her a stuffed pink dolphin and Kate an orange and white Nemo clownfish from the gift shop and leave a fifty-dollar bill on the counter.

She is happy.

Tomorrow isn't even a blip on her radar when we leave the gurgling sounds of the underwater oasis behind and climb back into the car so we can be shuffled back to the Four Seasons. She leans into me the entire ride up the elevator, and then we stop and check in on Kate, but she's sound asleep after drinking herself into a breast milk coma.

"I'll come back and get her in a few hours," I tell the babysitter.

And then I lead Ashleigh across the hall, pull her into our suite, and push her against the wall. "It's time to end the date,

Ash. Tell me what kind of promise you can give and I'll hand over a kiss."

She takes a deep breath and tilts her chin. The light is low in here, but her eyes sparkle a bit as she studies my face. "I can do a phone number."

I lean down and touch my lips to her cheek, lingering for a moment, letting her warmth radiate into me, then pull back. "I can manage a peck."

"Is it good enough for now?"

"It's more than enough. Do you trust me, Ashleigh?" I ask her one more time.

"Yes," she replies immediately. "I do, Ford."

"Good," I tell her as I stroke her cheek. "I'm so glad," I whisper in her ear, sending a shiver down her entire body. I untie the ribbon around her throat that's holding up her dress and the red fabric flutters to her waist, exposing her breasts to me. I squeeze, but this time I am kind and considerate and gentle. They are hard and full and the milk drips out. She moans because they are tender, even though my touch is light. "I will be very careful with you tonight, Ashleigh. The spankings might hurt for a moment, but I promise to fully satisfy you many times."

I kneel down and slip my hand over the top of her foot. She bites her lip and sucks in some air. I unbuckle her straps and slide it off, my fingertips lightly caressing the high arch and then her heel. She gasps again when I repeat the whole act on the other foot. Her dress is being held up only by the curve of her hips. It takes nothing more than a slight tug to make it whoosh to the floor at her feet. I lean forward and nibble her inner thigh and slip my hand around and cup her ass. I move up to the v between her legs and I bite her there too, gently, just above her most sensitive spot.

This time she moans.

"Do not come, Ashleigh." She's very close and I've barely touched her.

She bites her lip and nods her head, but her eyes are closed.

I stand up before she loses control and brush the hair away from her eyes. "Your nightwear is in the hall bathroom. Go put it on and join me in the bedroom when you're done."

I watch her as she walks off, her hips swaying gently, her thighs brushing against each other, like she's trying to stimulate herself. I smile at that. Because the first one will be easy. The first one will come out in a gush. She will writhe and scream. She will buckle her back and open her legs wider as she says my name over and over when I suck on her pussy. And then she'll be primed and ready for the more adventurous things I have planned for her tonight.

I'm going to take Ashleigh Li. I'm going to own her body in every way imaginable. I'm going to take her from behind. From above. From below. She's going to beg me for more, beg for my cock in her mouth, and beg me to do it again and again and again.

She will *never* forget me, even if she does walk out of my life tomorrow.

THIRTY-TWO

The master bedroom in our suite has a vast view of the Strip. I turn out all the lights and enjoy it for a moment, then flick on two small sconces above the headboard. The light is soft and amber in color. It will shower Ashleigh's beautiful body with golden light. At the foot of the bed is a bench upholstered in a plush light blue fabric that accentuates the aqua and cream color scheme of the room. There are some small throw pillows on the bed and I put a few within easy reach of the bench.

When I turn around to check on her, she's already there. Standing in the doorway wearing a black baby doll top that presents her full breasts, then flows down and stops just at her hips. Her panties are also black and are fully exposed.

I smile. A dimpled smile, but not a creepy one that says *I'm gonna fuck you*. It's a sincere one that says, "You are fucking beautiful."

"Thank you," she says softly.

I look down at her feet and notice she didn't put the shoes on. "I don't like them," she explains when she notices my gaze.

TAUT

"I have no complaints, Ashleigh." I beckon her with my fingers. "Come here." She bites her lip and then takes a deep breath and walks over and takes my hand. I lead her over to the bench at the foot of the bed. "Sit down."

She sits.

And she is the perfect height to do fun things with my *package*, as she likes to call it. She looks at my dick as it grows under my suit trousers, and then tips her head up to me.

Holy fuck, she is stunning. Her eyes are dark with makeup, but not too dark. Her lips are not glossy with lipstick anymore like they were at the start of the evening, but they are still stained a nice red color and that plump pout she has makes me want to nibble on them.

I control myself. I've lasted this long and I've planned her first real experience with me perfectly. Taking her in a fit of desire comes much later.

I pull one side of the bench away from the foot of the bed and straddle it. She watches everything I do, her chest moving up and down a little faster now. I imagine the adrenaline coursing through her body perfectly matches my own. "Get on your knees, Ashleigh. Place your chest on the bench and face me so I can see your eyes."

Her tongue flicks her upper lip and her breathing quickens, but she obeys without talking and lowers herself down to her knees and does exactly what I ask.

That turns me on so fucking bad, the fact that she will submit without me asking. It's like a gift. She takes a deep breath, closes her eyes, then opens them again because she knows I want to watch her watch me. "Are you ready?"

She nods first. "Yes. Ten spankings."

"Pull your panties down, Ashleigh. And leave them around your knees."

She keeps her chest on the bench and reaches back to pull down her black lace panties. The baby doll lingerie flutters below her stomach as she moves and then her ass is bare. I push the fabric up her back to get the full view of her curves.

"Would you like me to count for you? Or can you manage that tonight?"

She licks her lip again and if she doesn't stop that, I'm gonna lean down and bite her. "I can manage."

"Put your hands wherever you want, but once they're there, you may not move them. Understand?"

"Yes." She brings them up and then clasps them together at the small of her back.

I love her.

My left hand drags a few stray wisps of hair away from her face so I can see her better. She senses the pleasure she's giving me and smiles just as my right hand comes down on her right cheek with a loud smack.

She moans as I watch her ass turn red. "One."

She is perfect.

I massage her ass where the handprint forms and just as she relaxes a little I bring my hand down again on her left cheek.

"Two," she says before the moan this time.

Now both cheeks are red and I massage them in firm circles. My fingers slip between her legs and she opens up a little, moaning even more as I play with her folds. I slip a finger inside her and she is so wet I withdraw immediately so she won't come. "Did it hurt, Ash?"

"No," she says immediately. "Not this time."

"Tell me, Ashleigh. Tell me how it made you feel."

"Oh," she moans. "It was like last night in the bathroom. It felt so good, the pain was left behind."

"Get up off the floor and stand in front of me. I owe you a reward."

She stands up and the panties around her knees fall to the floor.

I change my position so I'm not straddling the bench anymore, but sitting normally, right in front of her. "Come here," I say softly as I open my legs up to give her room. She inches forward and her legs are brushing against mine, causing a flicker of excitement to erupt through my whole body. I reach up to the strap on her left shoulder and pull it down, then do the same with the right. Her breasts are far too full to allow the lingerie to fall freely, so I use both hands to pull the soft fabric down her arms and watch it flutter to the floor at her feet.

Her breasts. Holy fucking God, her breasts are spectacular.

I cup them, very softly. But she's so full of milk they drip.

I growl with desire. "Is it too uncomfortable? Do you need to take care of this?" I ask in a low throaty voice that betrays every dirty thought running through my mind.

She shakes her head. "I'm fine."

I squeeze a little harder then and she opens her mouth but it's a whimper that makes my dick so hard I might explode before she does.

I get up off the bench and loosen my tie. She watches every move I make. I take it off and put it around her neck, then slide the knot up to her throat, not tight, but enough. It curves over her breasts and falls down her torso where it flirts with her belly button.

She takes a deep breath.

"I won't hurt you."

"I know."

She's amazing.

I step out of her way and beckon to the bench. "Your turn to sit." She turns around and takes a seat, her hands fidgeting in her lap as she swallows and finally tilts her head to look up at me. I put a few throw pillows behind her. "Lie back, Ash."

She actually blushes a little and lets out a nervous giggle, but she bites it back as she chews on her lower lip and leans back, exposing herself to me.

"Open wider."

She obeys, but she moans as she does it. I laugh. "I swear to God, Ashleigh, I will spank the shit out of you if you come before my tongue touches your clit."

"Oh—"

I reach down and grab her nipple and squeeze. Milk shoots out and she gasps, but she stops moaning. "That was close. You are way too easy."

"I'm desperate, Ford. Please, just lick me already!"

I kneel down in front of her legs and she moans again, so I get back up and go to the basket of essentials I asked the concierge to provide in the bedroom basket. There's two black silk scarves in there and I bring them both over to her, setting one on the bed, and holding the other up to her face. She watches carefully. "I don't want you to come until I tell you to, understand?"

She nods. "Yes," she says as she tries to stay in control.

"You're never gonna last, Ashleigh."

She laughs. "I'm sorry, you—I just—Ford, just looking at you makes me come. I can't help it."

I shake the scarf. "Which is why we need this for now. I'll take it off in a little bit, but for now, you need it. Don't you agree?"

"Yes." She smiles up at me and I wonder if putting it on will make her release even quicker than leaving it off.

"Oh, for fuck's sake. Just try your best." I tie it around her eyes and let the long ends drape over her shoulders with her dark hair. I kneel down and her moaning starts immediately, I reach up and pinch her nipple again and this elicits a real whimper. A pain whimper and not an orgasmic one.

Round one to Ford.

I let go and part her legs, then lift them up and push her knees into her chest. Her scent is so erotic, I have to stop and breathe it in. It's sweet and intoxicating. "Hold your legs open, please," I ask her in a soft growl that betrays my hungry desire.

She obeys and I have to pinch her again to keep her focused.

She's not gonna last another minute, so fuck it. We might as well get this one over with so we can move on. I lower my mouth to her pussy and she gets the kiss of her life as I suck on her clit.

She comes immediately. She gushes into my mouth. Her whimpers and moans are not about pain, even though I'm squeezing the shit out of that nipple. Her whole back buckles and her thighs clamp down on my head as her fingers fist my hair.

I push her legs apart forcefully and caress her inner thighs for a few seconds before pulling back and standing up. "You could've put off the next two spankings for quite a while if you held it in, but it's too late now. Bend over the bench, Ashleigh. That's two spankings for me and one orgasm for you."

She whines as she pulls herself up from the bench and then kneels down, her hands behind her back, her face turned to the side. I straddle the bench again and pull her face closer to my crotch. Her breath is hot against my dick, even through the thick fabric of my trousers. "Do you know what number we're on?"

"Yes."

"Spread your legs this time, Ashleigh."

She does, no hesitation at all and before she's even in position my left hand pushes her face into my dick and my right hand smacks her hard on an upswing. It catches her pussy and both cheeks this time and she yelps, but her hands stay put at the small of her back. Her breath comes out in short gasps against me. My fingers dip inside her folds and she's dripping from her last explosion. I push two fingers inside her and she moans.

"You forgot to count, Miss Li. Let's try it again."

I smack her again and this time as soon as I'm done she says, "Three." I don't give her a chance to think, just swat one more time. "Four."

I lean down to her back and bite her shoulder blade and then stand up, still straddling the bench, and release the button and unzip my pants. "How many orgasms have I given you since we met, Ash?"

"Um…" She knows what's coming, so she takes a few seconds. "Four. No, five. You talked dirty to me this morning and that was not my fault."

I sit back down and whisper in her ear. "How many have you given me?"

She takes a deep breath and lets it out slowly. "None," she

whispers back.

"I'd like one now. Open your mouth."

She has to take a deep breath first, but she opens her mouth. I inch towards her and release my dick. It's fully hard. Hell, I was hard the minute she came in the bedroom. The head of my cock brushes against her lips and she leans forward, eager. I encourage her to take me as I fist her hair and push. Her mouth opens wider and then her hot, wet tongue licks my head and it's my turn to moan when she buries it inside her mouth. Her lips stretch around and seal against my shaft. She sucks, then pulls back, licking and swirling her tongue as the cool air replaces her heat.

She keeps her hands behind her back even though I could care less if she wants to use them or not at this point. I pull her upright on her knees and change my position so I'm facing forward and she's between my legs.

I lean back against the pillows. "Fuck me with your mouth, Ashleigh. Make me come and we can move on to your next orgasm."

I push her head and she opens up her mouth more, stretching her lips around my thickness. I push again and her tongue flattens out. This shit almost drives me over the edge. Her face is not panicked or in distress, so I fist her hair a little harder and she hums out a moan against my sensitive skin. The vibrations tickle and I can't wait any longer, I force her face into me so my cock in is in her throat and then reach down and shove my balls up to her chin.

She gags a little and I ease up and let her take a breath. If she complains I'll stop, so I wait for a moment.

No complaints. I push towards me again, her tongue flirts with my shaft, and then I ram myself up against her soft palate until she gags. I release, let her have a moment to recover, and do it again. Each time she tries to take more of me. On the fourth time with no complaints I gush down her throat and she swallows three times, once for each wave of semen.

I give her some air and then lean down to whisper in her ear.

"You OK? You do understand you can say no, right?"

She takes a few breaths and nods—her face turning up towards the sound of my voice. I wonder if her eyes are closed behind that blindfold? "I came too," she says softly.

I laugh. "You sneaky shit!" I smack her ass playfully and then let my fingers dip into her pussy and sure enough, she is dripping again.

"You said I'd get one orgasm for every two swats, and since I got three this time, I figured you owed me, so why wait?" She smirks from behind her blindfold and I smack her again and then pull the scarf down so it's around her neck with my tie. She looks down at my dick and that smirk grows into a shit-eating grin, then she brings that sneaky simper back up to meet my gaze.

She just checked me out and she liked what she saw.

Round two to Ford.

I get up, take off my suit coat and shirt, then drop my trousers. She watches me the whole time.

"Are you ready?"

She glances down to my cock, it's already getting hard again. She's small and I'm not, so I'm wondering if she's worried. But she just kneels down, bending over the bench with her hands behind her back for her spanking.

I am in love with her.

"Open," I command.

She obeys instantly.

"Wider," I command as I straddle the bench again.

She adjusts, her legs so wide her pussy is barely hovering over the floor.

"Perfect." I wasn't going to do this, but I think she'll like it, so take my chances and swing my palm upward until it connects with her clit. She squirms and squeals for this one, but I don't even need to check her pussy to see if she liked it, she's dripping.

"Five," she calls out before I can make a remark about the count. I smack her pussy again and this time she jumps a little.

"Six."

"Stay just like you are." I get up and grab the condoms and some oil from the basket. She says nothing. I kneel down behind her and open the oil and then drip it over her ass.

She whimpers and tries to sit up. "Ford—"

"Shhh," I say as I push her back down. My fingers go to her bare back and I trace out the kanji from our sleeping game last night. "Trust me, Ashleigh. I said I won't hurt you. Whatever we do, you will like it or we will stop."

She takes a deep breath.

"OK?"

"Yes."

I'm not gonna fuck her in the ass our first time, she's crazy. I'm trying to make her love me, not run away. But I am gonna play with it. I snicker at that and she looks over her shoulder at me with an annoyed expression.

I tuck down my amusement, because I'm winning and I don't want to give her any stupid reasons to rebel against my control.

I rub the oil onto her cheeks in wide, slow circles—my fingertips reaching past the boundary between sensual and sexual, then slip between her legs and massage her inner thighs. This makes her sigh with pleasure and she relaxes her head back down on the bench. I continue to knead the softest skin near her sex, sometimes passing innocently over her clit or up and down her slit. But mostly I keep it confined to her thighs and ass cheeks. After a few minutes I can tell she's totally relaxed and I push a finger inside her pussy, then slide it up to her asshole, push against her little pucker, let her gasp in surprise, then withdraw and go back to her pussy.

I do this again and again, and after the fifth or sixth time she starts to wiggle against my finger when I push against her asshole.

I slip it inside and she moans, but it's not a painful moan. I position my hard and throbbing cock against her clit and slap her pussy with it while I continue to play with her ass.

TAUT

"Ohhhhh," Ashleigh moans. "I want you to fuck me so bad, Ford."

I push my finger inside her pucker, farther this time. "I want you to come right now and clench your ass around my finger."

Her cheeks are squeezing before I even get the last word out.

I'm going to marry this girl.

I smack her hard before she's even done coming and she yells out, "Seven."

Holy fuck. She's perfect. I smack her again and this time, "Eight," comes out as a moan of pleasure.

"How many orgasms, Ashleigh?"

"Seven for me and one for you."

"Here comes eight. Stand up, please." I back away from her so she can stand and then take her spot on the bench. I tap her thigh. "Put your leg on my shoulder, Ashleigh."

She lifts her leg and the sight of her swollen clit peeking through her lips almost does me in. She rests the back of her ankle on my shoulder and lets out a long breath. "The sight of your wet pussy, your swollen clit, and your open legs is something I hope to see again and again, Ashleigh. I want this so fucking bad." I slide my hand under her lifted thigh and cup her ass, then grab her behind the knee of the other leg and lift her off the ground. "Other leg on my shoulder."

She obeys and my other hand follows her motion and cups that ass cheek as well.

"Oh, my God, Ford." Her arms wrap around my head and she scoots her pussy closer to my face. I stand and walk over to the wall of windows and press her up against them. "Lean back, love. Release your hold on my head and stretch your arms against the glass. Bare yourself to me, Ashleigh. Open yourself up to me completely."

She obeys but she's tense from being in this position.

"Trust me, Ashleigh. Relax. Think about people with binoculars and telescopes. People who train them on this suite, hoping against hope that one night they'll peek through and see your fantastic ass, my exceptional package, and my face between your legs giving you the orgasm of your life."

I pull her towards me until my mouth covers her clit and I lick and suck. She buckles and I have to take a step back to accommodate her writhing and twisting body. "Ford, oh my fucking God, Ford!"

My fingers explore her ass as I pleasure her folds with my tongue and she only lasts a few more seconds before her moaning turns into screams.

She takes her time coming, and I lick wave after wave of milky white juice dripping out of her pussy.

She is so fucking sexy.

I carry her over to the bench and sit down, then remove her legs, one at a time, and place her feet on the ground. Her knees wobble a little, so I set her on my lap instead. She rests her head on my shoulder.

"Ready to stop?"

"No, sir. You still owe me two more spankings."

"Mmmmmm," I moan into her hair. "Make me come, Ashleigh, any way you want."

She sits up and gets off my lap, then bites her lip as she thinks. She looks over at the condom wrappers on the floor, then reaches down and grabs one, rips it open, and places it over the head of my dick. She rolls it down, rubbing her palms against my shaft to get me going, and then stands up.

I can't stop the smirk, but luckily she's looking down at my dick when it comes out. She comes towards me, massaging her breasts. They're over-full and the milk drips out with the slightest touch.

"That might drive me insane. I have no idea why, or if it's normal, but I love it, Ashleigh."

She climbs into my lap once again, rubbing her pussy against me. She drapes her arms around my neck and before I even know what she's doing her lips crash against me. Her mouth parts and her tongue flicks inside, probing for a response from me.

TAUT

I pull back instinctively.

She dips her forehead against mine and then sighs. "Sorry, I forgot. I didn't mean to do that."

I cup my hands around her face and look her in the eyes. She looks afraid, like she might've ruined the whole night with her mistake. "It's OK," I say softly.

She bends down into my neck and takes her mouth to my ear. "I want a kiss from you. A real one. But I don't want to have to steal it." And then she lifts her hips up and places the head of my cock against her clit, dragging it back and forth a few times before positioning it under her pussy.

When she lowers herself on top of me, I know I can't ever let her go.

She sits up and my cock almost completely withdraws before she lowers herself again. She goes slow. She takes her time, she whispers into my ear. "Fuck me, Ford," she coos. "You are perfect, Ford," she insists. "You make me wild with longing. I want you so bad," she admits.

And with each confession I melt a little. My defenses break, the walls begin to crumble.

She moans when I lie back and thrust up against her—and then I pull her to my chest and slam my balls against her pussy. She comes first, I can feel the waves of shudders, but as soon as she starts I'm in my own personal nirvana as well and the only thing on my mind is how the fuck I can get this girl to move in with me so we can do this twice a night and every morning.

After, we rest for a few minutes, her head still on my chest, our rapidly beating hearts slowing together. I play with her long hair and drag my fingertips up and down her back. When I'm almost sure she's asleep I smack her ass twice, softly. "Nine and ten," she whispers.

I stand up and hold her close so I can carry her to the shower. I set her down on the stone counter top and she complains about how cold it is. I just smile and turn the water on hot. I remove the old condom and slip on a new one and then carry her into the shower, press her up against the wall, cupping her ass with one hand, her leg draped over the crook of my elbow. Her other leg wraps around my waist.

"Ashleigh," I hum into her ear. I slip my hand to her throat and enjoy the feeling of the hot water pulsing against my back.

"More, Ford. I still want you, *please*. More."

I slip inside her again, but this time I go slow. I pull out, pause, and then ease myself back into her beckoning folds until I'm buried up to my balls. "Ashleigh," I moan again.

She comes as I say her name and her groaning blocks out my words. But I hear them. And they echo in my head as I spill into her one more time. "*Stay*," I say. "*Stay with me.*"

We linger there against the wall. I press against her, eclipsing her small frame with my large one. And then I hoist her up and carry her to the bench to wash.

We are spent. I wash her hair and then her body, the luxurious bubbles coating her perfect skin. By the time I'm done, she's half asleep, so I dry her off and send her to bed wearing nothing but a pair of white panties.

I cover her up and pull on a pair of boxer briefs and jeans so I can go across the hall and grab Kate. The babysitter is out of milk and Kate is awake, but Ashleigh needs to nurse anyway, so it's no big deal.

Back in our room I place Kate up next to Ashleigh in bed and she wakes up long enough to position the baby against her full breast.

I turn the lights out, drop my jeans, and slide under the covers—pulling Ashleigh's ass up against my thighs. I wrap my arms around her, play with Kate's hair for a few seconds, and then I just drift away in my perfect thoughts of our perfect night.

The three of us fall asleep like that.

And I've never been so happy in all my life.

THIRTY-THREE

"Oh. My. God," Ash moans into her pillow.

"What's the problem?" It's still dark, so I'm not even in the mood to be awake right now, but Kate's unhappy complaints pull me right out of my peaceful post-sex slumber.

"She won't sleep. I've fed her, she didn't burp, and now she's cranky. I'm so tired. Please, Katelynn, *please* just let mommy sleep."

Exhausted Ashleigh is whiny.

I like it.

I'm not sure why I like it, since most guys would probably find it annoying, but I like her baby-begging. "Give her to me, I'll try."

"Be my guest." She rolls over and brings the baby with her and as soon as I lift Kate up, Ashleigh rolls her back to me and fluffs her pillow. I put the baby on my chest and pat her back. This is how long it takes Ash to start snoring.

She's not kidding about being tired. I have no idea what it takes to keep a baby content, but I imagine it's quite a task. And she's been doing it alone since Kate was born.

When I sleep with them, I wake up too, but I don't actually have to do anything. I just grumble and go back to sleep. But Ashleigh has to feed her, change her, and then probably entertain her if she isn't in the mood to sleep.

Kate lifts her head and shoulders off my chest with a frustrated whimper, and then collapses. I sit up a little so she's not so flat and pat her back a little harder. She lets loose a massive belch and I can't help it, I chuckle. "Nice one, Kate." She agrees and I feel her relax a little.

I've never felt this kind of closeness before. No wonder my parents were always touching me as a baby. That makes me smile. Until I realize how hard it must've been to have a kid like me. How would I feel if Kate hated for me to touch her?

Not good. I like this. Especially when she's relaxed and comfortable. It's like an accomplishment, keeping babies happy. Very satisfying.

The bedside table clock says it's four AM.

All this might be gone in a few hours. If we were in the car right now we'd be to LA by eight. Well, with traffic, probably longer since it's a Wednesday. I could make an afternoon meeting. And Old Ford might've jumped at that chance. This job is a big deal. Not because of the money, which is nice. It pays a hell of a lot more than fucking game and reality shows. But I don't need the money. I just need to feel fulfilled, and this career might be just what I need to get a little closer to that.

I admit, the projects I've done so far haven't been that satisfying. The only good thing about Spencer's show was Rook. And the game shows, fuck. As soon as I have something else to put on my resume, those will be the first credits to go.

So I'm really looking forward to being involved in this show. It's a science fiction pilot set on a future Earth. Sci-fi is a very popular film genre and it has a nice effects budget, so the whole project will be a huge leap forward for me.

But... I also like *this*. I like this *girl*. I like this *baby*. I like having these two people around me. I like sharing our meals, and traveling together, and shopping.

I like being responsible for them.

It's… intimate.

Very.

In fact, this trip with Ash and Kate is probably the most intimate thing I've ever done.

Something tickles my ribs and it takes me a few seconds to realize I was just drooled on.

I love it.

Kate squirms because I've stopped patting her back and she's letting me know in her own little baby way to get busy with it again.

I resume the patting because she asked so sweetly.

Fucking Merc would have my balls if he saw me now. Hell, even Spencer would rub my face in it. Up until this… diversion in my life… Ronin was the only one of my friends who ever wanted a serious relationship. He's always been looking for the future Mrs. Ronin Flynn. It was like a big joke a couple years back when we were working together regularly.

Ashleigh lets out a loud snore and then rolls over my way again. Even in the dim light she looks pale and exhausted. All this caregiving is draining her. She needs someone to care for *her*.

And really, that's what families do. They care for each other. So when the bad stuff comes they have someone to lean on. A family is really like a team. People you can rely on to have your back. At least that's how it was for me. My mom and dad always had my back.

I had a lot of fucking therapy as a kid. Mostly because I was defective. And weird. I refused to talk, I carried on when people touched me. I learned things too quickly. I never made friends. In fact, I just didn't get the point of friends. I didn't need them. I only needed me.

Or so I thought. Because obviously I just never understood

what it meant to have these other relationships in my life.

Spencer living across the street from me all growing up was a convenient friendship. That's how we became close over the years. And he never fucked with me. Ever. When I told him not to touch me, he shrugged and said *whatever.* Then went back to sorting through his Matchbox cars, giving me half—always the shitty ones. But he never questioned me. He was just there. And I suppose that's where that loyalty to him and Ronin stems from. Spencer's unconditional acceptance of me and my weirdness.

I never really appreciated him. Or Ronin, for that matter.

My therapists—all of my many, *many* therapists—they all warned me that being alone is not part of the human condition.

That's the word they used. Always. The human condition. Like it needs to be capitalized.

People are social, they insisted. And since I am a person, I need to be social.

It just never happened that way. I did get better at things. I can talk to people, obviously. I did well in school. I played on teams and learned that whole working together lesson. And there's no way you can produce shows and films alone. Even if you carry the camera and do the editing yourself, you have to have actors.

MIT never understood why I turned them down, but I knew accepting that offer was a dead end for me. I knew it instinctively. I knew that locking myself away in a lab curing diseases, or desperately seeking to understand the real significance of the Higgs boson, or looking up in the night sky trying to discern the percentage of nitrogen gas around distant planets—or any of the other millions of more worthwhile things I should be doing with my intellect than producing game shows—these things, these experiences would not be in *my* best interest.

Because even though people are social, the self has to come first or it all breaks down.

I went to film school to save myself from wasting my life away as a lonely, solitary introvert.

I joined my first team when I went to college. Not the baseball team or the occasional pick-up hockey teams. My first social team—Film Studies. That one step forward opened the door to Ronin, Spencer, and Mardee. My first, and only, professional team. Which led to Rook. Which led to Ashleigh.

And even though I'm here for my own selfish reasons—I like her, I want to fuck her nightly and again every morning—right now, this actual moment in time, I'm here because Ashleigh looks like she could use another team member.

I'd like to be on her team.

Kate squirms and I pat her back. She's already got me trained. If she wiggles a little she can get a part of the human condition we all crave.

Intimacy and love.

And since I'm part of the human condition, as well as a sucker for adorable babies who have moms named Ashleigh, I give in. I pat her back until she's sleeping so deep she no longer notices the lack of rhythmic thumping against her skin.

But since she's part of the human condition as well, she returns the favor. And I drift off to the beat of her heart against mine, feeling appreciated and satisfied.

THIRTY-FOUR

It's the French toast that wakes me. Kate is no longer on my chest—in fact, I'm face down in the pillow. Ashleigh is also missing. Which explains the French toast.

Four Seasons room service.

I roll out of bed, glance at myself in the mirror, stop to flatten down some bedhead, and then make my way out to the living area of the suite. The dining table is filled with food, but that's not what catches my attention first. "She sits!" I beam at Kate in her highchair and she shoots me a toothless grin and flails her hands in response.

Ashleigh is sitting at the table wearing a fluffy white robe, spooning some goop into Kate's eager mouth. "Yeah," she smiles over her shoulder. "She's four months today and I thought I'd see if she could manage the chair."

"Four months. You said three years."

"You asked when they could sit in a chair alone or something ridiculous like that. She can't sit up all by herself just yet. But probably pretty soon. They learn new things every day when they're this small."

I'm intrigued. "What else do they do at four months?"

"Roll over, so keep an eye out. And teeth will be coming soon, I think."

The table is filled with pretty much everything on the breakfast menu so I help myself to some eggs and waffles, pour some syrup, and take a seat on the other side of Ash. "So she's gonna be entertaining us daily? Nice."

"Yeah, well, she'll also start getting more demanding and stop sleeping so much too. This is when the hard part starts." Ash lets out a long sigh and I know exactly what that sigh says. She's gonna have to deal with all the bad stuff alone. And all the good stuff is just a little less fun when she's got no one to share it with.

"I'll help if you need anything. I got her to sleep last night, didn't I?"

Ashleigh looks up at me again. "Thank you. And…" She trails off a little and I swear she's blushing. "I'd just like to officially declare that last night was amazing. Except—"

I raise my eyebrows and swallow my eggs. "You have a complaint? How is this possible?"

She blushes even brighter. "You just said… and normally I would not bring it up, but you're the one who said…"

I wait, but she waves her hand in a never-mind gesture.

"Said? What?"

She shakes her head furiously and then giggles. She's too embarrassed to say the words.

I can't help myself, I laugh. "You have to say it or I'll punish you. Three swats for not finishing a thought, and one extra when it's about sex."

"Well, you said, back in the room in Utah, that you'd tie my ankles to my thighs."

I laugh.

"Ford, you made me come with words. That's not something you forget."

"I do not take requests, Miss Li. So I can make no promises."

"Whatever."

"But I'll do my best to fulfill your secret desires next time."

She rolls her eyes at me. "You have no idea what my secret desires are."

"No?"

"No, but I know what yours is." She smirks at me.

"I'm waiting."

"Me." The light dances off her mischievous eyes and then she bats her lashes.

God, she's cute. "You're right. You are my most secret desire." I lean over the small table and bite her earlobe, whispering in her ear, "Will there be a next time?"

She draws in a deep breath. "I hope so. But I have to see what happens today. I'm just not sure what's gonna happen."

"I understand." I bite her softly again, hoping *she* understands what that bite says.

Ashleigh wipes Kate's face, much to the dismay of the infant, and then scoops her up out of the high chair and saunters off. "We're gonna take a bath before we go."

I try to will myself not to feel disappointed, but I can't help it. This is it. This—whatever it is—is over. My food is suddenly unappetizing and I push the plate away and go out onto the balcony.

It's loud outside. Even though we're thirty-nine floors up, it's still loud. Most of the noise is wind, but the sound of a city as busy as Vegas can never really be drowned out. I lean over the railing, soaking up the sun for a while. It feels good after the blizzards in Colorado this winter.

God, I just don't know how to process this Ashleigh thing. She's the one who mentioned the possibility of a next time. She's sending such mixed signals. And part of me wonders if some of her actions and feelings towards me are only due to her unstable state of mind. She's definitely not one hundred percent in the emotional department, but then again, who is? Not me, that's for sure. I'm all over the place too. One minute I'm New Ford, team of one. And then the next I'm playing father to an infant whose real father is waiting for her in LA.

Maybe I should back off. Bow out gracefully and exhibit all those bullshit good loser manners my dad was always trying to teach me. I stare down at the traffic as I try and come to terms with my current reality.

A little while later Ash and Kate come out of the bedroom and I turn to watch them. Ashleigh is wearing a t-shirt of mine. This one says *When hell freezes over, I'll ski there too*. That makes me smile because it totally fits her. She's just flipping a big fuck you to the world. And then I notice Kate's wearing a pretty orange dress and she has matching bows in her hair.

I wonder if Ash dressed her up because she's gonna go see her dad today? It's ridiculous to be jealous, I realize this. I bought her the fucking dress. I might not've picked it out, but I fucking paid for it. She's wearing a dress I gave her.

But it's not enough. I need more. It's painful to think of losing these two. Especially so soon after the whole falling out with Rook. "Don't pack, Ashleigh," I call to her as I go back in. "The staff is going to box it all up and deliver it to LA tomorrow. Just take what you need for today."

I figure this will give me one more chance to see them if she walks away from me this afternoon. But if she suspects my motives, she holds it in. Because she's already telling Kate the latest news on the Itsy-Bitsy Spider.

Fuck.

I can't do this. I can't just give up with her like I did Rook.

Fuck Tony. I let Ronin have Rook because it's what she really wanted and I'd be the biggest dick in the world if I stole her from him just because I could.

But *fuck* Tony. I don't even know this guy. And yeah, Ash loves him. I respect that. But if he's not gonna take care of her and Kate, then I don't have to walk away.

I have four more hours on the road with her. Probably five with traffic. I go back to our bedroom and grab some jeans and a t-shirt Ashleigh packed for me from the Vail house. I laugh when I read this one. Fucking Ash. It says *Jedi in the streets, Sith in the sheets*. I don't even remember *owning* this shirt.

After I'm cleaned up and dressed I go back to the living room and Ashleigh is all ready, sitting on the couch waiting for me. I grab my keys and wallet and Ashleigh stuffs some pastries in her diaper bag and hoists it over her shoulder with Kate in her other arm. "Here," I say, grabbing the bag. "I got it."

"Thanks," she says, giving me a look as we leave the room and walk down the hall. "What's up with you, anyway?"

I pretend I don't hear her and just punch the button for the elevator. Luckily there's one waiting and the doors open up immediately so we are momentarily distracted by the process of getting ourselves inside.

The doors close and she's staring at me. "Ford."

"Yes," I say as I stare at my phone and pretend to text someone.

"What's wrong?"

I look up and smile. "Business, Ashleigh. Sorry. I have a meeting this afternoon that I should try and make. So I'm thinking about that. They've been planning production schedules all week without me. I'm playing catch up."

Ronin would be proud.

"Oh," she says, like that was not the answer she was expecting. I'm not sure what she was expecting, but I'm not in the mood to talk about it just yet. I'm not avoiding the topic of Tony, but why end this trip before we have to? We'll be in LA soon enough and I'm pretty sure Tony is the only topic on the table when we get there.

The elevator doors open and we walk out to the valet area. The Bronco has been washed. Actually, I'd call it detailed because it smells like *Guy on a Hot Date* and the tires are gleaming in the sun from an Armor All application.

Ashleigh buckles Kate in the back and then jumps up front with me. "If we're lucky, she'll sleep the whole way."

TAUT

"I could use some luck, so here's hoping."

She lets out a long breath and settles into her seat. I pull out and make our way to the 15 freeway that will take us all the way to the 10 in LA. It's warm out but not hot. The Bronco likes the extreme heat just about as much as it enjoys the extreme cold. So luckily, Vegas in January is mostly mild. As soon as we clear the city limits and are heading west, Ashleigh kicks her feet up, lowers her seat, and closes her eyes.

"You just woke up, how can you be tired already?"

"Ford," she says as she lowers the sunglasses the hotel gave us yesterday. "I'm a new mom. With anyone but you, I'd choose sleep over sex any day of the week, that's how fucking fantastic it feels to close my eyes and forget about life." I can see her out of the corner of my eye, but I don't want her to see my smile, so I keep focused on the road. "And I do not want to hear about my swearing today. Yesterday you called the shots so today it's my turn."

"Should we play a game to see who calls the shots?"

She slides her glasses back into position and sighs. "Me. I call the shots."

"You cheat, Miss Li. You only play until you win, then you back out."

"I'm too tired to entertain you today, Ford. I think you should entertain me."

I get a wicked grin.

"With my clothes on," she amends.

"I'm a master of entertaining. However, you still owe me something."

She snorts. "Like what?"

"My favor. You promised to tell me about school."

"Oh," she says with more relief than might be necessary. "Yeah, whatever. What do you want to know?"

"What kind of program, to start." She laughs, then covers her mouth and when I look over she's blushing. "What?" I ask, laughing with her. "You're getting a master's degree in porn or

378

something? Why are you blushing?"

"No, it's just kinda funny."

I wait for it.

"I'm a psychologist. Well, I will be if I ever finish grad school and pass my licensing exam."

Psychologist. I should not be surprised—she was reading my mind back in Vail just like I was reading hers. "Will you? Finish the program?"

She slides her sunglasses down her nose again. "No. I never wanted to be a stupid psychologist. But I had to pick something, and that was as good a major as any and it was all paid for out of my trust. It was a way to get money. A way to survive and become educated at the same time. Plus, it pacified my father when I left home."

"He needed pacifying. Why?"

She's silent for this one. For a long time, like more than a minute. When she finally speaks her speech has an edge to it. "You know that story about the boy who drew cats? Well, that's me. I draw cats. But no one wanted to let me draw cats and I never had the good fortune of having my cat drawings come to life to save a shitload of people to prove I'm worthwhile, so I had to do something else."

"So what do you really do? When you draw cats?"

"It's stupid." She turns her head to the window and watches the desert for a little while. I let her, because I'm not starting an argument on this ride. I'm deflecting. I'm in denial. I'm postponing. I'm stalling.

"You're super smart, Ford. I mean—Eagle Scout? Those equations in your bedroom? The sign language, the Japanese, and probably a lot more shit I have no clue about. I'm not a physics expert or anything, but I've taken my share of science classes and those equations were way up there on the genius level. So why did you become a film producer?"

"I wanted to draw cats, Ashleigh. And my dad didn't give a fuck what I did in school. He told me to choose something fun.

TAUT

I got offers from every top ten school in the country and quite a few big ones overseas as well. And I went to a public university in my hometown and studied how other people who wanted to draw cats make shit up and put it on film. Because it looked fun."

She settles back into her seat and sighs.

"I get it. I get *you*, Ashleigh. And you get me. I understand what it means to be misunderstood. So just tell me, what kind of cats do you draw?"

"Poetry," she whispers so softly I can barely hear her over the engine and the wind from the open window.

"Poetry. Do you have some with you that I can read?"

"No, I left my journal at the hotel because I'm tired of thinking about it. If I read that stuff one more time I might really go insane." She pauses, but it's almost an afterthought. Like she was going to say something but changed her mind.

I wait her out.

She presses the button for both our windows and rolls them up to quiet things down. "I can tell you one from memory, if you want. They're not complicated, Ford."

She says this like she feels the need to explain herself, and that saddens me. She should not have to explain why she wants to draw cats.

"I write them simple on purpose. Because my life…." She trails off for a few seconds, then sighs and gives it another shot. "My life is so, so fucked up. It's twisted and complicated, and filled with *shit*." She swallows hard. "Bad shit. But my poems are the opposite of that. When my life is unraveling, and everything about it is slack, my poems are taut. My poems take the fray and wind it back together."

"Taut." I say the word out loud as I scan the desert landscape.

"They're short and simple. Not long and complicated and pretty, but very concise and controlled. And honest. I usually take lyrics to songs that I love, choose all the words in that song that stand out, then make up my own poem using those words. That's how I like to write them. Every word is ordinary. But when

380

I mix the words up and put them together in a new way, that's what makes the difference. That's what makes them special. It changes everything."

I get off the freeway at the next exit, take the off-ramp over towards a truck stop, pull off on a dirt road, and stop the vehicle in the middle of the Nevada desert.

"What are you doing?" Ashleigh asks.

I pull the e-brake and turn to face her. "Listening."

She stares at me, her eyes darting back and forth across my face. "Did he send you, Ford? Please. You can tell me if he did."

"Who, Ashleigh? You've asked me that question three times now. Why the hell do you think someone sent me?"

"Why are you helping me?"

I throw up my hands and let out a long breath. "I don't know. I was there. I was reeling from a volatile conversation with Rook back in Denver and I just… I don't know. I just didn't have it in me to be a dick, I guess. I was too wounded to put effort into getting rid of you, so I just…"

Her expression changes from interested to disappointed. I owe her more than this. If I want her to trust me, I owe her more that this lame shit.

"I wanted company. You needed help. It made me feel… wanted. You were hungry that morning at the hotel and when I said I'd take care of your car you looked so… relieved. And thankful. And then when I told you to put the baby in the van after things were settled and you didn't question me, it felt good to be in control of two helpless people. It felt good to drive you to a house and get you inside. And buy things that you needed at the store. It felt good to take care of you."

"But…" Her eyes are all watery now and I just know she's gonna cry. I don't want to make her cry. "But you could've just given me money and left me at the hotel. Why did you take me *home* with you? And don't say they didn't have rooms, there's plenty of hotels in Vail and you can afford all of them. So why invest time in me?"

TAUT

I look back at Kate and shrug. "It was strange to see you take care of her. Even though you had nothing, you gave her everything she needed. You are her whole world. She is your whole world. The two of you are a team. And I was missing my team. Ronin and Spencer and Rook are my team. I wanted—I *want* to be a part of your team."

I release a long breath. I cannot fucking believe I just said that shit.

I turn away and look out the window.

Her words tumble out and when I turn back to her, she's got her eyes closed.

I feel the stress of an eager distance.
I clean the mess of a swelling indifference.
I raise the walls
And steal your love,
But it's never enough
To meet my needs,
Or heal me from
The ruin of rest and decline,
Falling through the fault line."

She opens her eyes and the tears are gathering. I swallow. "Who did you write that for?"

She sniffs, wipes her eyes, and then turns away. "My father," she says. "He prefers dogs."

THIRTY-FIVE

want more.

I want so much more.

I want Ashleigh, I want her baby, and I want a fucking house that is not filled with cold ultra-modern shit. Somewhere that isn't the suburbs, but I'd make allowances if that's what she wanted. I want dinner at a table with Kate in a high chair. I want Ash in my bed every night. I want to listen to her thoughts. I want to hear everything she has to say. I want her to write *new* poems, just so I can be the first one to read them and declare her brilliant. I might even want to get her pregnant. Make her tits and belly swollen with my child and then ravish Glowing Ashleigh until she begs me to leave her alone.

I want to keep her forever.

She turns back to me and Composed Ashleigh is in control. "We better get going, huh? You don't want to miss your meeting."

"Meeting?" The word barely registers.

"Yeah, you said you have an afternoon meeting and—"

"Right," I say, releasing the brake. "I'm not sure I'll make it, so there's no rush." I put the truck in gear and pull back onto the highway access road, then get back on the 15.

I am blown. I am destroyed. I am—

"Ford?"

I take a deep breath to calm myself. "Yes, Ashleigh."

"Do you think I'm crazy?"

"What?"

"For coming all this way just to see him? For not letting go? You can tell me, I get it. It's crazy. It's stupid. It's… it's… bordering on delusional."

"Delusional? Who said that?"

"My sister. She thinks she knows everything, but she's just a bitch. She's never had to deal with this type of situation. How would she know what's normal and what's not? I mean, I'm a psychologist. Maybe I don't have the master's degree and the license yet, so I'm not official, but I'm qualified in every other respect. I understand my reaction to this situation isn't quite… *textbook*. But I figure, it's my life, right? I'm allowed to live it the way I want. And if I need this last… whatever this is, then I'm not crazy. I just…" She trails off and does not pick it back up. I just glance over at her. I'm not sure what to say. She's staring out the window, looking down, like she's watching the road pass by.

"Just what, Ash?"

She swallows and takes a deep breath. She's been better about the crying since yesterday, but even this is a little warning bell telling me how fragile she is right now. She's held off the tears for one day and to me this is an accomplishment. "I just need to tell him, Ford. I just need to tell him how much I love him and what life has been like for me since he's been gone. And I do realize that I went about this the wrong way, I get that."

I squint my eyes down as I try to make sense of this conversation. I'm not sure what she's talking about now.

"I shouldn't have called my sister from Japan, that was my first mistake. I should've known she'd never understand. And then when I saw him at the airport, I just sorta freaked out."

"Wait, what? What are you talking about, Ashleigh?"

She looks over at me and shakes her head. "My road trip. Before you. I flew into LA and my sister had blabbed her mouth off, as usual, and my father sent a driver. I swear to God, I saw that sign that said Miss Li and I almost threw up. So I just walked past and got in a cab. He saw me of course, but what was he gonna do?" She shrugs. "Nothing, he could do nothing. And he was boxed in by other cars, so the cab just left, and I left, and..."

I wait, or at least I try to. "And then what, Ash? Then what happened?"

"I didn't know where Tony was. I needed to ask someone where he was. And I knew his friend's address in Texas. I made the cab drive in circles around the airport for about an hour, then I went back and got on another plane and went to Dallas. And they thought I was crazy too. I mean," she huffs out a sad laugh. "Carting this new baby all over the fucking world just to have a final conversation. I get it, Ford. It's crazy. But needing this... this crazy *plan* doesn't make *me* crazy. Desperate, maybe. But not crazy."

I let the silence grow as I try to understand what's happening.

What is happening? This is some sort of confession, I think. But of what?

"Anyway." She picks the conversation back up. "His friend told me where he was, and of course, it's in LA, so then I needed to get back there. But I figured flying was a no-go. They already knew I went to Texas, I'm sure. That's not hard to find out. So I took the last of my cash and bought that crap car and took the least likely route back to California."

I laugh a little. "Well, I bet you certainly threw them off your trail with Colorado."

She smiles and laughs a little with me.

"And then... I swear to God, I was sitting there on the side of the road and the tow truck guy pulls up and asks if I need help. I had no money. Like thirty bucks, maybe. It was pretty much over for me at that point. But he said no charge, just get in the truck.

So I did."

She looks over to me and smiles. "And he took me to you. We were getting off the freeway and that tow truck guy stopped to talk to you. And when he pulled away you know what he told me?"

"I'm almost afraid to ask."

"He said, 'That guy's a fucking genius. He has all the answers.' And do you know what I thought?"

"What?" I smile at her.

She smiles back. "I thought... *I need that guy.*"

A chill rockets through my body. I'm electrified by her words, by her admission, by her desire to have me. I look over at her and she's gazing out the window again.

"*I need those answers so bad*, that's what I thought. And then you appeared outside my car."

"And then I invited you in, and kept you warm. And took you home, and bought you clothes, and played games with your mind when the last thing you needed was my fucking mind games. I'm sorry for that, Ashleigh."

She looks back over at me and now she's grinning. "I'm a Gamer, Ford. I like the games. I've gone easy on you"—I laugh out loud at this—"because you seemed a little lost too. But I don't mind the mind-fuck. That's part of my job, right? I'm a mind-unfucker."

I bust out a guffaw. "Holy shit, you're so... so... so perfect for me." She takes a deep breath and I can feel the tension escape with the exhale. "Feel better? Got that shit off your chest?"

She nods, but she's still looking out the window. "Yeah. But there's more, Ford." When she looks over at me the smile is gone.

"You can tell me, Ash. I'll understand, no matter what it is."

"I know you will. I know that." She chews on her lower lip as she weighs her options.

"Is it a matter of trust? Or fear? You can keep it to yourself, too. If you want. I'm good with denial when it's necessary."

"OK," she says in her Sweet Ashleigh voice. "I'm gonna hold

the rest in for now. Just one more day, that's all that's left. In a few hours, all this uncertainty will be over." She looks over at me again. "And that's it. The end."

"The end of who? Us? Or you and Tony?" This question makes her fight the tears again. I reach over and take her hand. "It's OK, Ashleigh. You can keep that to yourself too."

She fights the emotion and her face scrunches up as she swallows down the bad shit. "I need to for now. It's so close, ya know. Why rush it?"

"God, that's the truth." I squeeze her hand again and she squeezes back this time. I'm not a hand-holder. I held her hand last night because that was her special request. But I'm not about to let go of her hand right now. This one's for me. I want to keep a hold of her for as long as I can.

We drive like that for a while. Just silent. Kate is passed out in the back. Every time I check on her in the rear-view her little mouth is open and her head pressed up against the head support thing. Ashleigh messes with my phone as she makes a playlist, then plugs it into the cassette player. The sad music comes on, that same stuff that had her walking off in the Middle of Nowhere, Utah two days ago. "*The Naked and the Famous*," I say absently. She looks over at me, waiting to see if I'll protest. "It's your day, Ash. You can listen to whatever you want. Today is all about you."

She smiles at that but her mood is somber.

"Where do you live? I mean, here, in So Cal, where do you normally live when you're here?" I need to get something out of her before we get to LA, otherwise she might slip away.

She tilts her head, like she's thinking about this for a moment, then shrugs. "We don't have any houses in LA right now. But there's a condo in downtown San Diego and the family house in Rancho Santa Fe."

I raise my eyebrows at her. "That's swanky."

"Where's your house?"

"Bel Air."

"Very swanky," she says back. "I think Bel Air trumps *El Rancho*."

"Did you go to school there?"

"No, a day school in La Jolla."

"Swankier."

She laughs at this. "I went where I was put, so it's not like I had a choice."

I don't know what to say after that. The whole Tony thing is just hanging in the air between us. Even Ashleigh seems a little bit uncomfortable. We pass by Barstow, blow through Victorville, make our way through the hills they call mountains out here, and then suddenly LA is looming in the distance. The gray haze of smog that lingers over the tall buildings looks even more ominous with the overcast sky and the traffic begins to slow considerably as we approach the 10. Californians freak out on the freeway if the weather changes. A little rain is a big deal, so I hope the fuck we get off the freeway before it starts pouring. "Westwood, right?" I ask Ashleigh.

"Yes," she whispers.

"You have an intersection, or an address you can put into the phone GPS?"

"Just take me to Strathmore and Kelton."

"Kelton, huh? Not sure where that is. Strathmore is over by UCLA, right? Do you have an address?"

"Strathmore and Veteran. Just take the 405 up to Wilshire. That's close enough."

"So you won't give me an address?"

"It's my day, remember?" She turns her head away a little more, essentially ending the conversation.

The traffic is horrific so it takes a good hour to get over on the west side of town. I get off at Sepulveda and head towards the hills, because the traffic getting on the 405 is a nightmare waiting to happen. "My house is not far, Ashleigh. You sure you don't want to go there first, rest up a little and then make a plan?"

"No," Sweet Ashleigh says. "I'm good. Just take me there

now."

I fight the street traffic for a few miles, then turn on Wilshire and take it up to Veteran. Ashleigh gives directions. Left, straight, right, left again. "Stop," she says.

"Where?" I ask, slowing down. There's no parking here, the place is a clusterfuck of cars and apartment buildings.

"Just pull over here."

I go up a half a block and then whip a bitch and pull into a red zone.

We sit.

And then she's a blur of motion. She's out of the car and walking back to the cargo area. I get out as she opens the tailgate and pulls out the stroller and then throws the diaper bag and her purse in the bottom area where there's room for baby supplies. I just stand there, not quite accepting what's happening. "Ashleigh, where are you going?"

She ignores me, just unbuckles Kate's seat and hauls it over to the stroller. She fits it on top of it somehow, like it locks into place, and then folds the canopy over Kate's eyes because a few drops of rain are falling. When all that's settled she finally looks up to me. "Thank you, Ford. I am so, so happy that I met you. We'll have to get together again sometime—"

"Whoa. Hold on. You're just taking off? No address or phone number?"

"I'll give you my number, call me later, we can make plans." I fish out my phone and place it in her waiting hand and she types in some numbers.

"What's this number go to, Ashleigh?"

"My cell," she says, like this phone actually exists. "I don't have it on me, I need to get another one. I'll probably do that right after I take care of stuff. So just call me later."

I put a hand on her shoulder. "Do you want me to wait? Just in case?"

She shakes her head. "No, Ford. I'm sorry it's so rushed, I just need to go." And then she grips her stroller and walks up the sidewalk to one of the apartment buildings. I watch her for a few seconds because I'm actually unable to move.

She just walks away.

When she gets to the door she grabs the handle and pulls, but it's locked. She glances nervously over her shoulder at me and waves. Then someone comes out the door and they hold it open for her.

I stand there like an idiot.

She just fucking left.

I get back in the truck and stare at the dashboard. I look over at the apartment building door and strain to see inside, but it's the wrong angle from here. A cop car pulls up next to me and rolls down the passenger window. I roll mine down as well, and a few raindrops hit my arm as I wait to see what they want. "You can't park here," one of the officers inside says.

"I'm leaving," I tell them. "Just get out of my way, I'm leaving." They pull up a few cars and then stop again, waiting to see if I pull out. I do. I whip a bitch and go the other way. If they are conscientious cops they should probably pull me over for that little move. Check out why the fuck I'd do something like that right in front of them. Maybe threaten me a little, write me a ticket. But they don't. I check the rear-view and they're already gone before I get to a little curve in the road, so I whip another bitch and pull over again.

"What the fuck just happened?" I just spent a week with a girl and her baby. Everything was awesome and now... she just walks away? I grab my phone and call the number she put in.

Errr-reeee-eeeeet. The number you have dialed is not in service. Please hang up and try your—

Fucking figured that much. The girl lives in Japan, she has no LA area code number.

I let out a long breath and shake my head. "Fuck!" I look down at the building again. I can't see shit, too many trees. And I'm just about to pull out and go see if I can get inside and somehow figure out where Tony lives when I see the stroller going down the road towards Strathmore. I watch and wait and when she gets there, she crosses that street and then continues down Strathmore towards Veteran.

I pull out and drive slowly after her. Where the fuck is she going?

I pull back into the red zone I just left and park the truck, then jump out and walk after her. This is a fairly quiet neighborhood, so there's no one around. When I get down to Strathmore and look for her, she's already walking around the corner of Veteran. I jog after her because obviously this was not the building where Tony lives. She gave me the wrong address so I wouldn't know where she was going.

When I get to the corner I almost expect her to be gone, disappeared like a ghost. But she's still walking. And if the clouds weren't black with the threat of a storm, she'd look like just another mother out for an afternoon stroll with her baby. I follow, staying back quite a ways, and she goes past a slew of apartment buildings. I jog a little to catch up and she crosses another driveway leading into the one of the large complexes that line one whole side of the street. I'm just about to give up being stealthy when she stops, looks both ways, and crosses Veteran. I keep walking, my eyes glued to her small body as she maneuvers the stroller over the curb and then approaches a gate in the long wrought-iron fence that lines that side of the street.

Oh.

Fuck.

No.

My heart crashes as she turns the handle and pulls the gate open, props it against her hip, and pushes the stroller through.

I want to drop to the ground, that's how much this hurts me. My chest is one gaping hole right now, and I don't even know how to process what I'm seeing.

Because Ashleigh just walked into the Los Angeles National Cemetery.

THIRTY-SIX

*T*ony is dead.
Tony is dead.
That's all I think about as I run back to the Bronco.
Tony is dead.

He didn't leave her, he fucking died while serving. And she was left overseas in a foreign country, all alone, pregnant, trapped.

My hands are shaking so bad when I get to the truck I can barely push the key in the ignition. The Bronco starts up and I take a breath to calm my racing heart.

Ashleigh. I need to get to her. Now.

I pull out and almost hit a fucking UPS truck. The guy honks and screams something derogatory at me as he passes by.

Calm down, Ford. Fuck. You're no help to her if you're dead too.

I follow the same route I did walking, but when I get to the gate it hits me. There's no way to get in on this side of the cemetery. I have to go all the way down to Wilshire and drive around. I try and look for Ashleigh and the stroller, but I can't see her and pay attention to the traffic at the same time. The turn lane I need to be in on Wilshire is impossible to get to because the far right lane is also the fucking on-ramp to the 405 and it's backed up past the street I'm currently on, so it takes me almost ten fucking minutes to make it to the cemetery entrance. I drive in cautiously, trying to decide which way to go. This place is massive—nothing but white headstones. Row after row after row of white headstones.

I decide to hit the gate where she came in and go from there. That's just straight back from the entrance, so I drive slowly, looking out both sides as I creep along. A large thunderclap jars me for a second and then the bolt of lightning that follows send eerie shadows across the darkening sky. I get to the end of the road and it just curves around in a loop so I stop and get out, then climb on top of the truck and look out over the sea of dead soldiers.

"Fuck, Ash. Where the hell did you go?" The rain starts as the last word leaves my mouth so I jump back in and drive. I go right this time, towards a large palm tree that looks like it's wearing the wrong uniform in a platoon of eucalyptus and scrub oaks. I follow this road as the rain pelts the roof and I can barely see anything. I slow down some more, take another road off to the left, and search both sides. I'm just about to give up and move to another part of the cemetery when I see her—way off in another section, just heading under some large trees. Another clap of thunder gets my ass in gear and I'm already heading that way when the next bolt of lightning flashes. I lose sight of her for a few seconds as I follow the road, but then the stroller pops into view again.

Ashleigh is nowhere to be found.

I panic. What the hell just happened?

I park the Bronco and jump out, heading over to the stroller at a full run. When I get there I see her, spread out on the ground in front of a headstone, lying completely still, her arms outstretched, like she's desperately trying to hug the grave. Like she's desperately trying to hug her dead fiancé who lies under it.

My world stops and all I see, feel, and hear is her pain.

The pelting rain competes with a screaming Kate for attention and the world starts up again.

"Ashleigh?"

She is soaked, I am soaked. Kate—I look over at her and she's half protected from the stinging drops by the canopy, but she too is soaked.

I kneel down in the grass and touch Ashleigh's back. "Ash?"

She takes a long gasp and lets out a wail punctuated by the crashing thunder overhead.

My heart is in pieces. I'm shattered into billions of pieces with the sight of her grief.

"Ashleigh, we need to go. It's raining. The baby—" I look over at Kate and she is in full-on wail mode right now. "I'll put her in the truck, OK? Stay here. OK?"

I grab the stroller and push. I try to hurry, run even, but the soggy grass is not cooperating and I just make it worse. When I get to the Bronco it takes me a few minutes to figure out how to get the fucking seat to detach from the stroller. Once that's done I buckle Kate into the backseat and shove the unfolded stroller into the cargo area. I do not have time to decipher that bullshit.

Kate roars her complaints. Her face is turning red from the crying and her little fists are shaking as she protests everything that just happened.

Fuck. I need to get Ash, but Kate—

I look around. I'm conflicted. How bad of a parenting sin is it to leave a baby alone in a vehicle?

The rain is still coming down hard, harder, maybe. I can't leave Ashleigh out there in the rain. She's falling to pieces on top of her dead lover. She needs me.

Kate is upset, she's loud with her crying, she's turning herself red—and that scares the shit out of me.

But Ashleigh is coming to terms with something life-crushing. Ashleigh is experiencing the worst moment of her life, maybe. I stand there, the rain running down my face, undecided. I'm back on that fucking mountain in Loveland and everyone I know is buried under a sea of white.

I slam the door of the Bronco and the sounds of the wailing baby fade. Kate is safe in the truck. She's not out in the rain. She's upset, but she is not hurt.

I turn away and jog back over to Ashleigh. She hasn't moved and the rainwater is starting to puddle up around her. I kneel down and put my hand on her back. "Ashleigh?"

There is nothing but sobs from her. She is face down in the grass, sopping wet, muddy, and dying of a broken heart. I lie down next to her and push my face into her neck. "Ashleigh, please."

She turns her head and I almost wish she didn't. Her eyes are so bloodshot they scare me. Her cheeks are covered in mud and stray pieces of grass, and her hair sticks to her skin. Long strands are wedged between her trembling lips. "I can't do it, Ford."

"Can't do what, Ash?"

"Live without him. I don't want to live without him."

Oh. My. Fuck. "Ashleigh—"

"I have so many things I need to say and I can't say them. There's nothing here, Ford. I thought I'd feel him here. I thought—" She hiccups and pushes her face back into the grass, then turns back and gasps for air. "But they never even found his body. He was blown up, into tiny little pieces. In some country filled with people who would do it again and never even blink. They blew up my Tony. He was the only one who loved me. The only one. And now I have no one. And he doesn't even know, Ford. He doesn't even know I had the baby. He missed it."

Her pain escapes as a long mourning wail.

And I have no idea what to do.

"I'd do anything, Ford. Anything, if I could just talk to him one more time. Just lie on his chest and have his arms around me one more time so I could tell him all these things he needs to know. Why can't we get one last moment? Why can't I have one last moment with him? I don't understand this. I don't understand why I had to lose him. I just need a moment. Just one moment."

I stare at her as my mind races with possibilities, solutions to this problem I know I can solve. I have all the answers, that's what Dallas told Ash that night. I'm the guy with the answers and she needs me.

I lie down in the grass next to her. "Come here." I grab her upper arms and she's like a rag doll, limp. Dead weight. Empty. I pull her on top of me and wrap my arms around her, her sobs rocking against my chest. "Tell *me*, Ashleigh. Tell me all those things you need him to know. I'll make sure he gets the message."

Her crying stops abruptly and she lifts her head to look me in the eyes. Snot is running out of her nose and she sniffs. "Did he send you, Ford? Did he send you to save me?"

I break again. All this time she was asking if her dead lover sent me to help her.

All I can do is stare and nod. Her dark eyes are filled with sadness. But for a fraction of a second there's hope there too. Hope that I can give her what she needs. I clear my throat and find my voice. "Yes, Ashleigh. He sent me."

She drops her forehead to my chest and cries again, but this time it has a feeling of relief. "I knew it. I *knew* it. I knew the moment you asked me to come in your hotel room. I knew he was there that night, looking over me. Trying desperately to stop me from making a big mistake. And he couldn't contact me himself, so he sent you. He sent you, Ford."

"Tell me what you need him to know, Ash. He can hear you. Tell me everything you need him to know."

"I have so much to say, Tony. I had so much trouble with the baby before she was born. I got sick at school and they took me to the hospital and wouldn't let me go home. I missed your last call. They kept me there, in that stupid little hospital. And then Kate was sick when she was born and they kept me even longer.

TAUT

I didn't even know you were dead. I didn't even know you were *dead*. I went home and I played my messages on the machine and your last call came on and you talked about happy things. Our holiday time we were planning. You said I was probably out shopping for Kate spending all kinds of money. And it made all that crap they put me through with the birth worth it. And then… and then… the message ended and there were so many more messages. All hangups. Until I got to the last message. It was a buddy of yours saying they didn't know how to find me and I needed to call them right away…"

She cries. She sobs. She loses it, just completely fucking loses it. And I let her.

What the fuck must that feel like?

I can't even imagine. With all those hormones still in her system. All alone in a foreign country.

"I tried to come sooner," Ash says, a little bit calmer now. "But I never got the paperwork done for the birth certificate and passport. I couldn't even come home to see you. I had to call my sister and beg her to help me. Get Kate a passport. And I missed—"

She sobs again.

"I missed the funeral because no one knew where I was. And I called your parents and they—"

"They what? They what, Ashleigh?" This I need to know, because just what the fuck? What the fuck is wrong with these people?

"They refused to talk to me. They sent me a letter with twenty thousand dollars and said that's all I was getting." She huffs out a laugh and yells, "I'm Damian Li's fucking *daughter*!" She lets out a sob and finishes less angry and more broken. "And they tried to buy me off with twenty thousand dollars." She takes a minute to inhale a few hitched breathes, then calms herself back down. "And I had to cash it, Tony, I'm so, so sorry for cashing that check. But I needed to see you. I just wanted to say goodbye, that's all."

She takes one long deep breath and whispers, "I needed to come talk to you. I'm sorry I took that money."

We lie there in the rain. Silent for several minutes. I know we should get up and go check on Kate, but I can't. I refuse to deny Ash this last moment. She needs to come to terms with reality in her own time, in her own way. I refuse to rush her.

"I love you."

"I love you too, Ashleigh." The words come out automatically, before I realize she's not talking to me, she's talking to Tony.

I've never said those words out loud to anyone. Ever. In my entire life. Not even my parents.

"I miss you so much."

"I'm right here, Ashleigh."

She breathes erratically for a moment and then settles down again. "I know, Ford. I know it's you. I'm not crazy."

I drag the hair away from her face and tuck the wet strands behind her ear. The rain is letting up now. We've managed to spend the entire storm lying on the grass in a cemetery. "Would you like to come home with me?"

She nods and holds in a sob. "Yes, please."

"Do you have anything else to say? Before we go?"

She lifts her head up from my chest. Her sobs are soft now. Just remnants. She leans in and kisses me. First on one cheek, then on the other. And then she stops and cups her hands around my face. "Just… thank you. For believing in me and bringing me here, and helping me say goodbye." She starts to cry again, her lower lip trembling so bad she has to bite it to try and maintain control. "I'm never gonna get over this pain, Ford. Ever. No one understands how special he was to me. No one understands that he was holding me together, all these years, since we were just kids. He always saw me, you know? He saw me when no one else did. And when I heard that message on the machine…"

She can't finish.

And I'm not sure I want her to finish. I'm not sure I can handle the image of Ashleigh losing her mind, still hurting from childbirth, a new baby to take care of, and no friends or family there to help. It rips me apart to even start picturing this scene.

So I picture her happy instead. I stare at her swollen eyes and mud-stained face and picture her happy and fulfilled.

I sit up but I clutch her close to my chest, then stand and cradle her against me, like I'd carry Kate.

She hugs me tight and rests her head on my shoulder. She is so small. When I get to the Bronco I open the backseat and set her down on the bench. Kate has cried herself to sleep but her breathing is hitched from her hysterical wailing. Ashleigh rests her head against the baby and I buckle her in, then close the door and take a deep breath as I look around.

She was right. There is no way to fix this. That life she had is over and this is where it ends.

THIRTY-SEVEN

I take the streets to get home. The 405 is a fucking parking lot from the rain. I cut up to Sunset, then catch Beverly Glen up to Bel Air. It takes us almost an hour to get there, but when I pull up to the gate all I feel is relief. I am so glad to be home.

I punch in the gate code and we climb the long and winding driveway up to the house. I park in the driveway and sit still for a moment, then look over my shoulder. The girls are sleeping, but they are both wrecked.

I have no idea what to do.

Obviously I need to get them both inside, but then what? Ashleigh left almost everything at the hotel. We need stuff. I pull out my phone and text Pam: *I need my spare room turned into a nursery. Like now.*

She doesn't text back, so I can only assume she's on it.

I drag myself out of the Bronco and open the back door. Ash is slumped down on the seat, all curled up in a little ball like a kitten. I pick her up and carry her to the front door, key in the access code, and walk all the way to the back bedroom.

TAUT

"Ashleigh, wake up for me, please."

"I'm awake, Ford. I just don't want you to put me down."

I take her into the bathroom and set her on the counter. "Sit here, OK?" I plug up the bath tub and start the water. "I'll be right back, gotta get Kate."

Ashleigh starts crying again, but I think it's because she might've just realized she forgot all about Kate in her grief. I go back outside, grab the car seat and bring her to the bathroom.

Ash is still sitting on the counter, her head bowed in defeat, her long hair falling over her face, hiding her. I set Kate down and go back to Ashleigh. It's not easy taking care of two people at the same time. "Lift your arms up Ash."

She obeys, but her head stayed bowed.

I pull her shirt up and over, then toss it into the corner. "Stand up, please." She scoots her butt off the counter and her feet drop to the floor. Her legs give out for a moment and I have to reach out and steady her. My hands drift down and unbutton her jeans. They are loose, so they come off easy. "Get in the tub for me." I hold her arm as she steps in and then I help her keep her balance as she lowers herself into the water. I grab some shampoo and squeeze a shitload of it under the running water. The bubbles froth up and fill in the space around her body, cocooning her in fluff.

Kate is still asleep, so that's how she will stay for now. There is no good reason to wake her up. So I pull off my shirt and drop my pants. I mess with the switches on the wall and the jets come on, swirling the bubbles up into a frenzy. I pull Ash forward and step into the tub behind her, then wrap my arms around her shoulders and pull her into my chest. "Relax now. We're just gonna relax for now."

She sighs. But it's such a bad, no-good sigh. It's not even an *I give up* sigh, it's a *please kill me now* sigh. I gently drag my fingertips up and down her arms and then lean into her neck. "I'm so sorry, Ashleigh. I'm so sorry this is happening to you." She turns a little so she can tuck her face onto my shoulder and her arms slip around my waist.

And we stop.

We just sit.

Pam comes. Or someone comes. I can hear them, trying to be quiet as they deliver things for Kate in the other room. It takes a while, and I have to add more hot water to the tub twice before the knock on the bedroom door startles Ashleigh from her sleep.

"You're all set, sir," Pam calls out in a whisper-yell.

I don't answer, but she's used to that and then everything goes silent.

"We're gonna stand up now, Ashleigh. OK?"

Ash shakes her head no.

"Yes, we're gonna grab Kate, take a real shower, and go to fucking bed. I do not care what time it is, this day is over."

And that's exactly what we do. Ash manages to pull herself together and get Kate out of her carrier, undress her, and then they meet me in the shower on the other side of the bathroom. I sit her down on the bench and cranky Kate sucks at her mother's breast greedily as I wash us with a soft sponge and luxurious soap that smells like a tropical island.

When we're done I turn the water off and wrap Kate and Ashleigh in my dark blue robe. They swim inside of it and it wraps around them almost twice, but it keeps them warm. I wrap a towel around me and then lead Ash over to the spare room.

Pam is a miracle worker. It's not the princess nursery Kate deserves, but it will do for tonight. There's a portable crib with soft bedding in it, a changing table, diapers, clothes, all that other shit I've seen Ash use but don't really know what it's for.

"You need help?" I ask Ashleigh as she sprinkles some baby powder on Kate's bottom and then fastens up her diaper. Kate is making little mad grabs at Ashleigh's hanging hair, oblivious to the pain her mother is enduring.

"No, thank you," Ash replies and then slips a pink t-shirt over Kate's head and picks her up. "But I'm not sure about leaving her in here alone."

TAUT

I point to the baby monitor. "We can turn that on if you want. Or she can sleep with us."

Ashleigh looks over at the baby monitor for several long seconds. "With us until she falls asleep, then I'll bring her in here."

I turn the light out after she exits and a little yellow moon flicks on near the crib. Pam thinks of everything.

Ashleigh takes off the robe and lies down in bed naked. She slips the baby up to her breast and nurses Kate again. I imagine it would be hard to give up the comfort she gets from having the baby with her at night. I bet she enjoys it just as much as Kate does. I get in beside her, lean over and click the bedside lamp off, then pull them close.

"I have no idea what I'm doing, Ford."

"Me either, Ashleigh. I'm making it up as I go."

"Should I go back to Japan?"

"Do you want to go back to Japan?"

"No."

"Then don't. Stay here. I'd like you guys to stay here."

"My father will want to see me."

"Do you want to see him?"

"No."

"So don't. Just stay with me. Let me take care of things. Let me take care of you two."

She leans back into my chest, her back pressed against me. "OK."

And that's it. We lie there in the dark, listening to Kate gulp milk and the low hum of distant cars far down on the road below.

And we fall asleep as a family for the first time ever.

THIRTY-EIGHT

I wake up to no Ashleigh or Kate. My heart pounds in my chest with this realization until I hear the soft whispers coming from down the hall. I lie there listening to Ashleigh sing a little song to Kate and can't help but wonder how long this can possibly last.

She is everything I wanted. They are both everything I've wanted.

A few minutes later Ashleigh tiptoes back into the room and slips into bed next to me.

I wrap my arm around her and pull her close. We're both naked and her warm body feels so perfect next to mine. Her skin is soft and she smells good enough to eat.

"Sorry," she says quietly. "I tried not to wake you when I got up."

"It was your absence that woke me, not the noise you were making."

She turns to face me, propped up on her forearms. "I'm so sorry you had to see me like that today, Ford. I'm—"

"Shh," I say, putting my finger to her pouty lips. "You do not owe me an apology. I know, Ashleigh. I understand you. You love him, he was your whole life. And now he's gone and you were absolutely right back in Utah. You got shit on. Bad. Life fucked you over and then kicked you when you were down. I'm surprised you're still functioning."

Her fingertips trace the muscles in my upper arms and it sends a chill through my whole body. "I know all that. I'm not sorry about that part. I'm sorry you had to listen to me carry on about him. It's not fair to you. I like you, a lot. And when I said I loved you, Ford, I meant you. And I know you said it back as Tony, but I just wanted you to know—"

My thumb against her lips stops her words. The moon is shining through the curtainless windows and the silver light illuminates her face, like she's a precious work of art on display in my bed. "I love you. I'm in, Ashleigh. I want you, I want Kate, I want this. I want to sleep with you every night and give you everything you want. I'm in."

I position myself so my bare chest is over hers and then both hands cup her face as I lean in. "I'm in, Ashleigh." And then I kiss her. I skim her lips with mine. And my heart almost stops at how soft they are. I nip her bottom lip and she sucks in a breath, then she wraps her hands around my head. I kiss her again, my tongue looking for hers, my eyes closing, trying to hold this feeling inside me for as long as possible. As the kiss lingers, breaks, and starts again, Ashleigh fists my hair, pulling it just enough to make me grow with desire. She inserts her thigh between my legs and eases it into my hard-on.

I pull back so I can look at her in the moonlight again. "You are beautiful. I could look at you all day long and never get tired of tracing the line of your lips with my eyes or imagining myself biting your earlobe."

"You take all the bad away for me, Ford. When I'm with you, all that stuff disappears."

My thumb traces small circles on her cheek and I watch her.

I'm fulfilled just gazing at her but I want her to be fulfilled too, so I slip my hand down her belly and stop over her mound. My hand splays out, feeling every part of her folds, then one finger traces the slit of her pussy and pushes inside her. She moans and I lean down and bite her shoulder, hard enough to make her cry out, but still just a nibble.

Her hands reach for me and I bite her again. "Grab the headboard, Ashleigh, and do not let go until I tell you." She obeys immediately and this makes me stretch to my full hardness. "You may moan, you may scream, you may whine, you may whimper, you may cry, you may laugh, you may show your emotions in any way you please. But the only words you are allowed to say are no and stop."

She nods her head and this makes me smile. The old Ash would smart off with a *yes, sir*. But New Ashleigh wants to please me.

"If you say no or stop, that's it, I stop. No questions asked."

She nods and grips the headboard a little tighter.

I throw the covers off and get out of bed. I watch her carefully as I do this, looking for any hint that she wants to stop, but while her eyes are exhibiting curiosity, they are not showing any fear whatsoever. I walk to the closet and grab all of my neckties. She watches me very carefully as I tie several end to end, then repeat the process so I have two long silk tie strands. I have rope, but I don't want to scratch Ashleigh's perfect skin.

I walk back to the bed and sit down next to her, then grab one ankle, wrap the tie carefully, but tightly. And then push her knees up to her chest and wrap the tied ankle to her thigh.

She remains still, hands holding onto the headboard, but she's paying close attention.

I repeat this entire process with her other ankle and then I sit back and enjoy her spread open for me. He eyes wander down to my cock and I feel it jump with excitement. My hands caress her calves and then travel up and grab her on each side by the waist and pull her whole body down a little so her arms are straining to hold onto the headboard. "Is this what you wanted last night?"

She nods. And then she smiles.

"I have a confession to make. Would you like to hear it?"

She nods again.

"I actually do take requests on very special occasions. And tonight is a very special occasion. Do you want to know why it's so special?"

She nods.

I lean down and kiss her pussy, then lick her slit and suck her clit, making her moan. I do it again and this time she squirms. I ease two fingers inside her and stroke her gently back and forth, then I turn my fingers around and beckon to her sweet spot.

This time she tries to hold the moans in, which only makes them more pronounced when they finally escape.

I love this.

I bury my face between her thighs, grabbing her clit between my teeth for a brief moment, but long enough to make her gasp loudly. I suck on it and then shift my attention to lapping against the forward wall of her sex with my tongue, before pulling back.

"It's special, Ashleigh, because you are the first woman I will make love to." I ease myself between her open legs, drag my cock across her exposed clit, letting it pause at her opening. I push it in slightly, then withdraw and start again. Her moaning gets louder with each pass but I withhold what she wants. "Do not come yet, Ash." Her expression is almost painful and I have to stifle a laugh. "Do your best, kitten."

Her pussy releases some of her juices when I use the nickname and this does so many things to me inside, I almost have no words. I drag the head of my cock over her clit again and she arches her back. I do it harder and faster, harder and faster. "Do you like it, kitten?" Hot liquid squirts out and floods my cock head with warmth.

"Oh, you are one sexy little surprise, Miss Li."

She blushes and laughs a little.

"Let's do that again." I whip her pussy with my dick, back and forth, several times, and with each pass she squirts a little more, her back buckles, her thighs begin to twitch from the restraints, and then one final pass is all she can take.

She explodes, screaming my name and panting hard as I thrust my cock inside her pussy. I ram it into her, pull out so far she's straining to move her body towards me and keep a hold of the headboard at the same time, and then I plunge into her depths again. Over and over, I pump and thrust, and over and over she says my name. "Ford, Ford, Ford," she begs.

I lower myself over the top of her breasts and suck gently. It's enough to make her cry, but not with pleasure this time. I adjust and let my tongue caress the hard nub as my cock fills her again and again. Her whole body tenses and I pull away, all the way out, and roll over. "Let go of the headboard, Ashleigh. Let go and ease your pussy over my cock, but do not sink down onto it. Do you understand?"

She rolls over, struggling to right herself in her bindings, and presses her hands on my chest so she can hover over top of me.

I squeeze her breasts, harder than I should, and the milk drips out and runs over her swollen curves and lands on my stomach. "Fill yourself with my cock, now, Ashleigh." She lowers herself on top of me and I squeeze her tits again and then massage the sticky liquid around her nipples.

"Take me in, Ashleigh. Take me in and come for me."

She lowers herself down on my chest, rubbing her folds back and forth across the length of my cock, then lifts up and slams down as I make her pussy and her nipples drip with wetness.

We moan each other's names as we climax together. "I might need to spank you for speaking," I tell her softly a few minutes later as I wrap my arms around her waist and breathe heavy into her neck.

"I know," she says with a resigned sigh. "I'm counting on it."

I laugh as I reach down and untie her legs. She stretches them out along my body when they loosen, but neither of us has the energy to remove the bindings from her ankles.

She falls asleep on top of me, satisfied, sticky, wet, and warm.

THIRTY-NINE

All three of us are twisted together in the morning. Kate is lying half on me and half on Ashleigh, her little mouth open and her tongue making that little suckling motion. Ashleigh's arms are above her head—*like they are when I fuck her*, I think absently—and she too is passed out cold. I wonder if Kate was demanding last night and that's why she ended up in bed with us?

Or maybe Ashleigh just likes sleeping with her. I lift Kate off me and place her on the bed next to Ashleigh, then grab some running shorts from the dresser and stick my phone in my pocket. It's bright out today and the sun is shining in the large south-facing windows. The back of the house has a fantastic view of LA.

I'm just about to head out and go for a run on Mulholland when Kate starts getting cranky.

"Katielynn, you're not hungry, baby. You just ate," Ash says in her *I'm too fucking tired for this* voice. "Shhhh. Go back to sleep. Shhhh."

"I got her." I pick Kate up and lean in to smell her. She's still good, thank God. I open the sliding door that leads to the pool and slip outside into the sun. Kate tucks her face against my chest to avoid the brightness and I take a seat in a lounge chair. I look down at the baby. Her little fists are clutching at my upper arms and she's looking up at me with those big browns. "What's up, Kate?"

She blinks.

I laugh. "I like you. I want to keep you. Would you like to live here? It's not a bad place. It's got a great view, it's centrally located to all the best studios. And it's got a pool, right? You could do worse."

She blinks.

"Oh yeah, I'd keep your mom too. No worries. She's the milk machine." I hear some snickering from the bedroom door and Ashleigh is peeking her head out the door.

"Quit sneaking and come out here."

"I'm naked."

"So? I thought you likes the exhibitionist stuff?"

She gets over her shyness, or maybe she just wants to drive me crazy, because she steps out and walks over to us. "I heard that, you know," she says taking a seat on the lounger next to me. She pulls her legs up and Kate immediately starts whining to go to her. I hand the baby over and she gives her the breast. "I guess she was hungry after all."

"So do you?" I ask. She just stares at me. "Want to stay here?"

"I'm not sure you understand what you're getting in to. I'm a single mom."

"I'm a single guy."

"I have Kate and—"

"And I want Kate, Ashleigh. I do. I want you both."

She watches Kate nurse in silence for a few seconds and then turns to look out at the view. The back patio is not large, not by Colorado standards anyway. Our yard in Park Hill is ten times this big. But this place has an infinity pool with an unobstructed view.

"I'll call in child-proofers, Ashleigh. We'll get a cover for the pool, and fence that part of the hill off so she can't get into trouble." Holy shit, I don't even know where that came from. I've never said the word child-proofers in my life.

"That's not it, Ford."

My phone buzzes in my shorts and I check the call real fast. Jason in Vail. Probably to tell me about Ash's car. I press silent and go back to the conversation. "Then what?"

She shakes her head. "I'm a mess. Just a total mess."

"You're not a mess, Ashleigh. In fact, you're coping better than most people would in your circumstances. Do you feel any better today?"

"I do," she nods. "I do feel better. But I'm still so sad. Just picturing his face is enough to make me cry. Just all of it, the whole thing was just… traumatic. And I'm pretty sure you're not gonna be happy if I'm moping around all the time thinking of the man I lost." She looks up at me and shrugs. "I know I'd feel weird if the tables were turned."

I think about this for a while and Ash leans back and closes her eyes. She is so beautiful. "I'm not jealous of him." And as soon as the words come out I understand Ronin. It's strange. It's like this realization hits me out of nowhere. I'm not jealous of Tony because Tony isn't a threat. Tony makes Ashleigh whole, but Tony is gone. And that's not something that will ever change. Ronin must feel this way about me. I make Rook whole, but he knows her heart belongs to him. He wants me in her life to make her happy. Because he loves her.

"Tell me how you met."

"Who?"

"You and Tony."

"Why would you want to know that?"

"Because you love him and you miss him. And I'm sure you're dying to tell anyone who will listen about all the things that made him so special. And I'd like to listen, Ashleigh. Because… because I want to make you happy. I want to know because he's part of you and Kate, and I want you and Kate. I'm hooked. I can't even imagine leaving you behind."

She just stares at me.

"So tell me. Start from the beginning."

She hugs baby Kate a little tighter, much to the dismay of the hungry infant, and then looks out over the valley. "I was fourteen years old. And he was sixteen. My father told me I had to join a sport when we finally settled in Rancho Santa Fe and I started going to a local school. So I joined basketball."

I laugh.

"I know," she says, smiling. "I'm five foot two." And now she laughs. "But it was winter and it was either that or cheerleading. I took my chances with basketball. Anyway, we would travel to the other schools in the area for games and stuff, and Tony went to another school. Co-ed. Mine was all girls, remember?"

I nod. I have not gotten the image out of my mind and now I'm picturing her in a basketball uniform. But it's probably inappropriate to say that when she's telling me how she met her first love.

"I sat the bench for every game. The coach knew I was only on the team to please my father, so she never made me play. But every time we went to play against the girls at Trinity Day I'd see this guy. Total hotness, jock, already built like a man."

"Tony."

"Anthony Fenici." She blushes at his name. A decade later and the simple act of saying this guy's name is enough to make her blush. "That first game I was just minding my own business, warming my bench, and then the coach asked me to go out to her car and get her notebook. So I took her keys and went out to the parking lot, got the stuff, and I was walking back when I saw hot-assed Anthony Fenici making out with a girl against the building. And when I walked past, I was staring. I was young, I'd never kissed a boy, so I was sorta gawking at them. And then I noticed that Anthony Fenici was watching me gawk at him. Even as he stuck his tongue down this other girl's throat. And then he winked at me."

What a player.

"Anyway, I was hooked from that moment on. He tortured me that whole year at every game we played against Trinity Day by being around, making me notice him, acknowledging that I noticed him, and then promptly ignoring me. And when basketball season was over, I joined track in the spring, just so I could go to those away meets with Trinity. And the next year came, and I was in ninth grade, and I did it again. I joined basketball and track. Only now I'm getting a little better at b-ball, right? I had a year of practices under my belt, plus all that damn running in the spring gave me endurance. So I played a game or two that year. And every time I made a basket, which was not often, but every time that fucking Anthony Fenici would stand up and yell *Li Li scores!*"

Suddenly she's crying. Her face is all red as she tries to stop, but can't. "I'm sorry, Ford."

I pull my lounge chair over to her and put my arm around her. "It's OK, Ashleigh. You're allowed to cry."

She wipes her eyes and takes a deep breath. "And he did that all season. And then in the spring, he was at the finish line every time I crossed. I did cross-country that year. But he never talked to me. Not once. He was just *there*, encouraging me. And that's not something I got a lot of, ya know? I was not encouraged. My father never came to my games, he had no idea what I was doing in school. But Tony, he was *there*. He was always there. And the next year, I was in tenth grade and he was a senior. And this is when everything changed. Because he asked me to homecoming at Trinity Day."

I smile as I picture her getting asked on that date. "Sounds like a perfect start to a perfect relationship."

"Anthony Fenici is the son of a prominent man. Just like I am the daughter of another, equally prominent man." She looks over at me with a sad smile. "Our fathers are business rivals."

"Legal business?" I ask.

She shrugs her shoulders. "Mostly. My father runs an"—she does air quotes—"import-export business. Black-market drugs. Not like cocaine and heroin, more like non-FDA approved treatments. Hormones mostly, for doping, fertility, anti-aging. His business services hospitals in Mexico, Costa Rica, and others."

"And Tony's father?"

"Your basic Italian stuff."

I laugh. "Straight Sicilian mafia?"

"Yeah."

"So you two were a modern-day Romeo and Juliet?"

"No, he wanted out and I had no intention of ever doing anything remotely related to what my father does. My sister is in the business, she's an accountant, which comes in handy, I hear. My educational trust came from my mother's estate. It was not conditional, so I left, picked a major that would never be useful to my father and got on with life."

"And Tony?"

She smiles up at me. "He joined the Marines. We did go to dances and he always showed up at my games when they were at Trinity Day, but we never *dated* in high school. Not like most kids do. We knew it was impossible, so instead of dating, we planned our future and talked on the phone and met up every once in a while for sports or a dance. He joined the Marines when I was in eleventh grade thinking he'd get out after two years and join me wherever I was going to school. But…" She looks up at me and tries to force a smile, but fails. "He liked it, Ford. He enjoyed the combat stuff. He told me he felt part of something real, something like a family. Something he never got from his home life. This was something I could relate to. I understood, so I thought the right thing to do was to encourage him. When his two-year Marine contract was up he applied for SEALs, he got in the BUD/S program and the whole time I told myself, he'll never make it. They never make it. Almost everyone fails. But he didn't fail, he wasn't top of his class, but he was not bottom either. It wasn't easy, he said, but he'd do it again in a heartbeat. And then before I knew it, he was over the hardest parts and that was that. He was *in*."

She stops and lets out an I-give-up sigh. "What could I say? Nothing. I had to support him. This was his dream. He put himself through hell to achieve it. What could I do?"

This pause is much longer and I can only assume she's thinking up all the ways she should've discouraged him. Maybe she'd have crushed his dream, but he'd still be alive.

"I was already in Japan by then, and we saw each other when he could make the trip. And two years later here I am. Alone."

It takes me a few minutes to put all this information together and she pats Kate on the back, waiting patiently to see what I'll say. "It's pretty unconventional, Ashleigh. I'm not discounting how you feel about him, but that's not exactly a dream relationship. When did you do all the fun stuff?"

"I know what you're trying to say, and I'm not saying I disagree, I'm just telling you I love him and that's how it happened."

I nod. "Fair enough. But there's more to life than that. Ash. There's more to love than that. Maybe you don't like me, and that's cool. If you don't I'll totally understand. I'm not for everyone. But if you like me, Ashleigh, then hear me out."

She closes her eyes as she continues to pat Kate on the back. "I do like you Ford. A lot. But I'm complicated."

"I'm complicated too, shit. I'm like the King of Complicated."

She laughs and then opens her eyes and looks at me. Sees me for the first time this morning. "I don't know, Ford. I'm not sure what I'm doing right now. I'm just drifting. I'm completely unraveled, I'm nothing but slack. Everything about me is frayed at the moment. So, I'm not sure I'm ready for life just yet. I just don't know. Maybe, Ford."

All I hear is yes. *Yes, Ford.* God I love it when she says my name. "I can pull you taut, Ashleigh. Like the poems. I can bring you back together. You are so fucking delicious, Ashleigh. So fucking perfect. I wish I could take this pain away from you, really, I swear I feel your sadness and it makes me crazy. Do I ask for more information and risk the tears? Do I pretend it's not happening and risk you feeling ignored? Tell me what to do." The words surprise me as much as they do her and all I can do is shrug. "I don't understand what you need, Ashleigh. And I feel like it's my job to provide for you and I don't know how to do that. If you know what you need, tell me."

She snuggles her face down into Kate's neck and I can hear her draw in a long breath, smelling the sweet scent of the baby's skin. "I just don't know, Ford. I feel like I'm stumbling along, waiting for something to happen."

We sit like that for a few silent minutes. My head is spinning with all these revelations that have happened over the last twenty-four hours. Tony, Kate, her family. I reach over and take her hand. "Come here."

"What?"

I pull on her arm, tugging her harshly. "Now, Ashleigh. Sit in front of me." She thinks for a moment. "It's not a request, Ashleigh. I want you here, between my legs. *Now*."

Ash stands and then kneels on my lounger. I pull my knees up so I can box her in, and she leans back, her naked body pressing against my chest. Kate's head is resting on Ash's shoulder, her eyes trained on me. I smile at her and she gives me gums as her eyes twinkle. I have to hold back the urge to just squeeze her plump little cheeks because I'm trying to be serious.

"If you don't know what you want, and you won't tell me specifics, then I'll tell you what I think you need. You're mine now, Ashleigh. I'm claiming you. I'm claiming Kate too. If you want to be with me then I call the shots. And I've made my first decision."

Ash turns her head a little to try and look at me but I clamp my knees against her waist and hold her tight so she can't shift her position. Her whole chest expands and then it's like she flips a switch and the tension melts away. She relaxes.

But that's not a yes, so it's not enough.

"I'd like to fuck you right now. I love that you're outside naked. I love that you're holding Kate like this. Oblivious to the world, just existing. Following my orders. I know you're not submissive, Ashleigh. It's why I didn't fuck you until I made up my mind that I liked you. Because I knew we'd have to have this conversation. I'm a control freak. I like to call the shots. Most people don't like that. Most people want to tell me to fuck off. You're free to feel that way, you can tell me to fuck off. I'll still take care of you until you figure out what you want. But if that's your decision then this potential relationship is over and it won't go any further."

Silence.

"Thoughts?"

"Is this about sex or things like what to make for dinner?"

"It's about what's good for you."

"How do you know what's good for me?"

"I don't, not yet. I hardly know you. I'm not perfect, I'll make mistakes. But relationships aren't something I normally do. I do sex. I do fucking. I do blow jobs, I do bondage, and I keep pets. I keep girls as pets, Ashleigh. I never get their names, I never ask them out on a date. They're given a time and a place, they meet me or they don't. If they don't show up and I feel like fucking, there's always another girl on the list."

She blows out a long breath of air. "Holy shit, Ford."

"I told you, I'm not a nice guy. I'm Fucking Ford. It's practically a nickname. This is how I operate."

"So I'm just another one of your pets?"

"Do you think I'd be having this conversation with you if you were just another pet?"

"Then what do you want from me?"

"Wrong question, Ashleigh. The real question is what do you want from me." She wriggles, trying to turn and see my face. I box her in again and put my arms around her shoulders, but she continues to struggle until Kate begins to get upset. I let Ash go and shake my head. "What are you doing?"

She shushes Kate as she leans in to kiss her cheek, and then turns her whole body so she can watch me properly when she speaks. "I want love." She stares at me, her dark brown eyes a little bit watery.

I'm probably a total dick for having this conversation after all the shit she's been through, but I can't stop myself. I'm a greedy bastard and I need to nail this down or let it go, and I need to do that right the fuck now.

"I want to be loved," she whispers. "I want to be kissed and I don't want to have to play a game to get one. I want you to show me—*tell me*—everyday that you love me. Because I *had* love. And maybe you don't approve of the relationship I had with Tony, but your opinion hardly matters. It doesn't count. It was enough for me to know he was mine. That when he came home, I was the only thing he thought about. He wrote me love letters and poems. And before you fucking shake your head or roll your eyes, Ford, he was a Navy SEAL, he grew up in the mafia, he was as manly as they fucking come."

"You want me to write you poems?"

"No, I want you to give up a little piece of yourself to make me happy. Just like you're asking me to give up a little bit of myself to make you happy. It's a give and take, Ford. You might be someone's master, but not mine. I like you. You're almost perfect."

"But…"

"But… I want to know what your level of commitment is. I'm not looking for a boyfriend. I have no use for a boyfriend right now. And I'm not looking for a master, either. I can make my own decisions. I might make mistakes but I'm smart, I learn from them. It's just that emotions sometimes overwhelm my brain and I do irrational things. Like this trip. But…" She swallows. "This trip is a new way forward for me. One way or another. So it's not a completely crazy waste. I'm in a new place, I'm a mother, I'm flailing, Ford. I'm standing at some fucking crossroad looking at all these choices, and I have no way to know which one is the best route. They all have risks, but some risks are higher than others." She looks away for a second, then gives me a sideways glance. "You're a big risk in my mind. I can't commit to you without something… something big. Like a grand gesture, Ford. I *need* a grand gesture."

"So leaving you alone in a foreign country to have a baby, that's the grand gesture you're looking for?"

She hardens at my sarcasm and I'm instantly sorry, but it's too late—the words hang in the air between us, creating a gulf.

"What part didn't you hear? He showed up at my games and competitions for an entire year and got absolutely nothing back in return. Not a kiss, not a conversation, nothing. He was patient and concerned and so… so… *open*. He didn't care that his whole school heard him encourage me at the basketball games. Or that his friends laughed at him standing there in the rain at the finish line of a cross-country race. He did it anyway. He did it because he only saw *me*, Ford. He took me to two dances a year because that was as many as we could get away with. He showed me I mattered before he asked me to give up a little bit of myself to make him happy. I gave up my fear of him dying as a soldier so he could pursue his dream. And maybe these things aren't as fancy as what you have in mind, but I don't care what you think about it. He made me feel special—we made *each other* feel special."

"You want the fairy tale, then?" I shake my head.

"I want to be won, Ford. If you can win me, you can have me. I'll be yours and you'll have earned it."

I stare at her and say nothing.

The grand gesture. Ashleigh wants a Jedi and all I'm capable of giving her is the Sith.

She reads my introspective silence as her answer and gets up and takes Kate back into the bedroom.

FORTY

When I go inside she's dressed and sitting on the couch with Kate watching something on TV.

"Ashleigh, look, I'm not—"

My phone buzzes in my pants and I take it out and look at the name. Jason.

"Who is it? A pet who needs to be fed and walked?"

I silence the phone and stick it back in my pocket. "Cute." I sit down next to her. Fuck. I am so bad at this shit. What the hell do I say? I feel like I'm losing her, right now, this very moment. I feel like she's slipping away and I have no idea what to say.

"Just tell me what you're thinking. Start there, Ford."

She's a mind-reader. She's a fucking psychologist for fuck's sake.

"If you can't do that, then I'm just wasting my time."

"What the fuck do you want from me? I said I wanted you. How is that not telling you how I feel? I fucking want you to live here, move in. Be with me. Let me help with Kate."

"In what capacity, Ford? What is Kate to you but some pet's

423

offspring?"

"That's enough," I glare at her. "Don't talk shit to me because you're insecure."

"You're the one who's insecure. You want control to suppress your social inadequacy."

"Fucking don't do that either. If I wanted a psych evaluation I'd go see a therapist."

"So I'm supposed to pretend that I didn't just go to school for six years to get a degree in psychology? Just pretend that I don't see all the issues you have?"

"Issues I have? Ashleigh, please. If I'm fucked up, then you're right there with me. We're both—"

The gate alert buzzes and cuts off my words. "Fucking people are here from the hotel to drop off our shit, I bet." I get up and go over to the security panel near the door and press the button that opens the front gate. I peek out the window but the driveway is long and we're at the top of a hill, so I can't see the gate from the house. "You and I are the same, Miss Li. We both have issues. So don't push me away with that excuse."

Ash says nothing and I peek out the window again as a large black Mercedes pulls up. "Who the fuck is that? I'm pretty sure hotel couriers don't drive an eighty-thousand-dollar Mercedes."

"What?" Ashleigh jumps up and hurries over to the window just as a tall man in a black suit gets out of the back of the car. He's older, maybe early fifties, has jet-black hair, and as soon as he turns around I know who he is by the color of his eyes.

"My father is here." A blonde woman gets out after him. "And my fucking sister. Oh, God. Ford, listen to me." Ash pulls on my arm. "Listen to me, OK? Do not open the door, do not open the door!"

"Why are they just standing there?" I ask as we peek out at them.

And then a cop car comes up the driveway.

"What the fuck is going on?"

"OK, look, I left some things out of my story… Ford!" She

grabs my arm again but I'm watching these fucking people talk to the cops, probably about me, in *my* fucking driveway. The cop nods and then puts his hand on his Taser. Ashleigh is still talking but I don't hear anything she says because the fucking cops are walking up to my door with Ashleigh's father and sister looking like they're in the mood to take my shit out.

The doorbell chimes. They're looking right at us through the window, even as Ash continues to freak out and tell me all kinds of shit that just never even registers in my brain.

Fuck.

What if they have dirt on me? What if this father of hers found out who I am and has fucking dirt on me? Ronin, I need Ronin. I pull out my phone to call him when the doorbell rings again. Kate begins to cry because Ashleigh is so upset and before I can press Ronin's face to place the call another call comes in.

Fucking Jason, *again*.

"Mr. Aston," the cop says, his muffled voice coming through the closed window. We're only like three feet away from him. "Mr. Aston, Mr. Li here just needs to have a few words with his daughter. Can we come in?"

And then an ambulance rolls in behind the cops. What the fuck is going on?

"Ford! Are you listening to me?" Ashleigh practically screams it and poor Kate begins to wail.

"What?" I'm still not listening because two paramedics get out of the ambulance and another guy with a suit. I finally turn to Ash. "Tell me what the fuck is happening."

But before Ashleigh can answer, Mr. Li is standing in front of the window. "She's very sick, Mr. Aston. I know you've taken good care of her, but you need to know she is very sick."

I swear, I almost fall over. "Sick how?"

"Don't listen, Ford!" Ashleigh is pleading. "Please, don't listen. I'm sorry for what happened, I was not thinking clearly, but please, don't listen!"

Mr. Li takes out a folded piece of pink paper and Ash loses it.

She starts crying and pleading with me. Her father holds it out in front of the window and I can't help myself. I open the window, push the screen aside, and take it. Ashleigh goes wild, jumping with the baby trying to get it from me.

"Ashleigh," I say sternly. "Stop it. Right now."

"I don't want you to see that, I don't want you to read that!" She's hysterical.

"OK."

She stops, like literally holds her breath for a few seconds. "OK?"

I nod. Mr. Li is talking to me, but I reach over and close the window back up. "But you need to tell me what's going on. What's in here." I hold up the paper and she snatches it away. "Tell me what it says and tell me why all these people are here. Why is your father saying you're sick? Do you have a medical condition?"

"Tell them to leave first. Tell them to leave!"

"I'll tell you what she wrote in the note, Mr. Aston," Li says. When I look back he's opened the window so his voice is loud and clear.

Ashleigh crumples and I reach down and grab Kate before she hits her head on the white tiles.

I look back to Li. "You need to leave. Whatever it is you have to say, I'll hear it from her first, and I'll hear it when she's ready. Not like this."

"We need to take the baby, Mr. Aston. Ashleigh," her sister says in a soothing voice from outside. "Ashleigh, honey. We're concerned about the baby. If you don't let us take her, we're going to do what we talked about last time. Do you understand, Ashleigh?"

Kate grabs at my face, still upset and crying. "You can't take the kid," I say, shaking my head.

"Mr. Aston," the cop chimes in. "Miss Li has written at least two suicide notes in the past three weeks. She's highly unstable and the *family*"—he stresses this word, like he's reminding me that I'm not family—"will back off and not pursue an involuntary psychiatric detention if Ashleigh allows herself to be evaluated and hands the child over to be cared for by her sister."

Oh. Fuck.

"I have authority to hold her, Mr. Aston. Pursuant to California Welfare and Institutions Code, Section 5150, she might need a mandatory seventy-two-hour detention for evaluation and treatment in a psychiatric facility. Now, the family is willing to forgo that extreme measure if Ashleigh agrees to come home and bring the baby with her so the family doctor can monitor her."

"We only want to keep her safe, Mr. Aston," her father says. "Please open the door and allow the officers in. We do not want to commit her."

I just stare at him.

"Ashleigh," he says calmly. "Open the door and come home, or we will be forced to send you away for an evaluation. It's for your own good, we only want to keep you safe. You're been running wild for years and now there's another life involved. A baby who is my own blood. And I will not stand by and let you endanger her." He looks up to me. "No offense, Mr. Aston. I realize you've taken very good care of them, I'm grateful. But this is over now. She's coming home, whether or not we have to—"

The door opens and Ashleigh walks out. "I'll go, just please don't take me away from Kate. She's all I have left, please don't take me away from Kate. I'll go."

The sister comes in and pries a red-faced Kate from my arms and she starts to wail.

Oh God. This shit is really happening.

I stand there in a state of shock and watch her being loaded into the black car. And then two minutes later the driveway is empty.

My house is empty.

And they are gone.

FORTY-ONE

I stand there looking out at the driveway, waiting for the world to rewind and bring them back. But that doesn't happen. What does happen is a van drives up, knocks on the door, then drops off a box that says Four Seasons Las Vegas.

Our stuff. But there's no *our* anymore.

Holy fucking shit. What just happened? Did I freeze? I didn't say anything. I was stunned silent. What could I say? They wanted to incarcerate her in a psychiatric facility. I spy the folded pink note on the floor, forgotten in the midst of chaos. I walk over and pick it up and then grab the box from the front door. I take them both back to the couch and sit down to try and calm my racing heart.

I don't want to read this note, I really don't. It feels so invasive, like I'm betraying her if I read it. But I have to. I need more information. I unfold it slowly, and then take in the sight of her handwriting. It's a beautiful cursive with lots of flowing lines and loops.

TAUT

The angel of A D D
Kills the baby inside of me
The angel of A D D
Blames the baby inside of me

I sail, I sail, I sail into the dark

You're not listening
And that kills me
You're not listening
My mind is sailing inside of me

I sail, I sail, I sail into the dark

The angel of death breeds
A sickness inside of me
The angel of death breeds
Killing the baby inside of me

I sail, I sail, I sail into the dark

It's a poem. A dark one, for sure. But it's a fucking poem. It's not a suicide note. And she says that she takes words from songs she likes and creates new poems out of the same words. I go in the office and start up the computer. It's not anything special, just your run-of-the-mill home setup. But it's got internet and that's all I need. I put the first line in the search bar and press enter.

Nothing. I add the refrain, since it's repeated three times and it makes the poem look more like lyrics.

Bingo. A song called *Sail* by AWOLNATION.

It's not even a dark song, it's kinda techno and catchy. The video is actually quite stupid. Some shit about aliens. But Ashleigh's arrangement of the words is disturbing when taken out of the context of where they came from. I can see why her family was upset.

I grab the box and open it up, looking for the journal she said she left behind when we left. It's under a bunch of clothes, smells a little bit like dirty socks, and is bulging at the seams. Three thick rubber bands hold it together and prevent all the loose papers from escaping. I remove the rubber bands and it spills open as soon as the tension is released. Two passports fall out. I open the first one. Katelynn Li. She's got just one stamp. USA. She entered the country on Christmas Eve. It's even got a little baby picture of her.

I smile. God, I miss her already.

I put that aside and open Ashleigh's. Her book is almost full, only a few pages left. She's been everywhere. Most of them say USA and Japan, but she's got a lot of Hong Kong and she looks totally different. The date of issue says 2006 and she's got a punk haircut. Those bangs that drive her crazy now are short and dyed a hot pink. She's got some black eye makeup on, and from the look of her pupils, she might be high. She's wearing something revealing on top, I can't see much of her clothes, but that's because the shirt is cut very low. Sixteen-year-old Wild Ash is sexy as all fucking hell, but I'd spank her ass hard if she went out in public like this in front of me.

There are pictures too. All of Tony and Ashleigh. He's a big guy and in every one he's looking down at her tiny body like he won the Powerball.

He loved her. I have to concede that, he must've loved her. She's right. She had love, she knows what it feels like and there's no fucking way she'd settle for my pathetic bullshit as a second-hand substitute.

My phone buzzes and I quickly take it out and check the call hoping it's Ash.

Jason. Fucking pest.

"Yeah," I answer.

"Ford! Fuck, dude! I've been trying to get a hold of you all day! Some people were here looking for you and that girl you left with. I didn't know it was a big deal, I swear. I told them you had a place in LA, man. I'm fucking sorry. Did they come to your house?"

I sigh loudly. "Yes, they did."

He babbles on and on for a few minutes, explaining how he entered the VIN number into his computer and it downloaded as a Carfax database report.

Bam. Her father was on that shit quick.

I hang up with Jason after promising I'd come back and see them when things settled down.

Right.

My phone buzzes again. Pam. "Yes?"

"They'll start looking elsewhere if you don't show up today, Mr. Aston. Breach of contract."

I almost snort thinking of me threatening Rook with the same thing last year when we did the STURGIS contract. She'd get a kick out of this, I'm sure. "Thanks, Pam. I'll be in after lunch today."

I go back to the journal and open it to the first page. It's called *My Worry Book.*

I read that journal from front to back. It's a series of letters to Tony and God, alternating, one after the other most of the time.

The letters to Tony tell him how scared she is that he'll die on duty. Things she'd never tell him to his face because this was his dream and she wanted to support him.

The notes to God are nothing but begging. Begging God to spare her lover's life in any number of ways. *Please don't let him be shot. Please don't let him be captured. Please don't let him get blown up.*

God was not listening, because Tony did get blown up. Into so many pieces nothing came home to be buried.

I read her fears and it breaks my heart that this is how she lived for three years. In between the journal entries to Tony and God are the poems. All sad poems. The Sail poem is there too, and it says flat out that it's about death. It's about Death taking her Tony and ripping away her innocence. It's dated last year, not even related to this trip at all. That pink note was a desperate attempt to let people know how she was unable to cope with the loss.

The journal entries during the last months of her pregnancy were pretty happy. Ashleigh believed Tony was in a safer position, her worries were mostly about gaining weight, the baby not being healthy, being sick at the end.

And then… the day.

The day she learned about Tony's death.

It says only one word over and over—*Why?*

No other entries until New Year's Day this year.

It's a note to God.

Dear God,

> *Thank you for sending me Ford.*
> *He's perfect.*
> *Thank you so, so much.*

Ashleigh Li

TAUT

Below that is another poem.

I've been searching for you
It's always been you
Hearts and grace
You take me from this broken place

I'll search for you
It will always be you
On my way home, all alone
In everything I do, I'll search for you

I want your lips in a kiss
It's true, I love you
I'll always be searching for you
Because you are my saving grace
You take me from this broken place

I stare at those words for what seems like hours. I read it over and over and over. And then I go back to the computer and look for this one too. It takes me a while to find the original online because there's two versions of this song. I listen to both several times before deciding this poem came from The Maine, *Saving Grace, Take 2.*

This song just rips my heart out.

And she thanked God for *me*. I am her saving grace?

I toss the journal down on the couch and go take a shower so I can get dressed for work. I'll be useless today, but all they want is the appearance that I give a shit about this project right now.

I do give a shit about this project. I want this project. We're leaving in a week for New Zealand to start filming. They're just rehearsing right now, a part of the production I'm not required to participate in, that's the director's job. But they want me to show an effort? I can do that.

I dress in my best suit, then stumble over that little yellow ducky as I come out of the closet in the bedroom.

Kate. God, no more Kate. No more Ash. And the last fucking impression she'll have of me is being a controlling asshole, making demands of her out by the pool.

She wants the grand gesture. She wants the fairy tale.

But she's in the middle of a nightmare right now. I only hope they took her home and not to some hospital.

I lock the door behind me and get in my Audi. I need the air conditioning today. It's warm and I don't want the windows open. I want to block out the world and not participate in it. The studio is not that far away and when I get there I go through the motions. I shake hands, laugh about my ridiculous luck in getting to LA in the Bronco. Explain my emotional attachment to the truck and why I needed to save it. They are all sappy artists, they totally understand my eccentricities. That's one thing I always loved about being in the art community—they pretty much accept everyone. It does not matter how weird you are, they like weird.

And I think this show will be a hit. It's got every popular trope going right now.

I waste hours chatting these people up, but on the inside I replay Ashleigh's words over and over in my mind.

I want to be won, Ford. If you can win me, you can have me. I'll be yours and you'll have earned it.

TAUT

I hold it together until the day is finally over at six-thirty, and then get back in my car and drive home. I stop at the gate, but not because I need to enter a code.

It's open.

Did I close it before I left?

My heart races as I drive up the hill, hoping that somehow Ashleigh found a way to come back, but when I get up to the house I almost crash the car into the garage door before I snap out of my surprise.

Rook is sitting on my doorstep.

FORTY-TWO

She stands up and waits for me to get out of the car but I just sit for a few seconds, staring at her. Why is she here? Did she leave Ronin? I open the door and get out, then close it gently, like noise will disrupt the fabric of the universe and bring it all crashing down upon me. I walk over to her and stand there. She's got her hands in the pockets of her jeans, her shoulder slightly hunched, and her eyes are wide with expectation.

"I'm so sorry," she whispers.

"For what?"

"For taking advantage of our friendship. For taking you for granted. For not giving more. I'm sorry, Ford. I had no idea I was hurting you. I do love you, you have to know that. I do. It's just…" She stops to take a deep breath. "It's just… you're right. It's not the same way that I love Ronin. Not that it's bad," she adds hurriedly. "It's not bad, just different. And I can't stand the thought of you not being in my life. I'm going crazy here, Ford. I'm desperate to prove to you that I'm more than just a Taker. I'm a Giver, Ford. I want to give you whatever it is that will make you happy and bring you back into my life. I do."

"Where's Ronin?"

"Back home."

"Does he know you're here?"

"Yes. I told him I needed to sort this out."

"How long are you staying?"

"As long as you want me to."

"What do you want from me, Rook?"

"I want for you to love me, Ford. Like you did before this happened. I want for you to love me like that again. Because this"—she waves her arms in the air in an all-encompassing gesture—"this is not working for me. I can't stand this, Ford. I need you. You're my best friend."

I unlock the door and wave her in, then follow. "Have you eaten?" She looks like she's lost some weight.

"No, I'm not hungry."

I throw my keys down on the counter and shake my head. "I have no idea what to say to you, Rook. A week ago I would've been thrilled that you came all this way to see me." I look over at her face as she internalizes this and fuck. She's upset.

She turns away and walks over to the door, but I'm there before her hand touches the handle. "No. No, you're not walking away. I'm not running away. We're gonna have to figure this out, Rook. Because I do love you. I do. I'm not sure what it means, but you're important to me and what I did to you was wrong. I was—" I breathe deeply. "I was just hurting so badly that night. And I had that speech prepared, I was planning that escape. And even though I told myself it wasn't to confuse you and make you feel what I was feeling, that's exactly why I did it. I wanted to hurt you. I wanted you to miss me and regret not choosing me."

She looks up at me with tears in her eyes and I feel like total shit. Rook is not a crier. She holds pretty much everything inside, so the fact that I'm making her cry right now… well, that's painful too. "Don't. Please. Don't cry over this. I'm not worth it. I'm a total piece of shit."

"Ford," she says in a soft voice. She turns into me and throws her arms around my neck and hugs me. "You are worth it. To me, you are worth it. I can't stand this. I can't stand knowing that I was making you so upset all those months. All those months I was so happy and content and you were miserable. It—" She chokes back a sob. "It breaks my heart, Ford."

I hug her back. "Did you leave Ronin?"

She pulls back to look at me. "Do you want me to leave Ronin?"

"Answer my question. I'm tired of the games."

"No, I didn't leave him. I love him. He's my one, Ford. But you're friendship is important to me. I need you. I can't picture my life without you. Please, just tell me what I need to do to make this better."

I am the biggest piece of shit alive. I win all the piece of shit awards.

I hug her close and breathe her in. "Rook, you're a living goddess to me. You're the most tragically beautiful creature I've ever seen. I love you so much. I'd do anything for you, you know that right?"

She pushes back a little so she can look up at me.

"But you're right. It's just a very special friendship. We're friends. It's taken me a while, but I finally get it. You belong to Ronin, Rook. And I'm so sorry that I caused all this bullshit with my childish actions." She nods into my chest and breathes out a long sigh. "I might've found my one in this girl I was on the road with. But the shit just hit the fan this morning and to be honest, I could use a friend's advice on what to do about it all."

She turns her head up to me again and then wipes her eyes. "You can ask me, Ford. I'm pretty bad at making good decisions, but I'll do my best to help you sort it out."

"Let's go eat first. You look so thin, Rook. I don't like it."

"I know," she says, sniffling. "I can't eat when you're mad at me."

"I'm sorry. But I'm not mad anymore, so let's go get steaks at

Mastro's. Have you ever been?"

She snorts. God, I've missed her snorts. "Every time I come to LA, I hit up Mastro's first."

And just like that our fight is wiped away. We drive down the hill into Beverly and have dinner. Ashleigh is still weighing heavily on my mind. I feel like I'm wasting time, like I need to be doing something right now. But it's not good to act impulsively. I need information and advice. And Rook is my sounding board. I tell her everything. We are friends. Best friends. And that's exactly how it feels. Like this girl is the only person on this whole planet who won't judge me, no matter what I tell her.

She listens to the entire story—laughing at the funny parts, crying her blue eyes out when I describe Ashleigh at the cemetery, and then sighing with sadness when I describe the scene this morning at my house.

"What should I do, Rook?"

"She wants you to sweep her off her feet, Ford."

"Yeah, but she's gone. How the hell?"

"You're the genius," she says, taking a drink of her soda. "I'm sure you can come up with something. There has to be a way to get her away from them and not have her committed in the process. Can't you just hack into her father's shit and fuck it up?"

I laugh at her silliness. "No, he's big time. He's dirty, like me. He's not going to sit back and let me fuck with his multi-billion-dollar pharmaceutical business."

"So you have to make it personal then, right?"

"Yeah," I sigh. I look down at my watch. "Pam has you booked first class on the eleven-fifteen flight back to DIA. You can't spend the night. Ronin will be pissed."

She takes my hand and pouts. "Are you sure, Ford? I can smooth things out with Ronin if you need my help."

"No, I need to think. I'll drive you to the airport."

It's hard to say goodbye to Rook when I drop her off at LAX Departures, but she needs to go home where she belongs and I need to come up with a plan, and that plan involves another phone call to Merc. I take out my phone and press Adam.

Merc answers on the second ring. "Yeah."

"I need a big Merc."

"I hope to God that baby-fucking-sitter didn't steal your kid and you went apeshit and killed her and now you need to escape the country under the assumed name of BJ Cobbledick." He pauses. "Or something."

I know better than to feed Merc's insults so I ignore that whole fucking outburst. "I need dirt, Merc. Lots of dirt."

"What's the name?"

"Damian Li, owner of Li Pharmaceutical Imports, based in Tijuana. How fast can you get it?"

"Depends, Ford." I hear keystrokes and know he's looking right now. "He's big time. You sure you wanna mess with him?"

"I'm in love with his daughter and he took her away this morning."

"Give me a few days."

"I'm leaving for location filming a week from today. I need it before then."

"Got it."

I press end on the phone and tuck it back into my coat pocket. I finish the drive home in silence. I'm missing them. I'm missing Ashleigh's antics and Kate's gummy smile. This is the first night in a week that we've been apart and I am missing them.

I park the Audi and look longingly over at the Bronco, picturing our road trip. Those were the best seven days of my life. Truly. I get out and go inside, not even bothering to turn on the lights until I get to Kate's room.

It's wrong for it to be empty. Just wrong.

I think about my plan as I take in her things. Her little crib that is not nearly good enough for her. She deserves something fancy and pink. This one is just a portable fold-up thing that Pam got in a hurry. No love went into choosing it. If I get them back, we'll buy all this stuff again. We'll spend lots of time mulling over every little detail.

TAUT

But right now I need to think about the job. Because the risks this time are so much higher than money and prison time.

This time, I'm risking my heart.

FORTY-THREE

The downtown San Diego office of Damian Li, CEO of Li Pharmaceuticals is not what I expected.

One, it's not an office building like one might imagine houses other large corporations around the world. And two, it's not some waterfront warehouse that one might imagine houses an international drug smuggler.

No. Damian Li's office is actually a craftsman-style bungalow in Hillcrest.

A house. A fucking house smack on Sixth Avenue, in the middle of one of the largest gay communities in California, across from Balboa Park, with no fucking off-street parking. I drive past to make sure I know where the place is, then hang a right onto Laurel and go down a few blocks until I see the brightly colored lavender building and hang a left into the alley where a tall, thirty-something blonde woman waves out a hello. I unlock the doors and she opens the passenger side and gets in with a whoosh.

"I told you it was easy to find," she says, dragging her seatbelt across her chest. California has its people trained well. We are going two blocks down the road, but the seatbelt action is instantaneous and automatic.

"Well." I nod up at the building. "It's the only fucking purple office building on Laurel. Not exactly stealthy."

"No, we're not about being stealthy here." She chuckles at her inside joke.

"Right." I look over her clothes and give her the once-over, then proceed down the alley so I can get back over to Sixth Avenue. "Well, you clean up nice. That outfit is perfect."

"Thanks, I had a little help, but yeah. I like the business classy look. I might adopt it in the future."

"Good for you," I say absently as I search for an on-street parking spot. "Who the fuck has an office with no parking?"

"I thought you said he does business in TJ?"

I shoot her a dirty look. "Just remember when we get inside, no talking. You nod or look to me for guidance, got it?"

She waves her hand at me like I'm the one annoying *her*. "There!" she exclaims, pointing. "That guy's pulling out. Quick, put your blinker on and—"

I reach over and place my hand over her mouth. "No. Talking. I know how to parallel park, for fuck's sake. Stop mothering me."

She rolls her eyes when I move my hand and wait for the car to pull out, then I slip in and straighten out the Audi. I let out a deep breath and look over at my accomplice. "Please, just whatever you do, don't fuck this up. I only have one chance."

She holds up three fingers on her right hand. "Scout's Honor."

"That is just so unnecessary."

She snickers.

Please, God, I know I don't check in often since I'm pretty good at figuring this life shit out myself, but please, do not let this woman fuck up my plan. I beg you. You totally owe Ashleigh.

And then I get out of the car and walk down the street and cut over to Sixth Avenue to Damian Li's home office. It's a modest place for a man of his stature, but real estate is at a premium here, so it's a much bigger deal than it looks like from the street. I walk up the expansive porch supported by the signature craftsman-style pillars, and then tap the large square knocker on the equally impressive front door.

Mr. Li greets us personally.

How quaint.

"Mr. Aston." He smiles a fake smile. I might not be Ronin, but I can finger the fakeness as well as anyone. "It's nice to see you again. You're looking well." He steps out of the way and waves me forward. "Come in, please."

He eyes my companion with a slight narrowing of his eyes, but that's all. To her credit, she says nothing. We are directed through the reception room and down a hallway to the office. "Do you live here?" I should not be worried about it, but I can't help myself. What the fuck is up with the house-slash-office in Hillcrest?

"No. It's a business property, used for... recruitment."

"Ah," I say with a little too much enthusiasm. "I see."

Li takes a seat at a massive desk. There are diplomas on the wall and this is yet another thing that takes me off task. "You're a doctor?"

"Not my certificates, I'm afraid. I have employees who man this house when it's in use. Please," he says, motioning to the two chairs in front of his desk. "Sit." And then he looks at my accomplice and nods. "I don't think I've had the pleasure."

"Yes, well, she's my secret weapon, Mr. Li. Pam, my personal assistant, has been with me since I graduated college. I can't do anything without her these days."

My good little assistant is busy texting on her phone and does not even grace Mr. Li with a polite hello.

She's perfect. *Thank you, God.*

"Well," Li says clasping his hands together like this is a pleasant social call. "What can I do for you?"

I take the passports out of my pocket and hold them up in the air. "I just wanted to return these to Ashleigh. She left behind all her stuff, mostly just old clothes and baby things that are easily replaced, but getting a new passport is a bitch. I figured she'd want them back."

"Yes," he says reaching across the desk. "I can take those and deliver them the next time I'm up at the family home."

I tuck the passports back into my inside pocket. "Well, Mr. Li, that's great. Really great. I'll be relieved to be relieved of them, but to be perfectly honest, I'm not here to return the passports."

He smiles, like my pathetic passport ruse was so amateur.

"I'm actually here to request one short visit with Ashleigh and Katelynn. I'm worried, Mr. Li. You see, Ashleigh mentioned that she was not on speaking terms with you or her sister. So I'm wondering if something nefarious is going on. I like Ashleigh. I'd like to make sure she's OK, and I'd like to request a visit today, if you can swing it. One fifteen-minute visit, and then I'm afraid I have to be going. I'm leaving the country, we're filming on location for the next six weeks."

He stares at me. His eyes narrow. His face whitens just a smidge. His hands steeple under his chin and he smiles. He senses the trap. "I'm afraid I'm going to have to refuse, Mr. Aston. She's not well. She's recovering from a severe depression."

"Is she medicated?"

He pauses again, mulling over what kind of danger answering this question could lead him into, then decides none. "No. She's combative in that regard. The…" He pauses. "The breastfeeding. She's still breastfeeding because the child won't accept formula. The transition hasn't been as easy as we'd hoped."

Transition to what?

But I lock that shit away. *Later, Ford,* the voice in my head warns me.

"Fifteen minutes. I'm going to have to insist."

And this time his smile is real. Because I just laid out my hand. I'm here. I want something. I'm not leaving until I get it.

Li opens his top desk drawer and removes an envelope. He places it on top of the immaculately varnished wooden desk, then pushes it in my direction with a single fingertip. "Your compensation, Mr. Aston. For taking care of my youngest daughter when she was ill."

"Thank you." I smile and nod but do not take the money. I don't know what the fuck he thinks I am, but desperate for a few thousand dollars is not it.

"It's two million dollars, Mr. Aston. You might rethink your reluctance."

"Was she checked into a facility, Mr. Li?"

He pushes the envelope a little closer.

"I need a face-to-face, Mr. Li. I'm worried about her. You see, my father was a rather well-known psychiatrist and he had a lot of friends in So Cal."

His eyes narrow again.

"I called them immediately after she was taken away. They've been keeping tabs on all the local facilities. Now maybe you took her to a place far away, that's entirely possible. But if that's the case I need to know where. I need to check up on this and I won't let it go. All I want is fifteen private minutes, then I walk away, get on my plane, and never bother you again. But I will get that visit, Mr. Li. I have another associate, one with skills that match or exceed my own, who has been doing a little digging." I stop here to see if this registers.

He tips his chin up in a defiant gesture and that's my proof that yes, it does in fact make a difference.

"He's been researching you, Mr. Li. Or should I call you Dr. Matigan?"

He looks quickly over to my assistant who is still busy on her phone. He studies her for several seconds before dragging his gaze back to me.

"She's deaf, Mr. Li. That's why she's so valuable."

"Mr. Aston," he says in a totally different voice than the placating one he's been using on me since I arrived. "You have no idea what you're getting yourself into."

I'd like to laugh in his face. And if I wasn't so close to getting what I want, I might. But now is not the time for childish antics. Ashleigh needs me. "I'm afraid I do. And that's why I will insist on a visit. Right now. I already know she's in the Rancho Santa Fe house. It's a forty-minute drive up, a fifteen-minute private visit, and then we'll be out of your life."

He looks over at my assistant again, hesitating.

"I do not go anywhere without her, so the answer to your next demand is no. She stays with me. We follow you up or you give us permission to go up without you. Whatever works."

"Mr. Aston, there is nothing nefarious going on here. Ashleigh is sick. She's been mentally ill her whole life. She's been in and out of treatment facilities, she's been on medication since she was a small child for attention deficit disorder, she's run wild over in Japan with no therapists, no mood-stabilizing drugs, doing God knows what. She's out of control. She got pregnant out of wedlock by a man whose family would just as soon kill her as look at her. My mortal enemy, Mr. Aston. She had a baby with the son of my mortal enemy. She endangered that child by going off on that half-cocked road trip and they'd probably both be dead if you weren't there. And now that the Fenici family understands the scope of Anthony's deception, they are *very* interested in that baby. They want her. And they will not get her. So my eldest daughter has stepped in and we're taking care of it. She will legally adopt Katelynn and the Fenici ties will be broken."

He waits to see what my response is, but this is not the time or place for a statement. So I shut my fucking mouth and wait.

"So," he says as he exhales a long breath of held-in air. "What do you really want?"

"I want what she wanted when she came back to America. A chance to put things to rest."

"And that it's?" He watches me with a critical eye.

"That's it, Mr. Li. That's all I want. I'm very busy. I'm supposed to leave the country tonight, but I will cancel and wait this out. I don't need this job. I don't need to work, as I'm sure you're well aware. It's a hobby for me. So I'll wait. But one thing's for certain, I *will* get a final word with Ashleigh. Somehow, some way."

He's silent for a long time and I know I've won. He's running the logistics around in his head. Finally, after several full minutes he delivers his terms. "You can follow me to the family home and if Ashleigh is willing, you may have five minutes."

"Agreed. That's more than enough."

Li relaxes back into his seat and smiles. Confident.

"I'm ready now, Mr. Li."

He stands and gives me an open gesture with both hands. "Proceed."

We walk back out of the office and we hit up the back door this time. "Where's your car?"

"One street over on Fifth."

"I'll drop you off and you can follow me."

FORTY-FOUR

I don't know," my deaf assistant says as we follow the black Mercedes up the 5 freeway.

"I don't care. Just shut the hell up about it."

"He's dangerous. What if he comes after me?"

"He thinks you're Pam, Evelyn. He has no idea who you are."

"But he will as soon as this shit is over. I've got a license. He can check up on me."

"You're coming with me afterward. What's the fucking problem?"

"Who the hell are you? Just some rich kid, some spoiled rich kid. You're a movie producer. How are you going to take care of this?"

"Evelyn, you're *in*, dammit. You cannot back out now, he already saw you."

She's silent for a while and I feel bad. *Ford*, that stupid inner voice says. *She's helping you out, reassure her.* "OK, look, here's my assessment of Li, OK? He loves his daughters. He's worried about Ashleigh's state of mind and the new genetic ties with that

451

other crime family, right? He's just trying to make things right in his own way, but when we do this—*together*," I emphasize—"he'll see we're right, he's wrong, things are good, and no hard feelings."

I look over to catch her reaction and she's rolling her eyes. "You're full of shit. He's a white-collar mobster, he's got people who kill for him, and he's coming after us as soon as we pull out of his driveway."

I chew on this for a second. "Yeah, probably."

She shoots me a *what the fuck* look.

And then we both laugh. Because honestly, it's crazy as shit to mess with this guy, but I have no choice. Ash said fight for her. I just have no choice, I have to show the fuck up and fight for her.

We follow Li's car when he gets off at the Solana Beach exit. We bypass all those fools turning left who think living near the ocean is an acceptable trade-off for the congestion and traffic and turn right to head up into the eucalyptus-covered hills of Rancho. The road winds like crazy around the canyons and finally we come to a stop in front of an exquisite stone-walled property with an equally impressive gate.

A house guard appears with a sidearm and I can tell Evelyn is getting nervous again. "Just relax. This is not the time to panic. We'll be fine."

Li's car moves forward and the guard shoots us a dirty look as we follow and pass by. Ashleigh was lying when she said my house in Bel Air trumped this massive piece of prime real estate in San Diego County. They must have ten acres at least. Ten acres in Rancho Santa Fe. It's mind-boggling. There are tall trees on both sides of the driveway and it takes a full minute to actually reach the house, that's how long and windy this driveway is.

"You think he has all this land so when he kills people like us, no one hears it?"

I shoot her another *shut the fuck up* look, but it's actually a pretty good question.

We follow Li around a circular driveway, and then I make a point of pulling up past his car, so I'm in front and pointing down the driveway. Just in case I'm wrong and Li's not all about the mental health of his youngest daughter and we need to make a quick escape. "No talking until everything's in place, got it?"

She nods but keeps silent.

We exit the car together and walk up to Li who is waiting at the head of the long stone-paved walkway that leads to the front door. "Beautiful home, Mr. Li. Did you build it yourself?"

"No," is all he says.

I'm assuming that's him giving me the *shut the fuck up* response. I oblige him, it's the least I can do.

We enter the foyer and I'm staring at an elegant curved staircase that leads up to the second floor. Evelyn looks around like an idiot and I want to pinch her right now, but I can't. "Nice," I say to take Li's attention away from my gaping assistant. "Is Ashleigh upstairs?"

"No, Mr. Aston. I called ahead. She's in the library waiting for you. You have exactly five minutes and then this is over."

I smile and walk towards the closed door that he's pointing to. Evelyn follows, her head buried in her phone again, her fingers clicking out something to keep up the ruse.

He opens the door and I walk in.

Ashleigh is standing by the window, her back to me. "Ash?"

She doesn't turn and I look over my shoulder to see her father is still behind us. "Private, Mr. Li."

"Your five minutes are ticking," he barks as he backs out and closes the door.

"Ash?" I walk over to the window and notice Kate is sleeping in a portable crib. "Ash?" I ask as I tap her arm. She turns slowly around, her head down and her shoulders slumped. "Are you drugged? Did they drug you?"

She shakes her head. "No. I won that battle."

"Look at me, Ashleigh."

She lets out a breath and then tips her head up. Her eyes are bloodshot, her face pale, and her hair is all askew. Like she just rolled out of bed. Her clothes agree with my assessment. She's got on some leggings and a large t-shirt. Last week this was cute as all hell because she was smiling and happy, and most of what she was wearing belonged to me.

But now, this is a sure sign that the depression is worse. I wrap my arms around her and pull her close.

"Ford," she says through her sob. "I'm not gonna make it. My sister is adopting Kate and—"

"No, Ashleigh. No. Your sister is not adopting Kate." Ash looks up at me and then notices Evelyn behind me. "That's Evelyn, Ashleigh. And she's here to help me."

"Help you do what?" Ash asks, confused.

"Fight for you, kitten. I'm here to fight for you. Your sister isn't going to adopt Kate. I am. And you're not gonna live here anymore, you're coming with me."

"But—" She looks hopeful, scared, and defeated all in the same moment. "My father won't let me leave," she whispers. "He's giving my baby to my sister and I have to go back on the drugs as soon as she's weaned off the breast milk." She covers her face with her hands so I can't see her cry.

"Ashleigh," I say forcefully. "You're leaving here with me. But I have to ask you something first."

"What?" she asks as she frantically wipes her eyes.

I tip her chin up to force her to look at me. It takes her eyes a couple of seconds to catch up with her head, and then I see her clearly for the first time since she was taken away. "Can I be on your team?"

She squints.

"I have a ring," I say hurriedly, because she's looking confused and not the least bit excited. I pat my coat pocket and remove the black box and then open it up and present it to her. "I'm not very good at this stuff, Ash. I'm sorry, I should take you up in a fucking balloon or get down on a knee, or do it on Valentine's Day, or bake it in a cake, or pretty much any other way than this right here." I sigh and wave Evelyn over. "Begin," I tell her.

"Ashleigh, I'm authorized by San Diego County to provide a

California Confidential Marriage License on site to couples who wish to have a private and immediate ceremony. All you have to do is accept Mr. Aston's proposal, and I will sign the paperwork and declare you married."

"It's a shitty way to do this, right? I get it, Ashleigh, It sucks. I hate it. You deserve so much more. I love the shit out of you, I love Kate, and I miss the fuck out of you guys. I'm desperate, Ashleigh. Desperate to get you two back. And I prepared a whole fucking speech to sweep you off your feet and show you I'd fight for you and win you, but fuck. I forgot it. I have a photographic memory and I forgot the fucking proposal I spent all night working on. I'm nervous, can you tell? I'm sorry, I suck at this romantic shit. I'll let you draw cats and answer all your questions and I'll let you inside my sphere and—"

"Stop," she says, putting her little hand against my lips. "Stop talking, you nerd." And then she laughs and I swear to God, it's the most beautiful thing I've ever heard. "You had me at *I will call the police and report you for child abuse.*"

"Is that a yes?" Evelyn says.

The library doors open and Mr. Li interrupts. "Your time is up, Mr. Aston."

"Yes," Ashleigh says.

"Ashleigh Li and Rutherford Aston, by the power invested in me by the State of California, I pronounce you married. Sign quickly." She presents a marriage license and thrusts two pens into our hands." We scribble our names as Mr. Li rushes across the room towards us. Evelyn looks up at me. "You know what to do."

I do know what to do. My hands cup Ashleigh's face and she comes up on her tiptoes, and I kiss her. On the lips. With no coercion or games or tricks.

Damian Li punches me in the side of the head and I go stumbling sideways, hot blood dripping out of my ear and down my neck. This should piss me off, but I won. And nothing can touch me right now. "It's done, Li." He's seething with anger. Like that shit is about to drip out of his pores, that's how pissed off he looks. "She's mine now. And if you doubt my plans, let me spell it out for you. She's not on any medication. No doctor examined her, did they, Ashleigh?"

She shakes her head now as she glares at her father.

"No doctor examined her and pronounced her unfit. Unless of course you'd like to count your fake credentials hanging on that wall back in your San Diego office." I wait a beat but he keeps quiet. "She's not mentally ill, Damian."

"She is, Ford. She's sick. And you think this is cute and romantic? Taking her away like this? It's not, because she needs serious help."

I shake my head. "No, you're wrong. She's not sick. She's sad." I look down to Ashleigh and take her hand. "You're not sick, kitten. You're sad. And that's OK, because life shit on you. And you do need serious help. But not in the form of drugs and therapy, Ashleigh. You need time and permission to feel what it feels like to lose someone who meant the world to you, that's all. And we've got our whole lives to get it right and be together. I'll grow old with you, Ashleigh. We'll do this together."

Her lip starts to tremble and she swallows down the pain and nods her head in agreement.

"You're brave, Ashleigh. And strong. And very, very sad. But it's OK now. You can be sad about what you lost all you want, until you're ready to let Tony go. Because I'm gonna take care of you and give you all the time you need. You're not sick, Ash. You're sad. You don't need drugs, you need Kate. And me. You need us, your team. We'll get through this, I promise. Just trust me."

She grabs hold of my neck and then jumps up and wraps her legs around my waist, her head buried into my neck, just under my ear. "I have never trusted anyone more than you, Ford Aston. I swear to God, I'm yours."

FORTY-FIVE

I was right about Damian Li. For now at least. Ashleigh screamed and her sister came and cried over Kate. It was not pretty. At all. In fact it was a blubbering mess of female hormones and in the end Li and I had to break out a decanter of 1946 Macallan. I'm glad Ashleigh had no fucking idea how special that whiskey was, because I'd never live down offering her a few shots of ten-thousand-dollar 1939 when her father had a dusty decanter of the stuff that costs half a million dollars.

But I was right in the end. They do love her. Damian Li was doing his best to protect everyone involved.

He sucked ass at it, unlike the God-man that is me. I kicked the shit out of that day.

And now we're in New Zealand. Evelyn and her girlfriend came along as far as Sydney. They're staying on my dime until Evelyn is really convinced that Damian won't come after her for performing the confidential marriage. Let's just say that's not anytime soon. They got jobs and an apartment. But Li seemed calm about it. I'm not too worried and I usually have a pretty good inkling whether people are holding secret grudges, and I didn't get that vibe from him.

Kate pulls on my ear and shakes me out of my daydream. She's getting so big. Five months now. Pretty soon she'll be crawling. And in a few weeks we'll go home and real life will catch up to us.

My professional team—as I like to call Spencer, Rook, and Ronin—are all eager for me and my domestic team to return home. We have a lot of loose ends to clean up this spring. We've pissed off quite a few very important people trying to dig ourselves out of our past mistakes. And this is it. These next few months will dictate the rest of our lives. And all of us are important, even Ashleigh and Kate. Because they're what I live for these days. Not money, not jobs, not pets, not sex, not control.

Just them.

Ashleigh walks out of the ocean in front of me. She's taken up open-water swimming to help her through her pain. I hate it. I dream about sharks eating her, I dream about enchanted seaweed wrapping around her ankle and pulling her under, I dream about Charlie horses, and stomach cramps, and swallowing too much seawater, and sunburn. Fuck, I worry about everything. And it sucks.

But it also feels awesome because it means I'm capable of feeling.

Love is a risk and I can live with it.

"Wow," Ash says as she comes up to us on the beach, "that was my best time ever! Did you see me?"

"My eyes never left you, love. Never." And I had a boat trailing her the entire time. Love might be a risk, but I'm all about risk-management.

She takes the towel I hand her and flops down in the sand. I sit next to her and place Kate in between my legs. Kate grabs the sand and immediately tries to eat it. Ashleigh freaks out, but I figure, it's sand, right? She'll figure out pretty quick sand is not yummy. It doesn't take a genius.

I'm one of *those* parents. Calm and lenient.

I love parenting. I love everything about it. I play the peek-a-boo game and give Katie daily updates on the Itsy-Bitsy Spider. I live for her squealing laughter.

Ashleigh wraps her hands around my upper arm and leans into my neck. "I love you, Ford."

"I love you too, Ash. More today than yesterday."

"I'm so glad God sent you to save me."

I smile at that. I thought she was talking about Tony, but she was talking about God. "Well, I have a confession about that day. When I told you he sent me to save you back at Tony's grave, it was a lie."

"No," she whines.

"Yes," I say back, looking down at her scowling face. I lean over and put my palm against her neck, feeling her life force rushing through her body. She thrills me. Everything about her thrills me. I kiss her forehead, then her nose, then her lips. We linger like that, and then both of my hands have her head and I hold her still so I can look directly into her soul as I tell her the truth.

"God never sent me to save you, Mrs. Aston. He sent you to save me."

And then I kiss her thoroughly. With tongue and biting and a promise of very dirty things to come tonight.

This paperback interior was designed and formatted by

E.M. TIPPETTS BOOK DESIGNS

www.emtippettsbookdesigns.com

Artisan interiors for discerning authors and publishers.

CPSIA information can be obtained
at www.ICGtesting.com
Printed in the USA
FSOW02n1248250416
19655FS